THE
Sweetest Rain

FLOWERS OF EDEN . BOOK ONE

MYRA
JOHNSON

www.FawnRidgePress.com

DEDICATION

For Zoë, my first-born granddaughter and definitely the artist in the family. I treasure each and every one of the beautiful pictures you've given me. Every grandmother, mom, or aunt should have a girl in her life as precious as you!

For as the rain and the snow come down from heaven, and do not return there until they have watered the earth, making it bring forth and sprout, giving seed to the sower and bread to the eater, so shall my word be that goes out from my mouth; it shall not return to me empty, but it shall accomplish that which I purpose, and succeed in the thing for which I sent it. —Isaiah 55:10-11, NRSV

$$\text{🙚} \quad \text{I} \quad \text{🙚}$$

EDEN, ARKANSAS
AUGUST 1930

S now, beautiful snow! Cold and wet and heavy, each puffy flake brushing Bryony's cheeks like an icy kiss. Pure delight swept through her, and she twirled and twirled and twirled, her bare feet stirring the rapidly rising drifts until the airy crystals rose all around her in a wintry cloud—

"Bry. Bryony!" Something hard landed square in the center of Bryony's chest. "Move over, will you? It's hot enough without you breathing on me."

Her sister's words didn't register at first. *Hot?* Only a moment ago she'd been dancing through snowdrifts!

Then reality returned, along with the stifling heat of the August night. Bryony rolled onto her back and rubbed her breastbone, still smarting from Larkspur's elbow jab. Come December, when frost covered the ground and winter winds rattled the windowpanes, they'd all be wishing for a taste of summer's warmth.

Except maybe not *this* summer's.

Bryony drew up her knees and fanned herself with the hem of her thin cotton gown. How they survived this miserable heat was

I

beyond imagining—and it wasn't over yet. Even the crickets' inces-sant chirping sounded like one long complaint.

Blowing out a sigh strong enough to lift the heavy, damp strands off her brow, Bryony shoved herself upright and dropped her legs off the edge of the narrow cot. Beyond the porch screen she could just make out the shadowy tree line at the far edge of the cotton field. Glimpses of pink through the branches told her dawn wasn't far off. No sense trying to grab another half-hour of sleep when this was surely the coolest part of the day. May as well get up and get cracking.

Careful not to disturb her two sleeping sisters, Bryony edged past their cots, eased open the screen door, and padded across the dry, stubbly grass. After a quick visit to the outhouse, she drew a bucket of well water and splashed her face. Not as refreshing as the snowflakes she'd been dreaming of, but at least it was wet. As droplets trickled down her face and throat, she looked toward the creek and strained to hear the ripple of water over stones as the creek wended its way toward the river. Not much water to speak of in the creek these days, and the river was down, too. Bryony couldn't remember the last time they'd seen rain.

A movement caught her eye—a dark form rising and stooping along the rows of cotton. It could only be Grandpa, getting a head start on another long, murderously hot day. He paused, looked her way, and waved. There wasn't enough daylight yet to see his smile, but she knew it was there. Grandpa Rigby smiled not because he was happy but because he refused to lose hope. "Every day we're breathin' is a gift," he'd say. "We ain't dead yet, so's we gotta keep on keepin' on."

Bryony wasn't sure she subscribed to Grandpa's brand of cynical optimism. She wanted to believe something better awaited at the end of this drought, and she fervently hoped it encompassed more than merely "keepin' on."

The sere summer air had already sucked the dampness from her skin, just like it was drying up those cotton stalks Grandpa kept nursing along. The harvest would be pitiful at best, and surely wouldn't bring enough at the cotton gin to sustain them through the winter.

Winter . . . snowflakes . . . Bryony yearned to be cold again, just for five minutes.

Groaning under the weight of the water pail, she carried it to the vegetable garden and portioned out minuscule sips to each stunted plant. "Drink up, y'all. You never know when the next drop could be your last."

By the time she finished, Grandpa had made his way back to the house. Sweat soaked his yellowed undershirt beneath faded denim overalls. He fanned his reddened face with a wide-brimmed straw hat that had seen better days. "Cotton looks ready for pickin'. Best get the girls up so's we can start."

"Yes, sir." Bryony could just imagine how thrilled her sisters would be with the news. They all had to pitch in or the work wouldn't get done. It had been that way for twelve years now, ever since Mama first brought them to live on Grandpa's tenant farm on the Heath family's Brookbirch Plantation.

Grandma had already gone to her eternal reward by then, and not quite four years ago Mama joined her. An old man and three skinny girls trying to keep a farm afloat? Insanity. Sheer and utter insanity.

"Lark. Rose. Get a move on." Bryony let the screen door slam behind her, and both sisters bolted upright.

"For pity's sake, Bry." Raking stiff fingers through her matted blond hair, Larkspur growled her irritation.

Rose, the family redhead and at sixteen the youngest, hopped off her cot with an eagerness Bryony envied. Of all of them, Rose loved the farm best, maybe even more than Grandpa.

Already dreading a hot day of picking cotton, Bryony started for the kitchen. "Rose, get the milking done, and see if the hens favored us with any eggs this morning. Lark, set the table for breakfast."

"Always so bossy," Larkspur grumbled as she swept passed Bryony.

The remark stung, and Bryony bit back a snappish reply. Tears nipped at the corners of her eyes.

"Don't mind her." Rose gave Bryony a hug that was long enough to be encouraging but quick enough to avoid sharing too much body warmth. "It's the heat. Makes us all testy."

Testy didn't begin to describe it. "We're about to get a lot hotter. Grandpa says the cotton's ready."

Two conflicting emotions flashed in Rose's eyes: anticipation followed instantly by comprehension. "It's gonna be bad, isn't it?"

Bryony knew her sister wasn't talking about the hot day ahead. She nodded slowly. "It's gonna be bad."

"We'll make it, Bry. Somehow we'll survive. God can't let this drought go on forever."

With a quiet sigh, Bryony followed her sisters into the bedroom, where she shucked her damp nightgown and wiggled into a thin housedress. After running a brush through her hair, she twirled the thick strands into a bun. Standing before the highboy, she glimpsed her sisters' reflections in the mirror. They were an odd bunch. Bryony had inherited Mama's ebony waves, while Larkspur took after their fair-haired, blue-eyed father. Redheaded Rose, who at sixteen already had the womanly figure neither Bryony nor Larkspur could ever hope for, bore a startling resemblance to photographs of Grandma Rigby in her youth.

And their personalities were as disparate as their looks. Rose was the eternal optimist, Larkspur the dreamer, and Bryony . . . Bryony just kept doing her best to hold what was left of her family together.

❧

Hours later, her back aching and sweat dripping from every pore, Bryony winced as the sharp spikes of a cotton boll tore at the exposed skin above her leather gloves. After stuffing another handful into the long, heavy bag dragging behind her, she straightened with a moan and mopped her forehead with the sleeve of her chambray shirt. Peering at the sky from beneath the wide brim of her sunbonnet, she estimated the time to be nearing five o'clock.

Relentless. No other word described the sun's ferocity. Heaven help her, she couldn't last much longer in this heat. Her heart pined for the way things used to be. Before the drought. Before Papa was killed in the Great War. Before Mama uprooted them from their comfortable home in Memphis and brought them to the farm. She imagined sitting on their Memphis front porch, a stately elm blessing her with its shade and a pleasant breeze wafting the curling tendrils off her neck. She'd sip from a tall glass of cold lemonade with real ice cubes while a handsome beau kept the porch swing swaying gently with a push of his spit-shined brogues.

"Ouch!" Rubbing another scratch from a cotton boll, Bryony decided she'd better pay more attention to her cotton picking and less time dreaming about what would never be. Not to mention mooning over nonexistent beaux. *This* was her life now, taking care of Grandpa and her sisters on a struggling tenant farm in Eden, Arkansas.

One row over, Grandpa paused to ease his back and gulp a swallow of water from his canteen. Shifting the strap of his cotton sack, he whistled out through his teeth. "Fraid it's worse than I thought, Bryony. We're gonna be in a world of hurt this year."

She angled a glance toward the canvas tarp at the end of the row, where they'd been emptying their sacks. After a full day of toil, the pile remained heartbreakingly small, and she could no longer hold back the tide of worry that had been building all summer. The cow's milk was drying up, the hens had all but stopped laying, and what she'd canned from their vegetable garden wouldn't begin to last through the winter. With this cotton crop, they'd counted on at least breaking even. Now, those hopes were gone as well.

Fatigue and despair stole the last of her strength, and she sank to her knees in the dirt. She'd cry if her body could spare the tears. Tipping back her bonnet, she scanned the field until her gaze settled upon her sisters, working side by side several rows over. After the Thanksgiving Day tornado of '26 that took Mama's life, Bryony swore on her mother's grave to take good care of Larkspur, Rose, and Grandpa.

But with food growing scarce and no money in the bank, what was she supposed to do—let them all starve?

There had to be an answer, some way to provide for her family until this cursed drought ended and the farm turned a profit again. Maybe if she talked to the landlord, explained their dire situation, he'd show a little compassion and give them extra time to cover the rent. He might even help out with a loan to get them through next spring's planting season. Might be a long shot, but she had to try. She'd walk over first thing in the morning.

She wouldn't tell Grandpa, of course. It would hurt his pride to think his granddaughter had gone begging. First off, she'd need an excuse for leaving Grandpa and her sisters to pick cotton without her. She could take a jar of pickles from the cellar and say she was going into town to trade it for a sack of flour so they could have biscuits and gravy for supper. Except rumor had it Mr. and Mrs. Heath used to be quite partial to Grandma's bread-and-butter pickles, and Bryony wasn't above bearing gifts if it would soften their landlord's flinty heart.

After a swallow of water too warm to be refreshing, Bryony adjusted her bonnet and returned to picking cotton. If her seventy-year-old grandfather could keep working like a dog, she could, too. She had to. Their very lives depended on it.

⚘

Mornings on the west veranda, then move to the east side for the afternoons. It was the only way Michael Heath could abide the cruel turn this summer had taken. Sketchbook propped on his knee, he adjusted his glasses and leaned forward to study the sprig of elongated leaves he'd laid upon the porch rail. *Itea virginica*, more commonly known as Virginia sweetspire. Even shaded by the house and carefully watered and cultivated, the shrub showed signs of distress.

Michael debated whether to draw the leaves exactly as they were, with brown and shriveled margins, the tips curling inward as if in self-protection, or to render them supple, green, and healthy, as they were meant to be.

Maybe some of each, because nothing was ever perfect. Not in this life anyway.

As he chose a light umber pencil from his artist's kit, a whisper of breeze carried someone's tuneful humming to his ear—"Singin' in the Rain," a popular but woefully inappropriate ditty for the summer they were suffering through. Lifting his head, he peered down the long, tree-shaded drive and saw a woman strolling toward the house. A floppy straw hat with a ridiculously wide brim shaded her face. A loose curl the color of the darkest burnt umber fell across one shoulder.

Véronique? A torrent of memory engulfed him, and for a heart-stopping moment he was sitting at an outdoor Paris café.

Eyes squeezed shut, he poked two fingers up under his glasses and rubbed furiously. No . . . no, he was home in Arkansas. Paris and the war remained in the distant past, along with everything else he'd consciously chosen to forget.

He pried open his eyes and saw the woman more clearly now. Not Véronique, but the resemblance had certainly taken him aback. Whoever she was, Michael's next impulse was to gather his supplies and slip inside before she noticed him. He didn't care for social callers, didn't care much for most people in general. Since coming home two years ago, he did well to tolerate the company of his own parents, who mostly let him be, thank goodness. His glance fell to the withered sweetspire leaves.

The woman's footsteps crunched on the gravel. "Good morning," she called, sounding entirely too cheerful for eight o'clock in the morning.

Too late to escape. Michael laid his sketchbook on the table next to him and stood. His throat dry and raspy, he asked, "Can I help you?"

Ten feet from the bottom of the veranda steps, she froze, her mouth dropping open. "Oh. Guess I've been squinting into the sun too long. I thought you were Mr. Heath."

"I am Mr. Heath." Michael's lips twitched. Not really a smile, but he couldn't miss the irony of being mistaken for his father. "You're looking for the elder Mr. Heath, I'm sure. Tell me your name and I'll fetch him for you."

"You're his son?"

"Michael. Yes."

"I heard you'd come home awhile back. Pleased to make your acquaintance." Marching up the five steps, she shifted a cloth-covered basket to her left arm and extended her right hand in greeting. "I'm Bryony Linwood. My grandfather, George Rigby, is one of your tenants."

"Bryony, or *bryonia*, a genus of flowering plant in the gourd family."

She blinked, a surprised grin brightening her soft features. "You know what my name means?"

"Sorry, bad habit." Hesitantly, Michael accepted her handshake, then quickly withdrew. "I'll get my father."

He marched to the screen door and yanked it open, then made his way through the rambling first floor of the family mansion to his father's office—not his favorite place to be and one he avoided if at all possible. "Dad, there's a woman here to see you. Her grandfather is—"

An upraised hand silenced him. His father took another few seconds to study some figures in the account book lying open on the desk. "Mm-hmm, mm-hmm . . ." He removed his round tortoise-shell glasses and looked up. "Yes, Michael, you were saying?"

He repeated his announcement. "Rigby, I think the name was."

"George Rigby. Yes. Falling behind on his rent." Tiny beads of perspiration dotted Sebastian Heath's broad forehead. He whipped out a handkerchief and blotted his face. "Wouldn't be surprised if he sent his granddaughter to plead for another extension."

"I wouldn't know." Michael couldn't bring himself to care much about his father's business dealings. He edged toward the door. "Should I send her in?"

The elder Heath brought both palms down on the desk with a resounding slap. Eyes narrowed, he shot Michael a pointed glare. "No, son, I want you to *bring* her in, and then you will sit down and pay attention to how this plantation is managed. It's long past time you took an interest in your future inheritance."

Michael braced for the queasiness he'd come to expect when such conversations arose. "Dad, please—"

"Don't argue. If you want to continue living in this house, you'll do as I say." With a meaningful *ahem*, his father returned to his accounts.

Stomach churning, Michael backed out of the office, then strode several paces down the hallway before pausing to take a calming breath. *In . . . out . . .* He couldn't do it, couldn't be the son his father wanted him to be, and no amount of hammering, bending, or twisting would ever force this square peg into a round hole.

Gathering what composure he could, he returned to the porch, where he found their visitor twirling the sweetspire sprig, a pensive look turning down the corners of her full lips. She'd removed her hat and laid it on a chair, and now her long, lustrous hair, secured off her neck by a faded azure ribbon, cascaded down her back.

She looked toward Michael as he stepped through the screen door. "So sad, isn't it? Everything's drying up and withering away."

Michael swallowed and tore his gaze from the ribbon at her nape. "My father said to show you in, Miss . . ."

"Linwood. Bry—"

"Bryony, I remember." He smiled in spite of himself, curious why her parents had chosen such an unusual name. Somewhere in his sketchbooks he had a drawing of the greenish-white, star-shaped *bryonia alba* blossoms. A hardy plant with medicinal properties, yet deadly poisonous if misused. How much resemblance did the woman bear to the specimen for which she was named?

"Excuse me, you're staring." Laughing softly, Miss Linwood laid the wilted leaves on the railing where she'd found them. "You were going to take me to see your father?"

"Yes. Right." Giving a huff, Michael held the door, then led Miss Linwood through the foyer and past the curving staircase. As they rounded a corner, he stopped abruptly and pointed down the hall. "Last door on the right. Can you find your way from here?"

"I'm sure I can. Thank you." Her confident air wavered. With a tremulous breath, she drew back her shoulders and strode toward the office.

Michael watched discreetly until she tapped on the open door and was invited inside. If indeed she had come to ask for a rent extension, he could understand her trepidation. Father was an uncompromising businessman and not easily swayed by sob stories.

Not even those of his own hurting children.

Seeing a motion at the end of the hall, Michael ducked into the foyer, barely escaping his father's keen glance. He winced at the carefully modulated tone of the query that followed: "Michael? Are you joining us?"

Without answering, Michael slipped out to the veranda, hurriedly collected his sketchbook and drawing supplies, then darted down the steps and along a shady path to the river. No doubt he'd have to explain himself later. For now, though, he'd avoided one more of his father's continual and utterly futile attempts to manipulate him into some semblance of normalcy.

Normal? For Michael, his last hope of living a normal life ended the day a creeping yellow cloud descended upon his foxhole. Though by some miracle he'd been spared the worst, two days later, three of his closest friends were dead from the agonizing effects of mustard gas.

Nothing had been the same since.

Knuckles whitening from her death grip on the basket handle, Bryony fought not to look away from Sebastian Heath's frosty stare. "I know it's a lot to ask, sir, but times are hard—"

"Times are hard for everyone, Miss Linwood. All my tenants are suffering as this drought drags on." The whirling blades of an electric fan stirred the man's iron-gray hair. He shifted, angling his body in a dismissive pose. "If I make an exception for your grandfather, I'll be expected to do so for the others as well. And then what kind of businessman would I be?"

"A kind and sympathetic businessman, Mr. Heath." Bryony lifted her chin, though her shaking knees belied her show of confidence. "A landlord who cares not just about present circumstances but about the future. Because your tenants *are* your future, sir. Where would Brookbirch Plantation be without us working the land?"

One brow hiked, he slanted her a glance that might be contempt . . . or it might be appreciation. Then he chuckled softly, leaned back in his chair, and briefly looked toward the ceiling. "My, my, a woman who isn't afraid to speak her mind. Blatant honesty can be a dangerous thing, you know."

"Decent human beings should never be afraid of the truth."
Already sitting ramrod straight, Bryony sat up even taller. "And the
truth is, I'm not leaving here without assurance of your support
until times change for the better."

"My *support*." The man gave his head a disbelieving shake. "My
dear, don't you think you have it backwards? The tenant farmers
are supposed to support the landlord. That's the way this system
works."

Bryony opened her mouth to disagree but then snapped it shut
again. Clearly, this circular argument would get her nowhere,
besides the fact that Mr. Heath appeared to take morbid pleasure
in their verbal sparring.

She looked down at the basket on her lap. Slowly, she drew
aside the flour-sack dishtowel, then set the jar of pickles on the
desk. "I've heard tell, Mr. Heath, that you once had quite a liking
for my grandmother's homemade bread-and-butter pickles."

Eyes narrowed, he stared at the jar. "I liked them very much.
The crunchier, the better."

"Well, sir, these pickles are the crunchiest and tangiest you'll
ever taste. Same recipe my grandmother always used. She passed it
down to my mother, God rest her soul, who passed it down to me."
With the tip of one finger, she nudged the jar closer.

"Are you trying to bribe me with pickles, Miss Linwood?"

She noted the subtle softening of his tone and pressed her lips
together in a tight smile. "Is it working?"

"You are persistent, I'll give you that." The landlord leaned
forward, one elbow on the desk as he reached out with his other
hand to trace the raised lettering on the Mason jar. "All right, I
have a proposition for you. One of our housemaids went and got
herself in a family way, so we had to let her go. If you want the
position, I'll count the hours you work against what your grandfather owes."

Bryony gulped. This certainly wasn't an option she'd anticipated. "I'd need to talk it over with my grandpa. We just started

picking cotton, and if he's left shorthanded, it'll put him in an even worse bind."

Mr. Heath rose and came around to Bryony's side of the desk. He hovered over her, close enough that she could smell the starch in his crisply pressed white shirt. He reached for her hand, and when he turned over her wrist and saw the red scratches from cotton bolls, he snorted. "Tightfisted old man, sending a delicate thing like you into the fields. He should have hired help."

Indignant, Bryony jerked her hand free. The chair screeched across the wood floor as she bolted to her feet. "If my grandpa could afford to hire help, I sure wouldn't be here begging you for leniency. And delicate?" She crooked a finger under Mr. Heath's nose. "Come pick cotton alongside me and my sisters for a day and we'll see who's still standing come sundown."

A dark look crossed Mr. Heath's face, but before he could respond, the staccato click of a woman's shoes sounded in the hallway. Moments later, a prim, petite woman appeared in the doorway. "Sebastian, dear, why didn't you tell me we had a guest?" She graced Bryony with a welcoming smile. "How do you do? I'm Fenella Heath."

"Ma'am." Bryony tipped her head.

Mr. Heath swiveled to face his wife. He took her elbow as if he wanted to hurry her from the room. "Miss Linwood isn't a guest. She's here on business. Her grandfather is one of our tenants."

"Oh, how delightful!" Mrs. Heath ducked past her husband and clasped Bryony's hand. "I rarely have the chance to meet our tenants. Sebastian falsely assumes I wouldn't want to be bothered. But it does get lonely so far from a city of any decent size, and I do miss female companionship. Don't you, Miss—"

"Linwood. I'm Bryony Linwood, ma'am." She liked the woman already. And liked her controlling husband even less than she did five minutes ago.

"Linwood, of course. I knew some Linwoods once. Darling, have you offered her tea? No, I can see you haven't." Mrs. Heath gave her husband a playful slap on the arm. "No manners, none at all," she whispered loudly at Bryony. "You just come along with me to the parlor and—"

"Ma'am, really, I can't." Feet planted, Bryony tugged her hand free. "You're so kind to offer, but I still need to settle my business with Mr. Heath, and then I absolutely must get back to the farm."

One arm around his wife's shoulders, Mr. Heath steered her toward the door. "She's right, dearest. Run along and find Michael, why don't you?" Irritation flickered in the man's eyes, whether toward his wife or his son, Bryony couldn't tell. When Mrs. Heath's footsteps faded, he returned his attention to Bryony. "I believe we still have an offer on the table. Are you interested in the housemaid position or not?"

Bryony chewed her lip. She knew right well what Grandpa would say. It was one thing to put his granddaughters to work harvesting the crops that were their livelihood, and quite another to hire one of them out as a housemaid to the landlord. Spending her days amidst all this finery in a fancy mansion twenty times the size of Grandpa's two-bedroom farmhouse? Why, she'd almost feel like a traitor.

Except she'd be saving her family from starvation and utter destitution.

What was it Mama used to say? Sometimes it's easier to seek forgiveness than to ask permission. Besides, Bryony was a grown woman of twenty-two, and now with both her parents in heaven with Grandma, she had responsibilities she couldn't shirk.

She thrust out her hand. "You have a deal, Mr. Heath. Soon as the cotton's in, though. Can't start before then."

"Very well." A twisted grin skewed the man's features as he gripped her hand for a firm shake. "I look forward to seeing you again soon."

Showing herself out, Bryony paused on the veranda to collect her straw hat. Now came the hard part—telling Grandpa. The long walk home would give her time to frame her words.

As she started toward the steps, the toe of her shoe sent something skittering across the painted gray boards. She bent to retrieve the stub of a green colored pencil and remembered she'd seen the younger Mr. Heath with a sketchbook. The sketchbook was gone, but the twig with the wilted leaves still lay on the railing.

A curious fellow, intriguingly taciturn, and Bryony had the sense Michael Heath and his father didn't get along too well. The thought brought an unexpected sadness, a lonely ache in Bryony's chest. It was just plain wrong for a father and son to be so distant. As long as they both had breath, nothing should be allowed to come between them. She still missed her own father horribly.

Laying the pencil on a nearby table, Bryony looked up as Mrs. Heath strolled into view at the north end of the veranda. The small woman waved and hurried over. Bryony waved back. "Hello again. I was just leaving."

"Oh, please don't. Are you a new neighbor come to call?"

Bryony's eyes widened. "No, ma'am. We met earlier. I had some business with your husband, remember?"

A blank look flattened the woman's features. She touched a hand to her temple as if searching her memory, then forced a shaky smile. "Yes, yes . . . Well, I do hope Sebastian settled everything to your satisfaction."

With little confidence Mrs. Heath remembered her at all, Bryony nodded. "I'll just be going, then. Nice meeting you, ma'am."

"Come back anytime, dear. We'll have tea and a nice, long visit."

"Yes, ma'am." Bryony backed toward the steps and waved again before hurrying on her way.

Oh, my. What was she getting herself into?

⊚❦⊚

Returning to the house through the north gardens, Michael glimpsed his mother standing on the veranda, a vacant look in her eyes. He trotted up the side steps, then slowed as he approached. "Mother? What are you doing?"

She gave a tiny gasp as she spun around to face him. "Oh, Michael. Have you seen Tillie? I've been looking all over for that girl. I need to go over a few details about tonight's soirée."

Michael knew good and well there were no festivities on the evening's agenda. He also knew that, thanks to an indiscretion with a neighboring plantation owner's hired man, Tillie was long gone. He laid his art supplies on a table, then gently took his mother's arm and steered her toward a wicker rocker. "Come sit, Mama. You're getting overheated. I'll fetch you some water."

"Yes, it's terribly hot, isn't it? You're such a good boy, Michael." She patted his hand as she sank into the chair. "Such a good boy."

His mother's failing memory worried him. He'd first noticed it about a year ago, but since Dad didn't seem overly concerned, Michael first assumed Mother's problem was ordinary forgetfulness. Over time, though, she began to forget what day it was, or whether she'd had breakfast. Lately she often forgot entire conversations only hours old. How long before she slipped away from them completely?

Hurrying through the house to the kitchen, he found Odette, their salt-and-pepper-haired cook. "Mother's having another spell. She needs something cool to drink."

"Surely, young sir." Odette clucked her tongue as she took a glass from the cupboard. "Lawdy, that poor woman done scared me silly this mornin' already. Found her standing right yonder at the stove and fixin' to boil water in a china bowl."

Stomach knotted, Michael waited while Odette dropped a chunk of ice into the water glass. He should have another talk with his father about Mother's condition. But the thought of attempting any kind of conversation with the man made him physically ill. They didn't understand each other, never had. Even after his release two years ago from the rehabilitation hospital in Raleigh, Michael would have been better off staying as far away as possible from the plantation he cared nothing about inheriting.

As Odette handed him the glass, she studied him with

narrowed eyes. "You lookin' like you could use a cold drink your-self. You been out wandering in this heat, haven't you?"

"Just down to the river. It's cooler by the water." Or so he'd convinced himself.

"Mister Michael." Odette set one fist against her ample hip. "How long I been workin' for this family? You think I cain't see when a boy's avoiding his pappy? Not that I blame you," she added under her breath. "But this ain't fixin' nothin'. You need to—"

"I *need* to take Mother her water." Michael swirled the ice in the glass, the *chink-chink* a subtle distraction from the cramp in his belly. "Thank you, Odette."

Shaking her head and muttering, Odette turned to check what-ever she had cooking on the stove. The last words Michael caught were, "Yes, indeedy, two stubborn ol' coots livin' under the same roof means nothin' but trouble."

Michael couldn't argue with that.

Returning to the veranda, he found his mother exactly where he'd left her in the rocking chair. She stared into the distance as if seeing a completely different scene. "Mother," he whispered with a light tap on her shoulder, "here's a cool drink of water for you."

Her eyes lit up in recognition as she accepted the glass. "My dear Michael, such a sweet, sweet boy."

His tension eased slightly as he settled into the chair next to hers. He reached for his sketchbook and opened it to the last drawing he'd been working on, a detail of the peeling, cinnamon-colored bark of a river birch. Tomorrow he'd return to the tree to sketch the leaves. Though the White River rode low on its banks during this hot, rainless summer, at least along its winding path everything grew a little bit greener.

"Show me your drawings, son." Mother leaned toward him, one elbow propped on the arm of the rocker. As he slowly paged through the sketchbook, she asked him to explain each picture. "Lovely . . . lovely," she repeated, often commenting on his color choices.

When he came to the last page, she cast him a clear-eyed smile.

"I knew you'd grow up to be an artist. You always drew me the prettiest pictures. And then . . ." She looked away and heaved a long, tremulous sigh. "And then everything went all wrong."

Michael closed the book. "Those times are in the past, Mother. Let's leave them there."

After a moment, she swiveled to face him again, all traces of sadness dissipating. "The young lady who came by earlier—she's George Rigby's granddaughter?"

Pleasantly surprised, Michael sat forward. "That's right. You remember her?"

"Well, of course!" She laughed as if his question were utterly ridiculous. "The Rigbys have farmed our land for . . . oh, my, must be close to forty years. Remember, Violet Rigby worked here for a while as nanny for you and Miranda."

The mention of his sister's name brought a pang of regret. "I was too young to remember Violet very well."

"I do miss Violet's pickles. How long has she been gone now?"

"I'm not sure." Michael drummed tense fingers against the sketchbook cover. "A long time."

"As I recall, your daddy was away on business and couldn't go to the funeral. But I took you and Miranda—"

Michael couldn't sit still a moment longer. "Let's go inside, Mother. Odette will have the noon meal ready soon. I'll take you upstairs and find Dancy to help you freshen up."

As he helped her from the rocker, she cast him a pitying look. But before she could open her mouth to speak, it was almost as if Michael could see the veil falling across her mind. "Yes, yes, and I must have a nap before the party tonight."

❦

Larkspur Linwood stuffed another handful of cotton into her sack, then peered across the field. What was Bryony doing in town all this time? Getting out of half a day's work, that's what. Grinding her teeth, Larkspur inched forward and plucked a boll from a withered cotton plant. Late summer in Arkansas was a miserable time of year even when they weren't in the middle of a drought. And picking cotton? Lord have mercy!

Another handful, another few steps, and Larkspur looked again toward the road. Finally. Here came Bryony, bobbing along like she didn't have a care in the world. Well, she'd just better get her perky little self out here and help them pick.

Twenty more minutes went by before Bryony emerged from the house in a long-sleeved shirt, leather gloves, and sunbonnet. Looping a cotton sack across her shoulder, she plodded along an adjoining row until she came even with Larkspur. "Sorry I took so long. I'll make up for it, I promise."

Larkspur gave a grudging nod. Bryony might be bossy, but she was no slacker. However, she'd chosen a most inconvenient time to decide to go for groceries. "How's things in town? Did you check our post office box?"

"Uh, no. Sorry." Shifting sideways, Bryony bent over a cotton plant.

Straightening, Larkspur studied her sister's back. "Then what exactly *did* you do in town?"

Bryony's shoulders rose and fell in an exaggeratedly long sigh. From beneath her bonnet, she slanted Larkspur a pleading look. "I didn't go to town."

"You didn't—" Snapping her mouth shut, Larkspur glared. "Then where, do tell, have you been all this time?"

"Keep your voice down, okay?" Bryony shot quick glances across the field. "I'll tell you, but you can't say anything to Grandpa or Rose until I have a chance to explain."

Larkspur plucked another cotton boll. "Bryony Faye Linwood, what have you gone and done?"

"I went to see Mr. Heath." She stole another look in Grandpa's direction. When Larkspur shot up with a surprised gasp, Bryony motioned her back to work, then continued in a raspy whisper. "I had to do something. You see how poorly the harvest is going."

"So what'd you do exactly?" Then, "No, Bry, you didn't!"

Both of them stooped over, Bryony met Larkspur's shocked stare through the dried-out stems of a cotton plant. "Larkspur Linwood, you get such abominable thoughts out of your head this instant."

Larkspur gladly discarded the image of her sister locked in a clinch with their fusty old landlord. This wasn't Hollywood, and anyway, prim and proper Bryony would never be the type to use the "casting couch" method of persuasion. "Well? Are you going to tell me or not?"

Bryony didn't answer until they'd each stuffed another wad of cotton in their sacks. "I'm going to work as a housemaid for the Heaths. My pay will go against Grandpa's debt."

"But that'll just leave—" Larkspur bit her lip and looked away. This couldn't be happening, not now. She had *plans*, for crying out loud!

"What is it, Lark?" Bryony stood erect and faced her sister. "Is there something *you're* not telling *me*?"

One hand on her hip, Larkspur pushed back her bonnet and drew her shirtsleeve across her forehead. "I can't bear it here any longer, Bry. I've applied to Henderson State Teachers College."

"Oh, Lark, that's wonderful!" Bryony stretched out her arms for a hug, and they came together across the prickly plants.

Larkspur's throat tightened, her eyes filling. "Are you sure? I was so scared to tell you."

"Hey, y'all." Rose's voice sounded behind her. "Lark, are you okay?"

Easing away from Bryony, Larkspur nodded and ran a knuckle under her eyes. A quick glance in Grandpa's direction found him looking their way with concern. She waved and struggled for a reassuring smile. "Everything's fine, Rosie. We'll talk about it later. Best we all get back to our picking."

Rose's lips puckered. "You think I can't tell when y'all are keeping secrets? I'm sixteen. You don't have to treat me like a baby."

"We're not, Rosie." Bryony patted the girl's arm. "It's just . . .

this isn't the time to talk. I promise, we'll tell you everything later. Now go back to work before Grandpa starts wondering what's going on over here."

Grumbling, Rose stomped over to where she'd left off picking. When she'd moved out of earshot, Larkspur turned to Bryony with a worried frown. "What if I *do* get accepted, Bry? If you're working at the Heath place and I'm away at college, it'll just be Rose and Grandpa. How will they manage?"

"They just will. My job's only temporary, until Grandpa's debt is covered. And I'll come home every night to do my share of the chores. It's not like I'll be a hundred miles away like—" Bryony smashed her lips together.

"Like I'll be in Arkadelphia." Larkspur's hopes were evaporating faster than the sweat dripping down her spine. "I won't go. It was a silly dream anyway."

Bryony's gaze grew steely. "It's not silly at all. You've wanted to be a teacher your whole life long. If you're accepted, I'll get you to college if I have to wheel you there in a hay wagon."

"Oh, Bry . . ." The words jammed in Larkspur's throat, and all she could do was grab her sister and pull her into another hug. They'd had plenty of quarrels over the years, especially since Mama died and Bryony assumed the role of keeping Larkspur and Rose in line.

But if Larkspur was certain of anything, it was Bryony's devotion to their family. Over and over, she'd sacrificed her own opportunities to make sure her sisters didn't want for anything. She'd even dropped out of school to help Grandpa on the farm so Larkspur and Rose could finish their studies.

Right then and there, Larkspur made a silent vow to stop complaining so much about her bossy big sister. If Henderson did accept her, in the days before she left for Arkadelphia, she'd work even harder around the farm to give her family as much of a head start for the coming months as she could.

❧

As Larkspur's hug tightened, Bryony choked out a laugh. "It's okay, honey. It's okay." Breaking free, she briefly cupped her sister's cheek with a gloved hand and offered a reassuring smile. Lark's ice-blue eyes spoke gratitude, and both girls returned to picking cotton.

Oh, no doubt about it, they'd have a struggle on their hands if Larkspur did go away to college. But how could Bryony ask her to stay? Ever since Mama had brought them to the farm, Larkspur had chafed beneath the rigors of hard work and scarcity. Fair-haired and fine-boned, she was the real beauty of the family. Lark was meant for finer things, and if becoming a teacher could get her out of Eden, Bryony would do everything possible to help make it happen.

The acceptance letter—of course. That's why Lark had asked Bryony if she'd checked for mail at the post office. Well, she would, first thing in the morning. Better yet, after they stopped for their noontime meal, she'd send Lark into town and give the girl a rest from picking cotton.

Pausing to survey the meager harvest, Bryony suspected they'd be lucky if they managed half a bale to the acre. A sinking feeling hollowed out the pit of her stomach. If the drought continued into next year, she might find herself indentured to the Heaths until her hair was as gray as Grandpa's.

❦ 3 ❦

T he expletives spewing from Grandpa's mouth set Bryony's ears aflame. "I forbid it, Bryony Faye Linwood. Downright forbid it! No granddaughter of mine is gonna clean house for rich folk. 'Specially the likes of Sebastian Heath."

Thanks to Bryony's announcement, the happy news of Lark-spur's acceptance to Henderson State Teachers College was all but forgotten. As Lark had hoped, the letter was waiting at the post office. As soon as she returned to the cotton field, she'd excitedly shared the news with Bryony, but they'd kept it to themselves until after the evening meal. Grandpa typically mellowed after he'd sponged away the day's dirt and sweat, then filled his belly with a hearty supper.

Oh, he'd been plenty proud to learn one of his granddaughters would go to college. Said they'd manage just fine while she was away over in Arkadelphia. Then Bryony, taking advantage of his good spirits, had slipped in her own news.

Big mistake. As Grandpa raged on, Bryony clutched Lark's hand under the table in silent apology. Rose, bless her heart, quietly gathered up everyone's dishes and carried them to the sink.

"Grandpa, please." Bryony raised her voice, hoping to get a word in edgewise. "Will you give me a chance to explain?"

"Ain't no explanation you can give that'll change my mind." Grandpa thrust out his jaw. "Lordy, girl, what on God's green earth possessed you to go begging that man for a job?"

"There's nothing *green* for miles, in case you haven't noticed." Her own annoyance mounting, Bryony plopped both forearms on the table and nailed her grandfather with a flinty glare. "Besides, I didn't go over there looking to get hired as a maid. I went because somebody had to do *something* if we're gonna make it through this drought."

"And you figured ol' man Heath would take pity on our poor, starving family and give us a pass on the rent?" Giving a snort, Grandpa crossed his arms and shifted sideways.

Now Larkspur slipped silently away to help Rose with the dishes. Bryony looked up in time to see her sister brush away a tear, then glowered at her grandfather. "If you aren't the stubbornest old man who ever drew breath, I don't know who is." She scooted around to Lark's empty chair so she could get right in Grandpa's face and lowered her voice to a rasping whisper. "And in case you haven't figured it out by now, Lark's college education won't be cheap. She's gonna need help—money we don't have. Grandpa, don't you see? This job is answered prayer. I'll be helping all of us."

He drew a hand down his face. "You have no idea what you're getting into. I'm telling you, Bryony, the Heaths aren't a family you want to go messing with."

"Oh, really?" Bryony stiffened. "Well, that certainly explains why you've been such a loyal tenant all these years."

"Loyalty's got nothing to do with it. A man's got to earn a living the best way he can, and when options are few, you make the best of what you got." Both palms on the table, Grandpa pushed tiredly to his feet. "Do what you want. You will anyway. I'm going to bed."

Watching him go, Bryony massaged her forehead. She'd expected resistance from Grandpa, but not this much. Not this pent-up anger, like the Heaths were evil, somehow. Was it only because they were rich, or was there something more?

Larkspur came to the table, sinking into Grandpa's empty chair. She twisted the edges of a damp dishtowel. "I heard what you said, Bry. I'll get myself through college. You aren't responsible for paying my way, and if working for the Heaths is going to make Grandpa so mad—"

"You don't worry about me and Grandpa. Besides, I'm your big sister and I *am* responsible for you. For both you and Rosie." Bryony eased the towel from Lark's fingers and laid it on the table, then took her sister's hands and looked her squarely in the eye. "You're the smartest of all of us, and I'm over-the-moon delighted you're going to college so you can become a teacher. And me taking a year or so"—she hoped that's all it was—"to work off Grandpa's indebtedness to the Heaths means next year will be better. The *last* thing I want is for you to get distracted worrying about us here on the farm and decide you can't finish your education."

"Bry—"

"You know it's true. One hint that we needed you, and you'd give it all up like that." Bryony punctuated her words with a sharp finger snap.

A dishtowel tossed over her shoulder, Rose came up behind Larkspur and squeezed her shoulders. "Bry's right. This is your chance, Lark. What Bry's doing will give us all a leg up." She stooped to kiss Lark's temple, then winked at Bryony. "Y'all leave Grandpa to me, okay?"

Their baby sister always could wrap Grandpa around her little finger. Rising, Bryony pulled Larkspur to her feet, then wrapped both her sisters in a hug. "We'll make it, you hear? We'll all make it just fine."

It would take another week or two to bring in the cotton, which they'd have to finish without Larkspur since she had to be at college by the first week of September. And once Grandpa learned exactly what their pitiful crop would bring them at the gin, he'd see Bryony's decision to work for the Heaths was a good one. A necessary one, if they were to survive another year.

Bryony just hoped she could survive both Grandpa's resentment *and* a full-time housemaid's job on top of her farm chores.

⚜

"And that wraps up the weekend sports news."

Michael twisted the radio knob to the off position. He'd never been much of a sports fan, but who could resist a comeback story? After five years of ending the season in sixth place, the Brooklyn Robins had begun 1930 with a bang, holding onto first place all summer long. Then in August, up against Pittsburg and Cincinnati, things went sour. But on Saturday the Robins had outscored the Phillies 22–8. They still had time to turn things around for a respectable season finish.

Would Michael ever turn his own life around for a "respectable finish"? The longer he stayed shut away in Eden and the memories, the less likely it seemed.

Odette came through the parlor with the coffeepot and refilled his cup. "Lawsy, how you can drink hot coffee on a day like this, I do not know."

"Habit, I suppose." One he'd developed during his rehabilitation to keep the nightmares at bay. Rising, Michael carried his cup and saucer to the window, where a sultry breeze stirred the curtains. From somewhere along the veranda came the *swish-swish* of a broom.

"Heard you listenin' to the radio. Who you think is gonna make it to the World Series?"

Michael shrugged. "Couldn't even hazard a guess."

"You ask me, it's gonna be them Phillies. Don't care that they lost on Saturday. They's—"

"Odette." Michael's father's sharp tone resounded against the high ceiling. "Don't you have something to do in the kitchen?"

Chin tucked to her chest, Odette murmured, "Yessir," and slipped out another door through the dining room.

Casting his father a cool stare, Michael shook his head and

turned back to the window.

His father's footsteps scuffed across the Oriental carpet. "You have an opinion about how I address the household staff?"

"What's to say?" Michael sipped his coffee. "It's no different from how you address your son."

An angry snort gusted from his father's nostrils, and he cursed. "For two years I've tried to talk to you, one man to another. But you're determined to close yourself off to me. To the whole world, it seems."

With a final swallow, Michael drained his cup, then brushed past his father. The cup and saucer clattered as he carelessly set them on a low table. "I'm not in the mood for this conversation."

"You never are, and that's the problem."

The note of defeat in his father's voice halted Michael's rush to escape. Hands low on his hips, he looked toward the ceiling and hauled in a steadying breath before turning to face the man he both loved and despised. "Why can't you—" Choking on the futility of it all, he lifted his hands and backed from the room. "I'm going for a walk."

Without bothering to grab the art supplies never far from his reach, he stormed out the front door, only to collide with a woman and a broom. Instinct alone made him grab her upper arms before she toppled over. Stumbling as well, he caught her against his chest and got a mouthful of silky brown hair.

"Oh. Oh! I'm so sorry!" Her quick breaths matched his as she found her balance and stepped back.

"My fault entirely." Michael straightened his glasses for a better look at the woman he'd nearly flattened. "Bryony. Bryony Linwood?"

Both hands wrapped around the broom handle, Miss Linwood smiled up at him. A natural smile, but not particularly friendly. More like it was expected. "Good morning, Mr. Heath."

The polite greeting hit him like a punch to the gut. His jaw clenched. "*Mister* Heath is my father." He motioned vaguely toward the broom. "And what are you doing with that?"

"Well, brooms are generally used for sweeping, and the best ones are made from broomcorn, because of how—"

Michael lifted one hand while suppressing the chuckle climbing up his throat. The rapid shift from exasperation with his father to bewilderment over Miss Linwood's presence had him reeling. "I meant, why are you here, sweeping our veranda?"

"I work here now. Just started this morning." Her brows knitted. "You didn't know?"

With a glance toward the parlor windows, Michael pursed his lips. Perhaps he would have, if he cared to pay more attention to plantation business. "Sorry, I wasn't aware."

"Well, it's my first day, and I want to make a good impression, so . . ." With an exaggerated shrug, Miss Linwood stepped around him and continued sweeping.

Michael absently rubbed the center of his chest. Why was it suddenly so hard to breathe? Losing his interest in the walk that only minutes ago he'd been so anxious for, he pivoted and went inside. He paused in the foyer long enough to determine his father's whereabouts—sounded as if Dad had returned to his office to take a telephone call—and then crept upstairs.

Solitude—what he craved most. And easily obtained once he'd closed himself off in his suite of rooms in the south wing. Except, blast it all, he'd left his drawing things downstairs in the parlor. He could fetch them himself or ring for one of the servants to bring them up. Or he could sit beneath the ceiling fan and brood.

Brooding won out. He was good at it, had lots of practice. The hardest part, as always, was corralling his wayward thoughts, which too easily tracked down forbidden paths: artillery fire, scorched earth, the screams of his dying comrades, the mustard gas . . . Twelve years had passed, yet some days—most nights—the past loomed all too real.

These were the times he envied Mother's failing memory. If he could obliterate scenes from his past with the ease of erasing an errant pencil line in his sketchbook, the present would be so much easier to deal with.

As for the future . . . easier not to think too far ahead.

Resting his head against the cushioned chair back, Michael closed his eyes and waited for the lingering tightness in his chest to abate. As his lungs had slowly recovered from the mustard gas, he'd experienced fewer and fewer such episodes, but every once in a while they caught him off guard, sapping his energy at best, priming him for a respiratory infection at worst.

This morning, he blamed the dust raised by Miss Linwood's sweeping.

Her image floated behind his eyelids, again conjuring up memories of a lovely brunette and a Paris café. Those, at least, were pleasant times—he and his army buddies sipping strong coffee while practicing their French with the local girls. Véronique spoke excellent English, though, and her American friend, an Army Signal Corps operator, sometimes joined them with her doughboy fiancé. Michael wondered where they were now. Probably happily married with a houseful of noisy kids.

A song floated up through his open window—"Singin' in the Rain," the same tune Miss Linwood had been humming as she'd strolled up the drive several days ago. Now she sang the lyrics in a velvety, almost melancholy tone.

So Dad had hired her as a housemaid, which meant Michael ran the risk of bumping into her on a regular basis—though he hoped not literally, as he had this morning. One sure way to avoid unnecessary contact was to spend more time ensconced in his rooms.

Which, for some crazy reason, no longer appealed.

❦

Working her way around to the south end of the house, Bryony was glad she'd started her sweeping on the east veranda, before the morning sun had risen any higher. She'd already taken well over an hour to complete the circuit of the expansive wraparound porch.

As she passed the open windows of Mr. Heath's office, the song she'd been quietly singing died on her lips. Grandpa hadn't let her forget his displeasure over her working for the Heaths. His parting words as she left the farm early this morning were a reminder to watch herself around the man.

"He can be hard, or he can be kind," Grandpa had said, his left eye narrowed to a mere slit. "Don't trust neither."

Bryony paused to rest her chin on the tip of the broom handle, her ears attuned to the heated telephone conversation Mr. Heath carried on. No eavesdropping about it. As loud as the man spoke, anyone within a half-mile of the house could surely make out every word.

When the next word out of his mouth singed Bryony's ears, she sucked in a startled breath and swept with rapid strokes until she'd arrived back where she'd started. Cutting across the crisp, dry lawn, she made her way to the kitchen, a squatty building attached to the main house by a short, covered breezeway.

"I finished the veranda," she said to Odette as she set the broom in the pantry. "What's next?"

"You's supposed to go see Miss Esther. She'll have your regular duties all lined up by now." The plump woman barely looked up from the mound of dough she rolled out.

Bryony made a half-turn, then reversed it. "Um, where will I find Miss Esther?"

"In the house." The rolling pin thunked hard against the floured countertop. "Hallway to your right. Cain't miss her office. Last door you come to."

Unsure what she'd done to get on Odette's bad side already, Bryony pushed a damp strand of hair off her forehead and marched along the breezeway to the back door. Making a right turn at a narrow hallway, she followed it to a tiny room at the end.

A bespectacled woman with a bronze complexion and tight auburn curls looked up from a rolltop desk. Her pleasant smile was a refreshing change from Odette's scowl. "You must be Bryony. Come in."

"Odette said you'd tell me my duties."

Miss Esther motioned to a chair, and Bryony sat, hands folded in her lap. "I'm sorry I wasn't prepared upon your arrival, but things have been difficult this summer." As Miss Esther spoke, she paged through a tablet filled with handwritten notes. "On top of losing one of our housemaids—the girl you're replacing—we've had to adjust work schedules. With this unbearable heat wave, there's only so much a body can tolerate."

"I've spent the whole summer working in the heat, ma'am. I'm used to it. So you just tell me what needs doing and I'll do it."

"I appreciate your eagerness." One brow arching, Miss Esther shifted her gaze to Bryony.

Suddenly conscious of her work-worn, sun-browned hands, Bryony tucked them deeper into the folds of her skirt.

"Very well, then." Tablet in hand, Miss Esther rose. "We'll start with a tour of the house, and I'll introduce you to the other servants."

Bryony followed the woman into the hall, scurrying to keep up with her surprisingly quick strides. "How many are there?"

"Well, you've met Odette, the family cook. A girl named Callie is our laundress and also sometimes helps Odette in the kitchen." Miss Esther paused at a doorway to point out the dining room and the front parlor just beyond. "Jeremiah is the butler and also Mr. Heath's personal servant. Dancy sees to Mrs. Heath's needs."

"They each have their own servant?"

Stopping in the foyer to straighten a crooked picture frame, Miss Esther cast Bryony a blank look. "You have a lot to learn about working for a moneyed family, don't you?"

"I suppose I do." Bryony clamped her mouth shut and vowed to listen quietly while Miss Esther continued the tour. It wasn't news that the folks in the big house enjoyed an easier life than their tenants. Bryony just hadn't realized how much easier.

They passed the library and a smaller sitting room. Then, from a discreet distance, Miss Esther indicated Mr. Heath's office. "You'll have to find a time when he is otherwise engaged before you clean in there."

Returning to the foyer, they took the curving staircase to the second floor. "The family's private rooms are on this floor," Miss Esther stated. "Mr. and Mrs. Heath share the largest suite, on the north end of the house. Young Mr. Heath occupies rooms in the south wing, and we have four guest rooms in between."

Bryony nodded. A nearby guest room door stood open, and she peeked inside. A middle-aged woman wearing a gray dress and crisp white apron ran a dust cloth over a mahogany dressing table.

"Alice," Miss Esther said, stepping past Bryony, "this is the new girl. As soon as we finish our tour, I'll send her up and you can show her the routine."

"Yes, ma'am, sure will." Alice offered a lukewarm smile, revealing a gap where her left front tooth should be. Tipping her head, she resumed dusting.

As they continued to the third floor, Bryony felt the increased warmth, even in the dim corridor. Miss Esther explained these were the live-in servants' quarters. She opened a door onto a narrow room to reveal an iron bed frame and bare mattress with faded ticking. On the opposite wall stood a highboy, one empty drawer sticking out at an odd angle. The furnishings appeared old and well used.

"This was Tillie's room," Miss Esther explained. "It's yours now if you want it."

"Oh, no. I'll walk over every day from home." Disguising a shudder, Bryony couldn't imagine spending one night in this bleak, stuffy room.

Miss Esther drew the door shut. "We'll see if you feel the same after a week or two of walking back and forth in this heat."

They finished the tour, ending in a windowless room across from Miss Esther's office. Opening the doors to a wardrobe, the woman swept Bryony with an appraising gaze and then selected a drab gray dress off a hanger. "This looks about your size. You'll be given two uniforms so you'll have a clean one to wear while the other is washed and ironed. As for your hair . . ." The woman frowned at Bryony's tresses, secured at her nape with a ribbon.

"Keep it off your face and pinned up. We can't have stray hairs falling about. Do you need some pins?"

Ten minutes later, Bryony emerged from the room, her blue gingham frock exchanged for an ill-fitting gray maid's uniform with white apron. She'd done up her hair as best she could, braiding and pinning it in a bun at the back of her head. Feeling frumpy and forlorn, she submitted to Miss Esther's inspection before trudging upstairs.

She found Alice plying a sweeper over the fancy fringed carpet running the length of the hallway. Alice shared another of her gap-toothed smiles. "See you got your official housemaid uniform."

"And the lecture about stray hair." Bryony twirled on her tiptoes like she'd seen Lillian Gish do in a motion picture Mama took them to see some years back, before times got so bad. The cotton crop had been bountiful that year, and with extra money in the bank, Mama said they could all go into Little Rock and buy new dresses and shoes. Bryony had long since outgrown the shoes, but since she'd mostly grown taller and not rounder, the dress still fit. Old and faded as it was, it looked a far sight better than the maid's uniform.

Alice pinched the excess fabric on either side of Bryony's waist. She screwed her mouth into a frown. "I got a sewing machine up in my room. After work's done tonight, let's go up and do some alterations."

"Really? Thanks. I do fine with cooking and cleaning, but I've never been handy with a needle and thread." Bryony wasn't sure why it mattered how she looked while cleaning house, but it did. Every year that passed and every change of circumstances carried her farther and farther from the way things used to be, the life she'd have had if Daddy hadn't been killed in the war and Mama hadn't brought them to Eden.

Eden. What a name for a dreary little town with not much more than a grocer, a feed-and-seed, and a church building that also served as the county school. Eden was Bryony's home now, yes. But paradise? Not by a long shot.

⚜ 4 ⚜

Rose leaned toward the open window over the sink and prayed for a breeze. She'd toiled all day in the fields with Grandpa, and now she stood in a hot kitchen hoping she hadn't ruined supper. Bryony made cooking look too easy. Larkspur was a pretty good cook, too, when she could tear her mind away from the books she loved to read every spare moment.

But Rose? Give her a cow to milk, a field to plow, seeds to plant. She didn't even mind washing up the dishes after a good meal. But no one should trust her for a second with a recipe and the ingredients it called for. Leastways if they valued their stomachs.

She glanced at the clock—half past six—then at the blackened stewpot bubbling like a cauldron on the stove. "Get home soon, Bry. Please."

"Land sakes, smells like burnt shoe leather in here!" Grandpa let the screen door slam behind him. Nose in a twist, he slung his straw hat onto the coat hook. Then his gaze met Rose's and every muscle in his face sagged. "Aw, sweetie. Don't you fret none. It's bound to taste better than it smells."

"No, it won't, Grandpa. It'll be horrid. You know I'm disaster in the kitchen." To prove her point, she dragged a wooden spoon through the sludge she'd hoped to pass off as beef stew. "See? The potatoes are mush, the peas have turned to slime, and the meat's burned to the bottom of the pot."

Grandpa took the spoon from her hand and cautiously sampled a taste. He smacked his lips. "Just needs a tad more salt."

"It'll take a lot more than salt to make this edible." Eyes narrowed, Rose snatched away the spoon and tossed it in the sink. "Least we have those leftover biscuits Bry made last night."

While Grandpa went to wash up, Rose set the biscuits on the table next to a tub of butter. One apiece for her and Bryony, two for Grandpa. If they could use the biscuits to force down a few bites of Rose's stew, it might hold them until breakfast.

Maybe she could talk Bryony into cooking up a whole week's worth of meals every weekend. Then Rose could just throw pans in the oven to warm and only have to worry about taking the food out before it burned.

The screen door creaked, and Bryony slogged into the kitchen. She homed in on the nearest chair and collapsed, head resting on the edge of the table. "Who knew working as a housemaid could be so exhausting? Picking cotton was easier."

Rose wanted to feel sorry for her sister, but at the moment she was more concerned about supper. She carried a tall glass of water to the table and patted Bryony on the shoulder. "Here, honey, this'll make you feel better. Take a minute to catch your breath, and then could you please come look at my stew?" She smiled sweetly. "It needs a little help. . . . Bry?"

Mercy sakes, if Bryony hadn't fallen asleep right where she sat. Rose slid her arms beneath her sister's. "Come on, honey, let's get you into bed."

Looked like Rose was going to have to figure out this cooking business whether she liked it or not.

Michael awoke Tuesday morning to the sound of Bryony's broom on the upstairs veranda. He assumed it was Bryony because he recognized her humming, only this song was not as cheery as the catchy tune she'd been singing yesterday. He tried to place the melody, but it eluded him.

What time had it gotten to be? Had he slept through breakfast? He rolled over to peer at the bedside clock and saw it wasn't yet seven. The live-in house help tended to start before dawn while this blistering summer held the South in its grip, but since Bryony had to walk from home, he hadn't expected her so early.

He couldn't blame her for electing not to move into one of the servants' rooms upstairs. Given the choice, he, too, would prefer to live anywhere but here.

When he sat up, the tightness his chest reminded him why he stayed. He refused to consider himself an invalid, but his lungs had plagued him all day yesterday, leaving him short of breath, out of sorts, and rather too dependent on the servants for his liking. He'd hoped a good night's sleep would bring relief, but he'd been awakened by coughs throughout the night, so things didn't look promising for a walk along the riverbank today. Which meant no escaping his father's accusatory frowns, unless Michael intended to spend another day of seclusion in his suite.

He coughed twice to clear his lungs, and the humming outside his window ceased. After a momentary pause, the broom strokes picked up speed and moved farther along the veranda. He peered through the blinds in time to catch the swish of Bryony's gray skirt hem before she disappeared around the corner.

A knock sounded outside Michael's sitting room. On his way to answer, he pulled on a lightweight cotton robe and knotted the sash. He opened the door to find Callie holding a breakfast tray.

"Odette sent me, sir." The girl curtsied. "She was worried you might not feel up to coming down to the dining room."

"Thank you, Callie." Michael held the door wider and motioned her to the table by the south window.

Soft-spoken and polite, her speech more refined than one

would expect of a fifteen-year-old, Callie wasn't typical of the folks around Eden who came looking for employment at the mansion. She'd come to work for the Heaths shortly after Michael returned home, and even then, he'd thought a girl of her intelligence ought really to be in school where she could make something of herself, not doing laundry and washing dishes for rich folk. Her long, dark hair and olive complexion hinted at Mexican or Central American ancestry. As long as prejudice reigned toward anyone who wasn't white, the girl's hopes for a better future were sadly limited—a truth that caused Michael no shortage of discomfort.

With quick movements, Callie arranged the dishes and silverware. She filled a china cup with steaming coffee. "Is there anything else you need?"

"Can't think of a thing." Forcing his thoughts to the present, Michael spread a napkin across his lap as he settled into a chair. "I'll bring the tray to the kitchen when I finish."

Hands clasped at her waist, Callie backed toward the door. "You don't have to, sir. I'll come back for it."

"I'm sure Odette has other chores for you." At her troubled expression, he smiled encouragement. "It's all right, Callie. I'll be sure to tell her you offered and I refused."

"Yes, sir." Another quick curtsey and the girl skittered out of the room.

Even after growing up with a houseful of servants, Michael had never felt completely at ease with his position. It was one thing to hire someone for a job you didn't have the time or skills or knowledge for, and quite another when you were perfectly capable of doing the job yourself. He suspected Bryony Linwood would return home each night to several more hours of farm and household chores.

Besides, in a house this size, the servants had plenty to do without Michael's adding to their workload. Weak lungs or not, he could certainly dispose of his own breakfast tray. However, he'd take extra steps to ensure both Odette and Esther understood Callie was by no means at fault.

He spread butter and strawberry jam on a flaky biscuit. When he bit into it, it fairly melted in his mouth. Odette's scrambled eggs were as fluffy and light as the rainless wisps of clouds drifting past his window.

The thought of another brutally hot day made him lay aside his fork with a groan.

Another knock on his door brought him to his feet. "Callie, I told you I'd—" The words died on his lips when he opened the door to see his father standing on the other side.

"Good, you're up." Sebastian Heath breezed past Michael and crossed the sitting room. He glanced at the remains of Michael's breakfast. "Finish up and get dressed. I want you to drive over to the Wieland farm with me."

"Today? Why?"

"Nels is four months behind on his rent. The sheriff's meeting us there, and we're evicting him."

Michael's interest in breakfast evaporated. He returned to his seat and lifted his coffee cup. The brew tasted as bitter on his tongue as his measured reply. "You don't need my help in throwing a family off their farm."

"No, but I need you to understand exactly what I deal with on a daily basis." Michael's father took the chair across from him and folded his arms. "Get a move on. I'm not taking no for an answer."

"I'm afraid you have to. I—I'm not up to leaving the house."

His father took a long, slow breath, clearly deciding whether he believed his son or thought Michael only used his health as an excuse. He flipped aside the napkin covering the bowl of biscuits and selected a plump, nicely browned one. "Pass the butter."

Michael did as he was asked. "Dad . . ."

"And your knife, too, if you don't mind." His father split open the biscuit and spread butter on both halves. He bit into one and chewed thoughtfully. After swallowing, he cut his eyes at Michael. "I'm not an ogre, son. I'm a businessman. As you will be, too, one day. I realize you've had a hard road recovering from all you endured during the war, and I've tried to be both patient and understanding. But the time has come for you to accept your role in this family. You've got to stop hiding behind your condition. More importantly, you need to quit wasting time scribbling in those drawing books."

"This *condition*, as you call it, is quite real." Michael nudged his chair back several inches and twisted sideways. Did his father assume he'd spent years under treatment in a private hospital because he wanted to? Because he was *hiding*?

His own thoughts accused him. Solitude, escaping with his botanical sketches—since the war, these were the only things that brought him any sense of peace.

His father dusted crumbs off his lap. "I never said you weren't sick. I'm just saying it's no longer a valid excuse for avoiding your family responsibilities." He stood and marched to the door. "Be downstairs in half an hour. The car will be out front."

⁂

With the porches swept upstairs and down, Bryony proceeded to the next task Miss Esther had assigned for the day, cleaning bathrooms. A house with real indoor lavatories—and not just one, like Bryony's childhood home in Memphis, but five! She'd endured trips across the yard to Grandpa's outhouse for so many years that she'd nearly forgotten such luxury.

She began upstairs in one of the guest baths. Rarely used, the porcelain sink and claw-foot tub needed only quick swipes with sponge and cleanser. She swished a brush around the bowl of the commode, dusted the windowsill, polished the mirror, and ran a mop over the mosaic tile floor.

Alice had already started on the bathroom across the hall, so Bryony decided to tackle one of the family baths next. The elder Heaths' door remained closed, but their son's stood ajar, which meant he must have already gone downstairs. All the same, she tapped on the doorframe before stepping into the room. "Hello?"

When no one responded, she set down her tote of cleaning

supplies and surveyed her surroundings. The blinds on the east end of the sitting room were shut tight against the blazing morning sun, while the wide, south-facing windows stood open to a sultry breeze. The remains of someone's breakfast sat on a tray atop a small table. Bryony made a mental note to collect the tray before she returned downstairs.

The closed door to her right must lead to the bedroom—the room she'd been sweeping outside earlier when she'd heard a man's cough. The idea that only a window screen and lowered blinds had separated her from Michael Heath in his bedclothes had been enough to choke off the song in her throat and hurry her on her way.

And now she must brave the closed door, enter his bedchamber, and clean his private bath. The intimate nature of such a task flamed her cheeks. True, she cleaned up behind Grandpa every day. But Grandpa was family. Michael Heath was her employer.

Rather, her employer's handsome war-hero son.

The man had intrigued her from the moment of their first meeting. His reserved nature, not to mention his hasty escape the morning Bryony had come over to speak with his father, suggested someone not entirely comfortable with the mantle of his life.

Not so unlike Bryony. Frowning toward the closed bedroom door, she felt decidedly *un*comfortable in this role she'd taken on as housemaid to Grandpa's wealthy landlord. Yesterday, working alongside Alice to sweep and dust in other parts of the house, she'd been too overwhelmed with learning her new responsibilities. Today, reality was sinking in. This would be her life for the foreseeable future.

The happy childhood she remembered growing up in Memphis had become a dream she could never return to.

With a resigned sigh, Bryony retrieved her cleaning tote. The sooner she completed this dreaded task, the sooner she could move on to something less . . . *personal*. She crossed the room and set her hand upon the doorknob, only to have it jerked away. The door opened inward, and she stood face-to-face with Michael Heath. His raised brows mirrored her surprise.

She cringed and covered her mouth. "I'm so sorry! I didn't know anyone was still here. The door was open, and I called out—"

"No harm done. I'm just leaving, so it's all yours." Michael opened the door wider and motioned her into the bedroom. He stepped past, and they traded positions. "By the way, what was the song you were humming earlier? I can't get it out of my mind."

Embarrassed that he'd heard her, Bryony looked away. A filmy haze of steam wafted from the open bathroom door. She quickly shifted her gaze and focused on the tip of Michael's starched collar. "Just a song my mother used to play, years and years ago when we had a piano. It's Chopin's 'Raindrop' prelude."

"Chopin, of course." Michael tilted his head, a curious grin twisting his lips. "You do have a fascination with rain, don't you?"

Bryony uttered a groaning laugh. "Lately, it's practically all I can think about."

"I understand completely."

An awkward moment passed as neither of them moved. Michael seemed disinclined to go on about his business, and Bryony couldn't bring herself to commence cleaning his bathroom while he remained anywhere in the vicinity.

"I should—" she began.

At the same instant, he asked, "Do you play piano?"

"Oh. Me? No." A strand of hair had escaped Bryony's bun. She nervously tucked it behind her ear. "Mama taught me some when I was little, but we sold the piano when we moved to my grandpa's."

"That's too bad."

Bryony nodded toward her cleaning tote. "I should get to work. Please don't let me keep you."

"And I'm keeping you from your duties. Forgive me."

"It's all right. I was just—"

Three sharp blasts from a car horn interrupted her.

Michael's lids fell shut. His chest rose and fell in a long, pained breath. "And that will be my father, impatiently waiting to haul me along on a disagreeable errand."

So the wealthy dealt with "disagreeable" duties as well, although Bryony doubted Mr. Heath and his son faced anything so odious as scrubbing toilets. She pressed her lips together in a tight smile and waited for Michael to leave.

He took three trudging steps toward the door before halting and turning to her with a troubled frown. "Are you familiar with the Wieland family who also farm for my father?"

"Yes, we've known them for years. Sad about Mr. Wieland, isn't it?"

Michael's brows quirked. "I'm afraid I know very little about my father's tenants. Did something happen?"

"He has a bad heart. Barely got his cotton crop in the ground this year." Knowing how the family had struggled as Nels Wieland's condition grew worse, Bryony's heart twisted.

Then she caught the sudden look of chagrin washing over Michael's features. "No," she whispered, then louder, "No! Please tell me you're not on your way over there to throw them off their land."

The horn sounded again, this time in one long blare.

"I'm sorry. Truly sorry." With a quick shake of his head, Michael marched out the door.

Bryony's cleaning tote hit the carpeted floor with a thud. She darted to the bedroom window and parted the blind slats. A shiny blue automobile with whitewall tires was parked on the drive below, and seconds later, Michael climbed into the passenger seat. The car sped away in a cloud of dust.

Without thinking, Bryony sank onto the unmade bed, one hand pressed to her roiling stomach. *Please, Lord, not the Wielands.* They didn't deserve another setback, not after everything they'd suffered already.

Then the thought struck her that if she hadn't agreed to come to work for the Heaths, it might be Grandpa facing eviction. How could a man be so unfeeling? Worse, it appeared Sebastian Heath was grooming his son to follow in his footsteps.

Except it wasn't callousness she'd seen in Michael's eyes, but compassion. He was nothing like his father—that much, Bryony knew.

"Bryony, you in here?" Alice's twangy voice rang from the sitting room.

Realizing where she sat, Bryony sprang up from the bed. She scurried over to where she'd dropped her cleaning supplies and snatched them up. "In the bedroom, Alice."

"Miss Esther's looking for you. Said to clean in Mr. Heath's office while he's out."

"Oh. But I haven't done this bathroom yet. Michael—I mean, the younger Mr. Heath—was still here."

Alice cast her an exasperated frown. "Don't tell me you been in here jawing with him all this time? Miss Esther has rules."

"It wasn't intentional. He asked what—" Bryony clamped her mouth shut. It was no one's business what she and Michael Heath spoke about. "I mean, it didn't last more than a minute or two, and then he left."

"If you say so." Alice strode over to the bed and tugged at the sheet and spread. She motioned to Bryony to help her fluff pillows. As they tucked the covers neatly into place, Alice clucked her tongue. "Don't know why young Mr. Heath won't let Miss Esther find him a manservant. Jeremiah's got his hands full tending to the master."

Bryony couldn't imagine why a grown man needed a personal servant. But there was a lot she didn't understand about how the upper class lived. Like why a family of three needed five entire bathrooms. And that didn't count the tiny lavatory next to Miss Esther's office or the one up on the third floor where the live-in house help resided. Her thoughts returned to the Wielands, who, like Bryony and her grandpa and sisters, subsisted with so much less than even a servant in this household.

Once again, she retrieved her cleaning supplies. "I'll hurry and finish up here, then do Mr. Heath's office."

"Don't dawdle. No telling how soon he'll be back." Alice marched out of the room, and seconds later, the outer door banged shut.

Steeling herself to scrub another toilet, Bryony blocked other thoughts from her mind, including whose bathroom she cleaned, and set to work. It was hard not to think about Michael Heath, however, as she rinsed a minuscule trace of shaving soap residue down the sink drain. His towels hung neatly folded in thirds from the towel bars, and she barely had to polish any spots from the mirror or faucet handles. His tidy habits shortened her cleaning time considerably.

On her way out of the suite, she noticed the breakfast tray still on the table. Alice could just as easily have collected it, but maybe she hadn't seen it. Bryony set down her tote and began stacking dishes. Her hand brushed against a pocket-size notebook and knocked it to the floor. It splayed open where a pencil had been tucked between the pages.

Annoyed with her clumsiness, Bryony gathered up the notebook and pencil. Her eye was drawn immediately to the delicate sketches filling the pages—leaves, flower petals, a cluster of berries. Each drawing illustrated one small, specific aspect of a plant. The lines were so meticulous, the details so accurate, that not even an actual photograph could have captured the image with more precision.

Had Michael drawn these? If so, his artistic ability was a true gift.

Someone rapped on the door. When it burst open, Bryony spun around, the sketchbook clutched to her chest. "Oh, Alice. You about scared ten years off my life."

"For pity's sake, girl, what are you still doing up here? Miss Esther don't tolerate slackers."

"I'm on my way to Mr. Heath's office right now. Just gathering up these dishes to take to the kitchen." She put the notebook back in its place, then looped one arm through the cleaning tote handle before hefting the breakfast tray. Ducking past Alice, she hurried toward the back stairs.

Not even two days on the job, and Bryony had managed to get on first Odette's and now Alice's bad side. She wanted to go home so badly it made her stomach hurt.

🙞🙜

Michael drummed stiff fingers on his thighs as the LaSalle bounced along washboard-rough country roads. "You're really going to evict them? Is it absolutely necessary?"

His father shot him a disgruntled scowl. "Brookbirch Plantation is a business enterprise, not a benevolent society. If the tenants can't pay what they owe, we rent the land to someone who can."

"But I understand Nels Wieland has health issues. Perhaps if you gave him more time."

A surprised laugh exploded from his father's throat. "So you *have* been paying attention."

All Michael needed was for his dad to assume he actually cared about learning the business. "Someone mentioned it, that's all."

"If the man's sick, all the more reason he doesn't need to be farming. Wieland can move his family into Little Rock or somewhere and start over."

"Start over doing what? More importantly, *with* what? If the man can't pay his rent, he certainly can't afford to relocate his family." Michael's ribs ached from the coughing spells he'd endured last night. Now he fought not to inhale too much road dust. He'd pay for this excursion with his father in more ways than one.

Dad didn't reply immediately. Eyes narrowed, he focused on the road ahead, one elbow poking out his open window. He blew a sharp breath through his nose. "What would you have me do, Michael? I already went against my better judgment by agreeing to let George Rigby's granddaughter work off his debt."

The mention of Bryony Linwood stirred feelings that Michael had best put a damper on right now. He hadn't dared let on how her appearance in his private suite this morning had affected him. Her naiveté was a refreshing change from the stiff, stuffy atmosphere that prevailed in the Heath mansion. Unlike the other servants—except Odette, perhaps—Bryony addressed him less like her superior than as one human being to another.

Too bad he and his father didn't communicate similarly.

Michael cleared his throat. "Would it tax your resources so badly to extend the Wielands a little grace? Besides, considering what the drought is doing to the state's economy, how likely are you to find another tenant who can afford the rent? You won't be any worse off if you wait until next spring to see if the situation improves."

The car slowed, and Michael's father turned into a rutted lane. Beyond a barren, sun-scorched field stood a weathered farmhouse. As they neared the house, Michael glimpsed the sheriff leaning against his vehicle. A skeleton of a man dressed in faded overalls stood on the porch, one arm draped around the tiny gray-haired woman at his side.

Michael's father eased the LaSalle to a stop next to the sheriff's car. He shut off the motor and stared through the windscreen at the Wielands for a long moment, then shifted his gaze to Michael and let out a tired sigh. "Stay in the car. I don't need you making cow eyes and trying to change my mind about this."

"Sorry, you insisted I come with you. You're not shutting me up now." Michael shoved open his door.

With an annoyed shake of his head, Michael's father unfolded his long legs and stepped to the ground. "Howdy, Sheriff Pollard. Thanks for coming out. You remember my son, Michael."

The sheriff met them at the front of his patrol car and offered Michael his hand in greeting. "Haven't seen much of you since you came home. Heard you had quite a long spell in the hospital healing from your war injuries."

"Years, yes." And recuperating from far more than just the

gassing. Doctors had few treatments for helping one through the guilt of surviving when so many others died, nor the waking nightmares after enduring such agony. "I'm mostly recovered, thank you. It's a time I'd rather not dwell on."

"Can't say as I blame you." Sheriff Pollard nodded toward the couple on the porch. "Best get this over with, eh?"

Michael cut his eyes at his father.

Ignoring him, Sebastian strode to the foot of the porch steps. "Nels, Jenny. I guess you know why we're here."

"Guess so." Nels hiked his chin.

Jenny's lower lip trembled. "Please—"

Nels's quick squeeze silenced her. "We knew this was comin', darlin'. No sense fighting it. How long you gonna give us, Mr. Heath?"

Though outwardly they had little in common, Michael sensed an odd kinship with the man. He stepped forward. "Do you have a place to go, Mr. Wieland? Any other prospects?"

"Prospects?" The wizened man gave a harsh laugh and spat. He motioned toward the empty fields. "Farming's been my life since I learned at my own pappy's side. You throw us off this land and I might as well lay down and die."

His wife stifled a quiet whimper and pressed her cheek hard against his shoulder.

Michael's father cursed under his breath. "You want me to feel sorry for you, Nels? Where are your kids? Why aren't they helping?"

Now Jenny Wieland burst into full-blown sobs.

Nels drew her against his chest and shielded her with his arms. "You got some nerve, Heath. You already forget we got two sons buried in that field yonder?"

Michael felt the couple's pain like a knife through his gut. If his father wouldn't show sympathy, he certainly could. He moved closer. "Mr. Wieland, I'm sure my father didn't mean any disrespect. We're just trying to find a solution here."

"Well, there ain't no solution. You seen what the drought's

done to us. My heart's giving out, we're dead broke, and our only living son's gone from sunup to sundown taking any odd job he can find just so's we got food on the table."

Michael's father turned aside and drew a hand down his perspiring face. Lips mashed together, he squinted at Michael with a look that said he wished he'd left him at home.

Michael refused to back down. Speaking directly to his father but loud enough for the Wielands to hear, he said, "This family has troubles enough. Let's go home and leave them in peace."

"All right, all right!" Sebastian Heath lifted both hands in resignation. "Nels, I'll give you another planting season to try to get yourselves out of this hole. But after that, no promises."

Mrs. Wieland cried harder. Nels merely nodded. He looked too worn down to care.

With a nod to the sheriff, Michael's father said, "Guess we won't be needing you after all."

Michael breathed a silent sigh of relief. Drained both physically and emotionally, he trudged around the LaSalle and dropped into the passenger seat. He waited while his father climbed in and settled behind the wheel. "Thank you," he murmured. "You did the right thing."

Jaw clenched, Dad started the car. He didn't speak until they'd turned onto the main road. Then, with a look of utter contempt, he growled, "Don't you ever back me into a corner like that again."

"Or what? You'll disown me as you did my sister?"

"Don't tempt me, Michael."

"Why should I care? Haven't I made it abundantly clear I'm not interested in my inheritance?"

"In case you have forgotten, the *source* of your inheritance is the same person who paid the exorbitant costs of the rehabilitation hospital that got you back on your feet after the war."

The reminder made Michael suck in a harsh breath. Of course he was grateful—and suffered even more guilt for costing his parents all those years of anguish and worry. He gripped the armrest as the car picked up speed. "Slow down, will you? I didn't survive mustard gas only to be killed in a crash."

When his father eased off the gas pedal, dust swirled through their open windows. Michael waved his hand in front of his face and barked a cough. He stole a glance at his father, but the man kept his gaze firmly fixed on the road ahead.

I don't even know you, Michael thought. He and his sister, Miranda, had grown up on the plantation. It was their livelihood, their legacy, but if things continued unchanged, Michael feared it would be his doom.

5

Finally, after two weeks of working for the Heaths, Bryony had a day off. Well, half a day, because as soon as they arrived home from Sunday worship, she helped Rose get dinner on the table, then faced a long, hot afternoon of washing, ironing, and all the other chores she hadn't had the strength to tackle after trudging home each day from the Heaths'.

"Go sit in the shade, Bry. You look about ready to pass out." Rose snatched the clothespin from Bryony's hand and finished clipping a muslin sheet to the line.

"Just for a minute, though." Bryony sank onto the porch step and fanned herself with the hem of her dress. She looked toward the garden, now overgrown with dull-colored weeds that didn't seem to mind the lack of rain. Everything else had shriveled and died.

At least she'd managed to salvage a middling crop of string beans, tomatoes, and cucumbers before heat and bugs got the best of them. The potatoes and onions had taken a hit, too, but with Larkspur away at college and one less mouth to feed, Bryony held cautious hope they'd make it through the winter.

The screen door banged shut behind her, and Grandpa joined

her on the step. "The Sabbath's supposed to be a day of rest. Lord knows you need one, girl."

She lightly rested her head on her grandfather's shoulder. "Show me one person in this county who isn't working like a dog every day of the week."

Grandpa harrumphed. "Sebastian Heath."

"Bet you're wrong. He may claim to own the plantation, but the real truth is it owns him. The man worries more over his account ledgers than I ever saw you fret about bringing in a harvest."

"But he ain't the one sweatin' up a storm to plow and plant and reap." Scowling in the general direction of the Heath mansion, Grandpa raised his voice. "He ain't the one struggling every day to keep flesh on bone."

When Rose looked up from the laundry basket with a concerned glance, Bryony cast her a tight-lipped smile. "Be right there, Rosie." To Grandpa, she said, "We're not starving, are we? Mr. Heath may be a hard man, but he's not heartless. You heard what he did for the Wielands."

"Nels said that had more to do with the boy sticking his nose in than any charity on Sebastian's part."

Bryony had heard the same from gossip among the servants. She'd wished several times she could have asked Michael Heath directly what happened that morning, but—besides the fact that it was none of her business—she'd scarcely crossed paths with him since then. She suspected Alice had said something to Miss Esther about catching Bryony snooping through Michael's things, because the next day Miss Esther informed her she wouldn't be cleaning upstairs for now and must also assist Callie with the laundry.

"Either way," she told Grandpa, "Mr. Heath let the Wielands stay on their farm. And he hired me, didn't he? Proves he's not above showing a little compassion when the need arises."

Before Grandpa could argue, she pushed up from the step and plodded over to the clothesline. By the time she and Rose had finished hanging sheets, the warm breeze had dried Bryony's drab gray maid's dresses. She took them from the line and went inside to the ironing board. Alice had altered the dresses so they weren't quite as shapeless on Bryony's figure, but apparently it had been the housekeeper's final act of kindness. To this day, Bryony hadn't a clue why both Odette and Alice had so quickly cooled toward her.

At least Callie remained friendly. The pretty young girl, barely fifteen, worked hard and didn't complain. She also didn't mind Bryony's chatter as they stood over a steamy vat of laundry or ran sheets, towels, and garments through the ringer. Callie liked to sing, too, and had taught Bryony some lively Spanish folk songs. In turn, Bryony taught Callie the words to "Singin' in the Rain," and they often joined in duets as they strung the wash on the line behind the kitchen.

About the time Bryony finished ironing her uniforms, Rose brought in a basketful of dry clothes. "Let me take over for a bit."

Bryony smiled her thanks as she straightened a dress on a wire hanger. "Soon as I put these away, I'll fix us some supper."

"No hurry." Rose set the iron on the stove to heat. "But could you write down some real simple meals I can throw together this week? That way, I could have supper on the table so you wouldn't have to cook after doing maid's work all day."

A chuckle bubbled through Bryony's chest. "Rosie, I love you dearly. But after the stew you made my first day at the Heaths', there's no way I'd ever come home so tired that I'd willingly eat your cooking."

❧

By mid-week, what little rest Bryony had squeezed in on Sunday was long forgotten. At least autumn's arrival brought relief from the heat, if not from the drought.

As she and Callie carried a tub of wash water out back to empty, something wet plopped onto the end of Bryony's nose.

Sputtering, she brushed it away, then laughed and flicked water at Callie.

Callie gasped. "Now what was that for?"

"You started it."

"Started what?"

"You know exactly what."

Together, they set the washtub down at the edge of the kitchen garden, and Callie straightened with a huff. Even so, her eyes sparkled with mischief. "I do declare, Miss Bryony Linwood, you are trying my patience something fierce."

"Don't turn this on me. You're the one who—" Another droplet hit Bryony's cheek. She looked toward the sky. "Oh, Callie, look! It's raining!"

"Praise the Lord!" Callie spun in circles, her arms stretched wide.

Bryony joined her as fat raindrops pelted them and spattered onto the hard, dry ground. Then she grabbed Callie's hands and belted out the opening stanza of "Singin' in the Rain."

"What in tarnation!" Odette stormed out the back door of the kitchen. "You two gone plumb loco? Get in here right this second afore Miss Esther catches you caterwaulin' like fools."

"But it's raining, Odette." Callie dropped one of Bryony's hands and reached for Odette's. "Come on, dance with us. We're celebrating."

Odette yanked her hand free, but the chiding look she gave Callie didn't hold as much conviction as the disapproving glare she cast Bryony's way. "I'm glad as you are for a little rain, but it ain't no excuse for wastin' time. Now both of you get on with your chores."

"Yes ma'am." Callie meekly dipped her chin but slanted a wink at Bryony.

Once Odette had returned to the kitchen, Bryony and Callie faced each other with barely suppressed giggles. The rain, hardly enough to get their clothes damp, had already slackened to barely a drizzle, but it had brought a much needed lift to Bryony's spirits, not to mention her flagging energy.

She helped Callie empty the wash water, then paused outside the kitchen door to poke loose pins into her straggly bun. Looking toward the main house, she glimpsed Michael Heath leaning on the balcony rail. He caught her eye and smiled.

Oh, Lordy, had he witnessed her acting like a nincompoop and singing at the top of her lungs? Gulping, she ducked into the kitchen.

Naturally, Odette was watching for her. "If you's through with your silliness, I got this tray needs takin' upstairs to Miz Heath."

Bryony eyed the delicate china tea service and plate of trimmed finger sandwiches. "Doesn't Dancy usually take Mrs. Heath her afternoon tea?"

"Dancy's feelin' poorly. Miss Esther sent her up to lie down." Odette waggled her fingers toward the tea tray. "How many times I got to tell you? Now go!"

Without another word, Bryony obeyed. She made sure to wipe her feet before entering the main house, then paused briefly in the servants' hallway to check her appearance. She hoped the water spots on her uniform weren't too obvious.

Upstairs, she knocked on the door to the Heaths' private suite. A feeble voice bade her to enter, and she nudged the door open with her hip.

"Good afternoon, Mrs. Heath. I brought your tea."

The woman reclined on a pale green velvet chaise and looked as if she'd been napping. "You're not Dancy."

"No, ma'am. It's Bryony. Remember?" Seemed every time she encountered Mrs. Heath, she had to remind the woman all over again that she was the new housemaid. She set the tray on a low table beside the chaise. "Shall I pour?"

"Please." The tiny woman eased herself more upright. "And pull a chair closer so we can visit awhile."

"Oh, ma'am, I can't stay. I need to—"

"Fiddlesticks." Frowning at the serving tray, Mrs. Heath

clucked her tongue. "Odette knew I was having company. Why on earth would she send up only one teacup?"

A male voice sounded behind Bryony. "Just an oversight, Mother, I'm sure."

"Mr. Heath, I didn't hear you come in." Bryony set down the teapot. "Are you having tea with your mother? I can fetch another cup."

Gray-green eyes twinkled behind the younger Mr. Heath's rimless glasses. "Not necessary. I'm not much of a tea drinker."

"Then can I bring up something else for you—coffee, a cold drink?" Bryony started for the door.

"Where are your manners, son?" With a reproachful frown, Mrs. Heath nodded toward a brocade chair. "This young lady is our guest. Please treat her as such."

Michael moved the chair closer to his mother's chaise and motioned for Bryony to sit. "Best humor her," he whispered.

"But Miss Esther—"

"Works for my mother. She'll have nothing to say about this." As Bryony reluctantly settled onto the front edge of the seat, Michael crossed to an ebony Oriental cupboard. He returned with another cup and saucer and placed them on the tray next to Bryony. "We keep extra china up here for just such occasions."

"You'll stay, too, won't you, Michael?" With a tittering laugh, his mother reached for her teacup. "Unless you can't abide gossipy women."

"Certainly, Mother, if you like." He brought a chair over next to Bryony's. As he sat, she noticed a small notebook protruding from his shirt pocket and wondered if it was the same one she'd come across in his room two weeks ago.

The one that had gotten her into so much trouble.

Mrs. Heath reached for a napkin. "Do have some tea and sandwiches, dear."

At Michael's reassuring nod, Bryony poured herself half a cup of tea. She eyed the sugar bowl. At home, she used sugar sparingly, and only when needed for cooking or canning. Never for anything as frivolous as sweetening tea or coffee! Today, though . . . why not? Using dainty silver tongs, she dropped a sugar cube into her cup and watched it melt away into nothingness. When she took her first sip of the fragrantly sweet brew, her eyes closed in sheer pleasure.

She hadn't realized she'd moaned aloud until Michael chuckled softly and murmured, "If it's that good, I may have to change my mind and have some."

Embarrassed, Bryony set her cup on the tray. "This was a mistake. I should get back to work."

"You'll disappoint Mother if you go."

"She certainly will." Mrs. Heath added another sugar cube to her tea. "Do remind me of your name, dear. I'm terribly forgetful of late."

"Bryony, ma'am. Bryony Linwood. I, um . . ." She glanced at Michael. "I live down the road. My grandpa is George Rigby."

"Yes, yes, of course. How is your grandmother these days? Violet makes the best bread-and-butter pickles I've ever eaten." Taking a bite of a finger sandwich, the woman's face lit up. "In fact, I can taste them in this egg salad."

Bryony wouldn't be surprised—probably the very pickles she'd brought over the day she'd come to plead for Sebastian Heath's forbearance. She decided as long as she was having tea, she may as well try a sandwich, too. She took one on a napkin and passed the plate to Michael. He declined.

"Did you bring your sketches, son? You should show Bryony."

Forgetting herself, Bryony swiveled toward him. "Yes, do. I'd love to see your drawings."

Michael's expression clouded. "They're nothing special, just something I do to pass the time."

"Nonsense," his mother burst out. "Fetch your pictures at once. The young lady—what was your name again?"

"Bryony."

Mrs. Heath rubbed her forehead. Bryony grabbed for the cup

and saucer before the woman's tea spilled across her lap. "I . . . I can't seem to remember anything of importance anymore."

"You should rest, Mother." Michael rose. "I'll see Miss Linwood out."

"No, no. Stay. I'll just close my eyes for a moment. You can entertain our guest." Turning her face toward the window, she rested her head.

Bryony studied the woman's pale profile. "Is she all right?"

"She has good days and bad." A thin coverlet lay across the foot of the chaise. Michael drew it up over his mother's legs. "I've asked Esther to make sure someone is with her or at least stays nearby, but it isn't always possible."

The tender look in Michael's eyes as he stood over his mother brought a clutch to Bryony's chest. "I'd be happy to help if Miss Esther would let me, but after what Alice told her—" She bit her tongue.

Michael cast her a curious glance. "Maybe you'd better enlighten me."

Bryony blew a sharp gust of air between her lips. "It was my second day working here. I didn't realize you were still upstairs, remember?" Though she kept her voice low so as not to awaken Mrs. Heath, her words tumbled out in a rush. "And then after you left I thought I'd collect your breakfast tray, but I accidentally knocked your little notebook off the table, and I couldn't resist looking at the pictures, and that's when Alice caught me, and ever since then—"

Michael was shaking his head, lips compressed into an annoyed frown.

Certain he'd inform his father and immediately have her fired, Bryony stood before him with folded hands. "It was an accident, truly. I never meant to pry. It won't happen again—you have my word."

With a glance toward his dozing mother, Michael took Bryony's arm and drew her out into the hall. Leaving the door slightly ajar, he faced Bryony, his expression stern. "You're in trouble with Miss Esther because you were looking at my sketchbook?"

Bryony nodded. "I'm only cleaning downstairs now and helping with the laundry. The only reason Odette let me bring the tea was because Dancy's not well." She looked toward the stairway, half expecting Odette or Miss Esther to come searching and demand to know why she'd lingered so long in forbidden territory.

After several moments of stiff silence, during which Bryony wrung her hands and vainly racked her brain for some other way to pay off Grandpa's debt, Michael finally spoke. "Would you sit with Mother awhile longer, please? I'm going downstairs right now, and I'll get this whole mess straightened out." He started for the stairs, then paused to look over his shoulder with a reassuring smile. "Don't give this matter a second thought, Bryony. Your job here is secure."

❧

Quietly seething, Michael made his way downstairs to Esther's office. He found her at her desk counting out petty cash for various household needs.

"May I speak with you a moment?" Without waiting for an answer, he moved an empty chair closer and sat facing her.

Esther, always prim and proper, smiled serenely as she tucked a stack of bills into an envelope and laid it aside. "Yes, Mr. Heath, what can I do for you?"

He summarized what Bryony had just told him. "No harm was done, and I see no reason for you to alter her duties due to lack of trust."

"Sir, we have strict rules—"

"None of which have been broken. I compliment Alice for her thoroughness, but in this case I believe she was overzealous and should not have assumed the worst." Hands on his knees, Michael pushed to his feet. "Oh, and one more thing. When Dancy is feeling better, please have her instruct Bryony concerning my mother's personal care."

Esther's mouth fell open. "I—I don't understand."

"This is no criticism of Dancy's competence, but as you are aware, Mother's forgetfulness is growing worse. From now on, anytime Dancy must attend to other duties, she is to leave my mother in Bryony's care." He angled one foot toward the door and lowered his voice. "I'd also appreciate it if you would speak to both Alice and Odette about their attitudes toward Bryony. She doesn't deserve their ill will."

Looking offended, Esther sat straighter. "I can assure you I do not tolerate rudeness from anyone employed in this household."

"Which is why I trust you'll see to this matter at once." With a curt nod, Michael exited the tiny office.

He took several rapid steps down the hallway before halting to draw a deep breath. Though he'd felt compelled to defend Bryony Linwood—even more, to bring her aboard to assist with his mother's care—involving himself in such matters strained his composure.

Not as badly as the day he'd prevented his father from evicting the Wielands, however. Those in a position of superiority walked a fine line between pragmatic detachment and the mutual concern for one another commanded in Scripture. Michael had witnessed the dichotomy firsthand while serving in the Great War—commanders who sent their troops into battle knowing how few of them would return alive, only to grieve inconsolably in the privacy of their quarters.

And Michael himself? Caught in the middle when the death of his sergeant earned him a battlefield promotion, and then it fell to him to order his closest friends into the fray.

The edges of his vision darkened. Before the unwelcome images returned, he tore his thoughts away from the past. A nice, long ramble along the riverbank would clear his head. Instinctively, his hand went to his breast pocket and the small sketchbook he kept handy for those moments when something in nature cried out to be captured on paper. He had a mind to make for the nearest door and escape, but if Esther didn't send someone to relieve Bryony right away, he didn't want her to feel stranded in his mother's room.

He'd look in on them briefly, let Bryony know about the arrangements he'd made with Esther, and then collect his larger sketchbook and pencil box for a trek down to the river.

When he reached his mother's door, a lilting feminine voice met his ears. He peeked inside to see Bryony seated on the chair next to his mother's chaise and reading aloud. Michael recognized the scene from *The Adventures of Huckleberry Finn* where Huck feigned his own murder and took off down the Mississippi. Despite a certain amount of envy of the fictional boy who so artfully took charge of his own destiny, Michael couldn't suppress quiet laughter at the theatrical inflection Bryony gave each line. His mother's face reflected her complete rapture.

Michael hesitated to interrupt, but before he could slip away, Bryony glanced up and caught his eye. She stumbled briefly over the next phrase, then continued until she reached a stopping point. She slid a finger between the pages and closed the book. "I saw this on the shelf and thought it might be a pleasant way to pass the time."

"It's a lovely idea. Thank you." Michael strode over and took his mother's hand. "Did you have a good rest?"

"Yes, and I feel so much better now. Bryony's been a dear to keep me company, but I've kept her occupied long enough."

Relieved that Mother seemed herself again, Michael looked across to Bryony. "Everything's taken care of with Esther. If you can stay and read some more, I know Mother would enjoy the company."

"Goodness, no," his mother chided, "or the poor girl won't have any voice left. Did you ever show her your drawings? I think you were about to when I nodded off."

With a self-conscious cough, Michael lowered his gaze. "I'm afraid I had other things to attend to."

"Then go and fetch them." His mother waved a hand toward the door. "I want another look, too." To Bryony, she said, "My son is gifted, truly gifted. He was meant to be an artist."

Moving toward the hallway, Michael didn't dare look up for fear of exposing his discomfiture. It was one thing sharing his sketches privately with Mother, who doted on him, and quite another to bare them to the scrutiny of someone he hardly knew. Bryony may have glimpsed a few pencil studies in his pocket note-book, but those were simple drawings compared to the intricate, full-color illustrations he limned in his larger sketchbooks.

Trudging the long hallway to his own rooms, he had plenty of time to ponder excuses for returning empty-handed. He could say he'd mislaid his drawings, which, since he was seldom parted from them, Mother would never believe. He could hope Mother would have forgotten about sending him on this errand in the space of time it took him to make the trek to his rooms and back—not an unlikely possibility these days, but one he didn't favor in the least. He hated what was happening to his bright, beautiful mother, and he'd do anything to preserve her health and memory for as long as possible.

In his sitting room, he went to the bureau where he kept his drawing supplies and selected his newest sketchbook, still only about half full. He started for the door, then backtracked for a second book, knowing as sure as he didn't bring it, Mother would send him for it.

Then, before he reached his mother's door, a rising sense of panic slowed his steps. All these years he'd kept to himself, first while in the hospital and now by avoiding everyone beyond imme-diately family and the servants. Others didn't understand—*couldn't* understand—what the war had done to him. Even as a young boy, conflict of any kind unsettled him, a cowardly character flaw in his father's opinion. But to be forced to kill another human being, to watch his companions die before his eyes? War had changed him in more far-reaching ways than what the mustard gas did to his lungs.

His hand froze on the doorknob. He tightened his grip on the sketchbooks clutched to his chest. These drawings of nature, of *life*, had been and continued to be his saving grace through the long years since the war ended.

And he wasn't ready to share.

⁂

As Bryony continued reading, Fenella Heath kept one ear tuned for Michael's return. What was taking him so long?

Then she heard the tiniest click of the doorknob and looked expectantly toward the door.

A minute passed. Nothing.

With a silent sigh, Fenella returned her attention to Huck Finn's current adventure. She should have anticipated Michael's reluctance to share his drawings. But he'd seemed otherwise at ease around Bryony, and after all, the girl wasn't *really* a stranger. She was Violet Rigby's granddaughter. Those years when Violet served as nanny for Michael and Miranda were such special times. Simpler times. Fenella wished she could turn back the clock and restore her children's innocence. Dear Michael, so beaten down by the war. And Miranda. If only things could have been different . . .

"Mrs. Heath?" Concern shown in the girl's warm brown eyes. Eyes that were familiar, somehow. "You're looking tired again, ma'am. Maybe we should stop for now."

"No, I'm all right. I just need to . . ." Fenella darted her glance around the room. Why was it so hard to remember things? Tossing aside the coverlet, she slid her legs off the side of the chaise and sat up facing . . . *who was this girl?* "Where is Miranda. Have you seen Miranda?"

"I don't know her, ma'am, but I'll be happy to go ask someone." The girl rose and laid a book in her vacated chair.

"No, no. Just get Michael. He'll find her." Panic squeezed Fenella's throat. Vague images danced at the edges of her mind, taunting her, beckoning her into an abyss of forgetfulness. "Where is Michael? He was here only a moment ago."

Footsteps pounded across the carpet. "I'm right here, Mother. I'm with you now."

She looked up into her handsome son's face—the face of a man, not a boy—and wondered where the years had gone. "I can't find Miranda. I can't find Miranda!"

6

One foot propped on the veranda railing and a half-empty mug of cold coffee on the table beside him, Michael sorted through his pencil box. For the toothed leaves of the *Ilex verticillata*, he needed a darker shade of green. He'd come across the thicket of winterberry shrubs while walking along the riverbank this morning. Bright red berries clustered along the stems and would provide a tasty winter feast for the birds.

Winter seemed a long way off yet. Though the heat of summer had mitigated, the earth remained parched, and a couple of recent short-lived rain showers had offered little relief.

At the sound of his mother's laughter, Michael glanced up. She sat at the opposite end of the veranda listening to Bryony read another chapter from *The Adventures of Huckleberry Finn*. The last few days had gone well. Dancy had voiced no objections to Bryony's helping with Mother. In fact, getting up in years herself, the maid emphatically welcomed the respite another pair of eyes and hands could offer. Caring for Mother couldn't have been easy these past several months, when one moment she clearly recognized her surroundings, and the next she slipped into another time and place.

Bryony had a calmness about her, though. When Mother's forgetfulness brought on a state of agitation, Bryony didn't over-react as Dancy sometimes did. The day Michael had returned with his sketchbooks to find Mother fretting over Miranda, he'd almost panicked himself. How many times would he have to tactfully explain that Miranda wouldn't be coming home? When Mother was in her right mind, she knew perfectly well why Michael's sister had been banished. And she knew Michael's father was to blame.

The circumstances, however, were not anything Michael cared to recall.

Returning to his sketch, he added a little more magenta to the berries, then deepened the shadow on the underside of a leaf.

Only when he felt a light touch on his shoulder did he realize Bryony stood beside him. He sat forward with a start. "Is Mother all right?"

"Yes, yes, she's fine. Dancy finished tidying your mother's rooms and took her upstairs for afternoon tea." Bryony leaned closer to peer at Michael's drawing. "Oh, my, how beautiful! It almost looks like it could sprout right off the page."

Flipping the sketchbook closed, Michael pushed to his feet. "It's no more than a hobby I picked up after the war."

"You never had the chance to show me your pictures the other day. I'm free for the next few minutes and I'd love to see more." She held out her hand for the sketchbook. "May I, please?"

Michael hesitated. He had no good reason for keeping his drawings private, only that sharing them felt too much like revealing the deepest part of himself. But Bryony's smile, full of innocence yet gently persuasive, slipped beneath his reserves. He handed her the sketchbook, then leaned against the porch rail with his arms tightly folded against his ribs.

Bryony took the chair he'd vacated and paged through the drawings. She lingered over each one with a kind of reverence, and her quiet murmurs of appreciation slowly drained away Michael's anxiety.

When she reached the last sketch, she glanced up at Michael

with parted lips, and strangely, his first thought was how closely the color of her lips matched the winterberries. His throat went dry, and now a different kind of anxiety made him tear his gaze away. He reached for his cold coffee—anything to distract himself from this sudden barrage of emotions.

Bryony was flipping pages again, must faster this time. "These are amazing. How did you learn to draw like this? And to know so much about each plant—did you study botany in school?"

"Never had the chance." Michael had always intended to go to college, until he'd abruptly changed his plans and joined the army. "I read a lot, though." Heaven knew he'd had plenty of time to study on his own while recuperating in the Raleigh rehabilitation hospital. One of the orderlies, working his way through school at North Carolina State, kept him supplied with books from the college library.

"Well, if I knew as much as you about flowers and trees and shrubs, I think I'd plant my very own Garden of Eden and never, ever leave." Bryony looked up suddenly. "Do you have a picture of my namesake, the—what did you call it?—*bryonia*?"

Michael cleared his throat. "I do . . . somewhere."

"Would you show me?"

"I'll have to go upstairs and look for it." He motioned vaguely toward the house, but he didn't move. It felt as if the soles of his shoes were nailed to the porch boards.

Bryony continued browsing through the sketchbook. "I wish Mama could see this. Grandma, too. They knew more about gardening than I'll ever learn. Now my sister Rose, she might come close someday. But Larkspur and I—"

"You're all named for flowers?" Chuckling softly, Michael shook his head. "Guess I shouldn't be surprised since your grandmother's name was Violet."

"And my mama was Iris. Told you they loved gardening." Bryony looked up with a wink. "Can't imagine what Mama and Daddy would have named a son if they'd had one."

Michael looked beyond the veranda toward a line of trees. "Perhaps Ash or Linden?"

"I like both of those. Manly yet elegant. Someday if I get married and have a little boy . . ." Face reddening, Bryony thrust up from the chair and handed Michael the sketchbook. "Listen to me carrying on like I've got all the time in the world. I'll get what-for from Miss Esther for sure."

Giving a quick tug to her apron, she darted into the house, and Michael felt suddenly deflated. How long since he'd actually enjoyed conversing with anyone so much? He argued with his father, attended to his mother, bantered with Odette, and simply tried to show kindness to the other servants.

But Bryony . . . Bryony was different. Though always respectful and a diligent worker, she had a single-mindedness about her, an air of purpose, as if working for the Heaths was a mere stopover on the way to something better. The other servants, especially those who'd been around the longest, went about their work with settled apathy. Michael didn't question their loyalty to the family, but he did doubt their enthusiasm. Even young Callie seemed resigned to the circumstances of her life.

Michael could relate to defeatism. It wasn't a trait he much admired, particularly in himself, but he blamed his own circumstances—the choices he'd felt compelled to make, the unavoidable consequences of those choices. He wished he had the strength to change things, but more than a decade of living in seclusion had left him with few skills of value to the greater world. And Dad's efforts to bring him on board with running the plantation? An exercise in futility, if only he could convince his father of the fact.

With a groan, he sank into the chair, opened his sketchbook, and turned to the winterberry drawing. Only a few strokes would complete the picture, but he couldn't find the motivation to pick up his pencils and continue.

Above him, a door opened onto the upstairs balcony, and Bryony's humming drifted down. *Bryonia alba*, a plant with medicinal properties. Odd how this woman he barely knew seemed to have a healing effect on him.

He gathered up his drawing supplies and marched inside. In his sitting room, he went straight to the bureau and rifled through his sketchbooks until he found the drawing he searched for. As he strode along the hallway toward his mother's rooms, he was already picturing Bryony's full-lipped smile when he showed her the pale, star-shaped flower she was named for.

◈

While Dancy helped Mrs. Heath into bed for a nap, Bryony gathered up the remains of afternoon tea to take down to the kitchen. She pulled open the outer door and found Michael on the other side.

He gulped. "I, uh, was just . . ."

"Is that what I think it is?" She nodded toward the sketchbook tucked beneath his arm.

He took a faltering step backward. "You're busy."

"Nothing that can't wait another minute or two." If Bryony let him escape, he'd undoubtedly find other excuses to avoid showing her more of his drawings. She swiveled to set the tray on a nearby cabinet.

When she glanced toward the door, Michael was still standing in the hall. His glassy-eyed expression suggested he was ready to bolt.

"Mr. Heath." Lips pursed, Bryony set her fists on her hips. "You promised to show me what a real bryony looks like, and you don't strike me as a man who goes back on his word."

He briefly looked away as if seeking the courage to step through the door. When he finally did, and Bryony closed it firmly behind him, he stood rooted to the spot.

She offered an encouraging smile. "Please. Show me."

Slowly, deliberately, he turned the pages until he found the one he wanted. With boyish shyness, he handed her the sketchbook.

"Oh. Oh!" Bryony pressed one hand to her heart while her gaze combed every pencil stroke of the drawing. "It's beautiful."

"*Bryonia alba* is a vining plant native to England," Michael explained. When Bryony carried the sketchbook to the table beneath the window and sat down, he followed and moved a chair next to hers. "It's sometimes called the British mandrake or wild hops." His voice strengthened as he warmed to his subject. "The flowers bloom in May, and over the summer the vines will grow several yards in length."

"And these little berries—are they edible?" Bryony ran her fingertip lightly over the area where he'd sketched a cluster of pea-sized scarlet berries.

"Deadly poisonous." Michael's tone became apologetic. "In fact, the whole plant is toxic."

Straightening, Bryony gasped. "I'm not so sure I like being named for a poison."

"But in carefully prepared tinctures, the plant has several therapeutic uses. I should let you borrow one of my botanical reference books so you can read about it."

"I'd like that. Thank you." Fascinated though she was, she decided she'd lingered long enough over the drawing of her toxic namesake. She stood and started across the room to gather up the tea tray

Just then, Dancy emerged from Mrs. Heath's bedroom. "Sound asleep already." She put a hand to her forehead. "And I'm fighting a headache. Wish I could—" Her eyes widened. "Oh, sorry, didn't know you was up here, too, Mr. Michael."

His voice sounded behind Bryony. "Go find some aspirin, Dancy. We'll keep an ear open for Mother."

At his use of the word *we*, Bryony suffered a moment of awkwardness. She certainly didn't need Dancy getting the wrong idea. "I'll keep busy tidying up till you get back."

Dancy had barely left the room when Michael appeared at Bryony's side, sketchbook in hand and a desperate kind of yearning in his eyes. "I have more drawings if you'd like to see them."

Flattered that he'd willingly offered, and sensing his deep-seated need for approval, she cast him a curious smile. He handed her the sketchbook, then motioned her back to the table. Hesitantly, she took a chair, then opened to a drawing that depicted a tall, spiky plant covered in bell-shaped pink and lavender blossoms. In the bottom right corner, Michael had penciled the name: *Digitalis purpurea*. "This sounds medicinal, too," she stated.

"Correct. A century and a half ago, a physician and botanist by the name of William Withering learned from an old woman in Shropshire that the plant could be extremely effective in treating patients with dropsy, better known as congestive heart failure."

"How interesting." Equally interesting was the way Michael's reserve continued to melt away as he described his drawings in greater detail. She turned another page and then another, asking more questions and noting the same response.

After reaching the last page, Bryony closed the sketchbook. She folded her hands atop the cover and tilted her head toward Michael. "Do you have any idea what a remarkable talent you have?"

He laughed nervously. "They're just drawings. A frivolous hobby."

"A *hobby*? Needlepoint is a hobby. Doodling is a hobby. But this —" She cast about for words, her voice dropping to a reverent murmur. "Your sketchbooks are a treasure chest. These drawings shouldn't be hidden away where no one else can enjoy and learn from them. Michael, you should publish them."

At his surprised glance, she threw her hand over her mouth. Had she *really* just called her employer by his first name?

She dropped the sketchbook onto the table between them and sprang to her feet. "I'm so sorry! I'm forgetting my place. I promise it'll never happen again."

While she held herself rigid, Michael sat forward, elbows on his knees. His ribs expanded with a slow inhalation. He lifted his head and slowly, tiredly, pushed to his feet. "I wish you wouldn't."

Here it came, the reprimand she deserved. She kept her eyes lowered.

"Bryony, look at me." When she reluctantly met his gaze, he smiled a sad, lonely smile. "What I meant to say is, it's a very rare thing to hear anyone other than family call me by my given name. It's nice to feel as if I have a friend again."

"But I work for you. We're not . . . I mean, we *can't* be friends."

A look of futility came over Michael's features. "No, I suppose not." He reached for the sketchbook and held it against his chest. "And once again I am keeping you from your duties. Please excuse me."

"Michael, wait—" Bryony flinched. Without even thinking, she'd done it again. Why did his Christian name fall so naturally from her tongue?

He halted and faced her, his eyes dark with pain.

She stepped closer. "We're not all that different, you know, each of us chafing against situations not of our own choosing." When he looked as if he'd argue, she hurried on. "Oh, yes, I've seen how your daddy tries to wear you down about learning the family business. And I know how every chance you get, you slip off with your drawing things so you won't have to listen to his nagging."

The slant of his shoulders deepened, reminding Bryony of the one and only time Grandpa had taken her into the woods with him to check his traps. They'd come upon a rabbit who'd likely been caught a day or two before, and the poor thing looked utterly spent and hopeless from its struggles to find a way out of the oblong box. The rabbit's dazed surrender had upset Bryony so badly that she had bad dreams for weeks afterward and never went trapping with Grandpa again.

Now she saw the same hopelessness in Michael, and it was wrong—so wrong! He had wealth, he had smarts, and he had talent. He could be or do anything he set his mind to. And yet, for reasons Bryony could only surmise, he seemed stuck right where he was.

Just like her.

"I've spoken out of turn," she said, her fingers curled around the hem of her apron. "Thank you again for showing me your drawings. I'd best get on with my work."

"Wait, Bryony. Please." Michael reached for her hand.

She tried to swallow but couldn't force her throat muscles to work. "Y-yes, sir?"

His fingers tensed. "I liked it much better when you called me Michael." Gently, he drew her around until they were toe-to-toe. Still holding her hand, he shot a quick glance toward the closed outer door, then to the adjoining room where his mother napped. He lowered his voice to a murmur. "I would never jeopardize your employment here, but . . ." His Adam's apple worked. "What I'm trying to say . . ."

Bryony gave a nervous laugh. "I'm no mind reader, and I've dawdled too long already, so maybe you should just spit it out."

Letting her hand fall, he retreated a step. Her immediate impulse was to close the gap between them, and it took all her resolve to hold firm and wait for him to speak.

He cleared his throat. "You said we couldn't be friends."

"And you agreed."

"Well, I'd like to change my mind."

Friendship? No doubt a huge mistake, one they'd both regret if Michael's father ever found out. But something about Bryony had captivated Michael so completely that he began to live in hourly anticipation for the few private moments they could spend together.

More often than not, though, Michael had to share her company with his mother. Not that he minded, because clearly Mother was thriving under Bryony's care. While Dancy capably managed his mother's daily routine and saw to her personal needs, Bryony's role had begun to resemble that of a companion. She read to Mother, chatted with her over tea, escorted her on walks around the estate.

In fact, Michael realized with sad irony, it was almost as if Bryony were stepping into the role Miranda should have filled had Dad not banished her from the family.

"You look so serious," Bryony said one day. It was a sunny morning in early October, and they'd taken Mother out for a stroll. "What are you thinking about?"

He wanted desperately to take her hand, but who knew whose eyes might be watching? Besides, his talk with Esther had done little to temper the resentment Odette and Alice exhibited toward Bryony, resentment that appeared to grow continually worse. Michael suspected envy lay at the root of their ill feelings, but his mother's well-being mattered much more to him than rivalry among the servants.

"I was just thinking how well Mother is doing these days." He smiled toward the tiny woman bobbing along several steps ahead of them. "The cooler weather seems to have restored a measure of vitality."

"She hasn't seemed as forgetful the past few days either." Bryony stopped to examine a spreading, white-flowered shrub. "Tell me the name of this one. I know I've seen it in your drawings."

"*Baccharis halimifolia*, also known as sea myrtle. Showy, isn't it?"

Bryony stuffed her hands into her sweater pockets and cast Michael a frustrated frown. "I've half a mind to steal all your sketchbooks and send them to a university somewhere. I'm sure my sister at college could find out from one of her professors where you could get them published."

With a quick shake of his head, Michael kept walking. "Don't get too far ahead, Mother."

"Sure, you just keep on ignoring me." Bryony jogged to catch up. "If you want to go against Scripture and hide your light under a bushel, I guess that's up to you."

He couldn't think of an appropriate retort, so he clamped his mouth shut and walked faster.

Bryony matched his pace, and soon they drew even with his mother. "Don't overtire yourself, Mrs. Heath. Save some energy for the return trip."

"So you young folks think I can't hold my own?" The spry woman laughed. "Look who's been lagging behind all morning. What have you two been doing behind my back—stealing kisses?"

A choking cough erupted from Michael's throat. He didn't dare glance Bryony's way. In a gruff whisper, he said, "Mother, please."

"Don't 'Mother, please' me, young man." Michael's mother halted suddenly, causing both Michael and Bryony to stumble. She reached first for Michael's hand, then for Bryony's, and cast a chiding glance at each of them. "I have never seen two people try so hard not to show their true feelings for each other. Son, if you intend to court this lovely lady, you must do it properly."

Stupidly, Michael swung his gaze to Bryony. Her face went deathly pale before a crimson blush flared. He squeezed his eyes shut and swallowed. "I think it's time we turned back."

Mother didn't argue, thank heavens.

They arrived on the front porch as Odette came looking for them. "Thought y'all had done took off cross-country for Little Rock. Dinner's hot and ready to be served."

Michael didn't miss the haughty look she aimed in Bryony's direction. He slanted the cook a warning glare in return. Lips pursed, Odette tucked in her chin and retreated to the dining room.

"Where is Dancy?" his mother asked. "I would like to freshen up before we dine."

"I'll help you upstairs," Bryony said, taking her arm. After Mother's insinuations during their walk, Bryony seemed overly anxious to put some distance between herself and Michael.

And all he wanted was to be alone with her again.

This was insane. There were so many reasons he shouldn't feel this way toward Bryony Linwood. He didn't care that she was the granddaughter of his father's tenant, nor that she was his mother's maid. He didn't care that a similarly ill-suited relationship was the reason his father had disowned Miranda. He didn't even care that Bryony must be a good ten years his junior.

No, the greatest barrier standing between them was Michael himself. He no longer knew how *not* to be a recluse. Solitude had become his refuge from all the things in the world that seemed so wrong.

But now Bryony had brought a sense of *rightness* into Michael's life that he couldn't risk losing. Somehow, he must persuade his mother never to mention her perceptions again, especially to his father. If Dad so much as suspected Michael entertained feelings for Bryony, he would surely take swift action to remove Bryony from their household.

"Michael."

His father's sharp tone made him jerk his head up in surprise. "Yes, sir?"

"A word in my office before dinner, if you please."

He *didn't* please, not in the least, but he mutely followed his father down the hall. His father settled in behind the desk and opened a ledger. Michael remained standing, arms folded.

With a grimace, his father shifted the ledger around in Michael's direction. He tapped the page sharply with the tip of his index finger. "I wanted you to see exactly what your generosity is costing us. If the economy continues its current downward spiral, it could be years before we recoup our losses."

Michael gave the figures a cursory glance, secretly relieved they were discussing plantation business and not the direction his thoughts had taken earlier. He leveled his gaze at his father. "And how long do you suppose it will take the Wielands and our other struggling tenants to recoup *their* losses—if ever?"

His father slammed the book shut. "Why do I even bother?" Swiveling his chair sideways, he shot Michael a scathing look. "I've lost my appetite. Make my excuses to your mother."

"Gladly." Michael marched out of the office.

After their confrontation, he had little appetite himself. With a quick word to Odette, he retreated upstairs, intending to eat later when his stomach had settled.

His mother was just on her way down and met him at the top of the stairs. "Aren't you coming to dinner?"

"No, Mother, not right now." He looked for Bryony, but it appeared Dancy would accompany his mother to the dining room.

"Oh, son, are you unwell again?"

He patted her arm and forced a reassuring smile. "I'll be fine."

If only he could will it so. But the nagging sense grew that his life held no meaning, no purpose. He must believe God had spared his life during the war for a reason, and after twelve years any sane person should have figured it out.

Bryony Linwood made him want to, now more than ever.

❧

"That's the last of the cornmeal." Miranda Heath Vargas set a tin plate of cornbread and watery beans in front of her husband. "We've maybe enough dried beans for another week or so. I can stretch them if I make the soup a little thinner."

Daniel Vargas looked up, bitterness and disillusionment carved into every line of his features. He nodded toward Miranda's empty place. "Where is yours?"

"Not much appetite." She'd learned to lie with a straight face, to never let on to the man she loved how her own hunger gnawed at her belly like a starving coyote.

"*Querida*—my dearest. Sit down here and eat." Daniel's strong fingers locked around her wrist. He pulled until she had no choice but to sink into the chair catty-cornered from his. He broke off half from his slab of cornbread, dipped it in the beans, and handed it to her.

She nibbled a tiny bite, but the dry crumbs caught in her throat, right along with the tears she refused to shed. "I packed you a clean shirt and an extra pair of socks. You be sure to wash up and put a smile on your face before you go asking anywhere for work. First impressions matter."

He smiled for her now, the same broad grin that had stolen her heart all those years ago, and the hardness around his eyes eased a bit. "You will be all right, Mandy. You're a strong woman. You just have to hold on till I can get farther north where this drought hasn't got a foothold. I'll find work, and I'll send you money quick as I can."

The dam of her tears broke loose, and Miranda fell sobbing into her husband's arms. "Daniel, Daniel, I don't want you to go!"

"I've got to, *querida*, you know there's no other choice. There's no money in farming this year, and I will not let my family starve." Daniel gave her back a brisk rub, then pushed her upright. He ran his callused thumb along her wet cheek, and his own voice grew thick with emotion. "No more of this blubbering, do you hear me? How do you expect me to do what I must do if I cannot have faith you're holding your own?"

"I will." She nodded fiercely. "I promise I will be right here waiting for you."

"One more thing you must promise me." Daniel set his mouth, his coffee-brown eyes boring into hers. "If things get any worse, you go to your father. You *make* him take care of you like he should have done all along."

Anger and revulsion rolled through Miranda. With a shudder so violent it shook the table, she tore her gaze away. "I'd rather die than go crawling back to him."

"Now you listen here, wife." Daniel shoved to his feet and pulled her roughly against his chest. Fierce love filled his tortured expression. "Don't you dare cause me worry about coming home to find you in your grave. You must fight to live with all you have, Mandy. For the sake of our family, you must *fight*."

Fight? When she didn't even have the strength to argue? She lowered her forehead into the crook of his shoulder. Her arms crept around his lean torso, her fingers memorizing every rib, every sinew, every rock-solid muscle. She breathed in his masculine scent, a mixture of hard work, soap, and warm skin, smells she already knew by heart from years of loving this man.

How could she ever let him go?

7

"Unbelievable!"

At the sudden bellow from the other end of the house, Bryony almost dropped the folded sheets she'd just ironed. She could only hope Sebastian Heath wasn't badgering Michael again.

Then a burst of laughter rang out, and Mr. Heath shouted Jeremiah's name. "Did you hear that? Did you *hear*?"

"Indeed I did!" came Jeremiah's strident reply, "Lawsy, that Joe Sylvester—winning seven races in a single day!"

Of course—the horse races they'd been listening to on the radio. Bryony cast a weary glance heavenward.

Alice appeared at the other end of the hallway. "What in tarnation are they hollering about?"

Stunned that Alice had actually spoken to her, Bryony took a moment to respond. She smiled and heaved an exaggerated shrug. "Something exciting must have happened at the racetrack. Whatever it was, they're mighty happy about it."

"Humph. *I'll* be happy when the work's done and I can eat my supper and put my tired, aching feet up at long last."

Bryony nodded politely, all the while thinking about her long walk home once she finished for the day. Alice, who usually stayed at the mansion between her days off, could enjoy Odette's fine cooking in the kitchen, then retire upstairs to the servants' floor.

Bryony shifted the load of laundry in her arms. "I'd best get these sheets up to Mrs. Heath's room."

"Yes, I guess you *best*." The rancor had returned to Alice's tone. She lifted her nose in the air and started past.

Bryony had had enough of being snubbed. She blocked Alice's way. "I wish you'd tell me what it is you don't like about me."

"I like you well enough." Alice's gaze darted toward the corridor leading to Miss Esther's office. "You been tellin' on me? Trying to get me in trouble?"

"I would never do such a thing. But when I first started working here, I hoped we were going to be friends. And it's clear Odette has never much cared for me. I don't understand what I've done to deserve your unkindness."

Alice's mouth twisted like she'd just sucked on a lemon. "If you don't know, I won't be the one to tell you."

"That's unfair." Bryony huffed. "I'm working here for the same reasons as you, to keep food on my family's table and a roof over their heads. It's not like I took anything away from you."

"Not from *me*, but—" Alice clamped her lips together. "You just get on with your chores and I'll get on with mine. Ain't no law says we have to be best friends to work in the same house." With a parting sneer, she shoved past Bryony and marched out toward the kitchen.

Chin quivering, Bryony drew her shoulders back and continued to the rear staircase. If Alice and Odette didn't like her, there was little she could do about it, especially since they weren't forthcoming with reasons. But it sure didn't make working here any easier.

When she reached the second floor, she turned in the direction of Mrs. Heath's rooms as Michael stepped through the door.

His whole countenance brightened as he strode toward Bryony. "I was just showing Mother my latest sketches." Then he added hesitantly, "Would you like to see?"

Bryony tipped her head toward the bundle of linens. "Maybe another time." After her puzzling exchange with Alice, she only wanted to finish her work and go home. Tomorrow was Sunday, and she had another blessed day off. Even with all the chores waiting for her at Grandpa's, at least she'd be with the people who loved her best.

"Is something wrong?" Michael edged closer. His expression hardened. "Did Alice or Odette say something again?"

She couldn't meet his gaze. "It's been a long day, that's all. And still so much to do."

When she tried to slip past him, he cut her off. With his sketchbook tucked against his side, he relieved Bryony of the folded linens and dropped them unceremoniously onto a hall table.

"Michael, please." Keeping her voice low, Bryony scanned the upstairs corridor. "Do you want me to lose my job?"

"Of course not. But you have to be honest with me, Bryony. I can speak with Esther again—"

"No." Without the linens as a barrier, Bryony felt vulnerable, exposed. She inched backward, arms hugged tightly to her ribcage. "The situation is what it is. Nothing you say is going to make a difference." She suspected what he'd said already had only made things worse.

Abruptly, he turned away. He gripped the balustrade overlooking the downstairs foyer, and his shoulders rose and fell with an exasperated sigh. "This friendship of ours isn't working out so well, is it?"

Bryony had no answer, at least not one she thought he'd care to hear. "I tried to tell you."

"Yes, you did. I still think you're wrong."

She wanted to be wrong. Desperately so. But even if Michael wouldn't admit to everything that stood between them, it was all too evident to her. Silently, she gathered up the sheets and scurried toward Mrs. Heath's door. As she turned to close it behind her, she caught Michael looking back at her with the same profound hopelessness that daily threatened to choke the breath from her lungs.

"About time." Dancy's sharp tone startled Bryony. "I been waiting on you so we can get the bed sheets on before I need to go down and see to Mrs. H."

"Sorry, I got sidetracked." Offering an apologetic smile to the tall, dark-skinned woman, Bryony moved toward the bedroom. "Is she still visiting with her priest?"

"Think she's invited Father Dempsey to stay for supper." Dancy moved to the opposite side of the bed as Bryony shook out the bottom sheet.

"That's nice. I'm glad for her to have some company. It'll be good for her."

"*You're* good for her." Dancy moved to the foot of the bed to tuck in the sheets. "When I'm with her, she raves on and on about them stories you been reading." Her voice dropped. "Makes me sorry I never learned to read."

Bryony looked up from fluffing a pillow. "You don't know how to read?"

"Not good as you anyways. I know my A-B-Cs, and I can sound out easy words good enough to get by." With a heartless lift of one shoulder, Dancy reached for the comforter and smoothed it across the bed. "Been workin' as house help since I was old enough to push a broom across the floor. Never had no time for schooling."

"How old are you, Dancy . . . if you don't mind my asking?"

"Fifty-seven. Least I think so. Only reason is because I'm pretty sure I was about ten years old in 'eighty-three." Casting Bryony a skeptical frown, Dancy fingered an earlobe as if deciding whether to continue. When she did, a weighty sadness subdued her tone. "That's when a bunch of white men barged into our house claimin' my daddy spoke rudely to one of their womenfolk and hauled him away." She snorted an ugly laugh. "You think we got hard times now? Ain't much worse than watchin' your daddy get hanged from a tree and ain't nothin' you can do about it."

Bryony had no words, no context for the horrors Dancy and so many others of her race had survived, and her heart broke for them all.

They finished making the bed in silence, and then Bryony helped Dancy lay out soap and towels for Mrs. Heath's bath, along with a fresh nightgown, robe, and slippers.

As evening shadows encroached, Dancy switched on one of the bedside lamps. "You should head on home before it gets any darker."

Tired to the bone, Bryony wasn't of a mind to argue. The only part she dreaded was going downstairs to the kitchen to retrieve her sweater. The thought of subjecting herself to more of Odette's snide glances was more than she could handle.

Halfway to the door, she halted and turned to Dancy. "We get along all right, don't we?"

The woman dropped her jaw, looking at Bryony as if she'd grown another head. Then her brows turned down in a sympathetic frown. "You still gettin' the evil eye from that glorified potato peeler downstairs?"

"I don't understand it, Dancy. What did I ever do to Odette? Or to Alice, either?"

"It ain't you, believe me. They's just protecting their own."

"But it's not like I took away their jobs or food off their plates."

Dancy straightened a hairbrush on the dressing table before guiding Bryony out to the sitting room. She nudged her over to the sofa and sat down facing her. "There's things you don't know about the goings-on in this house. Things you're better off not knowing."

Fists knotted, Bryony heaved a groan. "You're talking in riddles."

"Listen to me, child." Dancy covered Bryony's hands with her own, the marked contrast between light skin and dark evident even in the failing light of evening. "See, we all been here working for the Heath family a long, long time. And I 'spect we'll go on the same for years to come. But you, honey—this ain't your life. Soon as this drought lifts and crops are thriving again, you ain't gonna stick around here. You'll go home to your grandpappy for a while, till one day down the road you fall in love with a handsome white boy. Then you'll get married and prob'ly move to the big city where he'll be a doctor or lawyer or something else real important, and your time doing laundry and scrubbing toilets at the Heath mansion won't be nothin' more'n a distant memory."

All the while Dancy spoke, Bryony shook her head. How could she dare to hope for a different life—a *better* life—when every day was such a struggle? True, her father had died honorably in the war, not strung up like a criminal. But nothing had been the same since the day she learned Daddy had lost his life in a German artillery barrage, and when the tornado ripped Mama from their lives, Bryony thought she'd die, herself, from the agony of her grief.

But giving in and giving up wasn't allowed. Bryony had her sisters to think about. Grandpa too. "You're wrong, Dancy," she stated, her spine straight as a broomstick. "This *is* my life. I'm not going anywhere."

❧

Michael came down for breakfast Sunday morning to find both his parents already in the dining room. He'd hoped to be early enough to avoid them, particularly his father, but apparently they'd been up awhile. Dad was dressed in a crisp white shirt and maroon silk tie, and Mother looked elegant in a dark blue wool suit that complemented her eyes.

Eyes that seemed exceptionally bright this morning, no doubt a carryover from her lively visit with Father Dempsey last evening. Michael's mother had always been a social butterfly. While he and Miranda were growing up, their mother had regularly hosted dinner parties here at the mansion. She'd been quite involved in organizing charitable events as well, and often made the sixty-mile trip into Little Rock for committee functions.

"Michael, dear." His mother patted the chair seat next to her. "If you hurry and eat, we can all go to Mass together."

Her memory must not be as clear today as Michael hoped. The last time he'd set foot in the red-brick Catholic church the family attended over in Brinkley was before he'd joined the army. But to keep from upsetting his mother, he simply said, "I'm afraid I can't this time. You'll have to go without me."

Concern clouded her expression. "Are you feeling poorly again?"

"Of course he isn't." Michael's father scowled as he stirred more cream into his coffee. "Our son is only being his usual reclusive self."

Refusing to be drawn into an argument, Michael turned to the sideboard and quietly filled a plate with scrambled eggs and pork sausage. He purposely took a seat at the opposite end of the table from his parents.

Michael's mother crumpled her napkin beside her empty plate. "Now look what you've done, Sebastian. Apologize to our son at once."

After a slow sip of coffee, Michael's father set down his cup. He drew his mouth into a thin smile and slanted a deferential glance toward his wife. Reaching over to pat her hand, he murmured, "Please don't trouble yourself, dearest. Let's be on our way, shall we?" He aimed a stern look in Michael's direction and added, "Trust me, I'll be sure to work things out with our son later."

Michael watched grimly as his parents left the dining room, Dad's hand solicitously braced against the small of Mother's back. Sebastian Heath might be many things, but one thing he was *not* was an uncaring spouse. Michael suspected the only reason his father seemed to disregard Mother's failing memory was that he loved her too much to accept he might be losing her.

If only he loved his children with equal devotion.

As Michael drained his coffee cup, Odette came in to clear the table. "You get enough to eat, young man?"

"More than enough, thank you." Michael pushed his chair back and stood. Bryony had begged him not to interfere again, but the torment on her face yesterday wouldn't let him keep still. He cornered Odette at the sideboard. "I need an answer from you, Odette."

Her eyes grew wide as she swiveled to face him. She tucked her hands at her ample waist. "What'd I do, Mister Michael? Wasn't the eggs to your liking? Or the coffee too strong?"

"I think you know this has nothing to do with breakfast." However, at the moment, his sausage and eggs weren't settling very well. "I've always known you to be a good and decent person, which is why your attitude toward Bryony makes no sense. She may be spending more time caring for Mother, but she works as hard as the rest of you. Why do you continue to treat her so unkindly?"

Odette's mouth twisted. She gave her attention to the serving platters on the sideboard, replacing warming covers, gathering up utensils. When she finally spoke, Michael had to strain to hear her murmured words. "Just cain't help it. She don't belong here, and besides—" She clamped her lips together and brusquely shook her head.

"Besides what? Finish what you were saying."

"It's—it's just what I said. She ain't one of us, is all." With fluttering fingers, Odette stacked platters on a wide silver tray. "Now you let me get on here or I ain't gonna make it over to town so's I can worship with my family."

Michael backed away, but he wasn't at all satisfied with Odette's answer. Before she escaped to the kitchen, he tried once more. "Please, Odette, as a favor to me, will you try to be more accepting of Bryony?"

The laden tray balanced against her hip, Odette darted a glance at Michael. "I reckon I can try. She been real nice to Callie, anyways."

Michael recalled the day he'd watched Bryony and Callie dancing in the rain, and the memory lightened his heart. "Yes, she has. And she gets along well with Dancy, too. So if both you and Alice could try a little harder . . ." With a half-shrug, he cast Odette a hopeful smile.

Tucking in her chin, Odette mumbled a quick, "Yes, sir," and then scurried from the room.

With a hand on his abdomen, Michael closed his eyes. He needed to get out of the house for a while, to draw fresh air into his lungs. Sometimes he wondered whether he suffered more from the aftereffects of mustard gas and the war, or from the oppressive atmosphere permeating this house. It infuriated him that he could summon up neither the will to stay nor the strength to leave.

He gave his stomach another moment to settle, then trudged upstairs to his room. There, he donned a nubby, well-worn sweater and tucked a sketchbook and box of pencils into a satchel. Soon he was on his way down to the river.

All thoughts of time or place faded as he lost himself in the nuances of an autumn leaf, the paper-thin bark of a birch, the delicate petals of a wild aster. He followed a trail through the woods and came to a field where brown stubble testified to the drought. A dirt road stretched along the far side of the field, and in the distance a cloud of dust marked the passing of an automobile.

Feeling slightly breathless from his cross-country hike, he decided the road would be easier walking than retracing his steps. By the time he reached the road, dust coated him from the soles of his brogans to his knees. He brushed off the worst of it and then took stock of his surroundings, not exactly sure where he'd ended up. Home had to be to his left, but he wasn't interested in heading there quite yet. He hoisted the strap of his satchel higher on his shoulder and turned in the other direction.

He'd gone a quarter-mile or so when he came to a dirt lane flanked by plowed fields. One appeared to be planted in potatoes, but the vines looked sickly. Another might be some kind of forage, which didn't look much healthier. Michael assumed the land belonged to his father and was farmed by one of his tenants. With the crops in such distress, how would the farm family make it through the winter?

His thoughts drifted to the Wielands, and he wondered how they were faring. Would Nels get the medical attention he needed for his heart condition? Probably not. They'd be more likely to spend what money they had on food.

Michael's stomach growled, and he realized with shame that he had no concept for what real hunger felt like. Even with the statewide shortages this drought had caused, Odette's kitchen remained well stocked. How was it fair that the wealthy should continue living so well while the very people on whom their prosperity depended were forced to suffer want?

Lost in thought, he hadn't noticed how far he'd followed the lane until he looked up to see a whitewashed frame house ahead. A rusted black farm truck sat next to a tilting barn. He considered quietly reversing direction and heading back to the main road, until from somewhere on the other side of the house a woman's voice drifted his way.

He recognized it immediately—Bryony, trilling the cheery lyrics of "Singin' in the Rain."

Cradling an armful of scrawny turnips, Bryony closed the gate to the vegetable garden. Though the drought lingered on, at least the fall temperatures weren't so cruel. Dear God, if only they'd get a decent rain!

"Hello, Bryony."

She looked up with a start. "Michael! What are you doing here?"

"Not sure exactly." His shy smile widened as he crossed the scraggly backyard. "I was out walking, and this is where I ended up."

The porch door creaked open, and Grandpa stepped out. "Who you talking to, Bryony? Thought I heard a man's voice. "

"It's Michael Heath, Grandpa. He just came by to . . . well, we haven't figured that part out yet." She narrowed one eye and aimed a curious glance toward Michael. Here in her own backyard, he seemed different—and she *felt* different, almost as if they really could be friends. "I'm about to cook up these turnips and get some dinner on the table. You hungry?"

A strange look crossed his face. Maybe he didn't care for turnips.

And maybe she was a fool for extending the invitation. But it felt . . . right. "Rose is frying up a chicken, too. Although when she's at the stove, you never quite know how it's going to turn out."

"Bryony." Grandpa wagged his head, telling her with his eyes that he didn't care to share his Sunday meal. "Young Mr. Heath prob'ly has dinner waiting for him at home."

"Actually," Michael began, stepping closer, "I'd like very much to join you. Provided you'll let me help."

Bryony motioned him toward the porch. "We can always use an extra hand in the kitchen. You ever cooked a turnip before?"

"Can't say I have."

With a brief nod, Grandpa held the door for Michael and pointed him to the kitchen. He stopped Bryony on the porch. "So this is Sebastian's boy, the artist fella you been telling us about? I ain't sure it's such a good idea socializing with your boss's son."

"I'm not either, Grandpa. But there's something about him. Kind of like an emptiness that needs filling. I'm thinking the Lord brought him our way for a reason, and I've a mind to find out what it is."

In the kitchen, Bryony found Michael introducing himself to Rose—and dodging the sizzling chicken leg she forked onto a platter. Rose gasped when grease spattered onto Michael's trousers. "Oh, sorry! I'm still all thumbs at this cooking business."

"These are my roughing-about pants. No harm done." Michael set his satchel on a chair.

"Bryony says you make pictures of plants and flowers. Did you bring some to show us?"

Bryony dropped the turnips into the sink. "After we eat. First, I'm going to teach Michael how to fix turnip greens."

Both Grandpa and Rose looked askance at her, then shared dubious glances with each other. Bryony ignored them and instructed Michael to remove his sweater and roll up his shirt-sleeves. Soon she had him scrubbing turnips and rinsing the greens. When he splashed water on his glasses, she laughed and slid them from his nose to dry them on her apron.

As she handed the glasses back, he tilted his head to study her. "It's good to see you smile again."

"You mean after yesterday?" She set a knife and cutting board on the counter, then nodded toward Grandpa and Rose. "I'm back with my family again. They always cheer me up. Only wish Lark-spur could be here, too."

"Larkspur, the sister who's at college?"

"Studying to be a teacher." A wistful tone softened Bryony's voice. "I'm so proud of her."

Michael handed her the turnips he'd washed, and she began by slicing one in half, then dicing it into bite-sized chunks. She handed him the knife and stepped aside. "Think you can handle it?"

He grinned. "I think so."

She didn't mention it was nice to see him smiling, too.

While he worked, she filled a pot with water and set it on the stove to heat. Then she took a paring knife to a puny little potato. "Cooking a potato along with the turnips helps with the bitterness."

"And the greens?"

"We'll fry them in some bacon grease while the turnips are boiling."

"Sounds . . . delicious." Michael's doubtful expression didn't match his words.

With Grandpa setting the table and Rose smoking up the kitchen with her fried-to-a-blackened-crisp chicken, they soon had dinner on the table. After an initial grimace when he tasted the boiled turnips, Michael pronounced them the best he'd ever eaten. He even complimented Rose on her contribution to the meal.

Bryony smiled to herself at her sister's flushed cheeks. "I have to admit, Rosie, old Henrietta didn't turn out half-bad."

Michael hiked a brow. "Henrietta?"

"One of our laying hens. Only she wasn't laying anymore, so this morning Grandpa . . ." Bryony's voice trailed off as Michael paled and put his napkin to his lips.

"Excuse me," he said, clearing his throat. "This is my first time to consume a chicken who was known by name. It feels almost . . . cannibalistic."

Grandpa and Rose joined Bryony in laughter. "I promise, Henrietta lived a good long life," Bryony stated. "She honored us by donating herself to the cause of filling our bellies."

Rose snickered. "Even a tough old bird like Henrietta fries up nice and juicy. Care for another piece?"

"Thanks, but this is plenty." Michael poked at the remains of the chicken thigh on his plate.

When the meal ended, Bryony rose to clear the table. Michael immediately stood as well, one hand steadying the back of her chair. The courteous gesture made her face warm, and she offered him a grateful smile. Turning to Grandpa, who hadn't budged, she wiggled her brows. "Looks like we have a real gentleman in the house."

With a twinkle in his eye, Grandpa lumbered to his feet. "Rosie, my sweet, may I assist you."

"Why, thank you, kind sir." Fluttering her lashes, Rose waited for Grandpa to pull out her chair, then stood to bestow a kiss on his cheek. She winked at Bryony. "See, you *can* teach an old dog new tricks."

"Humph. While you young whippersnappers clean up the kitchen, this *old dog* is taking his full belly to the parlor for a nap."

Bryony paused on her way to the sink with a stack of dishes. "Wait, Grandpa, not before you see Michael's drawings. Rosie, get a dishcloth and wipe off the table."

Grandpa grumbled but pitched in along with Michael and Rose to help Bryony wash dishes and clean up the kitchen. Then they gathered around the table again and waited expectantly for Michael to bring out his sketchbook.

As he laid it in the middle of the table, he glanced at each of them in turn, and Bryony saw the uncertainty in his eyes. She rested a hand on his forearm. "It's okay."

He nodded but remained standing. "I think I'll wait on the porch, if you don't mind."

When he'd taken his sweater and walked outside, Bryony heaved a sigh. With an apology to Grandpa and Rose, she explained as best she could Michael's reluctance to share his art. "I think he keeps it private so he doesn't risk belittlement. Lord knows he gets enough of that from his father."

Grandpa's mouth twisted in an ugly frown. "Doesn't surprise me."

Bryony turned to the first page and watched Grandpa's and Rose's eyes widen.

Rose extended her hand as if to touch the delicate yellow flowers in the drawing. "They look so real."

"Your grandma used to grow those." Grandpa's voice had turned breathy. "Every spring the trellis out back would be dripping with Carolina jessamine."

"I remember," Bryony murmured. "Seems so long ago."

Grandpa nodded, his gaze drifting toward the window. Bryony didn't have to turn her head to picture the bare trellis with its weathered and broken slats. When they'd first come to the farm, Mama had replanted Grandma's flowerbeds, and for a few years the old place had been awash in the varied colors of growing things. But since Mama died, nothing had been the same, and whatever life remained on this farm, the drought was slowly siphoning away.

8

Larkspur tapped lightly on her faculty advisor's open door. "Professor Keene? Is this a bad time?"

The darkly dashing professor looked up from a desk strewn with open books and messy stacks of paper. "Miss Linwood. Come in. I just read your essay on William Wordsworth's 'By the Sea.'" He waggled a red pencil in her direction and smiled. "Excellent work."

"Really? Thank you." Heart fluttering, she ventured into the office. "To say so much in so few words—I found the poem utterly beautiful in its simplicity."

"Precisely." Professor Keene laid aside the pencil and folded his hands atop the clutter. "Now, what brings you by my office this morning?"

"I wondered if you'd had a chance to make those inquiries I asked you about last week."

"Regarding the letter from your sister." The professor invited Larkspur to sit while he riffled through a pile of papers. "I spoke with Professor DeMarco in the science department, and he suggested a couple of university publishing houses in the East."

"That's wonderful!" Larkspur scooted to the edge of her chair.

"Ah, here we are." He hand her a wrinkled sheet of paper.

"Sorry for the stains. Professor DeMarco and I were visiting over coffee."

Larkspur tucked the paper into her handbag. "It's perfectly all right. I know Bryony will be so grateful for this."

When she didn't get up to leave right away, the professor cast her a questioning smile. "Was there something else?"

"I, um . . . that is, a friend mentioned your literature discussion circle, and I was hoping—"

"I'm so sorry. The circle is for second-year students and up." Lips pursed, Professor Keene massaged his jawline. "However, in light of the insightful essay you submitted, I might consider making an exception . . ."

Hope swelled in Larkspur's chest. She clutched her handbag with both hands. "I might not be able to contribute much to the discussions yet, but the opportunity to learn from others would mean the world to me!"

Professor Keene rose and came around to Larkspur's side of the desk. When he took her hand to help her to her feet, she felt certain he'd hear the thudding of her heart. "We're meeting again next Sunday evening. In preparation, you should read 'Ode Against Pleasure,' by Katherine Philips."

"The seventeenth-century English poet? What an interesting choice." When the professor's eyes lit with surprise, she smiled inwardly that her eclectic reading habits were proving advantageous. "I shall look forward to Sunday."

"As will I." Without releasing her hand, Professor Keene escorted her to the door. "You'll let me know what comes of your sister's correspondence with those publishers?"

"Oh. Of course." Larkspur had all but forgotten about the letter she must write to Bryony this evening. She patted her handbag. "Thank you again—for everything!"

In the days following his unplanned visit to Bryony's home, Michael wondered if he'd lost his mind. Not that the choices he'd made over the past decade hadn't already raised his suspicions. Anyone who avoided other human beings as resolutely as he did had to be slightly deranged.

No, what concerned him now was how avidly he awaited Bryony's arrival at the mansion each day. He'd even taken to rising early and watching for her from his bedroom window, then making sure to be downstairs in the vicinity of the back hallway when she reported in with Esther, just so he could bid her good morning. Nothing too formal, and nothing anyone would suspect as intentional, or so he hoped.

But he couldn't help himself. Bryony had awakened something in his spirit that no one had touched in years. Maybe it was her melancholy smile, or her slightly off-key humming while she worked. Certainly it had much to do with how enraptured she'd become with his drawings. At every opportunity she made a point to hover nearby whenever his mother asked to see his latest sketches. A yearning kind of sadness would fill her eyes, and her parted lips would turn up at the corners as she drew a blissful breath. The thought that his renderings could evoke such a visceral response in another human being both amazed and humbled him.

When he spied her walking up the drive early Friday morning, she happened to glance toward his window. She beamed a smile, almost as if she'd been hoping to catch his eye, and his heart beat a little faster. He wiggled his fingers in a tentative wave before closing the shutters and heading downstairs.

By the time he reached the back door, she had let herself inside. She nodded toward the veranda, then held up five fingers and tapped her wrist. She didn't wear a watch, but he got the message. Slipping on the light jacket he kept on a coat tree in the rear hallway, he went outside under the guise of catching a breath of fresh air.

A few minutes later, Bryony appeared with a broom. She swept the veranda floorboards with purposeful strokes, pausing every few steps to brush cobwebs from around the window frames. Michael had moved down to the south end of the house to wait for her, where there were fewer chances of prying eyes.

When Bryony rounded the corner, her eyes lit up. She leaned the broom handle against the house, then peered in all directions before tugging an envelope from her sweater pocket. "I have some wonderful news, Michael! I've been so anxious to tell you that I barely slept a wink last night."

He couldn't imagine what had her so excited. A sudden windfall, perhaps? An unexpected inheritance from a dead relative so she wouldn't have to work here anymore? Michael cringed at the selfish thoughts roiling to the surface. He stuffed his hands in his jacket pockets and forced a smile. "Then you'd better tell me what it is."

"I heard back from my sister at college." Bryony held the envelope to her chest and released a long, slow breath, her grin widening. "She sent me the names and addresses of two university publishing houses that might be interested in your drawings. Michael, you must contact them right away."

Swiveling sideways, he drew a hand down his face. "I . . . I told you, my drawings aren't for anyone but me."

"But you share them with your mother and with me. Why not the world?" Bryony moved to his side and peered up at him. "The Lord didn't give you this talent for you to hide it away in your cupboard. Please, Michael. Just write to these people. Better yet, call them on the telephone and tell them about your pictures. Ask if you can send them some."

The *Lord* gave him this talent? Michael shook his head. "How many times to I have to tell you, Bryony? I draw to keep myself sane. That's all."

"No. That *isn't* all." She opened her mouth to speak, then snapped it shut again. Tears glistened in her eyes. "Your pictures gave me back something I'd nearly forgotten. Something special. Something beautiful. Your pictures make me want to hope again."

Her softly spoken words hung in the air between them. He

searched her face, and the longing to caress her cheek and brush away the wetness gathering there became irresistible. When his hand cupped the curve of her jaw, she trembled but didn't move away. "Bryony . . ."

"Please, Michael." She covered his hand with her own and leaned into his touch, her gaze pleading. "For me. Do it for me."

It hurt to swallow. It hurt even more when he lowered his arm to his side. He still felt the warm wetness of her tears on his palm. He couldn't find his voice, but he lowered his chin and gave a resigned nod. What he wanted didn't matter anymore. If this small thing would make Bryony happy, he'd do it, and do it gladly.

Her whole countenance brightening, she thrust the envelope into his hands. "This is a good thing, Michael. I know it deep down in my soul."

Then, spinning on her heel, she snatched up the broom and busily resumed her sweeping. All too quickly, she disappeared around to the west veranda.

Michael tapped the envelope against his palm. His silent assent was as good as a promise, and now he had to follow through.

❧

Between washing and ironing with Callie, polishing silver with Alice, and taking turns with Dancy to watch over Mrs. Heath, Bryony hardly had a moment to ponder her encounter with Michael on the veranda. And it was a good thing, because when he touched her cheek, she'd imagined—utterly foolishly!—how sweet it would be if only he'd lean down and kiss her.

"Bryony, dear." Mrs. Heath patted her knee.

Startled out of her thoughts, she fumbled to find her place in *The Red Badge of Courage*. They sat in the small downstairs parlor with a cozy fire in the hearth. "So sorry. Where were we?"

Mrs. Heath smirked. "A thousand miles from the battlefront, it appears. Bryony, you're far too distracted this afternoon. Are you unwell?"

"Oh, no. My mind was wandering, that's all." Wandering to places she had no business visiting. She turned a few pages. "We're almost to the end of this chapter. Then I'll fetch your afternoon tea."

"Lovely." Mrs. Heath relaxed into her chair as Bryony continued reading.

Before she finished the next page, the parlor door opened. When Bryony saw Michael standing there, her voice wavered.

"Excuse the interruption." He stepped into the room. "Mother, I need to borrow Bryony for a moment."

"Now? This is most inconvenient, Michael. Not to mention rude."

"I'm sorry, but there's a . . . a problem in the . . . dining room. It shouldn't take long."

The wrinkle between Mrs. Heath's brows deepened. "Isn't Alice available? Ask her. For heaven's sake, don't impose on our guest!"

Sharing a concerned glance with Michael, Bryony placed a marker in the novel and stood. "Alice is so busy today, Mrs. Heath. I'll be happy to see what Mich—I mean, your son—" With the sudden heat searing her cheeks, she couldn't find the words to continue.

"Very well, go and see what he thinks is so pressing." Mrs. Heath shooed them out the door.

Bryony halted in the hallway. "Shouldn't we find someone else to sit with her until I get back?"

"I've already sent for Callie. She'll be here any minute."

The words were no sooner out of Michael's mouth than the girl appeared behind him. "You needed something, Mr. Heath?"

He turned a kind smile toward Callie, a smile filled with warmth and welcome, so different from the reserved glances he typically bestowed on the other house help. "I'd like you to stay with my mother for a few minutes. If she asks why you're there, say you're tending the fire in the grate. And take your time."

"I understand, sir." Callie dipped in a brief curtsey before slipping into the parlor.

Moments later, Bryony found herself ushered along the hallway toward the dining room. Once they were inside, Michael closed the doors at both ends. Mussing his hair with stiff fingers, he paced like a nervous cat, until Bryony seized his arm and yanked him to a halt in front of her.

"What in all creation has gotten into you, Michael Heath? I've never seen you so overwrought."

"Overwrought doesn't begin to describe what I feel at this moment." He rolled his eyes heavenward. "I did it, Bryony. I did what you asked. And they want to see my drawings."

Bryony felt the tremors beneath his shirtsleeve and immediately let go. She locked her fingers together to keep from throwing her arms around the man in a euphoric embrace. "Oh, Michael, that's wonderful! Which publisher? What did they say?"

He sank into the nearest chair and whipped off his glasses. He rubbed his eyes as if he still couldn't believe what he'd done. "I decided if I really intended to do this, I wouldn't be able to stand the idea of mailing a letter and waiting for a reply. So I telephoned the first name on the list. A very nice gentleman asked me several questions to determine the extent of my botanical knowledge, and once he seemed satisfied, he asked me to send samples of my work."

Squeezing her eyes shut, Bryony offered up a prayer of gratitude. Michael needed this. He may not realize yet how much, but Bryony knew it in the depths of her being. He'd shut himself away from the world for far too long, and the publication of his incredibly beautiful drawings could finally set him free.

"Bryony."

She opened her eyes to see him standing inches away. Her breath hitched.

He reached for her hand. His voice dropped to a tense murmur. "Bryony, this whole business terrifies me. How will I ever—"

With a finger to his lips, so warm, so soft, she silenced him.

"One step at a time is how you'll do this. Don't be afraid, Michael. You'll find your way."

"Will I?" His breath scalded her fingertip, and she let her hand fall away. "What if I'm not even sure I want to?"

"Don't talk like that." Time to shake off this spell his closeness had cast upon her and think in practical terms. She put some space between them. "The first thing to do is decide which of your drawings to send. You'll want a variety—flowers, trees, grasses, shrubs—so you can really show off your talent."

"No. I can't." Shaking his head, he gripped the back of a chair.

Bryony fisted her hips. "What do you mean, you *can't*? Of course you can. You *will*."

"I mean, I can't put my pictures in the mail. What if something happens to them? What if they're lost or destroyed or—"

The panic in his eyes made Bryony's heart wrench. Naturally, he wouldn't want to risk losing the drawings he'd poured so much of himself into. She massaged her temple. "Here's what you do. Choose the pictures you want to send, then make smaller copies of them, just as detailed, and mail those. You can do that, can't you?"

Gnawing on his lower lip, he stared at her for a long moment, then nodded thoughtfully. "Yes, I suppose."

"Good, good." Bryony linked her arm through his and propelled him toward the door. "Then get busy right now. You don't want to keep the publisher waiting."

Before she could reach for the knob, the door swung inward, and both she and Michael had to scurry out of the way.

Michael's father stood on the other side. "What in the name of everything holy is going on in here?"

"Nothing, Dad. Absolutely nothing." Michael roughly cleared his throat as Bryony slipped her arm from his.

Sebastian Heath looked from one to the other. "Then why do you both look so incredibly guilty?"

"It's my fault, sir," Bryony piped up. She ignored the subtle plea in Michael's glance while racking her brain for a plausible excuse.

"I needed to bring up a matter regarding something of concern to —to Mrs. Heath. We just stepped in here to talk—"

"And left my wife alone?"

"Callie's with her. I made sure of that." Michael stepped between his father and Bryony. "If you'll excuse us, Bryony was just returning to the parlor, and I have some things to attend to in my room."

"I'm sure you do," Mr. Heath replied, and Bryony cringed at the sneer creeping across his face. "Coloring more pretty pictures, I suppose."

Though nothing changed in Michael's stance, Bryony sensed his brief show of confidence slipping away. She wouldn't let it happen. She brushed past Michael and stood toe-to-toe with Mr. Heath. "How dare you disparage your son and his talent! Just because *you* can't draw a leaf that looks real enough to touch, or a flower so beautiful you can smell its fragrance like it was right there in front of you—"

"Bryony." Michael's fingers wrapped around her elbow.

"I'm not through yet." She shook him off, her gaze never leaving her employer's stunned face. "You need to respect your son for the man he is, not the person you want him to be, and it's high time—"

"Bryony!" This time, the desperation in Michael's tone drew her up short.

Sebastian Heath's shocked stare eased into a raised-eyebrow look of disdain. "Miss Linwood. Apparently you don't value your position in this household—not to mention your family's continued occupancy on my property—as much as you led me to believe."

She clamped her lips together and fought with all her might to screw down the lid on her boiling-over stewpot of emotions. "I do, sir. I promise you I do. I—I was—"

Michael intervened. "This is just a misunderstanding, Dad. Don't do anything rash."

For several seconds, the only sound in the room was Bryony's own ragged breath whooshing in and out of her nostrils.

Finally, through gritted teeth, Sebastian said, "Then, young lady, I suggest you hold your tongue and return to your duties at once."

Without another word, and most certainly without daring a glance in Michael's direction, Bryony ducked past Mr. Heath and through the door.

In the hallway outside the parlor, she collapsed against the wall to wait for her racing heart to slow. "You foolish girl!" she murmured, hands fisted against her eye sockets. No matter how badly she longed to see Michael find his own way and escape his father's narrow-minded control, she couldn't afford to risk her own family's security. Not when this job might be all that kept them from homelessness and starvation.

"She didn't mean any harm, Dad. Please let this matter drop. Don't take any action against Bryony or her family."

Michael's father stepped farther into the dining room and palmed the back of his neck. With a pained sigh, he cut his eyes at Michael. "If she weren't so good with your mother . . ."

"But she is, and you know it." Fingering the folded paper tucked safely away in his pocket, Michael studied his father's profile. Bryony had defended him to his father, and now he must make sure she didn't suffer because of it. "Surely you can see how much better Mother has been since Bryony started spending time with her. Her memory is better. She's more alert. She seems happier again."

"I know, I know." Michael's father hung his head. "I admit I've been avoiding the situation for too long, but I can't bear the thought of your mother slipping away from us."

"Nor can I."

His father faced him full on. "Which is why I've been pushing you so hard to take an interest in the plantation. I'm seven years older than your mother and that much closer to my eternal reward. When I'm gone, it'll be up to you—"

"Come on, Dad, don't talk like that."

"No, hear me out. Brookbirch Plantation is your mother's legacy, and your grandfather's and great-grandfather's before that. I came into the family business when I married your mother"—his mouth flattened as his glance slid away briefly—"and I don't take my responsibilities lightly. I intend to make sure the plantation stays in the family, and since you are my sole heir—"

"But I'm not." Michael ground out the words. "Miranda is still your daughter, and despite her poor judgment she doesn't deserve what you've done to her."

Knuckles white against the back of a chair, Michael's father seethed in silence for a long moment. "I will not have this conversation with you again, so hear me clearly. Your sister alone bears the guilt of her sin and the disgrace she brought upon this family. She deserves every misfortune that befalls her."

Without giving Michael a chance to speak, he straightened abruptly and continued, "I'm driving over to Little Rock in the morning for a planters' association meeting. I suppose there's no point in asking you to come along."

"No, sir, there is not."

As soon as his father left the room, Michael pressed a fist against his abdomen and sagged against the sideboard. Much as he loved his mother and knew he should respect his family's heritage, what was he supposed to do with an inheritance he had no use or aptitude for?

And where was Miranda now? After Dad threw her out, Michael had completely lost track of his sister. Nor did he have any knowledge of the Mexican groundskeeper whose attentions had resulted in banishment for them both. Had they eventually married, or did they part ways? Michael could only hope Miranda had gone on to make a decent life for herself.

If so, she'd done better than Michael. He suspected no one's definition of a *decent life* included self-imposed isolation.

He pulled the slip of paper from his pants pocket and read the address he'd jotted down during his telephone conversation earlier. Bryony was right—he *needed* to do this. Before he could talk himself out of it, he marched upstairs to find his drawing supplies.

❦ 9 ❦

The next few days kept Michael shut away in his sitting room as he painstakingly copied several drawings onto letter-sized sheets of paper to mail to the publisher. Bryony had suggested a variety of plant types, which he'd done. Among them was the *bryonia alba*, because Bryony had come to mean so much to him, along with a larkspur and a rose in honor of Bryony's sisters. He eagerly anticipated the smiles he hoped his selections would evoke.

With a sturdy manila envelope addressed and a handwritten cover letter tucked inside with the drawings, Michael paced before his bedroom window and watched for Bryony's departure Tuesday evening. As the shadows lengthened, he glimpsed her striding along the garden path toward the drive. He allowed her time to pass the first bend in the road, then grabbed a sweater and tucked the envelope under his arm. He made his way quietly but quickly out the front door and hurried to catch up.

"Bryony!" He called just loudly enough to be heard without startling her.

She spun around. "Michael, is that you?"

"I did it, Bryony." With long strides, he closed the distance between them. "I have the drawings ready to mail to New York."

"Really, Michael? That's wonderful!" Even with fatigue painting dark circles beneath her eyes, she seemed ready to burst with delight. She glanced toward the envelope. "Is this the package?"

He nodded. "May I show you the pictures I'm sending?"

"If you don't, I'll have to wrestle them out of your grip and see for myself."

"Patience, now. We can't have you destroying my hard work." With an anxious grin, Michael opened the envelope and slid out the sketches.

Bryony's glowing response didn't disappoint him. "Oh. Oh! These are perfect, utterly perfect." She looked at each one twice, then lingered over the *bryonia alba*, her smile widening. "When are you going to mail them?"

"Actually, I hoped I might ask that favor of you." He tucked the pages carefully back into the envelope, then pulled a small handful of coins from his pocket. "It's difficult for me to get away, not to mention I'd rather not raise more questions with my father, so I thought . . ."

"I understand." With a slow nod, Bryony took the envelope and the money. Her downcast eyes didn't conceal the disappointment he imagined there. A grown man who couldn't stand up to his father, much less make a trip to the post office to mail his own letter? No one could think less of him than he thought of himself.

He held out his hand for the envelope. "I shouldn't have imposed."

"Nonsense. I'll have Grandpa take this to the post office first thing in the morning." Her smile returned. "But not before I show him and Rose the pictures. I only wish Lark could see them, too."

Relief and gratitude eased the tension from Michael's shoulders. "When your sister comes home for a visit, perhaps I can bring my sketchbooks over."

"You're welcome anytime." Hugging the envelope, Bryony slid one foot behind her, then the other. "I should get going before it gets any darker."

Michael took a step forward. "I hate that you have to walk home alone."

"I'm used to it." She shrugged, and a loose curl tumbled across her cheek.

An ache formed at the base of Michael's throat. He stepped nearer.

She didn't move. Her lips parted. Could she read his tumultuous thoughts?

"Bryony." He barely recognized the sound of his own voice. His tongue felt thick, his mouth as dry as the dusty road beneath their feet. "I have no right, none at all, but I want so much to . . ."

Her gaze slid sideways. "Please, Michael. Don't."

But he had to, or he would explode into a thousand yearning fragments. Inching closer, he cupped her cheek and tenderly lowered his mouth upon hers. He didn't demand, didn't probe, only tasted. The kiss lasted less than a moment, but it was the most precious moment in all eternity, a memory to be savored, cherished, protected.

With his forehead resting against Bryony's and his hands tucked around her elbows, Michael released a soft sigh. "Forgive me."

"No, never." Bryony shuddered but didn't pull away. She still clasped the envelope firmly to her bosom. "I mean, there's nothing to forgive. I . . . I wanted this, too." Shoulders heaving, she straightened and met his gaze. Even in the gathering gloom, he saw the sadness in her eyes. "But we both know it shouldn't have happened. And it can't happen again."

"Bryony—"

Stepping back, she held up one hand toward him, palm outward. "I mean it, Michael—Mr. Heath."

He flinched.

"We can't be friends, and we can't be . . . *this*." Her voice shook. "I'm happy to get your letter mailed, but when I come to the house tomorrow, I'd appreciate it if you'd leave me to do my work without—without . . ." With a groan of frustration, she pivoted and quickly disappeared into the shadows.

Michael clutched at his chest. The brisk night air suddenly

made it hard to breathe. Or was it only that Bryony's parting words had chilled his heart? How could one woman make him feel so much like a man while at the same time exposing his every frailty?

Mr. Heath. Never had the title wounded him so bitterly.

❧

"This shouldn't take long, Grandpa." Rose climbed from the pickup. "Meet you at the feed store in a few minutes."

Grandpa leaned toward the open door. "If Heath didn't give Bryony enough for the postage, don't you be spending none of our money, you hear."

"Don't worry, I'll probably have change left over for Bry to take back." Waving her grandfather on, Rose climbed the steps to the general store.

Inside, she made her way past shelves, crates, and barrels toward the tiny post office window at the back. "Anybody home?" she called as she tapped the bell.

"Be right there." Joe, the store clerk, appeared from the back room. "Well, good morning, Miss Rosie. What brings you by?"

She slid the manila envelope beneath the grate. "This is going to New York. How much?"

Joe adjusted his glasses to read the addressee's name. Then his gaze shifted to the upper left-hand corner. He narrowed one eye at Rose. "Michael Heath? What are you doing mailing stuff for him?"

"Just helping out. He sent it home with Bryony last night." Rose pretended interest in a sack of rice on a nearby shelf. She squinted at the price. "Really? Coulda sworn rice was a penny a pound cheaper last week."

"When there's shortages, prices go up. How you folks doing these days?"

"Hanging on, like the rest of the county. Grandpa planted potatoes after we got the cotton in. But without rain . . ." Rose shrugged.

"I hear ya. Bad all over, ain't it?" Joe set the envelope on the scale. "Looks like fourteen cents should cover it. What's the Heath boy got in here, anyways?"

"Now, Joe, that's not any of our business, is it?" Rose winked as she handed him a dime and a nickel.

He plucked a penny from the cash drawer and passed it through the window. "Just curious. Ain't every day I handle a big piece of mail going all the way to New York." Resting his forearms on the counter, he leaned closer and lowered his voice. "Say, you actually seen young Mr. Heath around anywheres? I hear tell he ain't barely shown his face since he come back from that mental hospital where they sent him after the war."

"I met him once," Rose answered coolly. "He seems real nice." Though she'd begun to have her doubts after seeing the state her sister arrived in last night. Bryony had blamed her red eyes on being tired from working all day, but Rose was pretty sure she'd been crying.

And if Michael Heath was responsible, Rose wanted to know why.

She turned to go, then paused to look over her shoulder at Joe. "He was in a mental hospital? You sure?"

"That's what folks say. Took him years and years to get over shell shock. Plus he was real sick from getting gassed." Joe clucked his tongue. "Sad, sad thing, what the war did to our boys."

"Yeah, real sad." Rose didn't need reminding since the Great War had taken her own daddy. She'd scarcely been four years old when he'd shipped over to France. Now, she carried only the vaguest memories of the smiling, fair-haired man who used to bounce her on his knee.

Well, she was Grandpa's girl now, and the farm was her life. About time she quit jawing with Joe and get on down to the feed store.

She found Grandpa loading a sack of grain into the pickup bed. A tall fellow in overalls and a straw hat was helping him. When the man looked Rose's way, she halted with a gasp. "Caleb Wieland?"

An appreciative grin spread across Caleb's face. "Well, I'll be! Rosie Linwood, aren't you a sight for sore eyes!"

Grinning back, she strode toward him, arms outstretched to give her childhood friend a welcoming hug. And then, for no good reason, she suddenly took note of her own dusty denim overalls. She'd barely even taken time to comb her hair this morning, just wove it into a braid and stuffed it under an old tweed cap.

Too late. Her momentum took her straight into Caleb's arms, and he squeezed her for all he was worth.

"All right, you two." Grandpa harrumphed. "Plenty of time for catchin' up later. Rosie, we gotta get on home. Caleb, tell your folks I said hello, and if there's ever anything your pa needs, we're just down the road."

"Yes, sir." Caleb eased up on the hug but kept one arm firmly around Rose's shoulder. "Might be asking your help with the well pump one of these days if you can spare the time." Worry lines crept into the corners of his eyes. "That is, if we can scrape up the money for parts."

"Come over and we'll look through my shed. Might find something you can use to make do."

They said their goodbyes, and Grandpa and Rose started back to the farm. A couple of miles passed in silence before Grandpa remarked, "Caleb's looking real good, wouldn't you say?"

"Mm-hmm." Rose tapped a stubby fingernail on the doorframe. "You think he's gonna stick around for a while?"

"Seems so. His pa ain't in no shape for farming no more, so it'll be up to Caleb from now on."

A sigh whispered between Rose's lips. "That's too bad. Not that he's back, I mean, but I hate he's had to give up on college. He's smart like Larkspur. He could become a doctor or lawyer or something else important."

"Farming's important, too." Grandpa slowed to turn down another dirt road. "Somebody's got to grow the wheat to make the bread to set out on the rich folks' tables."

Rose frowned as they drove passed another field, the crop so parched and shriveled up that she couldn't even guess what the farmer had planted. "Well, if we don't get a decent rain soon, the rich folk aren't gonna be eating a whole lot better than us."

How Bryony survived the next couple of weeks, she wasn't sure. Mainly it was by keeping her head down, her attention on her daily tasks, and her mind off Michael.

No, *Mr. Heath*. The familiarity, even in the privacy of her thoughts, had to stop. She absolutely could not risk losing this job.

"Bryony, you're needed upstairs." Miss Esther set her arms akimbo and glanced around the library, where Bryony had been dusting. "Haven't you finished in here yet? It's been over an hour."

"Sorry, it's a big room. Just a few more shelves and I'll be done."

"It'll have to wait. Dancy has taken Mrs. Heath up for a nap. She has some other chores and needs you to sit with her for a bit."

"Yes, ma'am." Bryony gathered her cleaning supplies and ducked around Miss Esther.

After a quick trip to the storage closet, she started up the back stairs, only to stop short when the elder Mr. Heath's booming voice echoed from his office. "Michael! Where are you?"

Bryony cringed. Earlier, as she dusted the library shelves, Michael had come in search of a book. She'd nervously offered to clean elsewhere and return later, but he apologized for disturbing her and excused himself. Clearly, these unavoidable moments when they happened upon each other in the course of a day proved as awkward for him as they did for her.

If only he'd never kissed her!

If only she hadn't enjoyed it so much. Or relived it every day since. Or imagined a life in which their differences didn't matter and there were no barriers between them.

"Michael, do you hear me?" Now Mr. Heath shouted from the front hall. "Come down at once."

From somewhere upstairs, a door slammed, and footsteps

pounded along the hallway. "I hear you perfectly well, Dad. And so does everyone else in the house. What's all the yelling about?"

"Just get down here now. We need to talk."

Bryony's first impulse as she reached the landing was to make herself scarce, but if someone didn't put a stop to this shouting match, they'd surely disturb Mrs. Heath, and once she became agitated, it could be frightfully hard to calm her again.

Michael gripped the balcony rail. "All right, I'm coming. Keep your voice down." He glanced toward his mother's door, looking both surprised and embarrassed to see Bryony standing there. His lips flattened. He gave his head an almost imperceptible shake and then marched to the main staircase.

The door opened behind Bryony, and Dancy peeked out. "What's the ruckus? Mr. Heath on another tear?"

"Appears so." Bryony paused in the doorway, wishing she could follow and find out what had Sebastian Heath so angry. With a resigned sigh, she turned to Dancy. "Miss Esther said you needed me?"

Looking frazzled, Dancy pulled Bryony into the sitting room and shut the door. "I swan, that woman done run me ragged today. If I don't get out of here for a while, I'll be bald by sunset."

"I would have come up sooner, but Miss Esther's had me cleaning downstairs. I think she's trying to get a head start for Thanksgiving." Bryony looked longingly at Mrs. Heath's chaise. Maybe she could put her feet up for a bit while the woman napped in the bedroom.

"This family does do up a fancy Thanksgiving feast. Always plenty of leftovers for the house help, too." Dancy lowered her voice. "Now don't you be saying a word about it when she wakes up, or she'll start in on you with all her plannin' and arrangin' and you'll never get home to your kinfolk tonight."

Bryony shot Dancy a worried look. "You *are* coming back later, aren't you?"

Brows wiggling, the maid moved toward the door. "Might. Might not."

"Dancy!"

"Oh, you know I will." She gave a limp-wristed wave. "In a month or two!"

Before the gasp left Bryony's throat, Dancy darted through the door and yanked it closed behind her, leaving only the echo of her laughter.

Good thing Bryony knew the woman was teasing. During the weeks Bryony had worked here, their friendship had continued to blossom into mutual concern and respect. Bryony had learned Dancy's kin grew rice over near Stuttgart, and during this drought every penny she made working for the Heaths went toward their relief.

A situation Bryony understood far too well.

Stifling a yawn, she eyed the chaise. Mrs. Heath usually napped for at least an hour, sometimes two. If Bryony could rest for just ten minutes, maybe she could scrape up enough energy to finish out the day. Fighting twinges of guilt, she lowered herself onto the plush, pale-green velveteen. *Just ten minutes*, she reminded herself firmly, and with a contented moan let her head fall against the cushion.

⬥

"Bryony. Wake up."

Forcing open her lids seemed harder than dragging a full sack of cotton. She'd been sleeping so soundly. It couldn't be morning already.

But . . . this wasn't her bed, and this certainly wasn't her room.

"Bryony."

She pried her eyes open and blinked several times to shake off the grogginess. When she glimpsed Michael standing over her, the last traces of sleep vanished instantly, and she sat up in a panic. "Oh my. I'm so sorry! What time is it?"

"Half past four, I think." He sank onto the end of the chaise, elbows on his knees. His gaze wandered the room.

Still getting her bearings, Bryony fumbled with the loose pins in her bun. Stupid and irresponsible to let sleep sneak up on her like that. If anyone but Michael had found her—

She shot a glance at the closed bedroom door. "Your mother?"

"Still resting."

"I should check on her." Bryony jumped to her feet.

Michael caught her wrist. "She's fine. Please, sit down."

"But I—"

"Please." His eyes held an urgency that made her stomach twist. "There's no one else I can share this with. No one else I want to."

As she reluctantly sat down next to him, the guilt she'd managed to subdue long enough to shamefully fall asleep on Mrs. Heath's chaise came roaring back. She focused on the rough edge of a broken thumbnail. "Does this have to do with what your father was shouting about earlier?"

"It has everything to do with it." Michael's shoulders heaved. "A letter came today from the university publisher."

Bryony sucked in a breath. "Oh, Michael!" She didn't even care that she'd slipped and used his given name. "What did it say? Was it good news?"

"I suppose that depends." He pulled an envelope from his shirt pocket, and his hands shook as he unfolded the letter. "Here. Read it for yourself."

She skimmed the contents once, then again, her heart pounding louder and faster with each word. "He loves your drawings. He wants to publish them!" Without thinking, she clasped his hand. "Michael, this is wonderful news!"

"Is it?" He leveled her a look that carried equal portions of anticipation and dread. "I'm not sure I'm ready for . . . for any of this."

"Of course you are." Bryony gave his fingers a reassuring squeeze before returning her attention to the letter. She wanted to absorb every detail.

The final paragraph included information about a botanist the university press had commissioned to write an article for their quarterly journal. *Please contact Dr. Hazleton at your earliest convenience regarding the illustrations his article will require*, the letter stated. *We shall need full-sized, publishable-quality artwork from you no later than January 31, 1931.* The editor offered a substantial payment for each drawing, payable upon acceptance, concluding with a request for Michael to telephone immediately to confirm his agreement with the terms.

Bryony refolded the letter and pinched it between her fingertips. "Have you called him yet?"

Michael shook his head.

"But why—" Instantly, she knew exactly why. "Your father."

"He didn't read the letter, only saw the university logo and the New York return address, and assumed I had applied for enrollment. He wanted to ensure I didn't expect him to foot the bill." Michael snorted. "He thinks it's a bit late in life for me to consider broadening my horizons beyond the scope of plantation business."

"But you told him he was wrong . . . didn't you?"

"I told him the letter was none of his business but that he needn't worry about my going off to college." Looking away, Michael murmured, "As if I ever would."

The defeat in his tone and posture stabbed Bryony's heart. Laying the letter aside, she swiveled to face him and gripped both his hands in hers. "You can do anything you put your mind to, Michael Heath. *Anything.* You're smart and talented and a better man than your father will ever be. Don't let his narrow-mindedness infect you. Don't give him power over the one thing that brings you happiness."

His forehead creased as he slanted her an oddly twisted smile. "Thank you, Bryony. Thank you for believing in me."

For a staggering moment she was afraid he might kiss her, and she'd promised herself it mustn't happen again. She rose abruptly and pulled him to his feet as well. "Go and telephone right now, before the publisher's office closes. Tell him you're delighted to

accept his terms and can't wait to work with this Dr. Hasslewood
—Hazelberg—"

"Hazleton." Michael chuckled softly, then sighed. "What is it about you, Bryony Linwood? How do you manage to reduce the thorniest issues to their simplest, most straightforward solutions?"

She shrugged. "Guess I'm just practical that way."

If only she could find a simple solution to her feelings about Michael Heath.

❧ 10 ❧

Michael cared less about the burst of confidence this publishing opportunity had brought than the fact that Bryony had ceased avoiding him. Over the next several days she took advantage of every chance encounter to quietly ask how his drawings were coming along, and he delighted in telling her about each one. At least half of the illustrations Dr. Hazleton requested were of plant species Michael had already sketched and catalogued. He only had to replicate the drawings, sometimes with additional elements or seasonal studies, on the paper type and page size specified by the publisher. Obtaining the necessary materials hadn't been difficult, either. Michael regularly prevailed upon Jeremiah to pick up a few art supplies for him whenever he drove Michael's father into Little Rock on business. And Jeremiah, being the soul of discretion, could be counted on not to mention his little side trips on Michael's behalf.

The one aspect Michael liked least about this drawing assignment was the time it required, which prevented those cherished moments with Bryony from happening nearly often enough. Whenever he knew his father was out of the house, he'd leave his door ajar to listen for her. She'd taken to humming again, making it easy to know when her duties brought her upstairs.

Then he'd venture out to the hallway on the pretense of stretching his legs or inquiring about his mother, and if he detected no prying eyes, he'd sometimes offer Bryony a glimpse of his latest sketch. If their hands happened to touch, or if she held his gaze a moment longer than necessary, so much the better.

Dear God, was he falling in love with this woman? He had to be careful, because if the other servants noticed and started to talk, and if the gossip ever filtered back to his father—

The pencil Michael held snapped between his fingers. Dad must never suspect Michael's feelings for Bryony, or he'd bring a quick and painful end to the matter.

He brushed aside the pencil fragments and held his latest drawing to the light. *Rhaphiolepis indica*, Indian hawthorn, a flowering shrub tolerant of heat and drought. Per Dr. Hazleton's instructions, Michael had limned a composite study of the leaves, berries, and blossoms.

And now he had the first five drawings ready to mail, with a sturdy envelope addressed and waiting. Bryony had already agreed to meet him on the garden path later when she started home. Her grandfather would once again take the packet to the postal clerk in Eden, although since tomorrow was Thanksgiving, the mail wouldn't go out until Friday.

As Michael slid the page into the envelope with his other drawings, he wondered what Bryony and her family had planned for Thanksgiving—or if she'd have any time at all to spend with them, considering the festivities Mother had arranged. She and Dad had invited the usual array of friends and relatives for dinner, and Michael should be thankful his mother felt up to hosting such a grand affair. He only hoped it wouldn't prove too much for her this year.

Bryony's lilting soprano drifted along the upstairs hallway: "Come, ye thankful people, come . . ."

Michael's heart swelled with a special kind of thankfulness. He strode to the door and swung it open in a burst of anticipation, only to draw up short when he saw his father following a few steps behind Bryony.

"Good afternoon, Mr. Heath." She cast Michael a shaky smile before scurrying toward the back stairs.

Michael collected himself, no easy task beneath his father's direct stare. "How is Mother?"

"Quite well. We were discussing a few more details for tomorrow." One brow lifted. "You look a bit flushed. Perhaps I should inquire about *your* health."

"I'm fine. Perfectly fine."

"I'm glad." Gesturing toward Michael's door, his father moved closer. "Because there are some matters we should discuss, and since you've ventured from your cave at long last, now seems as good a time as any."

A heaviness settled over Michael's chest. He swallowed. "I was just about to . . ."

"Please, Michael, don't insult my intelligence by suggesting you have anything more important to do." His father stepped past him and reached for the doorknob.

Michael spun around, his brain racing to remember whether he'd left his pencils and sketchbooks lying out—or worse, the envelope addressed to the publisher.

His father strode into the sitting room. He sank into Michael's favorite overstuffed chair and stretched one leg across the ottoman. With as much nonchalance as he could muster, Michael walked over to the table by the window and, with his back to his father, laid the envelope upside down. Hands in his pockets, he slowly turned and waited for his father to reveal whatever was on his mind.

"Well, don't stand there gaping. This could take awhile."

Reluctantly, Michael moved to the sofa across from his father. He pulled the chain on the table lamp, well aware that the fading daylight meant Bryony would start home soon. "Please, do tell me the reason for this urgent visit."

"Is there no possibility of our carrying on a civil conversation?"

Michael almost missed it, the flicker of hurt in his father's eyes. "I know you don't believe I care about what matters to you, but you're wrong. You're my son, Michael, and I've always wanted what is best for you."

Michael ran his thumb along the braided trim of the sofa cushion. "What *you* believe is best for me—I'll grant you that."

Tense silence filled the room. Michael's father exhaled sharply through flattened lips. "I've given this a great deal of thought over the past several days, and I realize I was too quick to discard your interest in continuing your education."

"Dad—"

"No, hear me out. All those years you spent in the hospital have hindered you in ways I've scarcely begun to appreciate. Going away to school can only be good for you."

So this was about the envelope Dad had intercepted from the university. "I told you, the letter had nothing to do with a college application."

"I know what you said—'None of your business,' I believe were your exact words. But it got me thinking." Dad lowered his foot to the floor and sat forward, hands clasped between his knees. "The exposure to new vistas and ideas is exactly what you need to bring you out of your shell. I admit at thirty-two you're well past the age of a typical college student, but even so, the experience will make you much better equipped to assume your responsibilities here when the time comes."

"Don't you get it, Dad?" Michael shoved to his feet. "I'm not cut out for running the plantation. I never was."

"You say that now—and believe me, I've heard you loud and clear. But a few years at college, earning the degree you would have gotten if you hadn't been such an angry, cocksure kid all those years ago, storming off to go to war—"

"You should leave now." Michael strode to the door and yanked it open. "This conversation is over."

His father seethed for several moments before rising tiredly and fixing Michael with a withering stare. "God knows I've tried with you, son. But if you insist on wallowing in your bitterness over something that happened years ago, there is nothing I can do to stop you."

As soon as his father stepped through the door, Michael slammed it with a thunderous bang. Stomach roiling, he ripped off his glasses and furiously massaged his eye sockets. *God knows* . . . Michael wasn't sure what God knew anymore, or if he even paid attention to the goings-on under this roof.

Then he spied the envelope ready and waiting to be handed over to Bryony. Surely God had brought her into his life for a reason. She'd awakened feelings in him he'd never expected to experience again. Glimmers of hope. Promises of healing. A chance to *be* again.

Shoving the encounter with his father out of his thoughts, he grabbed a sweater, snatched up the envelope, and made a beeline for the back stairs.

Bryony paced the garden path, now in shadows as the sun sank below the western horizon. She hated walking home in the dark, but if Michael didn't come down soon, she'd have no choice. She peered around a shrub toward the veranda. Miss Esther had already switched on the outdoor lamps, and the long porch was bathed in a pale amber glow.

"Where are you, Michael?" When Bryony had glanced over her shoulder on her way downstairs earlier, it was obvious Mr. Heath had plenty on his mind. Had he cornered Michael for a lengthy father-son talk? Bryony prayed the two of them could work out whatever issues they had, but she worried what another confrontation would do to Michael's fragile veneer of confidence.

Gravel crunched behind her. Michael approached, and she let out a relieved breath. "Where have you been? Is everything all right."

"Fine, fine." But he didn't look fine. He looked terribly distracted.

"Is it your father? What happened after I saw you with him?"

"It's not important." Michael thrust the envelope into her hands. "I'm sorry I kept you waiting. It's getting dark. You need to go."

Shivering in the evening breeze, Bryony tugged at the collar of her sweater. "You're upset. Don't pretend with me."

The tiniest smile crept across his lips. He reached for her hand. "I *was* upset. I'm not anymore. I never am when I'm with you."

"Michael, we talked about this." Reluctantly, she slipped her hand from his grasp and clutched the stiff, oversized envelope. She pivoted sideways. "You're right, I need to go."

"Let me walk partway with you. I promise I'll be a gentleman."

The plea in his tone brought a catch to her throat, and she consented. They cut through the garden and came out on the lane several yards down from the house. The tree limbs arching above them were already bare. Fallen leaves, dry and brown, skittered across the road and crackled underfoot.

"I can't wait to see Lark again." Bryony quivered with anticipation. "She should be home by the time I get there."

"It's awful you have to work tomorrow." Michael's voice sounded hushed in the deepening dusk.

The reminder pulled at Bryony's shoulders. And now she wouldn't even have the half-day off Miss Esther had promised, but had been told to return early in the morning to help Odette with the cooking, then be on hand to serve dinner and clean up afterward. The hours she'd hoped to spend peppering her sister with questions about college life would be reduced to scant moments over the next few days when Bryony wasn't too exhausted to prop her eyes open.

Michael's arm brushed hers. "You've grown so quiet. What's wrong?"

She couldn't keep the despair out of her tone as she explained about Miss Esther catching her as she was leaving. "I haven't seen Lark since September, and now I'll hardly see her at all."

"This isn't fair. I'll speak to Esther as soon as I get back."

"No, don't." Bryony halted in the middle of the road and faced him. "I mean it, Michael. Things have been better lately. Don't give Odette or Alice any new reasons to resent me."

Michael slanted a brow. Before he could reply, the rumble of an automobile sounded behind Bryony, and headlights swept the road. Michael looped his hand around Bryony's elbow and pulled her to the side as the vehicle braked to a stop.

It was Grandpa's truck. The driver's window rolled down and Rose poked her head out. "Hop in, Bry!"

"What are you doing, Rosie? Does Grandpa know you're driving?"

"Of course he does. He said I could come get you." Rose grinned and waved. "Hey, Michael. How's it going?"

"Rose!" Bryony glared.

Her sister gave an exaggerated eye roll. "Sorry. *Mr.* Heath."

"Bryony, it's all right," Michael whispered close to her ear. "Hello, Rose. I was just seeing your sister partway home."

"So I see." A girlish giggle bubbled from Rose's throat. She turned toward someone else in the pickup cab, and more laughter followed.

Bryony stepped closer. "Who's in there with you? Grandpa?"

"Um, no." Rose leaned back as another face appeared in the window beside her.

"Larkspur!" Reaching through the window, Bryony caught her fair-haired sister in a hug. She barely noticed when Michael rescued the envelope before she crushed it.

"Hey, y'all are mashing me!" Rose croaked. "Just get in the truck, Bry. Plenty of time for all this mushy stuff later."

Lark broke free from Bryony's hold. "Now wait a minute. First I need to be introduced to Bryony's beau."

Searing heat blistered Bryony's face. No amount of money could have made her look in Michael's direction.

He came up beside her and offered his hand to Larkspur through the window. "Hello. Michael Heath, at your service."

"How do you do?" Lark's simpering smile was sweet enough to bake a cake with. "So you're the artist fella Bryony wrote me about. Did she give you those names I got from my professor?"

"She did, and thank you." With a polite nod, Michael turned toward Bryony and handed her the envelope. "See you tomorrow?"

Now it was her turn to roll her eyes. "You know where I'll be."

Michael walked her around to the passenger door and helped her climb in next to Larkspur. Glad as she was to see her sister, not to mention grateful she didn't have to walk the rest of the way home in the dark, she could do without two pairs of prying sisterly eyes watching an already awkward goodbye.

The door clicked shut, and Michael rested his palm briefly against the window glass before stepping off the road so Rose could get the pickup turned around.

"Oh, my heavens!" Lark bumped Bryony's shoulder. "He's even handsomer than I pictured!"

"Stop it right now." Eyes forward, Bryony rested her hands in her lap atop the envelope. She'd been so anxious to see her sister again, and now she only wanted to disappear.

"And you get to work at his house and spend time with him every single day? Tell me *that* isn't pure torture!"

Rose slowed for a bend in the road. "Don't tease her, Lark. Bry works harder than any of us. If you could see how tired she comes home every night, with hardly a day off—"

"I know, and I'm sorry." Lark slid her arm around Bryony and squeezed. "I'm just so glad to see you, sweetie." A smile crept into her voice. "But you have to admit, he *is* quite the looker."

No arguing the point. "He's really nice, too. And I can't wait to show you these pictures." Bryony patted the envelope. "Oh, Lark, thank you so much for finding out about the university press. I can't even tell you what a difference this has made in Michael's life."

Rose harrumphed. "Sure enough made a difference in *you*, Bry.

A few weeks ago, when you started coming home every night with your chin draggin' in the dirt, you had me and Grandpa worried."

Leaning forward, Larkspur peered into Bryony's eyes. "Bry, what's she talking about?"

"I was just tired, that's all." She turned her face toward the window, though little could be seen but her own dim reflection in the glass. Eyes full of longing gazed back at her, and her lips trembled at the memory of a kiss.

❦

Michael's neck chafed at the tight, starched collar of his dress shirt. He hadn't worn a tie in months, and wouldn't have today if not for the necessity of looking fashionably presentable for his parents' guests.

That is, if one could call a ten-year-old brown serge suit fashionable.

Father Dempsey turned from admiring the oil landscape over the mantel and took the wing chair next to Michael's. "Have I mentioned you're looking quite well these days?"

"Thank you, Father." Michael took another sip of coffee, then balanced the cup and saucer on his knee. Across the room, his mother chatted with a cousin and her husband who'd driven over from Memphis. Dad was out rambling about the countryside with a fellow plantation owner, no doubt bemoaning the sad state of their holdings. The man's wife arrived with a headache and had asked to lie down for a bit in one of the guest rooms. Michael figured he'd better not try the headache excuse for himself or risk another of Dad's lectures.

"There's always a seat for you at Mass." The pudgy, gray-haired priest leaned Michael's way and continued in a low voice, "I'm concerned for you, my boy. How long has it been since you confessed your sins and received the Holy Eucharist?"

Michael forced a harsh laugh. "Too long, Father. Entirely too long."

"This isn't good for the health of your soul. Scripture teaches that if we confess our sins, God is faithful and just to forgive us and cleanse us from all iniquity. However, if we say we have not sinned, we make God a liar, and his word does not dwell in us."

"I'm sure my sins are many." The direction of this conversation stirred Michael's restlessness. If he wouldn't appear rude, he'd find any excuse to take his leave. "Father, I do appreciate your concern for my soul, but the Lord and I . . . we're too far apart on too many issues."

"Easily remedied with penitent prayer." Father Dempsey smiled benignly as he rose. "And I will be praying earnestly for you, my son, for the continued health of your body and for the healing of your troubled spirit."

Michael bowed his head as the priest discreetly made the Sign of the Cross over him. When Father Dempsey pulled over a chair to join Michael's mother and the other guests, Michael took the opportunity to slip from the room.

He set his cup and saucer on the pedestal table in the foyer and then leaned against the banister while his nerves quieted. It was times like these he truly missed the monotonous routine of the sanitarium. So far from home, he'd never had to concern himself with friends or family dropping in for a visit, and even on holidays the nurses never raised a fuss if he chose not to mix with the other patients.

On the other hand, his doctor had plenty to say about his preference for solitude. "Shell shock doesn't simply go away, Sergeant Heath. You have to *want* to get well."

The problem with getting well meant eventually returning home, and for a long, long time, home was the very last place Michael wanted to be. Nothing had convinced him more fully of the fact than when his doctor declared him fit and personally escorted him to the depot to catch the next train to Little Rock. His homecoming had been predictable—Mother fawning over him as if he were still an invalid, while Dad immediately began pushing him to take an active role in plantation business. The two extremes only exacerbated his compulsion to withdraw.

Until Bryony. He still could hardly believe she'd convinced him to submit his drawings for publication. But she believed in him, saw something in him he hadn't had the courage to find within himself. Now, if only he could convince Bryony to give this thing between them a chance. Yes, their disparate circumstances posed difficulties, but his sister had given up everything for the man she loved. So why couldn't—why *shouldn't*—he and Bryony find a way to be together?

He only hoped Miranda was happy in her choice, safe and well somewhere, and that fate had been kinder to her than her own father had been. If anyone had sins to confess . . .

Before his stomach twisted itself in knots again, Michael barreled up the staircase. Just a little quiet time in his rooms, and maybe he could hold himself together long enough to survive the big feast. But when he reached the upper hall and turned toward his door, he found it standing ajar.

His gut clenched with a new worry. Stepping into the sitting room, he could tell at once that someone had been here. The cabinet where he kept his art supplies stood open, and it appeared more than a few of his sketchbooks were missing. Several loose pages were strewn across the table beneath the window, as if someone had been searching through his drawings. Surely none of the servants would have invaded his privacy in this manner. His father? Not likely.

Mother. Palming his forehead, he blew out sharply. It should have occurred to him that she'd want to show off her son's artwork to her Thanksgiving Day guests. Fine, so long as she did so while Dad was out of the house. But where had she taken them? He hadn't noticed any sign of his drawings downstairs.

So much for a peaceful hour before dinner. He'd get no rest until he found the sketchbooks and made sure they weren't anywhere in sight when his father returned.

Bryony would help him. He took the back stairs and crossed

the breezeway to the kitchen. Aromas exploded around him before he ever stepped inside—turkey and dressing, yams, buttered beans, yeast rolls, pies. Odette shouted instructions to Callie, Alice, and Bryony as they stirred pots on the stove, mixed sauces, counted plates, and laid out serving ware.

He called Bryony's name as she rinsed and dried a large china platter. She set it on the worktable and hurried over, the dishtowel slung across her shoulder. "You shouldn't be in here," she said, flicking a loose strand of hair off her forehead. "It's a madhouse."

"Clearly." Michael moved aside as Alice charge past with a wooden spoon dripping something white and gooey. "Sorry, but I need you to do something for me." In an anxious whisper, he explained his concerns about the missing sketchbooks.

"I'm about to take some things to the dining room. I'll try to look around then." Looking tired and flustered, Bryony shooed him out the door.

Michael had returned to the foyer and was about to do some looking around, himself, when his father's booming voice rang out from the parlor. Back from their drive, Dad and his friend were loudly commiserating about President Hoover's handling of the drought crisis.

"Sebastian, please," Michael's mother interrupted. "Today is a day to thank the Lord for our blessings. Save the politics for another time. Besides," she said as Michael stood in the archway, "after we dine, I have something wonderful to show everyone."

11

"This is the saddest Thanksgiving ever." Larkspur drained boiled turnips into a colander, the steam swirling up to fog the window over the sink.

"Not the saddest," Rose murmured as she took a serving bowl from the cupboard.

With a tender smile for her sister, Larkspur emptied the colander into the bowl. "I know, Rosie. Nothing could be worse than losing Mama. I just meant it's awful Bry can't be here with us. We've never been apart for the holidays."

"She'll be home tonight, and maybe they won't make her go over too early tomorrow, since the big doings will be over." Rose plopped a serving spoon into the turnips and carried them to the table. "Where's Grandpa? I'm starved."

"Where he is about this time every year." Heaving a mournful sigh, Larkspur nodded in the general direction of town.

"Oh . . . the cemetery. Guess we can keep dinner warm awhile longer."

Larkspur peeked in the oven, releasing a wave of heat into the room. "The rabbit looks done. Should be nice and tender, roasted slow in its own juices."

"Not the same as a plump, juicy turkey, though."

"Be thankful for Grandpa's traps, or we might be having a meatless Thanksgiving this year."

At the sound of tires on gravel, both girls looked toward the back window. Grandpa parked his old black pickup beside the barn and climbed out, his steps plodding as he started toward the house. He paused near the door to the screen porch and stared into the distance.

Larkspur's heart twisted at the despair etched on her grandfather's weathered face. This was more than lingering grief over the loved ones they'd lost. His expression mirrored her own feelings, the soul-deep sense that things were never, ever going to get better. She'd hoped college would be her escape, and in many ways it was. She'd traded the drudgery of endless farm chores for a world of books and classes and stimulating discussions with peers and professors. And how she did love those Sunday evening literature circles at Professor Keene's, especially the cordial way he'd welcomed her into the group.

But college life presented its own challenges. From the day she'd received her acceptance letter, Larkspur had made up her mind not to allow schooling expenses to burden her family any more than necessary. Upon arriving on campus, she set out immediately to find part-time work. Her job at the local grocer's didn't pay much, but the hours didn't interfere with her classes and study time. She was always bone tired at the end of a shift, though, which made it a real struggle getting up the next morning in time for her first class.

"He's coming inside." Rose nudged Larkspur away from the window. "Put on a cheerful face, okay?"

By the time Grandpa entered the kitchen, Larkspur had taken the rabbit from the oven and set the roasting pan on a trivet in the center of the table. She and Rose had laid out Grandma's prettiest lace-trimmed tablecloth, the one they always used for special occasions. Mama's porcelain dinnerware graced each place setting.

"Just in time, Grandpa." Rose hooked her arm through his. "Dinner's on the table."

Lips quirked, he gave a brief nod. "The rabbit smells mighty good."

"Rose is turning into a fine cook," Larkspur said as she pulled out her chair. "I snitched a taste of the peach pie she baked this morning. We're in for a treat." She wouldn't mention Rose had used the last jar of canned peaches from the cellar, plus most of the sugar they had on hand. Seemed they were running low on everything.

After Grandpa blessed the food, they filled their plates and ate like people who had no worries about where their next meal was coming from. Larkspur refused to dwell on what they didn't have but tried hard to enjoy this time with her family. All too soon, she'd be catching a bus back to Arkadelphia.

"More pie, Grandpa?" Rose reached for his dessert plate.

Rubbing his belly, Grandpa slid his chair away from the table. "Two slices is more'n enough. Let's save some for Bryony."

Larkspur rose to clear away the dishes. "Hope she's getting something good to eat over at the Heaths'. It's the least they could do for making their house help work on a holiday."

"Bet they had turkey and dressing and all the trimmings." The tiniest hint of resentment colored Rose's tone. "Real pumpkin pie, too, I bet."

Larkspur snorted as she scraped the leftover rabbit gravy into a smaller bowl. "Next you'll be telling me *you'd* like to work for the Heaths, just so you could eat their fancy food." She covered the bowl with a cloth, then winked over her shoulder. "Or maybe you've got your eye on Mr. Heath's handsome son."

"Don't be ridiculous. He's way too old for me." A mischievous grin crept across Rose's face. "But not for Bryony. Did you see how they looked at each other last night?"

Grandpa slammed his palm against the table. "No more such talk. Bryony knows her place. I reckon the Heath boy knows his, too. Ain't nothin' between 'em and there's never gonna be."

"But I thought you liked him, Grandpa," Rose said. "You were nice as could be the day he had Sunday dinner with us."

Larkspur's brows shot up. She'd just filled the dishpan and nearly dropped one of Mama's plates in the soapy water. "Michael Heath had Sunday dinner here?"

"And showed us his pretty pictures. Which reminds me." Rose went to the hutch where Bryony had laid the envelope she'd brought home last night. "Bry said we could look at Michael's drawings before we mail them tomorrow."

Curiosity aroused, Larkspur dried her hands and joined Rose at the hutch. Michael must truly be talented for such an impressive New York university press to commission his illustrations for their journal. And since Larkspur had played a key role in putting Michael in touch with the publisher, she took special interest in the outcome.

Rose carefully withdrew the protective folder containing the drawings. One by one, she laid them across the hutch, and both she and Larkspur oohed and aahed over each one.

"These are every bit as good as Bryony described," Larkspur said. "I can't believe he hasn't done anything with his talent before now. Why, it's—"

"I know." Rose's fingers hovered over the drawing of the Indian hawthorn. "It's almost like it's real."

❦

"My gracious, this daffodil looks almost real enough to touch."

Bryony tried to keep her hand steady as she refilled Father Dempsey's coffee cup. Following the sumptuous meal, the Heaths had brought their guests to the parlor for dessert and coffee, and once the pie plates were cleared away, Mrs. Heath had brought out Michael's sketchbooks from wherever she'd tucked them away. Now she sat on the sofa next to the priest, one of the books spread open across her lap.

"Our boy shows true talent, don't you agree?" Mrs. Heath turned another page. "And look at this one. I can smell the wisteria as if it were growing right here in this room."

Moving among the other guests, Bryony offered more coffee. Michael stood by the front window, his gaze riveted to his mother and a tense smile distorting his lips.

"Refill your coffee, sir?" Bryony nodded toward the cup and saucer Michael had placed on the windowsill.

"Thank you."

With her back to the room as she poured, Bryony murmured, "I'm sorry. Odette kept me so busy that I didn't have much chance to search for your drawing books."

"It's all right." Turning toward the window, Michael lifted his cup and saucer. "Or it will be, provided Dad and Mr. McIlroy continue chatting in the office awhile longer."

"Perhaps if I deliver more coffee and dessert, it'll keep them occupied."

"Would you? It's worth a—"

A loud guffaw erupted in the foyer, and Mr. Heath appeared with his companion. "Perfect timing," he said, ushering his friend into the parlor. "The girl is here with more coffee."

The girl. Bryony suppressed a resentful shudder. When Michael's eyes met hers, she read his apology. Steeling herself, she crossed to the side table where she'd set the coffee service. After filling two cups, she carried them to Mr. Heath and his friend. Neither acknowledged her with more than a stiff nod.

With the coffee urn nearly empty and nothing more she could do to help Michael, Bryony decided to return to the kitchen. Surely by now they could spare her long enough for a quick bite of turkey and mashed potatoes. The staff had been given permission to eat in shifts, and Bryony, having the least seniority, hadn't had her turn yet. Her stomach rumbled in anticipation as she scurried along the breezeway. She'd been smelling the delicious aromas ever since she'd arrived at the mansion at half past six, and if she had to wait one second longer, she'd keel right over from hunger pangs.

Odette relieved her of the coffee service. "They doin' all right in yonder?"

Bryony certainly hoped so. Whatever happened between

Michael and his father over the sketchbooks, there was little she could do about it anyway. Besides, she simply *had* to eat something or she'd never make it through the afternoon. With a plate of turkey scraps and small mounds of dressing, mashed potatoes, and butterbeans, she sank into a chair at one end of the long oak work table. Each taste brought a moan of appreciation, and she found herself shoveling in the food faster and faster.

Callie passed by with a stack of dirty dishes. "Slow down, Bryony, before you make yourself sick."

"But it's so good," she mumbled over a mouthful. "Best turkey dinner I've tasted since—"

A door slammed. Loud, angry voices thundered outside, and someone charged past the kitchen windows.

Bryony dropped her fork and shared a startled look with Callie before they both rushed to the window to see what all the commotion was about.

"That's Mr. Heath," Callie said. "What's he throwing in the incinerator?"

"Oh, no. Oh, please, no!" Bryony's stomach heaved. She slapped both hands over her mouth for fear of losing everything she'd just eaten. "He wouldn't—oh, God, don't let it be so!"

Odette joined them at the window. "What's all the fuss?"

Bryony tried to answer but couldn't form the words. She sucked in a gasp when Michael halted on the lawn a few feet outside the kitchen door. His chest heaved as he watched his father rip page after page from the sketchbooks. The flames rose higher and higher above the brick-lined enclosure, fragments of glowing ash circling in the gray smoke.

"Gracious, gracious," Odette murmured. "His daddy done it this time. He gonna break his boy's spirit for sure."

"Poor Mister Michael." Callie's voice broke on a sob. "We have to do something. We have to stop this!"

Odette slid an arm around Callie's shoulder. "Ain't our place, sugar. Those menfolk gotta work this out amongst theirselves."

But they wouldn't. Bryony knew they wouldn't, not as long as

Sebastian Heath held sway over this household. Heart hammering, she bolted through the door and ran straight for the incinerator. "Stop it!" she screamed, jerking at Sebastian Heath's arm. "Please, you have to stop!"

The man shrugged her off with no more concern than if she'd been a buzzing fly. He tore another handful of pages from a sketchbook and flung the wad into the fire. "This'll teach you to go behind my back. I warned you, Michael. Don't say I didn't warn you!"

Smoke stung Bryony's eyes. She spun around in search of Michael. Why did he just stand there? Why didn't he fight to stop this?

She tried again to grab the pages from Mr. Heath's grasp, but this time he shoved her away, hard enough that she stumbled and fell. Through her tears, she glimpsed another sketchbook lying at his feet. She crawled toward it, but he kicked it beyond her reach.

Someone grabbed her from behind and lifted her to her feet. "Let it go, Bryony." Michael's voice rasped against her left ear as he dragged her backward, away from the flames. "It's too late. It's over."

"But your pictures—you can't let him do this!" She fought to get away, but Michael held her fast. She could only watch in horror as Michael's father fed every last drawing into the incinerator's gaping maw, while orange flames licked the air like the breath of a greedy, ravenous dragon.

When Sebastian finally turned from the incinerator and came toward them, Bryony balled up her fists and shook them at him. "How could you! How could—"

"Enough, Bryony." Tightening his grip on her arms, Michael forced her to be still.

She crumpled against him. Unable to bear the sight of the man who'd so callously despised his own son's talent, she buried her tear-streaked face in Michael's shoulder.

Behind her, Sebastian's voice rang hard as iron. "Go home, Miss Linwood. Your services here are no longer required."

As his words penetrated, a disturbing deadness spread through her chest. Her tears had suddenly ceased, and now all she felt was stunned disbelief. She couldn't even seem to make her lungs work to draw a full breath. What hope was there for her family now?

Michael stroked her hair as it tumbled from the loosened pins. "Don't worry, Bryony. It'll be all right. I'll make sure of it."

"But how? Michael, he's a tyrant. You need to—"

He silenced her with a finger to her lips. "Please. Just go home." His voice held an unnatural calm. "Does Esther have you working tomorrow?"

"She did, but now—"

"Then come at the usual time." With an arm around her waist, Michael steered her toward the open kitchen door.

When they reached the threshold, she balked. "Michael—"

"Trust me, Bryony. Please."

She had no choice.

❦

"How am I supposed to go back there, after what he did to Michael?" Crumpled over the table in Grandpa's kitchen, Bryony hugged herself. Much as she needed her job, she couldn't bear the idea of spending one more day in the employ of a man who could treat his own son so cruelly.

Grandpa stood behind her and massaged her shoulders. "You don't never have to go back. We'll make it just fine . . . somehow." The waver in his tone told Bryony he didn't believe his own words.

"Have some peach pie, Bry." Rose slid a plate and fork in front of her. "We saved this big slice especially for you."

Bryony tried to smile for her sister's sake. "It looks wonderful, but I can't, not right now."

Larkspur paced between the sink and the back door. "What comes over a person like Sebastian Heath? When I told y'all my dream was to be a teacher and I wanted to go to college, you never so much as flinched. You've supported and encouraged me every step of the way."

"That's rich folk for you," Rose said with a sneer. Although she seemed to be quite enjoying the box of leftovers Odette had shoved into Bryony's hands as she left the Heath place.

"Not *all* rich folk." With a deep sigh, Bryony looked toward the window, but all she saw was the utter emptiness in Michael's eyes as he'd watched his work go up in flames. The numbness that had cloaked her while she stood in Michael's arms had soon given way to fury. She'd raged silently all the way home, while her tears fell in torrents—enough, it seemed, to fill every well in the entire county.

Larkspur stopped beside Bryony's chair and leaned close to plant a kiss on her forehead. "You're so tired, Bry. You do so much to take care of us. Now let me take care of you."

Legs limp as boiled noodles, Bryony allowed her sister to pull her to her feet and guide her to the bedroom. There, Larkspur eased Bryony out of the drab maid's uniform and into a soft flannel nightgown. With long, gentle strokes, Larkspur ran a brush through Bryony's hair, and the sensation slowly drained the cares of the day and lulled Bryony into a mindless daze. Awhile later, when she laid her head upon the pillow and Larkspur drew the quilt over her, sleep came quickly, and she wished she'd never have to wake up and face tomorrow.

Someone just wouldn't give up.

When the pounding on his outer door didn't stop, Michael rolled onto his side and groaned. If he could muster the breath to do so, he'd shout at whoever it was to leave him alone.

"Michael?" His mother's voice.

Oh, Lord, make her go away.

"Michael, I hope you're decent, because we're coming in."

When he tried to sit up, another cough rumbled through his chest. The coughing had kept him awake most of the night, his own fault for standing vigil as his very life went up in smoke. He lay back down, his lungs heaving. He hadn't felt this weak and breathless since his last bout of pneumonia.

Two pairs of footfalls thumped through the sitting room. Seconds later, the bedroom door opened, and Odette's dark face appeared. "Just like I thought, Miz Heath. He's still abed, and lookin' mighty peaked."

"Merciful heavens." His mother darted to the bedside. She bent over him, concern etching her face as she laid a cool palm upon his forehead. "He doesn't feel feverish," she said over her shoulder.

"I'm not sick, just . . . tired." Michael's voice rasped across his dry throat. He coughed again.

"Get him some water, Odette." Tiny as she was, Michael's mother wrestled him to a semi-sitting position and fluffed the pillows behind him.

Odette returned with a water glass from the bathroom. Michael sipped gratefully, but the effort drained him. He rested his head against the headboard and closed his eyes. "I just need to sleep some more."

"Oh, you poor, poor dear." His mother stroked the back of his hand. "I've told you time and again to stay away from the incinerator when your daddy's burning trash. See now what all that smoke has done to your lungs."

No doubt *trash* was exactly how his father viewed his drawings. He pried one eye open and looked at his mother, wondering how much she comprehended of what had happened yesterday. It had all begun so innocently, Mother chattering on about Michael's sketches while she showed them to Father Dempsey. When Dad first noticed, he'd done little more than shoot Michael a disapproving frown while continuing his conversation with Mr. McIlroy.

Then a loose paper had fluttered to the floor. The same instant Mother retrieved it, Michael realized what it was—the letter from the university press. Perhaps if he hadn't panicked and rushed over to claim it, his father would never have been the wiser. But Dad must have caught something in Michael's reaction. He intercepted the letter and began reading, his face growing more crimson by the moment.

"What?" his father had bellowed. "Now you're *selling* your pictures like some—some—two-bit hack?"

Fortunately, their guests chose discretion over curiosity and had politely taken their leave. Father Dempsey had been the last to depart, unable to hide his concern over Mother's increasingly agitated state. She hadn't understood what Dad was so upset about, and whatever clarity she'd maintained while entertaining their guests had degenerated into mumbling confusion.

Somehow, Michael had deflected his father's anger long enough to convince him to let Dancy accompany Mother up to her room. But once they were alone in the parlor, Michael's father had reamed him out over wasting his time on silly drawings instead of devoting himself to learning the family business. Then, as he gathered up all the sketchbooks Michael's mother had brought to the parlor, he shouted for Jeremiah and ordered the man up to Michael's rooms to get the rest, including Michael's pencils and other drawing supplies.

Minutes later, Dad was feeding everything to the flames, and Michael had found himself vainly trying to comfort Bryony while stifling his own screaming emotions before they flayed him bloody and laid his shattered soul bare.

"Let's let your boy rest, Miz Heath." At Odette's softly spoken words, Michael's lids fluttered open. The round-faced cook cast him a sympathetic frown, and she shook her head sadly.

His mother cupped his cheek. "Are you sure you'll be all right, son? Odette can bring you up some breakfast. I'll have her make you a steaming cup of hot tea with honey."

"Perhaps later." Michael tried to sound reassuring, when he had no reassurance to give. He motioned for Odette to escort his mother out but then called Odette back to the bed. Quietly, he asked, "Did Bryony come today?"

"No, sir. She been fired, remember?" Her lips pinched. "Gotta say I weren't happy to see her go. She been a hard worker. Better'n I gave her credit for."

Michael nodded slowly, appreciating the effort it had taken for the stubborn cook to admit she'd been wrong. "I need two favors, Odette. First, send someone for Bryony to let her know she still has a job here. If you tell her my mother needs her, she'll come. Make sure she understands how important it is."

"Yes, sir, but how you gonna get your daddy to hire her back?"

"That's the second favor." A cough shook Michael's chest, and he sat a little straighter. "Ask my father to come up. Tell him I'm ready to do what he asks."

12

After a mug of weak coffee and the slice of peach pie she'd had no appetite for yesterday, Bryony dressed in denim overalls, work boots, and sturdy gloves. Despite Michael's reassurances as he'd held her yesterday, she'd made up her mind that she couldn't bear even one more hour working at the Heath place. In which case, she might as well get busy on farm chores. Grandpa and Rose had been left with the bulk of the work for too long, and while they were out baling what they could salvage from the drought-damaged hayfield, Bryony decided to clean out the chicken coop.

Armed with bucket and shovel, she ducked through the wire gate and latched it behind her. One of their best brood hens, a grumpy old thing with half her wattle missing, strutted down the ramp from the nesting shelter. She cocked one eye in Bryony's direction as if to say, "Where's breakfast?"

"Sorry, Cornelia, you'll have to make do on scraps today—and you'd better be nice about it or you could end up like Henrietta." From the pocket of her overalls, Bryony pulled out a handful of shriveled turnip greens and the crumbling edge of her pie crust. Before the food hit the ground, Cornelia and three of her cohorts were battling over who got the biggest share.

While the hens pecked at the leftovers, Bryony started scooping up manure. She'd filled the bucket and was on her way to the compost pile behind the barn when she glimpsed a small female figure traipsing up the lane. By the time she emptied the bucket and started back to the chicken house, she recognized the visitor as Callie.

The girl smiled and waved. "Hey, Bryony."

Bryony set down the bucket and tried to smile back, but a sick feeling hollowed out her stomach. "What brings you by? Shouldn't you be at the mansion?"

"Odette sent me with a message for you." Hugging herself against the chilly morning air, Callie marched across the yard and stopped in front of Bryony. "She says you're to come back to work, just like before, and—"

"Wait, *Odette* said this?"

"That's right, she said to come soon as you can get there. I'm to tell you—" Glancing sideways, Callie pursed her lips as if trying to remember the exact words. She looked at Bryony and hiked her chin. "I'm to tell you Miz Heath needs you real bad and don't you worry about what Mr. Heath said yesterday 'cause Mister Michael promises everything's gonna be fine now."

Bryony couldn't for the life of her imagine how everything could ever be *fine* again, not after Sebastian Heath had destroyed the one beautiful, significant thing in his son's life. She retrieved the manure bucket and started toward the chicken coop. "I'm sorry you came all this way for nothing, Callie, but I've already decided I'm through working for the Heaths."

"But you have to." Catching up, Callie grabbed Bryony's arm. "Didn't you hear me say Miz Heath *needs* you? Odette said Mister Michael told her if I said that, you'd be sure to come back with me."

Fingers resting on the gate latch, Bryony frowned at the girl. "So this is all on Michael's say-so. Mr. Heath hasn't changed his mind at all, has he?"

"Odette didn't say." Callie withdrew her hand and inched back a step. "But she wouldn't have sent me to get you if it wasn't okay with old Mr. Heath, now, would she? If you won't come back to take care of his missus, I'll be in big trouble, sure enough."

Bryony didn't see how anyone could put the blame on Callie—after all, the girl was only the messenger. But then, when had the truth ever stopped Sebastian Heath from making up his own rules?

Again, she set down the bucket. With a kind but determined smile, she pivoted to face Callie and rested both hands on the girl's narrow shoulders. "What makes you so sure Mr. Heath won't toss me out on my ear the moment I show up over there?"

One eye narrowed, Callie stood taller. "Because Mister Michael promised, and he doesn't lie."

Bryony didn't even want to think what Michael's promise would cost him—what it had cost him already. She tugged off a glove and rubbed her forehead. "Even if I agreed, I can't come today. It's been too long since I had a whole day off, and I need to help my grandpa and sisters with farm chores. You tell Odette and whoever else gives a hoot that I'll show up bright and early tomorrow morning and not before."

Relief flooded Callie's expression. She gave Bryony a grateful hug. "Praise the Lord! I was already missing you something fierce."

Bryony sent the girl on her way with a skip in her step. Still shaking her head over this sudden turnabout, she finished cleaning out the chicken house, then started on the barn stalls. The outdoor labor felt good, a welcome change from dusting and sweeping and polishing silver. Bryony did enjoy the hours spent in Mrs. Heath's company, though, even when the woman's mind wasn't all there. Sometimes, as Bryony sat on one of those plush velveteen chairs to read to Michael's mother, she could almost imagine herself back in Memphis with her own mama, before everything changed.

By noon, Bryony had finished in the barn. She went inside to clean up and found Larkspur at the stove stirring a pot of soup.

"Who were you talking to earlier?" Larkspur asked.

"Callie, from the Heath place." Heaving a sigh, Bryony sank

onto the nearest chair. "She came to tell me I can have my job back."

Larkspur shot her a surprised look. "Is that a good thing, or a bad thing?"

"Haven't decided. Every hour I work there pays off more of Grandpa's debt, and the little bit extra I bring home—Lord knows we need every penny."

"Can't argue that." With a troubled twist to her lips, Larkspur spooned up some soup and watched the thin, watery liquid spill back into the pot. She laid the spoon aside and joined Bryony at the table, her tone subdued. "I've been thinking. I could put off college for another year or two, maybe find work somewhere—"

"No." Bryony smacked the table. "Larkspur Linwood, you're going to finish college and be the best teacher there ever was. Don't you dare give up on your dream."

Larkspur reached across the table and cradled Bryony's hand. "But Bry, what about *your* dreams? When is it your turn for happiness?"

Brushing at the wetness suddenly streaking her face, Bryony squeezed her eyes shut for a moment. "What makes me happy," she said, dredging deep for a smile, "is knowing my sisters are getting every possible chance for a good life. When Mama died, I swore on her grave to take care of you girls—Grandpa, too. And I intend to do just that, whatever it takes."

Before Larkspur could argue, Bryony shoved up from the chair, kissed her sister on the forehead, and strode back outside. Better to stay busy away from the house where no one could see the tears she couldn't stop from falling.

Michael slid off his glasses and pinched the bridge of his nose. A headache bloomed behind his eyes, as much from the strain of suffering beneath his father's scrutiny as from poring over account ledgers and agricultural journals for hours on end. As he'd promised his father in exchange for allowing Bryony to keep her job, he'd spent the last several days doing his best to grasp the minutiae of running a plantation.

"I'm sorry, Dad. I've got to stretch my legs." *And get away from all this for a while.*

His father raised a critical eye from the other side of the desk. "Don't be long. We still need to go over the tenant leases coming up for renewal."

"Fifteen minutes, all right? I'll bring back some coffee." Maybe a jolt of caffeine would get him through the rest of the afternoon.

Pulling the office door closed behind him, Michael paused to suppress a sickening wave of resentment. Yesterday, while his father was out for the morning, Michael had sequestered himself in the office to make a difficult telephone call. He'd regretfully informed the university press editor that he would not be able to complete the botanical illustration assignment, only to be bombarded with questions about *why*.

To which he could give no satisfactory reply. "Some . . . personal issues have arisen," was the best he could offer.

The editor then pressed Michael to at least submit the drawings he'd already completed, and Michael assured him the first five illustrations were in the mail. He didn't even care to be credited in the journal. Just knowing something of his art still survived would suffice.

"I should never have committed to an assignment I could not fulfill," he'd concluded. "All I can do is ask your pardon for putting you in such a bind."

It was no use tormenting himself, wishing things were different. With a muted groan, Michael put the phone call out of his mind and continued down the hall.

As he neared the small parlor, Bryony's melodic tones drifted his way. She must be reading to Mother again. The resentment vanished, and Michael felt only gratitude and relief that Bryony had consented to return. For her sake, and for his mother's, he'd fulfill the oath he'd made to his father.

The parlor door stood ajar, and Michael hurried past, unwilling to torture himself with a chance encounter. Since Bryony resumed her duties last weekend, he'd taken to keeping his distance again, careful to avoid whatever part of the house she happened to be working in. He'd kept an eye on her from afar, though, wanting to be sure that neither his father nor the other members of the staff made serving here any more unpleasant than necessary.

"Michael, is that you?" His mother's voice halted him.

He could pretend he didn't hear and slip quietly away—but then his foot landed on the one squeaky board at the end of the hall. He winced and held his breath.

"Bryony, do run and catch him," Mother instructed. "I've barely seen my boy in days."

Seconds later, Bryony peeked shyly around the doorframe. "You'd best come in and say hello."

"Of course." Steeling himself, Michael approached. He made himself look away from Bryony's searching gaze.

She moved aside to let him pass. "I'll be in the library looking for another book. We're almost finished with *Treasure Island*."

"One of my favorites." When his hand brushed hers and she flinched, he wanted to die. Death would certainly be preferable to the current state of affairs.

"Michael." His mother's sharp tone snapped him out of his morbid thoughts. "Come in here at once and tell me where you've been keeping yourself."

He glanced at Bryony, but she'd already crossed the hall to the library. Just as well. There was nothing more to be said between them. Drawing a quick breath, he turned and stepped into the small sitting room. "Hello, Mother. How are you?"

"I'll be much better if someone will tell me what's going on in this house," she harrumphed. "Your father treats me like a child, as do most of the servants. Bryony is the only one who gives me a lick of credit for knowing my own mind, but even she won't give me a straight answer."

Michael weighed his reply as he eased into the beige brocade wing chair opposite his mother. "What is it you think we're keeping from you?"

A confused frown darkened her expression. She fiddled with the ruffled cuff at her wrist. "I—I can't quite remember what happened on Thanksgiving. We were having such a lovely day, and then . . . your father became terribly upset about something. I just can't recall what it was."

"It wasn't important, Mother." Michael stood abruptly and leaned down to kiss the top of her head. "Really, there's absolutely nothing for you to be concerned about."

She looked as if she wanted to believe him. A shaky smile turned up the corners of her mouth, and she reached for his hand. "That's no answer, but if you say so, I'm relieved. Now, while Bryony finds us another book, why don't you show me what you've drawn today."

The request felt like a knife through Michael's gut. He stifled a moan. "I haven't had much time for drawing lately. Dad and I are . . ." He swallowed the bile creeping up his throat. "We have quite a bit of plantation business to see to."

"But your pictures—"

There are no more pictures, he wanted to shout. Instead, he quietly patted his mother's hand. "Dad's waiting for me. I'll send Bryony in."

This was exactly why he'd kept his distance all week. Mother's mental state was too fragile to let her deal with the truth. Just as he protected Bryony, he must also shield his mother from the strife between him and his father.

He stood in the hallway a full minute before finding the courage to call Bryony from the library. When she appeared in the doorway, a wisp of dark hair drifting across her brow and a hesitant smile warming her eyes, he knew for her sake he could carry on with this strategy indefinitely.

Striving for a casual air, he asked, "What book did you decide on?"

"In honor of the season, I chose Dickens's *A Christmas Carol*."

Bryony held up the slim volume. With a wistful glance toward the office at the end of the hall, she added softly, "It's good to be reminded there's hope for even the most callous of Scrooges."

His father chose that moment to step into the hallway. Scowling with impatience, he drummed his fingers on the door-frame. "Michael, I'm waiting."

"Coming, Dad."

The remainder of the afternoon dragged on interminably, as did the rest of the week. Several times as he passed the parlor door or traversed the upstairs hallway outside his parents' suite, he caught snatches of Bryony's dramatic rendering of *A Christmas Carol*, especially Ebenezer Scrooge's pronouncement of "humbug" upon everything Christmas-related.

Humbug certainly described Michael's attitude toward Christmas these past several years. There hadn't been much Christmas spirit in the trenches while Michael served in France, nor afterward as he recovered at the rehabilitation hospital. True, the nurses and orderlies did their best to bring good cheer to the patients, and twice Dad had brought Mother over to Raleigh for a Christmas visit. They'd even signed Michael out to attend the Christmas Eve candlelight Mass at a nearby church. But then, as now, Michael's heart was too full of bitterness. How dare his father sing of goodwill toward men while denying love and forgiveness to his own daughter?

By the following weekend, the servants bustled about unboxing ornaments and preparing the house for decorating. As Michael observed Alice arranging greenery and candlesticks along the mantel, he wondered how Bryony's family celebrated Christmas. Probably with a lot less pomp and pretense.

His father came up behind him in the foyer. "Get your coat, Michael. I'll be in the car."

"Where are we going?"

"The Wieland farm. Nels just had a heart attack."

Bryony was on her way to the dining room with the embroidered poinsettia tablecloth she'd just ironed. Overhearing Mr. Heath's words, she froze. *Please, Lord, not Nels!* The Wielands had endured so much already. When she saw Michael start for the stairs, she rushed over.

"Is it true?" she asked. "Will Mr. Wieland be all right?"

Michael paused, one foot on the bottom step and his hand only inches from hers on the banister. His gaze filled with sympathy. "I'm afraid I don't know anything more than what my father just told me."

"Will you come and find me the moment you get back?"

"Of course." He closed his fingers around hers, and though he tried to smile, Bryony could see the worry in his eyes. He'd stopped his father once before from throwing the Wielands off their farm. Now, with Nels so sick and possibly dead or dying, would Sebastian Heath change his mind?

Minutes later, Michael returned downstairs, and Bryony caught up with him at the front door as he pulled on a brown tweed jacket. She tucked a folded slip of paper into his palm. "Give this to Jenny, please, and tell her I'm praying."

Knuckles pressed against her lips, she watched through the sidelight until Mr. Heath's LaSalle disappeared around the first bend in the lane. Unable to think about chores or decorations or even sitting down to read Mrs. Heath another chapter of *A Christmas Carol*, she stole away to the library. The room was usually unoccupied this time of day, so she curled up in one of the leather armchairs and hoped no one found her for the next few minutes while she sent up a heartfelt prayer to her heavenly Father.

She prayed for Nels Wieland, and for his wife, Jenny. She prayed that if God called Nels home to heaven, he'd bless Caleb, their only living son, with the strength and wisdom to step into his father's shoes as man of the house.

And she prayed Jenny would swallow her stoical pride and accept the help Bryony had offered in her swiftly written note: *Call on us, Jenny—anytime, day or night. You don't have to go through this alone.*

Recalling her own words, Bryony released a muted laugh. Didn't they all go through life alone? For who could truly walk in someone else's shoes or know the deepest, darkest places in another's soul? How long had Bryony been hiding the hopeless resignation she couldn't seem to shake, the utter certainty that her life would never be more than what it was right now, a drab, colorless existence of drudgery?

For a time, Michael had helped her see beauty in her world again. His exquisite drawings reminded her of Mama's garden, of a time when trees and fields weren't burned brown by the drought, and flowers bloomed in a profusion of indescribable hues.

And it wasn't only Michael's drawings that had awakened Bryony's hope. It was the compassion she saw in him, his quiet kindness toward his mother, the respect with which he treated each of the household servants.

The pure and guileless attention he'd bestowed on her.

Oh, she didn't fool herself with presumptions that anything could come of this attraction. But it was sweet to recall, nonetheless. She lightly touched a finger to her lips at the memory of one unforgettable kiss, and a tear slid down her cheek.

"Bryony, there you are." Callie's timid voice startled her. "What're you doing in here? Miss Esther's been looking all over the house for you."

Jolting up from the chair, Bryony tugged at her skirt and apron. "I only sat down for a minute. I—I needed to—"

"You've been crying. What's wrong?" Callie's eyes snapped. "Did Odette say something mean again?"

"No, nothing like that." She sniffed and swiped a finger beneath one eye. "I overheard some bad news about a friend—another tenant farmer—and I came in here to pray."

Looking past Bryony's shoulder, Callie heaved a long, sad sigh. "My daddy's a praying man, but my mama—she's got no use for the

Lord. Says he's been too hard on us. Says he's as cruel and heartless as her own daddy."

"I'm sorry she's had such a hard life." Bryony welcomed the distraction from her own worries. "You don't talk much about your parents, Callie. Where are they?"

"They farm a ways up the river from here. Daddy's a sharecropper. Except they aren't doing so good. Mama sent word awhile back that Daddy's gone north looking for work."

"I've heard lots of folks are doing the same." Bryony cast Callie a sympathetic smile as she started for the door. High time she got her own miserable self back to work.

She found Miss Esther having it out with Alice over a broken lamp in one of the guest rooms.

"I swear it was an accident." Alice wrung her hands. "I was sweeping between the nightstand and the wall, but the corner's so tight and my elbow just—"

Clucking her tongue, Miss Esther set her arms akimbo. "Your excuses are worthless to me. Every item in this house must be accounted for, and the cost of the lamp will come out of your pay."

"But Esther, you know I got mouths to feed at home."

"It's *Miss* Esther to you. And you should have thought about feeding your family before you let yourself get so careless."

Hoping to deflect some of the head housekeeper's ire, Bryony edged into the room. "You were looking for me, Miss Esther?"

The small, wiry woman spun around, her amber eyes sparking. "Where have you been, Bryony? Dancy has been begging for relief for the past hour."

"I'll go right now, ma'am." No sense messing with explanations. "But first, would you mind if I have Alice look at the tablecloth you had me lay out in the dining room? I noticed some threads unraveling on one end, and since Alice is the best around here with a needle, I'm sure she could fix it up in a jiffy."

Looking like she'd just sucked on a lemon, Miss Esther whipped her gaze from Bryony to Alice. "Very well. Take care of it as soon as you clean up this mess." She drew her shoulders back and marched from the room.

Alice sagged as she bent to gather up the ceramic fragments. "I swear, that woman eats nails for breakfast."

Miss Esther could be strict, yes, but Bryony rarely saw her quite so perturbed. Must be the strain of Christmas preparations. They'd all been working extra hard lately. "I'd help you, but I don't dare keep Dancy waiting any longer."

"You helped plenty." Slanting her head toward Bryony, Alice offered a grateful smile tinged with a hint of remorse. She hadn't been altogether unfriendly of late, but Bryony could tell the woman hadn't fully released whatever she held against her.

Maybe after today things would change for the better, because it was hard enough working for the Heaths without also feeling snubbed by the help. Thank goodness for Callie and Dancy, her only real friends here.

If she didn't count Michael.

But oh, Lordy, whatever this thing was between them, it sure enough didn't fit any definition Bryony ever attached to *friendship*. No friend she'd ever had in her life made her pulse quicken like Michael did, or cause her to dream of warm kisses on chilly nights.

Or give her stomach aches from worrying over why in the name of everything merciful he hardly spoke to her anymore. Those moments earlier, when she'd caught him on his way out to see the Wielands, were the longest conversation they'd had since Thanksgiving.

Pain skewered her soul. Now she had one more tragic memory tied to a day that should only bring good times and grateful hearts. If she lived to be a hundred, she'd never be rid of the stench of Michael's beautiful drawings turned to smoke and ash.

Two months since Daniel had headed north, and Miranda hadn't heard so much as a word from him. Had he found work? Was he even alive?

She never doubted for a second that he loved her. Never doubted he'd sacrifice everything for the sake of his family. But if he didn't send money soon . . .

Miranda leaned against a wobbly fence post at the corner of the garden. She'd dug through the slowly shrinking turnip mound for a small one she could cook up for her supper. Going to bed hungry had become a regular occurrence, but if she was frugal, she might stretch out her food supplies another week or so.

As for surviving the rest of this winter, only God knew the answer, if he even cared.

Daniel's words came back to haunt her: *"If things get any worse, you go to your father."*

Well, things couldn't get much worse. Her husband had taken off for parts unknown, she was near starvation, and—*dear Jesus, why now?*—she was pregnant again. All the years they'd hoped for another baby, even knowing the struggles their children would face. But they'd convinced themselves the world would change someday, and the color of one's skin or the circumstances of one's birth wouldn't matter nearly as much as the condition of the heart.

Daddy sure had misjudged Daniel's heart. Miranda's, too, if her father thought he could bully her into turning her back on the only man who'd ever made her feel wanted and special. She'd never forget the day she went out to the stables to saddle her horse, Belle, for a ride, only to discover the mare was down with laminitis. She ended up spending half the morning sitting on a hay bale while Daniel patiently explained why alfalfa was good for some horses but poison for others, and that Miranda needed to stop giving Belle so many sweet treats.

A month later, with her horse on a new diet and back on her feet, Miranda had fallen in love with the quiet, gentle man who tended the livestock and worked alongside the groundskeeper.

Naturally, Daniel resisted at first. A penniless Mexican laborer and a rich white girl? What kind of life could he offer?

And, oh, when Daddy found out, it was like releasing the hounds of hell. He fired Daniel and forbade Miranda from ever seeing him again.

But all his raging and blustering couldn't make the baby growing in Miranda's belly disappear, and once Daddy realized he was about to become a grandfather whether he liked it or not, it was the last straw. That was the day he forever banished his daughter from his home and his life.

To say the love between Daniel and Miranda had sailed them painlessly into a future together would be an outright lie. Yes, they'd struggled. They couldn't stay in Eden, so Daniel had found farm work here and there until a landowner over near England, Arkansas, took him on as a sharecropper. Life continued to be hard, but they'd survived, proving every day, at least to each other, that love was stronger than hate.

Miranda began to doubt, though, that love would be enough to get her through this year of drought and deprivation.

Where are you, Daniel? I need you, honey, like I never needed you before.

One hand on her swelling abdomen, Miranda conjured up an image of the tall, muscled man with walnut-brown skin and a smile that never failed to fill her with hope. Daniel was meant for better things than sharecropping, scraping a living off land that took more than it gave. He should have been a horseman, with one fine stallion and a whole herd of broodmares suckling prize-winning foals that took top dollar at auction every year.

Miranda sighed and wondered what had ever happened to sweet Belle. Knowing Daddy, he'd probably sold the mare to a glue factory out of pure spite.

❧ 13 ❧

Two weeks before Christmas seemed a terrible time to have a funeral. Yet here Bryony stood alongside Grandpa and Rose as the preacher committed Nels Wieland to the earth. Last Friday, Jenny had found him collapsed on the floor of the toolshed, but Nels made her wait a full day before letting her send Caleb for the doctor. By then, there was little to be done. He'd hung on for five more days while his wife and son prepared themselves to say goodbye.

When Rose skirted the grave to take Caleb in her arms for a hug, Bryony could barely hold back the tears. She once thought Caleb and Larkspur would end up together, but Lark was too bookish and Caleb too much of a tease. Now, seeing her baby sister acting so grown up, and knowing how much responsibility Rose had taken on when Bryony went to work for the Heaths, she had a sudden vision of a future where her family had moved on without her. Lark would be a teacher someday, and Rose would marry and have a passel of kids.

And Grandpa wasn't getting any younger. Bryony wondered how much longer he could survive the rigors of tenant farming. If the strain didn't kill him like it had Nels Wieland, it sure enough would cripple him to the point he'd have to give it up and depend on others for support—something a proud and independent man like George Rigby would resist to the bitter end.

Someday it might only be Grandpa and Bryony, the two of them scrabbling for a living on what Bryony could earn as a housemaid.

Grandpa, dressed in his black wool suit, a moth-eaten old thing and the same one he'd worn at Mama's funeral, tucked a hand around Bryony's waist. "We best pay our respects to Jenny and be on our way."

She nodded and dabbed at a tear with the corner of her handkerchief. They waited while one of the other neighbors offered a word of comfort and then made their way past a mound of crumbling dirt clods covered with a tarp. Bryony wondered how anyone had managed to force a shovel into the hard, dry ground.

"Thank you for being here." Jenny's voice broke as she clasped Grandpa's and Bryony's hands, her stiff fingers like talons. "I don't know what I'm gonna do now. Oh, Lordy, I just don't know!"

"You're gonna survive," Grandpa stated. "The good Lord'll give you strength."

"Thank the Lord I still have Caleb." Releasing Grandpa, Jenny reached out to draw her son into the circle.

Rose snuggled in close on Caleb's other side. "Y'all should come on over to our house. Grandpa trapped another rabbit last night, and it's all ready to go into the roasting pan."

Nodding vigorously, Jenny stifled a sob. "I'd like that a lot. We'll be along soon. I—I want to stay while the grave's—while they—" Another sob, and her knees buckled.

Caleb held her fast while she wept into his shoulder. "It's all right, Mama. It's gonna be all right."

"Y'all come on along when you're ready, then," Grandpa said. He motioned Bryony and Rose toward the pickup.

As they turned to go, Bryony glimpsed two figures standing silently near the cemetery gates. Wearing overcoats and with dark fedoras pressed low on their foreheads, they looked like a couple of revenuers. Then one of the men removed his hat as they both stepped forward.

Recognizing Michael and his father, Bryony faltered. She caught herself before Grandpa noticed, but there was nothing she could do to avoid meeting them on the path.

Grandpa didn't so much as flinch. "Good day to you, Sebastian. Michael. Come to pay your respects?"

"We have," the elder Mr. Heath replied. If he took umbrage at Grandpa's use of their first names, he didn't show it. Guess Grandpa had been a tenant long enough that formalities didn't matter.

Rose hung back and tugged on Bryony's coat sleeve. Her wide-eyed look spoke her uncertainty about how she should act around Michael. Things had been so relaxed and friendly the day he'd come to the house and shown them his drawings. Now . . . everything had changed.

Nothing emphasized the fact more completely than the way Michael's cool gaze skimmed past Bryony, almost as if he hadn't seen her. Hands stuffed deep inside his coat pockets, he stood at his father's elbow, chin high, a noncommittal smile barely curving his lips.

With one arm looped through Rose's, Bryony tapped Grandpa on the shoulder. "We'll be in the pickup," she murmured. She had a feeling her grandfather had a few choice words for his landlord, and she'd just as soon not end up in the crossfire.

The moment they passed through the gates, Rose leaned close, her tone incredulous. "I don't understand him, Bry. It's like we were invisible."

Bryony yanked open the pickup door. She let her sister climb in first, then slid in beside her. "He's been like this since Thanksgiving. It's breaking my heart."

"What do you suppose Grandpa's telling Mr. Heath? I sure hope he doesn't get us kicked off the farm."

"I doubt it'll come to that." However, looking toward the three grim-faced men, Bryony had to wonder. Grandpa could be quite outspoken when the mood took him, and from all appearances he wasn't giving an inch to the Heaths. Michael, on the other hand, had backed off a pace or two.

Then Michael nudged his father's arm and motioned toward Jenny and Caleb. They tipped their hats to Grandpa and parted ways.

As Grandpa shuffled toward the pickup, Rose shivered. "I'm so scared, Bry—for us, and for Caleb and his mama, too. We've never had a year this hard."

"We'll make it, honey." Bryony drew her sister close in a reassuring hug. "We'll just keep putting one foot in front of the other and pray for better times."

◦※◦

The day after the Wieland funeral, Michael chose to have breakfast brought to his room. He'd almost decided not to go down to Dad's office at all today. Yesterday had been too draining. Torn between his compassion for the Wielands and the certain knowledge he'd see Bryony at the gravesite, he'd come close to talking himself out of accompanying his father. In the end, the difficulty of making his excuses solved the dilemma. Easier to act the part of the dutiful son and heir than to endure another dressing-down for any perceived lack of commitment to the family business.

What a farce! As if he could contribute anything of value, much less make a lasting difference in how his father ran Brookbirch. Sebastian Heath was all about the bottom line, and with the general state of America's economy since last year's stock market crash and now this unending drought, Dad was even less inclined toward generosity.

Michael poured himself another cup of coffee and tried not to think about what Bryony would say about the pact he'd made with his father. All that mattered was ensuring security for her and her family.

When Callie came up for his tray, he hurriedly crumpled the scrap of paper he'd been doodling on.

Callie frowned as she gathered up the remains of Michael's breakfast. "You sure didn't eat much, Mister Michael. I thought you favored Odette's French toast."

"It was delicious, as usual." He fingered the wad of paper jammed deep in his pants pocket. "Guess I wasn't particularly hungry this morning."

"Can't say as I blame you, after the funeral yesterday and all. I was real sorry about Mr. Wieland."

"Do you know the Wielands?"

"Only in passing." Callie pressed her lips together. "You through with your coffee, sir?"

"Yes, thank you." Michael set his cup and saucer on the tray. He held the door as she hurried out.

Ten minutes hadn't passed before Michael's father showed up at his door. He rapped three times, then barged in. "You planning on lounging about all day, or can we get some work done?"

Teeth clamped together, Michael strove for a civil reply. "We buried one of your tenants yesterday, Dad. What could possibly be so urgent that we can't pause for reflection on a good man's life?"

"You barely knew Nels Wieland. Don't pretend you're grieving."

"I don't have to pretend. I feel his family's pain, as you should, if only you had an ounce of compassion in your stone-cold heart." So much for civility. Michael turned away, his fist tightening around the crumpled scrap in his pocket, the first feeble drawing he'd attempted since Thanksgiving—and it would be the last. Time hadn't erased the acrid smell of burning paper that clung to the inside of his nostrils and lay like bitter gall on the back of his throat.

His father remained silent for so long that Michael glanced over his shoulder to see if he was still in the room. Raw hurt simmered in his father's eyes. He shook his head slowly and walked out.

The man was an enigma. Michael had all but given up trying to understand how the same man who had brazenly laid waste to his own children's lives could also stand there barely blinking at the cemetery yesterday as George Rigby spoke his quiet threats—*"You best do right by Jenny Wieland and her boy, or you'll answer to me, Sebastian Heath."*

Afterward, Dad had approached Mrs. Wieland and her son with surprising kindness. He'd assured them they had a place to live at least through the winter while they figured out what happened next. And if Caleb truly had a mind to continue farming the land, they'd revisit the terms of Nels's lease at spring planting time.

Then, as they'd driven away in the LaSalle, Dad gave a snort. "I'll be surprised if they last till Christmas." Before they reached the house, he'd come up with several items of business he wanted to finish before day's end, including what to do about several more tenants who had asked for rent extensions. With his usual "I'm not made of money" rant, Dad had warned Michael not to try his patience with pleas for leniency.

And yet, so far Michael had been able to dissuade his father from following through with at least four evictions. If preserving roofs over these families' heads for another few months was the best Michael accomplished, that alone would be worth the sacrifice. He wished he could ensure they'd also have enough food to last them through the winter, but his father's acquiescence only went so far, and Michael knew better than to push his luck.

With that in mind, he decided both he and those tenant families would be better served if he bit the bullet and went downstairs to work with his father. Nothing would be gained, except a greater accumulation of rancor, by brooding in his rooms all day.

When he sidled into the office, his father barely looked up. He nodded toward a stack of papers on the narrow worktable he'd set up for Michael on the other side of the room. "Some correspondence you should look over. Decide what needs handling. File the rest."

Later, after Michael had sorted through most of the pile and had carried a stack to the filing cabinet, a screech sounded from the front of the house.

"Oh, Lawdy, help!" came Odette's shout. "Somebody come quick!"

Michael and his father shared panicked stares, no doubt both thinking the same thing—something had happened to Mother. Michael slammed the file drawer shut, and papers flew as he and his father raced down the hall.

Michael reached the foyer ahead of his father. The front door stood open, a cold wind sweeping through the house. Odette knelt over someone stretched across the floor—not Mother, praise God, but who? Michael's stomach heaved at the sudden fear it was Bryony.

He stepped around Odette. "Oh, God—*Miranda?*"

"Sho'nuf, Mister Michael, it's her." She tossed a glance toward Michael's father and cringed.

Michael fell to his knees and scooped his sister into his arms. Lifting her took no more effort than holding a wisp of cotton. "I'll take her to the sofa. Get her something to eat, Odette. She's skin and bones. And have Jeremiah send for the doctor."

"Now just you wait!" Michael's father blocked the parlor doorway. "She is not welcome in this house. If you want to play nursemaid to the tramp, you'll have to do it elsewhere."

Jaw clenched, Michael stared his father down. "Get out of the way, Dad, or so help me—"

"Sebastian?" Mother's anxious voice carried from the upstairs landing. "What's all the fuss about?"

Through tight lips, Michael told his father, "I suggest you turn your attention to Mother. Best she stays otherwise occupied until we sort this out."

His steely gaze never leaving Michael's, he called, "Everything's fine, Fenella. I'll be right up, dear." To Michael, he murmured, "I meant what I said. Don't forget our bargain, Michael. You'd be a fool to test me."

Slicing pain ripped through Michael's gut. How was he supposed to choose between Bryony and his sister?

Then Miranda moaned, her head lolling against his shoulder. In this instance, she must be his first priority. The rest . . . he'd figure out later.

The teakettle whistled, and Bryony grabbed a potholder. Folding towels and bed sheets with Callie had taken longer than she expected, and now Mrs. Heath's teatime was long overdue. Dividing her time between sitting with Mrs. Heath and helping the other servants with their chores kept Bryony's days from becoming too monotonous, but sometimes she felt pulled in too many directions at once.

Just then, Odette rushed into the kitchen, and Bryony nearly dropped the lid to Mrs. Heath's favorite china teapot. Breathing hard, the whites of her eyes shining bright in her dark face, Odette halted inches from Bryony. "Where's Callie?"

"Still in the laundry, I think." Bryony set the teakettle on a trivet. "Odette, what on earth has you so riled up?"

"Ain't got no time for questions." The large woman steadied herself against the oak table. Beads of perspiration popped out along her temples. "Miz Heath's tea's gonna have to wait. Fetch Callie in here, and y'all two warm up the leftover soup and bread we done had for lunch earlier."

"But who's it for? Is someone—"

"I done *said* I ain't got time to explain." Odette's worried glance swept the room, as if she was trying to work something out in her head. "Now, I gotta tend to some other stuff, but you bring that tray to the parlor quick as you can, hear me?"

"But Mrs. Heath's tea—"

"Send Callie up with it. Be sure she takes the back stairs. Things is crazy enough without throwin' her in the middle of what's going on out front."

An instant later, Odette hurtled through the breezeway toward the house, and Bryony could only shake her head in confusion. She went to the back door and called for Callie. The girl bustled in, a stack of folded flour-sack dish towels in her arms. As Bryony ladled soup into a pot on the stove, she relayed Odette's instructions.

After stowing the towels on a pantry shelf, Callie sliced some bread and buttered it. "Gracious, who's needing a meal so bad in the middle of the afternoon?"

"No idea, but Odette was fit to be tied." While the soup warmed, Bryony fetched the canister of oatmeal raisin cookies Mrs. Heath enjoyed so much. She arranged six of them on a gold-rimmed plate and set it on the tea tray. "Tell Dancy I'll come up to relieve her as soon as I can."

Callie left, and Bryony prepared another tray with the bread plate and a bowl of Odette's savory vegetable beef soup. Still with no idea whom she'd be serving, she shoved open the door with her hip and marched to the house.

Inside the back hallway, she found Odette and Miss Esther huddled together in deep conversation. The moment they saw her, they immediately grew silent.

Having enough of this mystery, Bryony strode over. "Will one of you please tell me what's going on?"

Miss Esther sniffed. "Odette, take the tray. Bryony, come with me."

Bryony had no choice but to hand off the tray and follow the petite head housekeeper to her office.

Miss Esther took her seat at the oak rolltop and motioned Bryony to a chair at her side. Hands folded in her lap, lips pursed, she inhaled long and slow. "A most unfortunate situation has arisen," she began. "Are you aware the Heaths have a daughter?"

"I don't recall . . ." And then she did. "I remember one day Mrs. Heath kept asking for someone named Miranda. She was quite upset she couldn't find her."

Eyes closed, Miss Esther nodded grimly. With another deep

breath, she met Bryony's confused stare. "It seems Miss Miranda has come home."

"Oh. Well, that's a good thing, isn't it? And just in time for Christmas, too."

"I'm afraid it is *not* a good thing, not in the least. There's bad blood between Miss Miranda and her father. He disowned her years ago and will not abide her staying a moment longer than necessary."

Bryony drew her lower lip between her teeth. "The food tray— it's for her?"

"The poor girl is near starved to death. It's the only thing would have ever brought her back."

"And now her father won't let her stay? Surely he can't be so cruel." Then the irony of her own words made Bryony gasp and clutch at her heart. After what Sebastian Heath had done to Michael on Thanksgiving Day, how could anyone not believe the man capable of so much worse?

Miss Esther reached across the space between them and caught Bryony's hand. Her amber eyes grew hard and dark. "You've worked here long enough to know how things are. We're holding off the master till we get Miss Miranda fed and on her way, but Lord only knows where she'll go from here. Worst of it is, Odette believes her to be with child."

Bryony furrowed her brow. "What about the baby's father? Is he not taking responsibility for his family?"

"Oh, he is, take my word. Best husband and father a woman could ask for." Turning her face away, Miss Esther rested two fingers upon her trembling lips. "Daniel's a good man, just trying to provide for his family the best he can."

As the pieces of Miss Esther's story came together, Bryony struggled to make sense of it all. Miss Esther must have known Daniel for quite some time to be so certain of his character. Maybe he and Miranda even lived somewhere nearby. And if the depression and drought had hit them as hard as it had other Arkansas families, no wonder Miranda had been compelled to come home seeking help.

Alice, who had been cleaning upstairs all afternoon, burst into the office. "Is it true—she's back?"

"Settle down, Alice. Yes, it's true." Miss Esther rose. "Where are Callie and Dancy? Is Mr. Heath still upstairs with the missus?"

"Yes'm, he is, and none too happy about it, from what I saw. Callie brought the tea and then went back out to finish the ironing. Dancy peeked out for a minute, but the poor thing's nervous as a cat with a bell on its tail."

It seemed everyone was intent on protecting Miranda Heath. Everyone except her own father, anyway. Bryony stood and moved her chair out of the way. "What else can I do? Would it help to pack up some food to send home with her?"

Now Odette filled the doorway, and the tiny office felt more crowded than ever. "Miss Miranda ain't in no condition to go nowhere. Mister Michael says if she don't get tending to, she could lose that baby."

Miss Esther palmed her forehead. "We don't dare keep her here or we'll all be fired."

"I got no room at my house," Alice stated. "Leastways, my man would have a conniption if I brought home another mouth to feed."

Bryony pictured Larkspur's empty bed. She spoke up before she could talk herself out of it. "One of my sisters is away at college. Miranda can stay with us until she's on her feet again."

All three women whirled to face her, their eyes lighting with gratitude. Miss Esther seized one of her hands and Odette the other.

"This is answered prayer," Miss Esther whispered.

Odette nodded fiercely. "I shoulda knowed the Lord sent you here for a reason. Hope you done forgave me for all o' my meanness."

Alice dipped her chin. "Mine, too," she added softly.

"Everything's forgiven and forgotten. I'm just glad to help."

Bryony only hoped Grandpa and Rose would be okay with the idea. They were already doing what they could to help Jenny Wieland. Now, to take in a helpless, starving pregnant woman?

But that's what neighbors did, and if Sebastian Heath refused to take care of his own daughter, Bryony couldn't imagine her grandfather turning Miranda away, even if it meant they'd all do with a little less for a while.

Odette must have seen the flicker of concern in Bryony's expression. "Don't you worry none, you hear? They's always plenty of leftovers here. I'll put some aside for you every night so's you'll have something to take home."

Bryony beamed her thanks. Their next concern was how to get Miranda to the farm. Miss Esther sent Alice to find Jeremiah and tell him to bring one of the cars around. Then, while Odette bustled out to the kitchen to pack up some food, Miss Esther and Bryony went to the parlor.

At the sight of Michael tenderly supporting his sister with one arm as he helped her to eat, Bryony choked back a sob. The poor girl was hardly more than a skeleton, skin stretched taut over every bone and joint. Only the small mound beneath her thin, faded dress gave any sign of the baby she carried.

As Bryony and Miss Esther neared, Michael set the tray aside. He helped his sister lie down and spread a coverlet over her legs, then turned to Miss Esther. "I don't care what my father says. We have to—"

"It's all taken care of," Esther said. "She's going home with Bryony."

Michael's gaze met Bryony's. His Adam's apple shifted, but no words came. Without warning, he took her in his arms and held on tight. She wasn't certain if the trembles she felt were his or her own, but it didn't matter and she didn't care. She only knew that right here, in this moment, was the only place she wanted to be.

14

Seated across from his wife at her prized antique mahogany table, Sebastian rubbed his thumb incessantly along the scalloped edge. He could barely sit still for wondering what went on downstairs, but he didn't dare go down, or no telling what he'd do or say that he might regret later.

Heaven knew he had plenty of regrets already. But what was a man to do when his own children showed such blatant disrespect for the family name he'd worked so hard to establish?

Fenella set her teacup down with such force that she cracked the rim of the saucer. "Where is Bryony? I invited her to tea, and she's late."

Dancy, hovering nearby, whisked away the cup and saucer. "She'll be along soon as she can, I'm sure."

Blast it all, Sebastian should be downstairs in his office with his nose buried in paperwork, not pacing his wife's sitting room like a caged tiger. He stood abruptly. "Dancy, go down and see what's happening."

"Yes, sir." With a quick glance at Fenella, the maid scurried out the door.

Fenella rose from the table and stared out the east windows. Sensing her ever-increasing agitation, Sebastian moved beside her and slipped an arm around her shoulders. The house cast long shadows across the gardens. Wispy pink clouds drifted across the sky.

When Fenella shivered, Sebastian guided her toward the chaise and unfolded a crocheted afghan. "Why don't you rest awhile, dearest?"

She halted beside the chaise and peered up at him. "Is it Bryony? Is she ill? Has there been an accident?"

"Nonsense. She's fine."

He'd barely settled his wife under the afghan when the door burst open. Dancy's eyes burned bright as she looked from Fenella to Sebastian. She opened her mouth and then quickly snapped it shut.

Sebastian bent down to kiss his wife's forehead. "I'll be back in a moment, darling. Just rest."

"I don't *want* to rest." Fenella tossed aside the coverlet. "You're keeping something from me, and I demand to know what it is."

Knowing she wouldn't be satisfied with anything but a semblance of the truth, Sebastian lowered himself to the edge of the chaise and cradled her hands in his. "I didn't want to trouble you, dearest, but we've had a . . . a beggar at the door."

"A beggar?" Fenella started to rise. "I must go down and see what's needed."

"Not necessary. The servants are dealing with the situation." Drawing up the afghan again, Sebastian eased his wife against the cushions. "It's better you stay here with me where it's safe."

Fenella gasped. "If there is cause for concern, we should send for the sheriff." She stretched a hand toward Dancy, who still waited by the door. "Where are the children? Go and make sure they're all right."

The knot in Sebastian's chest expanded to a throbbing ache. "The children are fine, dear. You rest here while I check on things."

When he felt her relax slightly, he stood and crossed to Dancy. With his back to his wife, he murmured, "What's the situation?"

"She's gone, sir." Dancy kept her eyes lowered. "Jeremiah took her away in the car."

"Good . . . good." Sebastian should feel relieved, but somehow he didn't. He clawed rigid fingers through his hair. "All right, then. Get Bryony up here with more tea and cookies before my wife asks any more questions."

Dancy swallowed visibly and inched back a step. "Sir, I can't. She's gone with Jeremiah to help."

Sebastian cursed under his breath. As he should have expected, Miranda's reappearance in their lives had completely disrupted his carefully managed household. A quick glance at Fenella assured him she'd been placated, at least for the moment. Her eyes were closed, and her breathing deepened.

"Stay with her," he ordered Dancy. He started for the door, then halted and held his finger directly under her nose. Teeth clenched, he ground out, "And if you hope to keep your position here, you will not, under any circumstances, mention Miranda's name."

❦

"Not a word," Michael said, his gaze drilling first through Esther and then Odette. They stood on the front porch, the late-afternoon sun angling through leafless trees and slicing razor-sharp across Michael's field of vision.

Both women gave firm nods. "We ain't gonna say nothin', Mister Michael," Odette stated. "Your daddy won't never know a thing."

"Make sure Alice and Callie understand, too. If my father finds out where Miranda is staying, it could mean trouble for all concerned."

"It's our secret." Esther laced her fingers with Odette's in a gesture of solidarity. "And you can be sure Jeremiah stands with us. There's not a one of us wouldn't do anything for Miss Miranda."

"Or you neither," Odette added quickly. "All us long-timers here loves you and your sister like you was our own."

Michael smiled his gratitude. He sent the women into the house, then turned to lean against the porch rail in hopes a few more breaths of clean, cold air would clear both his head and his struggling lungs. Staring down the drive, he wished he'd climbed into the car and gone with Jeremiah to Bryony's house. He craved more time with his sister, time to ask where she'd been all these years. He wondered what had happened to the baby she'd been carrying when Dad threw her out, if she'd married the man she'd given up everything for.

Instead, Michael had decided it best to stay behind and make sure his father didn't learn of the plan. After everything Michael had sacrificed for Bryony's sake, he didn't dare risk harm to her family because they'd taken Miranda in.

And what had Dad told Mother about the afternoon's excitement? Surely not the truth. Much as Michael knew his mother longed for the return of her wayward daughter, this wasn't news you sprang on a woman whose mind was even more frail than her aging body. Besides, Sebastian Heath would surely rather his wife forgot they had a daughter.

When the wintry evening air bit through Michael's wool sweater, he reluctantly went inside. The house stood deathly quiet, except for the muted tones of Mother's Victrola drifting from upstairs—Vernon Dalhart crooning "The Prisoner's Song." Snatches of the lyrics fell on Michael's ears, words about a man longing to escape prison walls and find his one true love.

With every day that passed, Michael became more fully convinced he'd found the love of his life in Bryony. Unfortunately, his "prison" wasn't so easy to escape. And now, he had to protect not only Bryony but his sister. The walls of his prison continually grew higher.

"Michael." His father stepped into the foyer. "My office. Now."

No use putting off the inevitable. Groaning inwardly, Michael followed his father to the end of the hall. While Dad situated himself behind the desk, Michael quietly closed the door. He remained standing, hands in his pockets so he wasn't tempted to throttle something . . . or someone.

Michael's father picked up a fountain pen and twirled it between his fingers. "I understand the situation has been dealt with?"

"The *situation* has a name." Michael's jaws ached from clenching them so tightly. "Or has your heart grown so cold that you feel not even a shred of concern for your own daughter?"

"Miranda ceased being my daughter the day she besmirched the Heath name by throwing herself at a hired man."

"Which part upsets you most—that she got pregnant out of wedlock, that the man she fell in love with was a Mexican immigrant, or that she stooped to give her affections to a common servant rather than the banker's son you'd hand-selected for her?"

Face reddening, Michael's father pushed up from his chair. He braced his hands on the desk and leaned toward Michael. "When you are sitting behind this desk doing everything in your power to preserve your family's legacy, *then* you can judge me. Now, get out before I change my mind about all those bleeding-heart charity cases you've tried to shame me into helping."

Anger mixed with hatred boiled like a cauldron in the pit of Michael's stomach. He wanted to tell his father he *should* be ashamed for treating other human beings, especially his own children, with such cruel contempt. But the man held too much power —not just over Michael but the people Michael cared most about. Without another word, he backed out of the room.

He slept little that night, the shame of his own weakness tearing him apart. If he were stronger, braver, more of a man than the broken shell who'd returned from the war, he might have done so much more.

A cold winter sun had scarcely peeked above the horizon the next morning before Michael dressed in his tromping-about clothes and slipped out the front door. Turning up his collar against the chill, he took the path toward the river, then cut through woods and fields to take a roundabout way over to the Rigby farm. He arrived as Bryony stepped out the back door.

She looked up with a startled gasp. "Michael!"

"I couldn't stay away a minute longer. How's Miranda?"

"Sleeping. And well fed, thanks to all the provisions Odette sent along with us yesterday." Shivering, Bryony snuggled deeper into her heavy wool sweater. "Go on inside. Grandpa's up. I need to get to your house. I'm late already."

"Bryony." Michael clasped her arms. "I don't know how I'll ever thank you."

Her tender smile quirked a little higher on the right to reveal a tiny dimple in her cheek. She opened her mouth to speak, then sighed and gave her head a quick shake. He thought he glimpsed a wet sheen to her eyes, but she hurried past him toward the road before he could say anything more.

When he looked toward the house, George Rigby stood inside the porch screen door. "Coffee's on," George said, holding the door wide. "Might as well make yourself at home."

Michael wasn't sure whether the invitation was issued in the spirit of hospitality or of obligation, but he wasn't of a mind to refuse. He'd foregone supper last night and hadn't taken time for breakfast this morning. The gnawing sensation in his gut evoked even deeper compassion for his sister. How long had she been subsisting on next to nothing and suffering hunger pangs a thousand times worse than this?

The Rigbys' kitchen was warm and homey, a welcome change from the stiff formality of the Heath mansion dining room. As Michael and George walked in, Rose turned from the stove. A welcoming grin spread across her face. "Good, you can help us eat up this mess of scrambled eggs and ham. I was just about to see if your sister's awake—"

"Michael!" Miranda's happy cry spun him around. A second later, she wrapped him in her arms, clinging with every ounce of strength in her emaciated limbs.

Michael was almost afraid to hug her back for fear her bones would shatter. Supporting her gently, he smoothed wisps of hair away from her face. Her eyes, shadowed and sunken, spoke volumes about the hardships she'd endured.

"Come sit down," he said, guiding her to the table. "Tell me everything—where you've been all this time, how you've been getting on—" Stupid, stupid question. She clearly hadn't been *getting on* at all.

A weak laugh bubbled up from Miranda's throat, giving Michael a glimpse of the lively, carefree sister he adored. She'd always been the resilient one, never afraid of a challenge or concerned about flouting convention, especially if it meant bucking their father's authority. "Oh, my dear baby brother, how you've grown up!" She lifted a hand to caress his cheek. "But the war was hard on you. I see it in your eyes."

"It isn't important. I'm worried about you, Mandy. You're skin and bones." His glance fell to the swell of her abdomen. "And . . . pregnant. Are you still with Daniel? Is he the father?"

Her longing gaze drifted toward the window. "I married him the day after Daddy kicked me out. He's a good and decent man, and I love him with all my heart."

"Then where is he? Why isn't he taking care of you?" Michael barely glanced up as Rose carried plates of ham and eggs to the table.

Miranda certainly noticed, though. She breathed deeply, savoring the aromas, then scooted up to the table and lifted her fork. "Oh, Rose, this looks wonderful!"

"Ham's a little crisp around the edges, but that's the way I like it." Rose returned from the stove with the coffeepot and filled the mugs George brought from the cupboard. "Y'all eat up while it's hot."

Michael wasn't to be deterred, even by his own growling stomach. "Answer my question, Mandy. Where's Daniel?"

Her lips trembled, and the fork clattered to the table. "I—I don't know. He went north to find work two months ago, and I haven't heard from him since. I'm terrified something awful's happened."

George took the chair across from Michael. He patted Miranda's arm. "Most likely he just ain't had a chance to send word. No sense thinkin' the worst."

The man's kindly tone seemed to take the edge off Miranda's fears. Her gaze drifted back to the plate of food in front of her, and she sighed. "If he knew I'd waited so long to ask for help, he'd be so angry."

"As well he should be." Michael tempered his gruff reply with a brotherly smirk. He lifted his fork. "Now eat up, or you'll have to fight me for those scrambled eggs."

For the briefest moment, a familiar spark lit Miranda's eyes, and she began a ravenous attack on the plate of food. Then, as Michael sliced off a bite of ham, it occurred to him she'd never once mentioned the child from her first pregnancy. Now, he hesitated to ask for fear of stirring more painful memories. There'd be plenty of time for questions as she grew stronger.

Sunday brought another day off, and Bryony couldn't be more thankful. Saturday had been tense as she went about her duties while avoiding Sebastian Heath at every turn and wondering how things were going at home with Miranda. The one bright spot was the almost miraculous change in Odette's and Alice's attitudes. Even Miss Esther showed Bryony a new level of kindness and respect.

Clearly, the difference had everything to do with their regard for Miranda combined with gratitude toward Bryony.

Miranda was still asleep as Bryony tiptoed into the bedroom to dress for church. According to Rose and Grandpa, the poor woman had done little but eat and sleep since her arrival. Probably the best thing for her—along with spending time with her brother yesterday. With a shiver of anticipation, Bryony considered that with Miranda as their houseguest, Michael might be expected to visit often.

Just as quickly, her excitement faded. She'd likely be toiling away at the mansion during Michael's visits and see even less of him than she did already.

Miranda stirred and sat up. "Good morning."

"Oh, you're awake." Bryony finished buttoning the front of her favorite Sunday dress, a pine-green shirtwaist that once belonged to her mother. "We saved you some flapjacks. I don't suppose you're up to going to church with us?"

"Not a good idea, considering my reputation around Eden." A regretful smile slanted across Miranda's lips. She reached for the borrowed flannel robe at the foot of the bed.

Bryony ducked her head. "Sorry, I wasn't thinking."

"Don't apologize. I'm plenty used to the stares and gossip, but there's no reason you should have to put up with it." Rising, Miranda straightened the bedcovers. "I don't know how much my brother has told you, but since you were kind enough to take me in, you're entitled to ask me anything you want to know."

"No more than what you're willing to share." Bryony sat on her own bed to buckle the straps of her Sunday shoes. When she looked up, Miranda stood over her, a thoughtful twist to her lips.

"You love him, don't you?"

"What?"

"Michael. You. You're in love."

Forced laughter burst from Bryony's throat. "Why, that's the silliest thing I ever heard." She sprang up and strode to the door. "We'll be home in a couple of hours. Coffee's made—well, it's mostly chicory, but it's hot—and there's warm syrup on the stove for your flapjacks."

In the kitchen, she went straight to the coatrack for her sweater and handbag. "Grandpa, Rosie, y'all about ready to leave?"

Ignoring their raised-eyebrow looks, she marched out to the pickup and climbed inside. She might thoroughly regret her haste if the day had been much colder. As it was, her breath puffed out in tiny clouds, but after Miranda's pointed observation, especially after knowing Bryony for so short a time, she needed time alone to compose herself. Bryony must not be as skilled at hiding her feelings as she'd hoped.

The pickup's windows had almost completely fogged over by the time Grandpa and Rose came out. Scooting to the middle, Bryony used her sweater sleeve to clear the windshield, then kept her eyes forward as Grandpa drove to church.

Bryony was glad to see Jenny Wieland and Caleb at worship. Jenny wept silently through most of the service, but she held her chin high like the proud farm wife she'd always been. Afterward, when they went out to the pickup, Grandpa retrieved a small covered box from beneath a tarp in the back and handed it to Caleb.

When Jenny peeked beneath the cloth, she gasped. "Oh, George, we can't accept this! Where on earth did you get so much food?"

"We were blessed, so let us bless you—and no questions asked or thanks needed, you hear?" Grandpa nodded for Caleb to put the box in their truck.

Bryony suspected he'd given the Wielands a small share of the food Odette had sent over with Miranda, and she doubted Michael would mind in the least.

As they neared the farm, Bryony's insides began to twitch. If Michael had come by again, could she keep her heart from beating out of her chest and revealing every secret hope she held inside?

"For goodness' sake, Bry." Rose slapped her hand down on Bryony's knee. "You're jumpier than a flock of fleas. What's got you so jittery?"

"I am *not* jittery." Bryony pressed her heels into the floorboard and locked her fingers around her knees. "Anyway, I'm not sure you'd call a bunch of fleas a *flock*."

"Well, I don't care what you call it. You *are* jittery, and don't tell me you aren't. Is it Miranda? You worried having her at our place might get you fired?"

The thought had occurred to her, yes, but helping the poor woman was a risk she'd gladly take—and not only because of her feelings for Michael. She'd have reached out to anyone in such dire straits, and ogres like Sebastian Heath be hanged.

Grandpa parked the pickup beneath the corrugated-iron shed roof, and while he stepped inside the barn to check on the livestock, Bryony and Rose went to the house.

The kitchen stood empty, and Bryony breathed a small sigh of relief. For a little while longer, anyway, she could keep a lid on her nerves. "If you'll peel the potatoes, I'll get the chicken in the oven," she told Rose as they shrugged out of their sweaters. "And we can use those ham drippings to flavor—"

Voices and feminine laughter from the parlor made her jerk her head around.

"Who else is here?" Rose asked.

"Can't be Lark—too early for her Christmas break." The only thing Bryony could figure was that one of the Heath servants had brought over more food. If this kept up, surviving the winter wouldn't be nearly as hard as she'd feared.

Miranda peeked into the kitchen. "Thought I heard y'all out here." Her eyes held a sparkle that hadn't been there two hours ago, and her cheeks creased in a cheery smile. She looked back toward the parlor. "Callie, come say hi."

"Oh, it's Callie." Bryony unscrewed the lid on a Mason jar of green beans. "I'm so glad you'll get to meet her, Rosie. She's the sweetest thing."

The girl appeared at Miranda's side. "I can't stay much longer, Mama. They'll be expecting me at the . . ." Callie's words trailed off as her gaze met Bryony's. She must have seen the confusion there.

"That's right," Miranda murmured, slipping her arm around Callie's waist. "Callie's my daughter. Mine and Daniel's."

"Wait. Then you're—" Bryony braced her hips against the counter while she tried to make sense of this. "Lord have mercy, you're the Heaths' granddaughter. Michael's niece."

"They don't know, of course," Miranda stated, stepping forward. "Please promise you won't tell."

"No . . . no, of course not." Through the back window, Bryony watched Grandpa amble across the yard. She shot Miranda a quick glance. "Maybe you'd better tell me who all does and doesn't know so I don't accidentally say something I shouldn't."

Miranda shared a look with Callie, and they both offered Bryony apologetic smiles. "Guess you're the only one working at the Heath house who *didn't* know," Miranda said. "Esther and Odette have known all along. Jeremiah found out about the time Callie was born, because he drove Dancy over to midwife for me."

"I see." Bryony chewed the inside of her lip. "What about Alice?"

"Alice found out when I sent Callie to ask for work." With a motherly touch, Miranda tucked a strand of the girl's dark waves behind her ear. Her hand lingered in a protective gesture that brought a pang to Bryony's heart. "I knew I wouldn't worry as much if she was with people I knew and trusted."

Rose, who had been busy paring potatoes while she listened, filled the pot with water and set it on the stove. Reaching for the jar of beans, she shot Bryony a pointed glance. "This is all as exciting as it can be, but my breakfast wore off about ten minutes ago. How about we get dinner cooking?"

"The chicken—almost forgot." Giving herself a mental shake, Bryony took a roasting pan from the cupboard. She wasn't sure what to say to Callie and Miranda anyway. Secrets and more secrets. What a crazy, mixed-up family the Heaths were.

About the time Grandpa strolled in, Callie hurried on her way, and Bryony decided to keep Miranda's revelation to herself until after they'd eaten and washed up the dishes. As Rose had so frankly pointed out, important conversations usually flowed better when stomachs weren't growling.

When she finally did tell Grandpa, after Miranda went to the bedroom to lie down and Rose had taken scraps out to the chickens, he voiced not the least bit of surprise. "Noticed right off they got the same eyes," Grandpa said. His smile warmed. "Just like you take after your own mama."

The reminder brought a tingle to Bryony's chest. Absently, she fingered the lock of hair falling across her shoulder. "But if it's so obvious to you, why haven't the Heaths seen the resemblance?"

"Callie's a serving girl. Long as she does her job, rich folk like the Heaths prob'ly don't give her no never-mind."

But Michael would have. *Should* have. With his kind heart and artistic eye, he must have noticed something about the girl.

And since Callie was family, he had a right to know.

❧ 15 ❧

"I had a right to know!" Michael paced the worn carpet in George Rigby's parlor, while his sister sat in a rocking chair and mopped her tear-streaked face with a handkerchief. "Your daughter—*my niece*—has been washing and ironing my shirts and serving my meals for more than a year, and not so much as a word!"

Miranda blew her nose. "I didn't want our parents finding out, so I made Esther and Odette promise not to tell you, either."

"But why, Mandy? Why would you put your child in service to her own family? She deserves better."

Miranda snorted. "Believe me, Michael, even in those cramped servants' quarters upstairs, my daughter's living a *much* better life than she'd have had with Daniel and me this past year."

Recalling the image of his emaciated sister collapsed in the foyer two days ago, Michael couldn't argue. "Still . . ." He removed his glasses and pinched the bridge of his nose. "I wish I'd known. I *should* have known, should have recognized my own niece."

Crossing the tiny room, Miranda wrapped her arms around him and snuggled into his chest. "What an awful mess we've made of our lives, haven't we, little brother?"

Another truth he couldn't deny. He tightened his hold and felt the soft bulge of her abdomen against his side. "If you could do it all again, would you?"

She was silent for a moment. "Some things, yes. I don't regret a moment I've spent with Daniel. And Callie—she's the light of my life. But there are days I wish I hadn't let Daddy have the last word. I wish I'd stood my ground and *made* him accept us."

Michael barked a sardonic laugh. "And exactly how would you have managed that? This is our father we're talking about. The man makes his own rules, remember?"

Miranda tipped her head to study Michael's face. "He's holding something over you, isn't he?"

"It doesn't matter, as long as—" A shadow in the hallway caught his eye. He looked up to see Bryony wearing a puzzled frown. She stood motionless for a moment, then shook her head slowly and backed away.

How much had she heard? Or seen? Miranda's question had stabbed deep, and Bryony might easily have read the answer in his eyes.

"I need a minute." Michael gently untangled himself from his sister's arms. He followed after Bryony, reaching the kitchen moments before she grabbed a sweater and bolted out the back door.

She was halfway to the barn before he caught up with her. When he snagged her wrist, she spun around and shot him a frosty glare. Her tone laced with hurt and accusation, she blurted out a single word: "Why?"

He released her hand. "Do you really have to ask?"

"I guess I do." Bryony hugged herself. "Please, Michael. Please tell me you didn't give up everything you've worked for, dreamed of—"

"What I've dreamed of is *you*, Bryony. Only you. Night and day, until I'm crazy with distraction." He moved toward her, every nerve and muscle fiber aflame with the need to hold her in his arms.

"Stop. Stop!" One hand shot up and jammed against his chest.

"I will *not* be the reason you gave up your art. I won't let you chain yourself to a life you despise."

Michael curled his fingers around her arm and tenderly guided it down to her side. With his other hand, he cradled her cheek. "It isn't your choice, Bryony. If doing the honorable thing for someone I care deeply for is what it takes for me to feel like a man again, I'll do it gladly."

Her face crumpled. Tears streaming, she leaned hard into his hand. He drew her close and pressed his lips to hers, their salty sweetness driving all other thoughts from his mind. But even as she returned his kiss, he sensed her resisting, pulling back, denying what so clearly they both felt for each other.

She broke the kiss, and with her forehead touching his, she rested the tips of her fingers against his mouth. "You *are* a man, Michael Heath, the kindest, most beautiful man I've ever known."

"Beautiful?" He couldn't suppress a dubious chuckle.

"Yes, beautiful." Bryony dipped her head, her breathy laugh warm against his neck. When she lifted her eyes, the deep brown irises flecked with glints of wintry sunshine, he thought his heart would burst. "I wish I was as good with words as you are at drawing, because then I'd tell you all the thousands of ways you're beautiful to me, and you'd never doubt yourself again."

An ache formed at the base of his throat. He wove his fingers through hers and squeezed. He would tell her here and now that he loved her, that he couldn't imagine life without her, if only he could be certain she wouldn't completely shut herself off from him.

The moment stretched long between them, neither speaking, neither moving, until finally Bryony slid her hands free and glanced toward the house. "You came to see Miranda. Go spend time with her while you can."

He nodded silently and started for the porch, but she didn't follow. As he opened the screen door, he looked back to see Bryony bend down to pick up a dead leaf. She twirled the stem in her fingers before crushing it in her fist. With the brittle, brown fragments sifting between her fingers, she sighed and walked away toward the barren fields.

Michael's knuckles whitened around the door handle. Lost in his own thoughts—grinding self-pity, if he were honest with himself—he almost didn't see George Rigby watching him from inside the porch.

"She's got a heart of gold, that one." Tipping his head in Bryony's direction, George fixed Michael with a narrowed gaze. "I'm not of a mind to see her suffer more hurt than she's already known, and that's aplenty."

"Nor am I." Michael stepped inside and let the door fall shut behind him. "I care about her, Mr. Rigby. More than I dare admit."

"Then see you treat her right." With a brisk nod, George shuffled to the kitchen.

Michael lingered on the porch while the older man's words echoed through his mind. Nothing he wanted more than to make Bryony happy, but he suspected the one thing that would please her most would at the same time bring devastation to the people she loved. For her sake, for her family's sake, he wouldn't take the chance.

***

Bryony stayed well away from the house until she saw Michael leave. He'd never come right out and admitted the truth, but she knew. Deep in her heart, she knew exactly what Sebastian Heath held over his son. Michael had chosen to lay aside his art and work alongside his father solely to protect Bryony and her family.

How could she let him continue this—this *abdication*, this denial of his very selfhood? Michael was meant to be an artist, not a ledger-keeping land baron. The war and its aftermath had already stolen so much, wearying him in both body and spirit. Sooner or later, the strain of living out his father's demands would crush him completely.

But wasn't she doing the same thing, sacrificing her own hopes and dreams for the sake of her family? The sudden realization nearly drove her to her knees.

What am I supposed to do, Lord? Is this truly your will for my life . . . for Michael's?

A vision of Jesus nailed to the cross shimmered behind Bryony's closed eyelids. *For God so loved the world . . .*

Love could be the only valid motivation for any act of sacrifice. And with sacrifice came the hope and expectation of a higher good. Bryony couldn't begin to imagine what blessings God may yet have in store for her or Michael or the people they loved. What else could she do but hold on in faith and keep doing the one thing she knew to do, to care for her family as best she could? If it meant working all day at the Heath mansion and coming home to farm chores every night, she'd carry on with her head held high.

The week wore on in just that way, not so different from the past several weeks except for the extra effort required to keep the truth about Callie from slipping out. Even while Bryony pitched in with laundry or kitchen duty, she guarded her tongue in case Mr. or Mrs. Heath happened to be anywhere within earshot.

Nothing changed much with Michael, either. As far as Bryony could tell, he spent most mornings ensconced with his father in the office. Sometimes they'd leave together in the car, most likely checking on tenants or meeting with other planters in the area. Usually late in the day, Michael would change into everyday clothes and walking boots and say he was off to stretch his legs. Only Bryony and the other servants knew his route, down to the river, then through the woods and across the fields to the Rigby farm.

On Thursday, one week before Christmas, Bryony met him returning along the road as she started home after work. As the sun set, the temperature dropped into the low thirties, and Bryony had her coat collar turned up and her hands tucked deep into her pockets. Preoccupied with watching her footing and thinking about how cold her toes were, she almost didn't see Michael until he stopped right in front of her.

He offered a boyish smile. "I was hoping to run into you. I've scarcely seen you all week."

"Are you sure this is a good idea?" She shot a nervous glance over her shoulder.

"I'm sure it's a *very* good idea." Michael inched closer. When he slipped his hands into Bryony's coat pockets and wrapped his fingers around hers, her shiver had nothing to do with the cold.

"Michael . . ." A hint of butterscotch laced his warm breath, so close to her face. "What if someone comes by?"

Heaving a regretful sigh, Michael withdrew his hands and stepped back. "I don't mean to make you uncomfortable. It's just . . . I've been missing you."

Bryony's pockets now seemed cavernously empty, her hands colder than ever. "How is Miranda today? I think she has a bit more color in her cheeks, don't you?"

"She's getting stronger every day. I can't describe how much I look forward to our visits."

"I know Callie's glad to have her mother close by." It felt as if they were making small talk, skirting the issues that didn't bear mention. Like Callie's servitude to her own grandparents.

Like the feelings between them that made Bryony's stomach so jittery she could hardly swallow.

To keep from jumping out of her skin, she started walking. When Michael fell in step beside her, she angled a glance his way. "Shouldn't you be going the opposite direction? You'll want to get home before Odette lays out supper."

"I'm afraid I've ruined my appetite with the cookies Rose baked this afternoon. Besides, I'm enjoying your company at the moment."

Bryony halted and stared at him. "*Rose* baked cookies? And with what?"

"I tucked some flour, sugar, and eggs into my coat before I walked over. The cookies were delicious, by the way. Hardly burnt at all. I hid some away for you in the pantry." Michael laughed softly. "Rose and Miranda were practically arm-wrestling each other for every crumb. Your grandfather ate his fair share, as well."

Looking skyward, Bryony shook her head. Part of her brimmed with giddy delight at the prospect of biting into a crisp, sugar-laden cookie, while another part struggled with guilt and sorrow for all the poor farm families who were barely scraping by this winter.

As if reading her thoughts, Michael offered a doleful smile. "It's all right to savor your blessings, Bryony. Certainly, after all you've done for my family and your own, you deserve this small indulgence."

"And what about you, Michael?" Biting her lip, Bryony looked deep into his eyes. She could no longer push aside the thoughts never far from the surface. "Where are your blessings in all this?"

He removed his glasses and began methodically polishing the lenses with the handkerchief he pulled from an inner pocket. When he finished, he met Bryony's gaze, tilted his head slightly, and smiled. "My blessing is hearing your soft humming as you go about your work. Pausing to listen outside the door as you read to Mother. Watching from my window every morning and every evening for a glimpse of you walking along the drive."

"Michael—"

"And the sweetest blessing of all?" He inched closer, his hands closing gently around her wrists. "Sitting at your kitchen table with a mug of your grandfather's strong, hot chicory and chatting about ordinary, everyday things. Even when you aren't there, I feel your presence. It's the most at home I've felt in so long, I can't even remember."

Bryony freed one of her hands to brush away a trickle of moisture on her cheek. "You're making me sad with such talk."

"Don't be sad on my account." With a muted groan, Michael glanced briefly in the direction of the Heath mansion. "Life is what it is, but I've made up my mind to snatch bits of joy anywhere I can." His smile returned. "Like these moments with you."

Shyly, she drew nearer, her arms creeping around his chest, her head settling so perfectly into the cleft of his shoulder. She breathed in the outdoorsy scent of his woolen coat and welcomed the feel of his arms holding her close.

I love you, Michael Heath.

What she wouldn't give to say those words aloud! But no, this could go no further, and it was pointless to hope otherwise. Michael's sister might claim to have no regrets about falling for a hired man, but look where it had gotten her—banished from home and family, with her own daughter now working as a maid and her husband nowhere to be found.

"Bryony, what are you thinking?" Michael's whispered words tickled her temple.

Palms pressing against his chest, she stood erect. "That it's late and I should get home. And so should you."

She could tell from his frown that he didn't believe her, but he merely nodded and said, "Of course. I shouldn't have kept you."

"I suppose I'll see you tomorrow." Bryony stuffed her hands into her coat pockets.

Michael did the same. "I'm sure. Take care walking home."

"I will. You, too."

Neither moved.

Then Michael slowly leaned forward, and Bryony held her breath as his lips neared hers. The kiss was feather-light, a lingering brush of warmth upon warmth. "Till tomorrow," he whispered, then turned and strode purposefully down the road.

❦

When Bryony finally walked in the door, it was nearly half past seven. Her family and Miranda had already sat down to supper.

"Your plate's in the oven," Rose said. "You're later than normal. Everything okay?"

Bryony answered with a noncommittal "Mmm" as she hung up her coat. After washing her hands at the sink, she found a potholder and carried her plate to the table. She sat down tiredly and then stared unseeing at the shriveled chicken leg and mound of greens.

Rose nudged Bryony's knee under the table. "I promise it tastes better than it looks."

She lifted her fork and tried to smile. "Your cooking's come a long way, Rosie. Heard you even baked cookies this afternoon."

The knowing looks passing between Rose, Miranda, and Grandpa made Bryony lay down her fork with a clatter. "All right, yes, I ran into Michael on the way. And it's a real good thing there wasn't anybody else out on the road, or—"

Rose wiggled her brows and grinned. "Or what, Bry? They might have seen y'all kissing?"

"Now, Rosie-girl," Grandpa interrupted, "don't be teasin' your sister like that."

Bryony's cheeks flamed. Lowering her head, she snatched up her fork again and plowed up a hefty bite of greens. "I was *going* to say"—she slanted a pointed look at Rose—"we don't need to be raising any suspicions that Michael's been coming over here to see Miranda."

"Mmm." Rose's echo of Bryony's earlier response wasn't lost on her.

Miranda cleared her throat. "Let me wash up tonight, Rose. And why don't you fetch Bryony those cookies Michael stashed away in the pantry."

Grandpa excused himself for his nightly prayer time in the parlor, but not before squeezing Bryony's shoulder. His soft-eyed look spoke sympathy and understanding.

Rose plopped a small tin near Bryony's place. "There's a little milk in the icebox. Hermione's completely dried up, but Caleb brought over a pint from their cow this morning."

"That was nice of him." Bryony couldn't help smiling as she bit into the chicken leg. Time to turn the tables on her sister. "Imagine that—Caleb Wieland using part of his busy workday to come all the way over here to bring you a pint of milk."

Rolling her eyes, Rose gathered up more dirty dishes. "Don't *you* go getting ideas, now. He was just thanking us for all the food we've been sending over."

"Mmm."

While Bryony finished her supper, Rose and Miranda made quick work of cleaning up the kitchen. Afterward, Rose joined Grandpa in the parlor, and Miranda settled into the chair at Bryony's left. The thin, dark-haired woman still had a bruised look beneath her eyes, but she seemed so much healthier than she had a week ago.

Bryony slid her plate aside and opened the tin. Four crisp cookies drizzled with caramelized sugar lay inside, cradled in a clean, white napkin. Bryony selected one and bit into it, savoring the crunchy sweetness.

"Want some of that milk?" Miranda started to rise.

"Maybe later." Bryony motioned for Miranda to keep her seat. "Right now, my taste buds are perfectly happy."

Smoothing a hand across her abdomen, Miranda sighed. "I'd feel so much guiltier about imposing on you if not for Michael making sure we all have plenty to eat. At least I can bless your family that way."

Bryony's heart clenched. She laid the rest of her cookie on her folded napkin, and her voice dropped to a reverent whisper. "Michael told me tonight about all the ways he feels blessed. It made me feel ashamed for how often I've grumbled about my circumstances."

Miranda looked askance at her. "The whole time I've been here, I've never heard you speak a word of complaint."

"Oh, but if you could read my mind!" With a self-conscious laugh, Bryony broke off a corner of the cookie and lifted it to her mouth. She chewed slowly, letting the crumbs almost melt in her mouth, while her mind lingered on those moments with Michael. Feeling his fingers entwined with hers. Tasting the tender warmth of his lips.

She straightened abruptly and blinked several times, extra glad no one could read her mind just now—although the funny smile on Miranda's face suggested she had her guesses.

Reaching across the corner of the table, Miranda touched Bryony's arm. "Michael needs you, Bryony. Please give him a chance."

"No," Bryony said slowly, "what Michael needs most is to draw again. Without his art, he's missing the best part of himself."

Now Miranda looked puzzled. "I don't understand. You're saying my brother is an artist?"

Bryony pursed her lips. "I shouldn't be surprised he didn't tell you. Not after what your father did to him."

"Then I think *you'd* better tell me, and right now."

As Bryony described the beautiful pictures Michael drew and how he'd been commissioned to illustrate an article for the university press, Miranda's eyes grew teary with pride. "I'd nearly forgotten how as a boy he used to make pictures for Mother. She'd pin them to the walls of her sitting room upstairs, until Daddy decided there were too many and he'd yank them down. But Mother always rescued them and tucked them away in her bureau."

Bryony could easily picture Sebastian tearing those childhood drawings from the wall, and it made her heart hurt for Michael all the more. Her throat clamped down, and the words came hard as she related how Michael's father had taken the sketchbooks and art supplies out to the incinerator. "But it wasn't just Michael's pictures going up in flames. He lost his hope that day."

By now, Miranda was holding back silent sobs. Horror filled her eyes. Her mouth trembled with repressed rage. "How could he? *How could he?*"

With no more appetite for cookies, Bryony replaced the lid on the tin. She sniffled and whisked away a tear. "Before I went to work for your father, Grandpa tried to warn me what a hard man he could be. But what he's done to you and Michael—I never dreamed anyone could be so cruel to his own flesh and blood."

"I don't understand him. I never will." Lowering her eyes, Miranda rested a protective hand upon her abdomen. "Once I hear from Daniel, I'm taking Callie and we're going to join him, wherever he is. And I hope it's far, far away from Eden, Arkansas."

"It isn't right. None of this is right." Bryony shoved back her chair and crossed to the window, where her own reflection shown dimly in the darkened glass. "Michael needs his art. Your children need the love of their grandparents." Face turned heavenward, she pressed her eyes shut. *Oh, Lord, why won't you do something to fix this?*

❦

"I need your help, Jeremiah." Michael had cornered the manservant in the workroom across from Esther's office.

Jeremiah glanced up from the shoes he'd been polishing. "What you be needin' on this beautiful Saturday morning, young master, and lookin' so serious about it?"

Pulling out a chair on the opposite side of the worktable, Michael sat with his knees splayed and his hands braced on his thighs. "I haven't been behind the wheel of a car since I drove for my commanding officer in France. It's high time I gave it another try, and I'd like you to teach me."

With a thoughtful frown, Jeremiah ran his fingertips across his salt-and-pepper beard. "Your daddy all right with this notion of yours?"

"I haven't mentioned it, but I doubt he'd object. After all, he does expect me to take a more active role in managing Brookbirch." Michael affected the persuasive grin that had rarely failed to win Jeremiah over to his boyhood schemes. "Say yes, and I'll help you finish all these shoes."

"You do know how to drive a hard bargain." Jeremiah passed a stained rag and a tin of shoe cream across the table. "Just don't you be telling your daddy you helped me."

"Our secret." Michael picked up one of his father's scuffed tan brogans and attacked the sole with a stiff brush.

They worked in companionable silence for a while, interrupted only by Jeremiah's occasional pointers about the fine art of polishing shoes. Michael had to laugh to himself, since everyone on staff knew this was the elderly butler's least favorite task.

In just over an hour, the gleaming leather of six pairs of shoes reflected the overhead lamp. After Jeremiah put away his supplies, he and Michael washed up in the servants' lavatory. While Jeremiah delivered the shoes to the master suite, Michael retrieved his coat. A few minutes later, he met Jeremiah in the garage.

Since Mother had persuaded Dad to drive her into Brinkley and call on some of their church acquaintances, the timing couldn't be better. Michael perused the remaining vehicles, the shiny green Chevrolet Superior catching his eye. He motioned to Jeremiah. "Think I can handle this one?"

With a dubious frown, Jeremiah shook his head. "I'm thinkin' not till I see how fast this driving business comes back to you. Ain't taking no chance on gettin' my pay docked on account of you putting a dent in this fine automobile."

Only moderately disappointed, Michael took the keys Jeremiah handed him for a Ford Model T truck. He climbed behind the wheel to wait while Jeremiah explained to their puzzled groundskeeper why they were borrowing his vehicle.

After a few jerky attempts with the clutch, Michael managed to back out of the garage without damage to either the truck or his pride. Shortly they were jouncing down the road at a good clip. Michael glanced over to see Jeremiah holding his breath and clinging to the door handle for dear life. He laughed to himself and pressed harder on the accelerator.

Jeremiah gave a low whistle. "Hold your horses, young master! I don't cotton to meeting my Maker upside down in a ditch."

Easing off, Michael settled into a comfortable speed. "Mind if we drive into Eden? I'd like to stop by the general store."

"Just you be watchin' traffic. Town's a lot busier than these country roads." A few more turns brought them to the main road into Eden. "If you be needin' something in town, you coulda just told me and I'd have picked it up." Jeremiah snorted. "Lots easier than scaring twenty years off my life. I ain't got that many to spare."

"Knowing you, Jeremiah, you'll still be kicking up your heels at a hundred and ten." Michael cast the butler an affectionate grin, only to be scolded for taking his eyes off the road and barely missing a mule-drawn farm cart.

Eden seemed little changed since Michael's last trip through town, the day his father brought him home from the train station two years ago. In truth, the town had grown very little since 1916 when Michael left home to join the army. The general store and the feed-and-seed were the main businesses, along with a gas station and the small church building that did double duty as a primary school for the local kids who weren't kept home for farm chores.

Michael and Miranda, naturally, received their education at a private boarding school. It would have been unthinkable for Sebastian Heath's offspring to attend classes with the children of sharecroppers and tenant farmers.

Michael braked in front of the general store and shut off the motor. Jeremiah followed him inside, watching with a raised brow as Michael ambled down each aisle. Reading prices, Michael grimaced. He'd seen in the account ledgers what his father paid the household servants, and at these prices their money wouldn't go far. Little wonder so many farm families struggled to put food on the table.

A balding store clerk meandered over. "You're Sebastian Heath's boy, aren't you? The one who went off to war."

"That's right." Michael hefted a sack of flour.

The clerk thrust out his hand. "Name's Joe. Pleasure to finally meet you. Yes, sir, I was mighty glad to take care of mailing your stuff to that fancy school up in New York." His wide-eyed curiosity turned the statement into a question.

Michael's jaw tensed. Before he could form a reply, Jeremiah cleared his throat forcefully and stepped forward. "Young master, we best be on our way, don't you think?"

Collecting himself, Michael accepted Joe's handshake. "In a few minutes, Jeremiah." He bestowed a cool smile upon the clerk. "If you don't mind, Joe, I'd like to confer with you about the status of our tenants' accounts."

Joe narrowed one eye. "What exactly are you asking, Mr. Heath? 'Cause when it comes to my customers' privacy, I got my principles."

"I wouldn't ask you to reveal anything confidential. However, perhaps we could discuss a mutually beneficial arrangement." The smile never leaving his face, Michael took the man's arm and guided him over to the counter. "If you'd just take a look at your ledger . . ."

By now, Michael had awakened Jeremiah's curiosity. The graying servant joined him at the counter. "What you doin' here, young master?"

"A good deed." Turning to Joe, he asked the clerk to tally up the account balances for all the families leasing farms from the Heaths. When Joe read him the total, Michael sucked air between his teeth. "That much?"

"It'd be a lot higher, 'cept I had to cut off credit or go bankrupt myself. As it is, lots of these folk ain't never gonna be able to pay down their debt. The drought's done us all a bad turn."

Head lowered, Michael pressed his palms hard against the countertop. "Here's what I want you to do, Joe. Open an account for me—in my name, not my father's—and transfer everything our tenants currently owe you over into that account. I can't promise how quickly I'll pay it off, but I guarantee it'll be a darn sight sooner than you'd get the money otherwise."

Wearing a doubtful frown, Joe stared at Michael long and hard. Then he turned to a clean page in the ledger, licked the tip of his pencil, and scrawled *Mr. Michael Heath* across the top line. Beneath it in the debit column, he wrote down the amount he'd just quoted.

Before Michael left the store, he added flour, sugar, dried fruit, beans, and a cured ham to his bill. When he and Jeremiah had loaded the purchases in the back of the truck, Michael handed Jeremiah the keys. "You'd better drive. I have some thinking to do."

"Like how you gonna explain to your daddy what you just done in there?"

"Who says he has to know?"

Jeremiah shook his head. "You just askin' for trouble, young master, and you know it."

He knew it well. But Christmas was coming, and these hard-pressed, destitute farmers deserved some relief. Despite the rhetoric spouted by Governor Parnell and President Hoover, Michael gathered from news reports that precious little aid had filtered down the pike. Even Red Cross efforts had been hobbled, since according to Hoover's philosophy the needy were better off relying upon their neighbors' charity.

Not a helpful solution when your "neighbor" was a heartless tightwad like Sebastian Heath.

"Let's drive by the Rigby farm," Michael said as they headed out of town.

"Humph, shoulda known." The twinkle in Jeremiah's eyes belied his gruff tone.

Settling deep into the seat, Michael shifted his gaze toward the window, but in his mind's eye, he saw only Bryony. He could still hear her lilting voice as she read *A Christmas Carol* to his mother, her gravelly growl with each "Bah! Humbug."

Michael doubted he'd ever see a change of heart in his Scrooge of a father, but Dad couldn't prevent him from performing his own acts of charity. Last week, a check had arrived in the mail, more than fair payment for the five illustrations he'd completed for the botanical journal. Until today's sudden impulse, he hadn't intended to touch the money, but now he had the chance to do something good with it—a start, at least, since his personal finances were limited to a small military disability pension. He'd have to do some finagling to pay off the balance he now owed the general store, but whatever it took, he'd find a way. His self-respect depended on it.

16

Nothing quite matched the crisp, clean smell of freshly ironed sheets. Bryony breathed deeply as she and Callie worked together to fold and stack the linens. Since Mr. and Mrs. Heath were away visiting friends, Bryony had spent most of the day either in the laundry with Callie or helping Odette with holiday baking.

Come to think of it, the temptingly sweet aromas of Odette's pies, cakes, and cookies definitely won out over the smell of clean linens.

Definitely one of Bryony's more pleasant workdays. Not that she didn't enjoy serving tea or reading to Mrs. Heath, but when the woman's mind slipped and Bryony had to pretend to be a visiting neighbor, the awkwardness got to be a strain.

Callie snapped the corners of a sheet together. "Five more days till Christmas. It's gonna be so nice having Mama nearby." With the Heaths away, she could speak freely. "Last year I didn't get any time off, not even Christmas Day."

"Really? That's terrible." Bryony passed her end of the sheet into Callie's hands, then grabbed the middle and did the same. "I never thought about how working here would mean holidays, too."

"Rich people expect to be served every day of the year."

MYRA JOHNSON

Callie's observation certainly didn't include Michael. Passing the servants' workroom that morning, Bryony had glimpsed him polishing shoes with Jeremiah, the two men chatting like old friends and laughing at each other's jokes. Then later they'd driven off together in the groundskeeper's truck—or rather, Michael had driven and none too expertly, if Bryony were any judge. Backing out of the garage, he'd given the shrubbery a mighty close shave.

With a sad sigh, Callie laid the folded sheet atop their growing pile. "Sure wish I knew where my daddy got to. And how's he supposed to get word to Mama since he won't know she's at your place now?"

"I'm sorry, Callie. I wish I knew." Bryony smoothed another sheet across the ironing board. From the first day she'd met the young girl, she noticed Callie's speech was more refined than that of the other servants. Now she knew why. Miranda had tutored Callie herself, teaching her the fundamentals of arithmetic, reading, writing, and elocution. Whatever obstacles the girl's ancestry might present, Miranda made sure Callie would never be hindered by a lack of education.

Miss Esther appeared in the laundry room door. "The mister and missus just sent word they'll be dining with friends this evening. I have their permission to excuse anyone whose work is done for the day." Hands folded at her waist, she shared a tight smile. "Since it appears you two are almost finished here, I'm certain you won't mind a little free time this afternoon."

Callie beamed at Bryony. "I can go see Mama!"

"She'll be thrilled." Bryony glanced into the wicker basket near her feet. "In fact, you should go right now. I'll finish the ironing and be along shortly."

Callie's bone-crushing hug spoke her thanks. She yanked off her apron and snagged her coat from a hook. On her way out the door, she nearly throttled Miss Esther with another quick hug, and seconds later she disappeared around the side of the house.

Stepping farther into the room, Miss Esther closed the door.

"You're a kind and caring woman, Bryony. Callie is blessed to have you for a friend."

"She's been a blessing to me, the only one who—" Bryony stopped herself. Long past time to forgive and forget.

"You don't have to say it, Bryony. I know some of us were unfriendly at first. Not that I'm offering excuses, but perhaps now you understand." Miss Esther helped to smooth another section of the sheet across the ironing board. "Callie is very dear to us. When you were hired as a housemaid, some thought you'd taken a position that rightfully should have been Callie's."

Bryony set down the iron. Her gaze bored into Miss Esther's. "Callie's *rightful position* is to be accepted and loved for who she is."

"I would not disagree. However . . ." Miss Esther heaved a tired sigh, her amber eyes darkening. "Perhaps you have surmised I'm also of mixed parentage."

"I wondered." Bryony glanced away.

"Unlike Callie's mother and father, my parents did not marry. My father owned the Birmingham textile manufacturing company where my mother worked. He led her to believe that if she didn't —" Hiking her chin, the woman drew a sharp breath. "Suffice it to say that love had nothing to do with my conception."

"I'm so sorry for you," Bryony said. "But Callie has two parents who love her. She has an uncle who'd do anything for her. How could her own flesh-and-blood grandparents turn her away?"

Miss Esther's sad laugh echoed against the hard stone walls. "This is the South. What more reason do you need?"

The woman left a few moments later, leaving Bryony alone with her tumbled thoughts and the unfairness of it all. Didn't Scripture teach that all were one in Christ? Why did race or color or class matter so much? Why were there divisions at all among the children of God?

By the time she finished ironing and folding the last of the linens, Bryony's mounting frustration had her stomach in knots. She could hardly wait to get home to the family who loved her unconditionally, the dear people who gave and gave and gave some

MYRA JOHNSON

more, even when they had so little of their own. Larkspur should be there by now, home from college for the holidays. The little farmhouse would be overflowing with warmth and good cheer.

After stacking the sheets in the linen chest upstairs, Bryony grabbed her coat from the back hallway, picked up her weekly pay envelope from Miss Esther's office, and hurried out the door. As she rounded the south end of the house, the groundskeeper's truck was just coming up the drive.

Jeremiah stopped beside her and rolled down the window. "You headed home already, Miss Bryony?"

"I am." She explained about being released early since the Heaths were away for the evening.

"Then you should hop in and let me drive you. When you got extra time off, no sense wastin' a minute of it."

Bryony wouldn't disagree. She'd been on her feet most of the day and hadn't looked forward to the long walk home. She thanked the man and scurried around to the passenger door.

Jeremiah winked as she settled in. "Just came from your place, matter o' fact. It's sure smellin' like Christmas over there. Them sisters of yours and Miss Miranda been baking up a storm."

She cast the elderly butler a grateful smile. "You must have taken more groceries over."

"Oh, not me, missy." Jeremiah steered the truck down the lane. "It was all the young master's doing. He near bought out ol' Joe's general store today." He cleared his throat and mumbled something Bryony couldn't make out. She thought it sounded like, "And that ain't all."

A twinge of uneasiness tightened Bryony's chest. "What's he done, Jeremiah? Please tell me it's nothing that will stoke his father's anger."

Jeremiah's forward stare and jutted chin gave the answer Bryony feared. He cut a quick glance toward Bryony. "That boy's got more heart than good sense, but when he puts his mind to somethin', they ain't no stoppin' it."

Bryony didn't dare guess what Michael was up to. Always, in

his own quiet way, he tried to make a difference. But his kindheartedness had already cost him so much. Bryony only had to close her eyes to be carried instantly back to the day at the incinerator.

When Jeremiah braked before the final turn, Bryony reached over to touch his arm. "Jeremiah, will you help me do something good for Michael?"

"I be glad to do anything for the young master. What you have in mind?"

"He's got to draw again. I know he won't be truly happy until he does."

The old man shook his head. "You know how that done turned out. If his daddy finds out—"

"He won't." Bryony delved into her coat pocket for the envelope containing her pay. "Michael told me you would sometimes pick up art supplies for him in Little Rock. How much would it cost for a sketchbook and a box of those colored pencils he likes?"

Jeremiah peeked into her envelope. His frown said she didn't have nearly enough.

"I've got a little more put aside at home. If you could—"

He silenced her with a gentle squeeze of her hand. "Miss Esther and I's s'posed to go into Little Rock on Monday to shop at the grocers there for things we can't get in Eden or Brinkley. We'll be right near the art store, so I'll see what I can find for the young master."

Bryony pressed the envelope into his palm. "Take this. If you need more, I'll pay you back."

The darkly spotted skin around Jeremiah's eyes crinkled with his merry grin. "I swan, Miss Bryony, your heart's 'bout as big as Mister Michael's. The Lord bless the day you came to the Heaths'."

Larkspur awoke before dawn on Christmas Eve morning, partly because the old settee in the parlor wasn't the most comfortable place to sleep, but mostly because Bryony dropped a pan as she started breakfast.

"Let me, Bryony," Larkspur said as she looped the sash of her robe. "There's no reason you should have to cook for us and then work all day for the Heaths."

"I'm fixing my own breakfast anyway. Least I can do." Bryony set a pot of water on the stove. "Especially since you refused to take my bed and let me sleep in the parlor."

"What are we going to do with you, Bry?" Larkspur wrapped her arms around her sister's waist. "Will you ever give up trying to take care of everyone but yourself?"

"Hmm, maybe when you're a full-fledged teacher and Rosie's married off to somebody smart and handsome like Caleb Wieland." Bryony measured oatmeal into the boiling water. "Then it'll be just Grandpa and me, and we'll sail off to Tahiti and sway in our hammocks beneath a sultry ocean breeze."

Grandpa's gruff laugh sounded from the back door. "Who's going to Tahiti?"

"Why, you and Bry, if she's to be believed—but only if we can get her out of the kitchen and doing for herself instead of everybody else." Larkspur snatched the wooden spoon from Bryony's hand and shooed her away. "Hey, don't you have a present to wrap?"

Bryony's annoyed frown instantly faded. Her eyes lit up like a lovesick schoolgirl's, and she darted from the room.

Grandpa hung his ragged wool coat and tweed cap on a hook, then took a mug from the cupboard and filled it from the pot of chicory simmering on a back burner. Larkspur didn't know how he could drink the bitter, nut-like brew, but as crops failed and grocery prices rose, real coffee had gone by the wayside. She smiled to herself, remembering the tiny bag of coffee beans she'd brought from Arkadelphia and wrapped as Grandpa's Christmas gift. There weren't many gifts under the spindly little evergreen Grandpa had cut last weekend and set up in front of the parlor windows, but they had a tight, warm house and food in their bellies. When so many were going without, how could Larkspur complain?

The oatmeal thickened, and Larkspur spooned it into bowls. A few minutes later, Rose burst through the back door, her cheeks ruddy from the cold. She sniffed appreciatively. "Those raisins Michael brought us would sure taste good in my oatmeal."

"Just a few, Rosie. Let's save some for the cinnamon rolls I'm making for our Christmas breakfast." Larkspur still couldn't believe all the groceries Michael had delivered last Saturday. Not to mention coming home from college to find his sister as their houseguest. Miranda was nice enough, but Larkspur worried where all this was leading.

She also couldn't miss Michael Heath's growing feelings for Bryony, and hers for him. Bryony had been giddy with excitement when she'd come home from work Monday night to find the sketchbook and colored pencils Jeremiah had brought back from Little Rock. She'd hidden the art supplies under her bed and made everyone promise not to mention a word about them to Michael when he visited.

Which, apparently, he did quite often. He'd come by every single day since Larkspur had arrived, and he never came empty-handed. First all those groceries on Saturday afternoon, then on Sunday the heel of a rump roast left over from his family's dinner. On Monday it was a tin of raisins and another sack of flour, and yesterday a burlap bag full of yams. What would happen if Sebastian Heath discovered where all this food disappeared to? Bad enough the cruelty he could inflict on his own son and daughter. Larkspur didn't want to imagine what harm he'd bring upon Bryony should he learn Bryony had encouraged Michael to draw again—or worse, for her part in protecting Miranda .

At the table, Rose stirred a meager spoonful of raisins into her oatmeal, then offered the tin to Larkspur and Grandpa. "Did I mention I saw Caleb in town yesterday when I went to pick up the mail? He told me the strangest thing. His mama sent him to pay what they could against their account at the general store, and Joe told him their balance was zero. *Zero.* Who'd do them such a kindness?"

Eyes in a squint, Grandpa peered from Rose to Larkspur. "Bo Jorgensen said the same thing happened to him."

"If I didn't know we're just as bad off," Larkspur said with a smirk, "I'd suspect you were responsible, Grandpa. But who *do* you suppose would have—"

"I'll tell you exactly who." Bryony stood in the doorway, dressed in her maid's uniform, her hair done up in a tight bun. Her eyes shimmered with the unmistakable glow of a woman in love, and Larkspur suffered a tiny twinge of envy.

So much for the talk she'd planned to have with Bryony before returning to college after the holidays. Michael may be nothing like his father, but Bryony needed to be careful nonetheless, because rich folk like the Heaths had the power not only to take away your livelihood but to destroy everything you cared about most.

But convincing Bryony to get Miranda out of the house, keep her distance from Michael Heath, and just do her job? Larkspur suspected any such advice given now would fall on deaf ears.

ॐ

Michael's father peered into his empty coffee cup. "Fool idea, giving the servants an entire day off."

"By all means, let me." Michael retrieved the coffeepot from the buffet and filled his father's cup. "I assure you, with all the food Odette prepared in advance, we aren't likely to go hungry." With a twisted smile, he added, "Merry Christmas, 'Uncle Scrooge.'"

His father's grimace told him exactly what he thought of the epithet.

When Michael rounded the table with the pot of tea for his mother, she beamed up at him. "I think it was a wonderful idea, the best gift we could have given the help. They deserve to be with their own families on Christmas Day."

"And we have our dear son to thank for this magnanimous gesture of goodwill." Michael's father lifted his cup in a mock salute. "I suppose you'll be serving dinner as well?"

"Unless I can twist your arm to assist." Ignoring another scowl, Michael took his seat and spread strawberry jam across half a biscuit. He started to take a bite, then lowered the biscuit to the edge of his plate. "Is there no hope for at least a tolerable Christmas in this house, if not a happy one?"

For the briefest of moments, Michael thought he glimpsed a shadow of remorse in his father's eyes. "It *is* a happy Christmas," his father stated. He reached across to hold his wife's hand and gazed at her with love in his eyes. "I'm here with my beautiful bride and our war-hero son—"

"Dad—"

"—who has at long last accepted his rightful place." The smile he aimed at Michael carried more warning than fatherly pride. "What better Christmas could a man ask for?"

"Oh, I do love Christmas." Mother's expression grew wistful. "If only . . . if only Miranda would come home. She's been away so long."

Michael cut a glance at his father but remained silent. He forced down part of his biscuit, the texture turning to cardboard in his mouth through no fault of Odette's. When he'd swallowed more coffee, he pushed back his chair and dug deep for a pleasant tone. "Mother, shall we go to the parlor and light the tree?"

"Yes, let's!" As Michael helped her from her chair, she winked at her husband. "Hurry and finish your coffee, Sebastian, so we can see what wonderful surprises Saint Nicholas brought."

Her remark brought back memories of childhood Christmases with Miranda. Every Christmas Eve, the family made their annual trek to Little Rock for candlelight Mass at the historic Cathedral of St. Andrew the Apostle. Afterward, they'd spend the night at a posh hotel, enjoy a delightful Christmas morning breakfast in the hotel's festively decorated dining room, then drive home. Michael and Miranda would race each other from the garage to the front parlor for a first glimpse of the treasure trove Saint Nick always left for them. Even as teenagers, they hadn't lost their eager naiveté. Michael sighed inwardly and wished he could return to those simpler times.

As usual, the space beneath the tree overflowed with wrapped gifts, most of them for Mother. Dad never seemed to tire of showering her with expensive jewelry, scarves, and various objets d'art. While Mother exclaimed over another bejeweled bracelet, Michael's father handed him an oblong box wrapped in sparkly paper. Inside was a silver fountain pen engraved with Michael's name.

"For your desk," his father said, and now the pride in the man's eyes appeared genuine. "Having you work alongside me these past few weeks has been . . ." Lips compressed, he gave his head a quick shake. "Words can't express what it means to have my son with me again."

Michael lifted the pen from its black velvet niche and tested its weight. Uncapped, it nestled easily into the groove on his middle finger worn deep from gripping art pencils. Swallowing hard, he laid the pen back in the box and closed the lid. "It's . . . exquisite. Thanks, Dad."

"There's another surprise coming," his father said. "I hoped it would arrive in time for Christmas, but it'll be another week or so. You won't be working at that rickety table or off the corner of my desk much longer. I've ordered us a partners desk."

Michael's chest tightened, and he could only nod. He didn't dare open his mouth to speak, not with Mother sitting right next to him. Instead, he knelt in front of the tree to retrieve the gifts he'd wrapped for his parents. Since he'd only been driving again since the weekend, he hadn't much opportunity for gift shopping, but he'd asked Jeremiah to look for a copy of Edna Ferber's latest novel, *Cimarron*, during his recent excursion to Little Rock. The book would be something new Mother and Bryony could enjoy together.

For his father, he'd been less imaginative. A pair of tan kid gloves and a wool muffler seemed perfectly suited to a man who valued practicality.

"What a lovely Christmas, just the four of us." Mother stood abruptly and went about gathering up boxes, paper, and bows. "Except . . . Miranda hasn't opened her gifts yet. She can't still be upstairs playing in her room. Did she forget what day it is?"

Dad rose and tucked his arm around Mother. His voice grew tight. "Miranda's away, dear. Remember?"

"At boarding school? But why haven't you brought her home?"

Michael could stand it no longer. Before he blurted out the truth, he excused himself to see what Odette had left for their luncheon. In the kitchen, he found sliced meats, condiments, and crusty bread, along with cold bean salad and two kinds of pies. Odette had laid out plates, napkins, and utensils on a serving tray, so all that remained was to set out the food. Michael made up his mind that as soon as they'd eaten, he'd claim the need for some air and a bit more driving practice, then slip away to Bryony's house.

He couldn't wait. His heart lifted at the mere thought of being with her again. And to know his sister was safe in the care of Bryony and her kindhearted kin made this difficult day more bearable. Soon, he'd be celebrating Christmas with a real family permeated by love.

Why, God? Why is my own family such a mess?

Michael hadn't prayed much since the day he turned his back on home all those years ago, at least nothing beyond the same desperate pleas every other doughboy sent heavenward as war raged on in France. After the mustard gas attack, while Michael lay near death in a field hospital, a young chaplain had sat with him for hours on end. Chaplain Vickary had witnessed the worst cruelty one human being could inflict on another, yet he hadn't lost his faith in the power of the Almighty to set things right.

What Michael wouldn't give for even a small measure of such faith. He almost wished he hadn't begged off last night when his parents encouraged him to attend midnight Mass with them. Bearing in mind Mother's frailty, they no longer made the drive to St. Andrew's but had attended Father Dempsey's church in Brinkley. Michael's parents had tried to get him to come along last year, too, his first Christmas home since he'd joined the army, but God had felt too far away for too long, and Michael hadn't the energy for pretense.

What do you suppose you're doing now, pretending to be the good son while subsisting on clandestine visits to a poorer but happier home?

He wanted to argue that his duplicity protected the people he loved most, but if he were being completely honest, he'd have to admit he protected himself as well. Because the longer he kept secret the glorious hours spent in the company of Bryony and her family, and now his sister and the niece he'd never known he had, the longer he could survive the rest.

❦

Stomach full from a delicious Christmas dinner of roasted rabbit, candied yams, and string beans, with not a turnip in sight for a change, Bryony helped her sisters wash up the dishes. Miranda and Callie had both offered to help, but Bryony insisted they enjoy what time they had together.

Larkspur passed Bryony a sudsy plate to swish through the rinse water. "You should get off your feet while you can, Bry. Tomorrow will come soon enough."

"I don't mind." She bumped shoulders with her sisters, Lark on one side and Rose on the other, then handed Rose the plate to dry. "I'd rather be right here with you two than anywhere else on earth."

Rose leaned forward and raised a brow in Larkspur's direction. "Hmm, do you think she means it? Or is she just biding time until Michael can come over?"

"Why, you—" Suppressing an embarrassed chuckle, Bryony flicked water in Rose's face.

Rose gasped and blotted her cheeks with a dishtowel, then snapped the towel at Bryony's arm.

"Ouch! Hey, I can still turn you over my knee if I need to, young lady."

"You started it!" Laughing, Rose danced away before Bryony could grab her.

Larkspur chided them both in her best schoolteacher voice. "That's quite enough, you two. Careful, or you'll break Grandma's good china."

With the table between her and Rose, Bryony feinted left and right, waiting for her chance. "You could save us all a lot of time, Lark. Come help me catch this imp."

"Oh, no, you won't get me mixed up in your catfighting."

"Spoilsport." With a wicked laugh, Bryony lunged for Rose's arm, barely missing. Her momentum carried her across the floor and straight into Grandpa's arms as he stepped in from outside.

He stumbled backward and wrestled Bryony upright again. "Lordy, what's going on in here?"

With an eye roll and a deep breath, Bryony straightened her dress. "We were just cutting up a bit. No harm done."

"Sure hope not, seein' as how more company just drove up." Grandpa shrugged off his coat.

Bryony glanced at the pendulum clock—half past two. "Didn't think the Wielands were coming over until later."

"Ain't the Wielands." One corner of Grandpa's mouth turned up. He fixed Bryony with a meaningful look.

Her heart plummeted to her toes and then soared again—*Michael!*

"For heaven's sake, breathe, Bryony." Rose patted her back.

But try as she might, she could barely force air into her lungs. Only days ago, a sketchbook and colored pencils had seemed the perfect gift to restore Michael to himself. Now, wondering how he'd respond, she was terrified.

Then he was there, standing behind Grandpa in the open door, a shy smile on his face and his eyes bright behind the lenses of his glasses. "I hope you haven't had dessert yet." Stepping around Grandpa, he offered Bryony a cloth-covered dish. "I brought a pie."

❧ 17 ❧

S trange, how a cherry pie exactly like the one he'd sampled an hour ago when serving dessert to his parents could taste so much better here at George Rigby's table. Michael scraped up more filling with the side of his fork and slid it between his lips with a contented moan. And though he had yet to develop much of a taste for chicory, he didn't mind at all the bitter nip it added when brewed with the real coffee Larkspur had given her grandfather for Christmas. Michael felt privileged to be invited to share.

"More coffee, Mister Mi—I mean, *Uncle* Michael?" Callie's cheeks took on a pinkish hue above her happy grin.

"Careful, Callie." Miranda lightly touched her daughter's arm. "Best not get too comfortable calling him that, or you'll forget one day when it matters."

"I know, Mama, but it just feels so nice not to hide the truth anymore. At least not here, away from . . ." Callie's wistful gaze conveyed what she couldn't speak aloud, the regret over grandparents who would never acknowledge her.

"Just half a cup, if you please, Callie." Michael eased back his chair. "Then you and your mother must open your gifts."

Miranda puckered her lips. "What have you done, Michael? You know we had no means to get anything for you."

He tried to say something about how spending Christmas with them was the best gift he could hope for, but the words jammed up behind the lump in his throat. Instead, he shook his head and focused on sipping his coffee.

When he'd drained the cup, he made a hurried trip out to the Chevrolet and returned with the gifts. Jeremiah had kept them hidden for him in a workroom cupboard, and they were small enough that he could conceal them beneath his coat when he left the house.

Bryony suggested they move to the parlor. She and her sisters carried in extra chairs from the kitchen, while George stoked the fire in a potbelly stove. Soon they were all gathered in the cozy room, Michael on the settee between Miranda and Callie, George in a padded rocking chair, and the Linwood girls all in a row. A fragrant cedar, decorated with a hodgepodge of glass and wooden ornaments and with a white-robed ceramic angel at the top, sat before the front window.

Michael handed a wrapped box to Callie and another to Miranda. "I wanted to do so much more—and I will someday—but I'm afraid I'm a little out of practice."

Miranda slid him an understanding smile as she eased the ribbon from the box and tore off the paper. She lifted the lid to reveal a baby's christening gown. "Oh, Michael," she cried, hugging it to her chest, "this was yours, wasn't it?"

"It's a little yellow with age but only worn once," he said with a wink. He turned to Callie, who stared at her unopened gift as if she couldn't quite believe it was real. "Go ahead, open it."

Reverently, she peeled back the bow and wrapping paper, then lifted out the leather-bound volume of poems by Henry Wadsworth Longfellow. Thumbing through the pages, she spoke various titles aloud, each time breathing out a blissful sigh.

"I'm afraid the book isn't new, either," Michael apologized. "I was just a year or two younger than you when my mother gave it to me."

"I'll cherish it forever." Misty-eyed, Callie shifted and started to lift her arms toward him, then hesitated.

Before she could draw back, Michael swept her into the hug he could see her hungering to give. "It's all right, Callie. You're my beloved niece, and here you need never pretend otherwise."

Sniffles sounded across the room. Larkspur stood and reached for Rose's hand. "We, um, we should go check on . . . something."

"Oh. Right. Grandpa, we might need your help."

George grumbled as he shoved up from the rocking chair. "Always somethin' with those girls. Best go see what they're up to."

Miranda dabbed moisture from beneath her eyes with the cuff of her sleeve, then folded the christening gown and tucked it neatly into the box. She planted a kiss on Michael's cheek and smiled her thanks. "I'll just go put this away," she said, rising. "Bring your book, Callie, and you can read me some of those poems."

As they left the parlor, Michael looked up to see Bryony still sitting across from him. Her lips twitched. Her throat shifted with a nervous swallow. She shot him a quick smile and then glanced away.

It finally dawned on him that the others had intentionally left them alone together. And now *he* was nervous—anxious and curious and pleased all at once. He was about to cross over and sit beside her so they could talk . . . or perhaps steal a kiss . . . but then she popped up from the chair. She strode to the Christmas tree, and as she knelt, her thick, dark tresses spilled across her shoulder. She looked so beautiful there in profile, color rising in porcelain cheeks, skirt tucked demurely around her lovely calves.

Darting a glance his way, she reached far beneath the wispy branches and brought out a large, flat gift wrapped in wrinkled brown paper and tied with a red ribbon. Without rising, she swiveled to sit on the floor at his feet. She laid the gift on his lap. "Sorry the package isn't prettier, but we ran out of Christmas paper, and this was the best I could do."

215

Michael gripped the sides of the gift, the shape and feel of it painfully familiar. His chest ached. "Bryony . . ."

"Please, Michael, open it."

He didn't think he could, but somehow he forced unwilling fingers to loosen the ribbon and tear away the paper. His hands shook as he lifted the lid on the box of pencils and hesitantly ran his fingers over the multicolored array. Now, as difficult as it had been to open the box, it became even harder to close it. He slid the sketchbook and pencil box toward Bryony. "I can't keep this."

"Of course you can." Edging closer, she nudged it back into his hands, then rose up on her knees and scooted onto the settee beside him. "Michael, you can't let your father win this battle. You can't let him browbeat you into giving up your beautiful, amazing, God-given talent."

"He's already won, Bryony." Coldness seeped into Michael's bones, a frigid stiffness not even the stove's warm glow could penetrate. "I'm doing what I have to do . . . for the sake of the people I love."

"I know you are, and I know why." Bryony's tone hardened. "But it doesn't have to be the end of the story. You can still be *you*." She reached for the pencil box and laid it aside, her voice becoming as tender as her movements. "Let this be your safe place, just like it is for Miranda and Callie." She turned back the cover of the sketchbook, revealing a pristine white page. "You *need* your art, Michael. You need to draw again, same as you need air to breathe." She handed him a dark green pencil, closing his fingers around it when he seemed to have forgotten how.

Then, almost beyond his control, his hand began moving across the page, the whisper of pencil across paper mesmerizing. A spiny, serrated leaf took shape, and another, and another. He traded green for burnt umber and sketched stems spreading through the leaves. Then a different shade of green, then strokes of yellow and tan. With red, maroon, and pink, he fashioned a cluster of holly berries.

He didn't know he was crying until Bryony took a handkerchief from her pocket and dabbed a teardrop that had fallen onto the page. He stilled his hand and gazed at her, hardly able to fathom the depth of love swelling his soul. "How . . . how?"

She circled her arm around him and rested her head on his shoulder. "I had a little help from Jeremiah."

His eyes fell shut, and a tiny, aching laugh bubbled through his chest. "Of course you did."

Bryony raised her head, and with her other hand cradled his cheek, giving him no option but to look deep into soft, brown eyes as wet with tears as his own. "Promise me, Michael Heath. Promise me you'll draw more pictures. Lots and lots and lots of them."

He couldn't speak, could only nod . . . and lower quivering lips onto hers in a kiss laced with deepest gratitude and undying love.

This was wrong. So wrong. Allowing herself to fall in love with Michael Heath could only result in heartache. It didn't seem to matter, though, because Bryony couldn't stop what was happening even if she wanted to. Every moment she spent with him, she loved him more. Loved the way his glasses sometimes slid down his nose when he was concentrating. Loved the feel of his long, strong fingers intertwined with hers. Loved his mixed scents of aftershave, wool sweaters, and pencil shavings.

And now, every single day when she finished work, she could look forward to finding him at her kitchen table, sketchbook and pencils laid out before him and a new drawing taking shape. She worried at first that Sebastian would grow suspicious about Michael's late-afternoon departures, especially since more and more often he stayed at the farm well past the supper hour. If Michael's father discovered the goings-on at the Rigby farm, they'd all be in for a heap of trouble.

"He won't find out," Michael assured Bryony a few days after Christmas. "As far as my father is concerned, a daily hike through the woods or a drive around the countryside is my fair reward for putting in the requisite hours on plantation business."

Then on the following Friday, the second day of the new year, as Bryony started to the small parlor to read to Mrs. Heath for a while, a delivery truck pulled up in front of the house. *Clarkson and Sons, Fine Furnishings for Home and Office*, read the dark blue lettering on a white background. Four brawny men in khaki coveralls piled out, and Jeremiah showed them down the hall to Mr. Heath's office.

Moments later, Michael emerged from the office, arms crossed and lips creased. He caught Bryony's eye briefly and gave his head a quick shake before shrinking into an out-of-the-way corner. From within the office came rustling and scraping sounds, along with Mr. Heath's barked instructions.

As Jeremiah made his retreat, Bryony called him aside. "What's going on?"

"Mr. Heath's getting a new desk." A noisy sigh expressed his irritation. "Excuse me, Miss Bryony, but I gotta unlock the loft over the garage so's they can move the old one up there."

Before she could ask why they were moving the old desk out instead of leaving it for Michael, Jeremiah bustled on his way.

The door to the small parlor opened. "'Bout time," Dancy said with a huff. "Miz Heath's asking for the next chapter in y'all's story before she goes up for her afternoon rest. And, Lawdy, if I don't need to put these tired ol' feet up for a spell."

With an anxious glance in Michael's direction, Bryony prayed whatever new arrangements Sebastian had set in motion wouldn't keep Michael from his drawing—or his regular after-hours visits.

"Dear Bryony, you've come at last." Mrs. Heath sat forward, peering past Bryony as she slipped into the parlor. Then her face fell. "I hoped you'd bring your grandmother this time. Have you told her how I long to see her again?"

"I'm so sorry. Grandma is—" Bryony bit her lip. Mrs. Heath's lapses in memory seemed worse again and never failed to cause awkward moments and uncomfortable replies. This time, Bryony was able to provide a satisfying but truthful answer: "She's gone to be with my parents."

"Oh, that's good of her. Violet is such a kind and thoughtful person." Mrs. Heath patted Bryony's hand. "Just like you, dear. Now, do sit down and let's find out what new adventures are in store for Yancey and Sabra."

Funny how the woman never lost track of the characters and events in whatever novel they read together—*Cimarron* at the moment, Mrs. Heath's Christmas gift from Michael. But who'd have thought a lady of such refinement would be so enamored with a story about the Oklahoma land rush?

Bryony picked up reading where they'd ended yesterday, but it grew difficult to concentrate with all the racket going on outside the door. Bryony longed to lay the book aside and take a peek at this magnificent new piece of furniture Mr. Heath had ordered. It must be something huge, considering how the floor shook with four sets of pounding footsteps, not to mention all the heaving and grunting.

When a loud thud rattled the figurines displayed in an ornate breakfront, Mrs. Heath gasped. "My word, are we having an earthquake?"

"No, ma'am. It's just the furniture movers."

A puzzled frown turned down the corners of the woman's mouth. "I don't recall . . ."

"Jeremiah said Mr. Heath is getting a new desk." With one finger marking the page, Bryony closed the book. "I'm sure they'll be finished soon. Shall we wait to finish the chapter when it's quieter?"

"Perhaps we should." Mrs. Heath's annoyed expression suddenly brightened. "Oh, of course! It's the partners desk for Sebastian and Michael. They're working together now, you know. Someday Brookbirch Plantation will be Michael's, and he has so much to learn."

A partners desk. No wonder Michael had looked so chagrined. One more sign of the iron grip his father had on his life. Retrieving the needlepoint bookmark she'd been using, Bryony slid it between the pages and laid the novel on a side table. "I'm sure you'd like a nap before teatime. Let me take you—"

"Sebastian took to plantation management right away," Mrs. Heath interrupted, eyes glazed with a faraway look. "I had no brothers, you see, so Brookbirch came to me—but only if I married by the time my father passed on." Her tone hardened. "Otherwise, my good-for-nothing eldest cousin would inherit."

Not sure she should be hearing any of this, Bryony shifted uneasily.

But Mrs. Heath wasn't through talking. Looking toward the tall east windows, she smiled wistfully. "Sebastian didn't have much when we met. Not much except unquenchable ambition and a shrewd, quick mind for business. When Sebastian first asked if he could court me, my daddy was adamant with his refusal. 'Sebastian Heath?' he said with a scowl. 'That poor tenant farmer's son will never amount to anything.'" She laughed softly. "But my Sebastian was persistent, and it didn't take long before Daddy realized this was a man who loved the land, a man who understood not only planting and harvesting but how to turn a profit and keep the plantation going strong. Daddy told me if I didn't marry Sebastian, I might as well join a convent."

Bryony had heard little else after the words *tenant farmer's son*. Hard to picture Sebastian Heath as anything other than the wealthy landowner he'd become. She ground her back teeth together and exhaled sharply. He *knew*. Knew exactly what it felt like to live from season to season, never knowing if the next hailstorm or drought would wipe you out. What had changed in him that he could now ignore his own tenants' struggles? His own *daughter's*?

And now a new question arose: How much about their father's past did Michael and Miranda know? In Bryony's conversations with Michael, he'd never so much as hinted that his father wasn't everything he appeared to be.

"I must say," Bryony began slowly, "Mr. Heath has made quite the name for himself around these parts."

"Indeed." A wistful slant to her eyes, Mrs. Heath kept her gaze fixed on the window. "As Scripture says, no prophet is accepted in his own country. If Sebastian had stayed in Conway, he could never have escaped his roots. Here, he had a chance to truly be somebody."

Somebody? Bryony would rather be a nobody for the rest of her days than turn out like Sebastian Heath.

"He's always felt he had to work like the dickens to earn the respect of our tenants," Mrs. Heath went on. "Had to take a hard stance so they'd learn they couldn't take advantage." The woman's voice fell to a whisper, and Bryony was no longer certain if she realized anyone else was present. "But the children must never know. They adore their father, and it would destroy Sebastian if he ever lost their regard."

Such a feeling of wrathful anguish rose up in Bryony's chest that she could barely keep from crying out. When the man clearly had no regard for his own children's happiness, how dare he expect them to love and honor him in return?

She needed to get out of this room right now, before she blurted out the angry, hurtful words ready to strangle her. Rising on shaky legs, she balled her hands into fists. "You must excuse me, Mrs. Heath." Her voice quavered breathlessly. "I—I'm not feeling well. I'll send for Dancy."

The gray head swiveled slowly in Bryony's direction, and questioning eyes, now clouded with forgetfulness, looked up at her. "I'm so sorry, dear. We'll have tea another time, when you're feeling better. And . . . bring your grandmother next time. I do miss Violet so."

Michael's father stood on his side of the massive partners desk and drew his fingertips admiringly along the burnished mahogany that framed the hand-tooled leather inset. "Well? What do you think?"

Michael doubted his father really wanted to know his thoughts at the moment. He tugged on one of the ornate brass rings and peered into an oak-lined drawer. "It's . . . big."

A burst of proud laughter spilled from his father's throat. "It is, isn't it? Sure glad this room isn't any smaller, or we'd have to knock out a wall." He rubbed his palms together. "Pull up a chair and let's get settled in."

"Dad, it's after four. I think I've had all the excitement I can stand for one day." Michael edged toward the door. "It'll be dark soon, and I'm desperate to stretch my legs."

His glance hardening, Michael's father rolled his padded-leather chair up to the desk and sat with a thud. "These extended evening jaunts of yours are growing tiresome."

"I've told you, after spending all day hunched over ledgers and agricultural journals, my eyes are tired and I'm stiff from neck to knees. I promise, I'll organize my side of the desk first thing in the morning."

"Did you forget already? Tomorrow's the planters' association meeting in Little Rock, and this time I insist you go along. It'll be valuable education for you." Michael's father pulled a stack of file folders from a cardboard box and slapped them onto the desktop. "This meeting is an important one. There are rumors of growing dissatisfaction among tenants and sharecroppers about food shortages."

And that surprises you? With a silent groan, Michael settled in on his side of the desk. Though the idea of attending the meeting of uppity plantation owners made his stomach heave, for once he felt it essential. He might be only one voice among many, but someone had to speak on behalf of the struggling farmers. With the Red Cross stretched to its limits, where else could these people turn except to their landlords?

It was one thing for Michael to quietly pay off their tenants' outstanding credit accounts at the Eden general store. It would be quite another to speak out in a public forum, where he would undoubtedly embarrass his father in front of his peers. Whatever Michael did or said must be with the utmost tact, because he couldn't risk Dad taking out his fury on their tenants—especially Bryony and her family.

He reached into the box at his feet, and when his hand closed around the slender box containing the engraved silver fountain pen, the sick feeling in the pit of his stomach intensified. He needed to get out of here, needed more than ever to escape to Bryony's. She'd still be working for another hour or so, but Miranda would be there.

Along with his sketchbook and pencils.

If the doctor at the rehabilitation hospital had never laid a blank sheet of paper in front of him and told him to draw, if he'd never stumbled across an old book of botanical illustrations in the hospital library, if Bryony Linwood had never walked into his life . . .

He slid the fountain pen into the center drawer and silently pushed it closed. "I'm sorry, Dad. I can't do this today. If I don't get some air, my head will explode."

His father glanced up from arranging files in a lower drawer, and the downturn of his brows reflected genuine concern. "Yes, of course. Sometimes I push too hard, I know." He motioned toward the door. "Go on, then. This will all be here when we get back from Little Rock."

Ten minutes later, Michael climbed behind the wheel of the Chevrolet and backed out of the garage. He caught a brief glimpse of Bryony through the kitchen window, but she was too busy to notice his departure. Just as well, since they both must be careful not to call attention to themselves. He'd bide his time with Miranda and his sketchbook until Bryony made it home.

With the window cranked partway down, he steered the car toward the Rigby farm and let the chill evening breeze sweep away the last remnants of the day's tension.

Sebastian continued filling desk drawers and arranging his workspace until Odette announced the evening meal. He joined Fenella in the dining room and bent to kiss her temple before taking his chair. "How was your day, my dear?"

"Violet's lovely granddaughter visited again." Fenella plucked at her folded napkin as Odette ladled fragrant, golden-colored soup into their bowls. "We're reading *Cimarron*—did I tell you?"

"That's nice." Sebastian spoke through tight lips, each sign of his wife's failing memory a stab to his heart. With a forced smile, he dipped his spoon into the soup and sampled it. "Pumpkin?" he asked with a glance toward Odette.

"No, sir. Squash."

Fenella clucked her tongue and sent him a chiding glance. "Darling, we haven't said grace."

With an embarrassed cough, Sebastian laid down the spoon and clasped her hand. "Sorry, guess I got carried away thinking about my empty stomach." He lowered his head and muttered a quick prayer of thanks, hoping both his wife and the ever watchful Odette would be satisfied with his piety.

Odette returned to the kitchen, and they finished their soup in silence. Fenella dabbed the corners of her mouth with her napkin, then heaved a sigh. "I miss the children when they don't dine with us. Where are they tonight?"

"Other plans, I suppose." Best to change the subject. "Tell me about *Cimarron*. Is it a story I'd enjoy?"

"I'm sure you would!" Fenella's eyes sparkled in the light of the chandelier. "Yancey Cravat, the hero, reminds me a little of you."

Sebastian's chest warmed. He found his wife's hand beneath the table and cradled it on his lap. "Really? How so?"

"Why, you're both adventurous, self-made men"—she winked—"with clever wives always there to keep you in line."

Beneath the graying hair and the age lines etched into her face, Sebastian still saw the woman of beauty and poise he'd fallen in love with nearly forty years ago. His throat thickened. "I owe everything to you, my dearest."

Odette returned with the main course, and Sebastian immediately collected himself. Dangerous letting his emotions take control. Too much responsibility lay upon his shoulders. Michael didn't understand the half of it, the fine line a landowner walked to keep tenants mollified and crop production at its peak.

And this blasted drought! The tenants weren't the only ones suffering. Sebastian had only to look at his account books to realize he'd soon have to cut a few corners, himself, to keep the plantation afloat. Growing up poor had instilled in him the necessity of setting money aside and making prudent investments, so for now they were holding their own. But if the stock market didn't rebound and the drought continued into next spring and summer—

"Sebastian, what's wrong?" Fenella's forehead creased in a worried frown. "You've barely touched your dinner, and you know Odette's fried chicken and gravy is your favorite."

He drew a hand down his face and stared at the peppery cream gravy congealing over a mound of mashed potatoes. A nagging pressure swelled his chest, this unabated urgency to succeed at all costs, to prove himself worthy of the life he'd married into, the wife he adored beyond reason.

Grunting a laugh, he sliced off a bite of meat. "Mind's wandering, that's all. My goodness, this chicken's melt-in-your-mouth delicious, isn't it?"

"Odette's the best cook our family ever had." As Fenella sipped from a glass of white wine, a confused look clouded her eyes. Slowly, she looked toward Sebastian. "Why haven't Miranda and Michael come down to dinner? Please, darling, ring for Violet and have her fetch them from the playroom."

The mouthful of chicken lodged in Sebastian's throat. He forced it down with a gulp of water, but the pain remained. And with it came the realization that he was afraid, more afraid than he'd ever been in his life.

18

When Bryony arrived for work Saturday morning, Callie told her Michael and his father had left before dawn for Little Rock. Bryony's shoulders drooped at the thought of not seeing Michael all day, but she still carried the memory of last night's visit. She'd arrived home just as he burst out in gloating laughter over taking the last trick in a Pinochle game against Grandpa and Rose. Seeing his twinkling eyes and cheeks crinkled with mirth had brought a clutch to her throat. She wanted always to remember him just that way, happy and free-spirited and without a care in the world.

As she and Callie filled the washtub with a week's worth of towels, Callie blew out a mournful sigh. "Miss Esther says I can't go see Mama again until next week. I hate she's so close by and I'm stuck here."

"I'm sure Miss Esther's just being cautious. Your mother sends her love, though." Bryony added detergent to the load. "She was up early this morning. Had bacon and grits on the table by the time I was dressed."

"So she's feeling all right? I mean, with the baby and all?"

"Seems so." Leaving the electric washer to do its job, Bryony and Callie started for the kitchen. Some days, Bryony couldn't stifle her envy over how easy the rich had it. Electric washers, electric lights. A whole big house kept warm by a furnace instead of a wood-burning stove that barely took the chill off the room you were in.

Callie's steps slowed. Eyes downcast, she murmured, "Sure wish we'd get word from my daddy."

Halting, Bryony took Callie by the shoulders and stooped to meet her gaze. "Don't you lose hope. Grandpa sent word to the postmaster over in England"—the Arkansas town about sixty miles away, where Daniel had farmed—"and if any letters come from your daddy, we'll find out soon enough."

"If he isn't sick or dead." Callie sniffed and swiped away a tear. "Can't help it, Bryony. I'm scared for him. For Mama, too."

"I know you are, honey." Bryony scooped the girl into a hug. "But don't you forget, the Lord's watching over him just like he is you and your mama. God brought your mama to a safe place, didn't he? He'll do the same for your daddy."

In the kitchen, they found Odette kneading a mound of bread dough. "Y'all's just in time. They's two more lumps rising in the oven." She lowered her voice and winked at Callie. "And one more I'm bakin' up to send home for your mama, sweet thing."

Bryony spent the rest of the morning up to her elbows in flour and dough, the aroma of baking bread filling the kitchen and making her stomach growl. When Odette wrapped up one of the loaves in a clean napkin and tucked it away where Bryony would find it later, Bryony wondered again how her family would have survived the winter without these extra rations. One thing for sure, they'd have had their fill of turnips and wild rabbits by now.

By early afternoon, Dancy was anxious for Bryony to take over with Mrs. Heath. "She ain't doing so good today," Dancy said with a worried frown. "Kept askin' me to hunt up Miranda so's I could measure the hem of her Confirmation dress. Lordy, that was nigh on twenty years ago!"

Bryony could tell the moment she entered Mrs. Heath's upstairs sitting room that something wasn't right. The tiny woman seemed even more agitated than usual, flitting about the suite and peering out the windows front and back as if expecting someone's arrival any minute.

"Sit down for a bit, and let's read some more of *Cimarron*," Bryony urged. She folded back the afghan on the chaise and patted the embroidered head cushion.

The woman halted mid-stride and cocked her head at Bryony. "Violet? Oh, thank heavens it's you!"

"No, ma'am, it's—"

"Sebastian's gone to town, and I can't find the children. Are they napping in the nursery?"

Bryony chewed her lip. She'd cause less stress if she simply played along. "Mrs. Heath, the children are fine, nothing to worry about." She circled the woman's shoulders with one arm and guided her to the chaise. "Come now, and put your feet up for a bit. You'll overtire yourself with all this fussing."

Her soothing tones finally calmed Mrs. Heath. She laid her head back and closed her eyes, and Bryony spread the afghan over her legs. With tender strokes, Bryony smoothed wisps of silver-streaked curls off the pale, furrowed forehead.

"Dear Violet, such a good friend." Eyes still closed, Mrs. Heath reached for Bryony's hand and patted it. "What would we do without you?"

While the woman dozed, Bryony busied herself straightening the things Mrs. Heath had set askew during her nervous pacing. She'd just sat down with a magazine she'd found in the bedroom when the outer door swung open and Mr. Heath barged in.

Seeing his wife, he stopped short. "She's asleep?"

Bryony stood and laid the magazine on the chair. "It's been a bad day," she whispered.

"Hasn't it, though?" From his shifted glance and tight-lipped scowl, Bryony guessed he had even more troublesome things on his mind. Then, as if shaking those worries off, he strode silently across the carpet to stand by the chaise. He looked across at Bryony. "Has she been worse than usual?"

"I'm afraid so, sir. Thought I'd never get her quieted." Bryony swallowed, wondering how much she should say. Then, resolutely, she lifted her chin. "She misses her children." *Emphasis on the plural*, she wanted to add.

Mr. Heath didn't reply right away. He breathed out long and slow, then turned toward the door. "Let me know when she awakens and I'll send Michael up. We'll be in the office." The grim lines around his mouth deepened. "Yes, I'm afraid it's been a *very* bad day."

Bryony's heart stuttered. Had he and Michael had words again? Had he found out about Miranda?

But no, if he'd learned Miranda was staying at Bryony's house, he'd have said something—more likely, fired her on the spot. She had no choice but to bide her time until Dancy relieved her and hope she could steal a private moment with Michael to ask him what had happened. She hadn't expected to see him at all today, and was frankly surprised he and his father were home so early from their meeting.

And now she felt as jumpy and unsettled as Mrs. Heath had been earlier.

※

Hearing his father's footsteps behind him, Michael turned from the office window. "How's Mother? I hope you didn't worry her with this news."

"Of course not." With an annoyed frown, Michael's father slumped into his desk chair and stretched out one leg. His gaze drifted, weariness stealing the starch from his usually erect posture. "Your mother is resting. According to Bryony, we aren't the only ones for whom this day has gone awry."

Michael closed his eyes briefly. He'd like to go up and see his mother for himself, but Dad had made it clear they needed to discuss their own response to the food riot over in England, Arkansas. News of the disturbance had interrupted the planters' association meeting, and after several landowners voiced loud harangues over the failure of Hoover's relief policies, the meeting had broken up.

Michael was thankful Miranda wasn't anywhere near England right now, or she might well have been caught up in the frenzy. Word was a tenant farmer named Coney got het up with righteous anger when a poor, starving woman came to his door saying she had nothing to feed her children. He'd rounded up some neighbors and driven into town to demand help from the Red Cross, but the local office had already exhausted its resources. As more and more irate farmers converged on the town, a mob scene threatened to erupt, diverted only when store owners began distributing food at no charge.

"Eden wouldn't survive a similar incident," Michael's father said tiredly, "nor would this family's reputation." He sat forward and rubbed his eyes. "Much as it pains me to admit, your do-gooder attitude toward our tenants is likely what's going to save us all. Now, we need to see if we can do more."

Eyes narrowed, Michael eased into the new leather-upholstered chair on his side of the desk. He removed his glasses and twirled the stem between two fingers. It took him a full minute to digest the fact that his father had finally seen the wisdom of generosity. Sebastian Heath may not have fully embraced the concept of ordinary human decency, but his concern for the bottom line would always win out.

With deliberate movements, Michael laid a lined tablet in front of him, then opened the center drawer and took out the silver fountain pen. He uncapped it and glanced across at his father. "Shall we list some ideas?"

For the next hour, they tossed the possibilities back and forth. Setting up a food collection center in one of the storage rooms off the garage. Creating their own voucher system to distribute to their tenants. Making the rounds to each farm no less than weekly to identify and address any urgent needs.

Michael had filled half a page when a knock sounded on the

door. He found Callie standing on the other side, her sweet smile all the more special because she was his niece. With his back to his father, he gave her a meaningful smile of his own. "Yes, Callie, what is it?"

"Bryony said your mama's awake and asking for you."

He glanced over his shoulder, a questioning look in his eyes.

"Go," his father said, reaching across the desk for the tablet. "I'll make a few more notes and be up shortly."

Bryony stopped him at the sitting room door, arms folded and a tired slant to her shoulders. Leaving the door ajar, she edged into the corridor. "I have to warn you, she's expecting a little boy, not a grown man. She's been confused all afternoon."

Tight bands of worry squeezed Michael's lungs. "Will it only confuse her more if I go in?"

Bryony shrugged. "Maybe seeing you will bring her back to the present."

With a muted groan, Michael rested his forearms on the railing overlooking the foyer. "She's slipping further and further away. Today, for the first time, I saw genuine worry in Dad's eyes."

"I saw it, too." Bryony eased up beside him, her nearness both comfort and torture. "Of course, he doesn't say much to me, but I've noticed a fear about him that wasn't there before."

Michael couldn't hold back a snort. "My father, afraid?"

"He loves her, and he's scared to death of losing her."

Shoving away from the railing, Michael strode to the opposite side of the hall. He found himself staring at an oil painting of a vase of roses, vivid pinks and reds on a velvety, blue-black background. Some of the flowers were in full bloom, others drooping and past their prime. The artist had added a faded blossom, the petals turning brown at the edges, lying on the table next to the vase, and the sadness of it all stirred Michael's ever-present compulsion to retreat to the cocoon of his rooms and never come out.

He couldn't give in, not now. His future might be spinning off in a direction he would never have chosen for himself—still wasn't certain he could endure—but the years of solitude were over.

With a resolute sigh, he turned away from the painting. "I'll go in now. Wait here, but stay close."

❧

She'd recognized him, at least. But Michael had a difficult time dancing around the truth about Miranda. With all his heart, he wished he could tell his mother that Miranda had come home, if only briefly, and now resided only a short distance away.

When his mother grew restless, tossing off the afghan and pacing the suite like a cornered animal, he called for Bryony. She came upstairs moments later with the tea tray.

"It's later than usual, but I thought this might help." She edged past him to set the tray on the table by the east windows.

The distraction proved exactly what his mother needed. As she took her place at the table, she peered up into Bryony's eyes. "Wait . . . you're not Violet, are you?"

"No, ma'am. Violet's my grandmother." Bryony passed her a teacup. "I'm Bryony, remember? We've been reading *Cimarron* together."

With a clear-eyed smile, Michael's mother shifted her gaze to him. "I remember. You gave me the book for Christmas, didn't you, son?"

He could melt with relief. "Yes, Mother, that's right."

He took the chair opposite his mother, and as Bryony served him a cup of tea, she cast him a private glance, misty-eyed and heavy with meaning.

The three of them enjoyed tea and gingersnaps together, and about the time they'd emptied the teapot, Michael's father sidled into the room. Jaw set, he stood to one side as if uncertain whether he should stay.

Michael couldn't say what prompted his actions—perhaps the

hint of loneliness in his father's eyes—but he held out the cookie plate. "There are two left. Come sit with us."

Her face lighting up, Michael's mother clasped her hands beneath her chin. "Oh, darling, do! We're having such a lovely chat. You know Bryony, don't you—Violet's sweet granddaughter?"

Looking suddenly nervous, Bryony stood. "I'll fetch more tea."

"Not necessary." Michael's father cleared his throat as he circled to the far side of the table and pulled out the fourth chair. "Stay, Miss Linwood. I wouldn't want to break up the party."

"I'm sorry, I can't. It's getting late, and I have . . . other things to see to." Bryony gathered empty cups and plates onto the tray. Under her breath, she added, "I'll find Dancy and send her in."

Michael slid back his chair and laid his napkin on the table. "If you'll excuse me, Mother, I'll see Miss Linwood out."

"Thank you, dear." She patted her husband's hand. "We've raised such a gentleman, haven't we, darling?"

Dad angled his head toward Michael, one eye narrowed in a knowing glimmer. His silent appraisal stretched interminably, until he muttered a tight-lipped "Indeed."

All the way to the door, Michael felt his father's gaze drilling through his spine. Bryony strode purposefully in front of him, all her attention focused on the tea tray. She didn't look back until the door closed behind them, and even then, she didn't stop. Michael could barely keep up with her hurried descent down the back stairs.

Reaching the bottom, she whirled around abruptly. Dishes clattered on the tray as Michael took a hit to the abdomen. He grabbed the tray handles, his fingers closing around Bryony's and both of them struggling for breath.

"He knows, Michael. Did you see the look he gave you?"

A weary sigh raked Michael's lungs. He ushered Bryony into the deserted workroom down the servants' hall, then pried the tray from her grip and set it on the table. Taking her by the shoulders, he looked deeply into her panicked eyes. "I can handle my father.

Whatever he *thinks* he knows, I promise you, it won't stop us from being together."

"Don't say things like that." Bryony wrenched away. "There's too much at stake—Miranda, Callie. Your art."

He encircled her from behind, his cheek nestled against her messy bun. When he exhaled softly across the top of her ear, she shivered and snuggled closer. "What about you, Bryony? What about *us*? You've made me come alive again, given me hope when I had none. I won't lose you."

She swiveled and burrowed deeper into his chest. Her whole body trembled with suppressed sobs, while he stroked her hair and feathered her forehead with tender kisses.

Her nearness undid him, awakening needs he'd denied for too long. His breath grew shallow, his pulse a staccato counterpoint. Hand at her nape, he drew her head back and gazed into irresistible pools of dusky brown. His glance skimmed her tear-streaked cheeks, the curve of her nose, the bow of her lips. With a quivering sigh, he lowered his mouth upon hers and tasted the salt of her tears. The kiss, gently insistent at first, intensified with a hunger he couldn't control, and her pliant submission told him she wanted this as much as he.

"No . . . we mustn't," she whispered against his lips. Her fists came up between them, and she lowered her head against his breastbone.

Michael forced his breathing to slow and his mind away from thoughts he had no right to be thinking. "I'd never hurt you, Bryony. Please believe me."

"I do," she said, lifting her head. With a regretful smile, she widened the space between them and cradled his cheek with her palm. "But can't you see what a dangerous game we've been playing? You're dividing yourself between two worlds and trying to keep one secret from the other. What happens when the secrets are out? How many people—you, most of all—will be hurt then?"

A part of him knew she was right. The strain of pretense wore on him daily, but he'd convinced himself the rewards were worth it.

Now, he saw clearly how the duplicity ate at Bryony. After all she'd done for him, for his family, he couldn't bear it.

While he wrestled with answers, anything to fix this horrible mess piling up like rubble around him, Bryony quietly retrieved the tea tray. "I have to go," she stated flatly. Before he could stop her, she bustled out the door.

◦◦◦

"You been crying." Callie's words carried both concern and accusation. "Tell me right now, did Mr. Heath find out about Mama?"

"No, nothing like that." Bryony concentrated on not dropping the teacup as she swished it through soapy water. She knew her eyes must be red and swollen, and hoped the same wasn't true of her bruised lips.

Callie set down the basket of folded laundry she'd brought in from the line, then whisked off her sweater and reached for a flour-sack dishtowel. She joined Bryony at the sink. "Then why? Are you in trouble about something?"

"Callie Vargas, you ask way too many questions."

A door slammed behind them, and both girls spun around. Half hoping and half afraid it might be Michael, Bryony sagged against the sink when she saw it was only Odette.

The plump cook shook her finger at Bryony. "Y'all don't be bandying the Vargas name so loud. Around here she's just Callie, and we best not forget."

More evidence of the fine line they walked to keep Miranda's secret. "I wasn't thinking. I'm sorry." Turning back to the sink, Bryony rinsed a saucer and handed it to Callie.

Dear God, she was so tired! Not just from cleaning and laundry and tending to Mrs. Heath, but from the sheer effort required to hold in all these emotions screaming for release. Outrage at Sebastian Heath for the cruelty he'd inflicted on his own children.

Despair over her powerlessness to stave off Mrs. Heath's decline. Constant anxiety for her family's security and wellbeing.

Frustration with Michael for making her want something she could never have.

They put away the last of the dishes, and Callie hefted her basket of laundry to take upstairs. Bryony's final task of the day was to help Odette get supper started. Once she'd peeled the potatoes, rolled out biscuit dough, and set the table, she grabbed her coat and made a hasty exit. The need to get home to her own loving family sped her steps down the darkening road.

For the first time since Miranda's entry into their lives, Bryony prayed Michael wouldn't intrude upon their evening. He made it impossible to think clearly, when it grew more urgent than ever that she must.

There was a simple answer, if not an easy one. She'd hired on at the Heaths' with the hope of protecting her family, but now every day working there only compounded the risk to her loved ones . . . to her own heart.

But if she quit, how would her family survive? Winter hadn't brought the hoped-for end to the drought, and Grandpa couldn't afford another year of failed crops. They might do all right as long as Miranda stayed and Odette kept sending over extra food. But what would happen if Miranda's husband returned, or if he sent word for her and Callie to join him up north—or if Sebastian found out and put an end to this whole situation once and for all?

And Larkspur, studying to be a teacher. Bryony wouldn't risk destroying her sister's dream for anything.

When she turned up the lane toward home, a glimmer of lantern light shone in the parlor windows and reminded her of the words from a psalm: *Thy word is a lamp unto my feet, and a light unto my path.* The path before her seemed so dim these days, and fraught with stones and potholes ready to trip her at the first misstep. More than ever, she missed her happy childhood in the cozy cottage back in Memphis, with Mama and Daddy always near and her only worry keeping her little sisters from kidnapping her favorite doll.

Then, arriving home, she trudged through the back door and faced a whole new set of worries.

Grandpa sat at the kitchen table with a bloodstained cloth pressed to the side of his head. He shot Bryony a stubborn glare. "Don't get yourself all in a lather. It ain't that bad."

"Not that bad? Grandpa, you're hurt!" Bryony slung her coat on an empty chair as she rushed over. Roughly, she moved his hand so she could examine the wound. "What happened? Who did this?"

Miranda brought a clean, wet cloth and exchanged it for the soiled one. "We just got back from England. Folks there were getting carried away trying to get food, and someone accidentally hit your grandpa with a rake handle."

Bryony gasped. "You got hit with a *rake?*"

"I said to calm down." Grandpa shoved Bryony's probing fingers away and held the cloth to his wound.

"It's my fault," Miranda said. "I couldn't wait a day longer to find out if Daniel's sent word, and I also wanted to get a few things from my house. Your grandpa offered to drive me over. We had no idea what we were getting into."

"Well, I hope it was worth it." Weak with worry, Bryony sank onto a chair.

Miranda's lower lip trembled. "It was. Daniel's letter came yesterday."

Sorry for her outburst, Bryony reached for Miranda's hand. "Thank the Lord! Is he all right? Did he find work?"

"He's fine, and he did." Miranda's eyes glistened. "He made it nearly to Milwaukee before he did, though. Times are tough every-where, but he finally got hired to work the loading dock at a canning factory."

"That's . . . that's good. I suppose he'll be sending for you soon."

"Not right away. He needs to save up enough for our train tickets." Miranda turned her attention to Grandpa's injury, inspecting it with much more gentleness than Bryony had used.

"Well, you can certainly stay with us as long as you need to." Hoping to conceal her surge of relief, Bryony strode to the stove, where a kettle of thick soup simmered. She gave it a stir and inhaled the rich aromas of potatoes, onions, and savory bits of left-over ham, extravagances they'd have to forgo when Miranda left. "This looks delicious. Where's Rose?"

"Doing *my* chores," Grandpa said with a growl.

Miranda clucked her tongue. "You should let me stitch this up, Mr. Rigby. I've tended worse for Daniel."

The relief Bryony felt moments before made a sudden, nause-ating shift toward jealousy. This was *her* home, *her* family, and the idea that Miranda Heath Vargas had supplanted her as matron of the house and caregiver to her loved ones—well, it just wasn't fair!

Yes, her response was illogical and entirely out of proportion, but Bryony couldn't quell the tumult of emotions. One hand on her roiling stomach, the other pressed hard against her throbbing temple, she made for the bedroom before another flood of tears gushed out.

It wasn't long before Rose tiptoed in and sat on the edge of the bed. Her overalls smelled of straw and manure. "Bry, are you sick? Grandpa said you flew out of the kitchen like the devil himself was chasing you."

"I'm tired, Rosie. Just so tired I could die."

Rose laid the back of her hand against Bryony's forehead. "You don't feel feverish. Want me to bring you some soup?"

"Not hungry." Sniffling, Bryony mopped her wet cheeks with the hem of the pillowcase. "Just leave me be, okay?"

"I *won't* leave you be. Bry, you're scaring me."

Knowing her baby sister was too stubborn to give up, Bryony heaved a groan and rolled onto her back. She reached up to tuck one of Rose's wild copper curls behind her ear. "Don't mind me, honey. It's been a hard day, that's all."

Rose's mouth hardened. "I wish you never had to go to work for the Heaths."

"I wish a lot of things were different. But they're not, and there's nothing we can do to change them." Bryony turned onto her side again, facing the wall. "Go have your supper, Rosie, and stop fussing over me. By tomorrow I'll be my old self again."

❧ 19 ❧

Rose set Grandpa's morning oatmeal before him, then shot another glance toward the bedroom. "Bry was so tired last night. I don't have the heart to wake her, but if she doesn't get up soon, she'll be late for work."

"Let her sleep." Grandpa sipped his chicory. "After breakfast, you take the pickup over to the Heaths' and tell 'em Bryony's ailing. They'll have to do without her for today."

Miranda took the chair across from Grandpa. "I wish I could do more to make things easier for Bryony. At least I'm getting stronger, thanks to your kindness."

"You've helped plenty already." Rose sat down to her own bowl of oatmeal. "Lord knows I'm grateful not to be doing all the cooking. Gives me more time to help Grandpa with farm chores."

"What there is left of this ol' farm," Grandpa said with a snort. "Ain't lookin' good for spring planting, 'less we get some good, long rains between now and then."

Rose didn't like hearing her grandpa talk that way, and she didn't like the worry lines around his eyes every time he looked skyward in search of nonexistent rainclouds. It was hard enough keeping her own spirits up when Grandpa seemed more discouraged every day. And now Bryony, who'd always been the family's pillar of strength—to see her so beaten down and despondent made Rose's heart clench with fears she didn't want to name.

She staved them off for the moment by giving all her attention to downing her breakfast. After dropping her dishes in the sink, she grabbed her coat and a tattered wool cap and headed out to the pickup. Fifteen minutes later, she parked in front of the Heath mansion and set the brake.

Rose had never seen the house up close before, and now it loomed over her like a magnificent palace. She probably should have parked around back and looked for the servants' door, but she had as much right to ring the front bell as the next person. The Heaths might be rich, holding sway over a big chunk of Monroe County, but she was pretty sure ol' Sebastian pulled his pants on one leg at a time just like everybody else.

She was more than a little disappointed when Jeremiah, not Sebastian Heath himself, answered the door. The aging manservant cocked a brow. Worry flickered behind his dark eyes, but he kept his tone friendly, giving nothing away to listening ears. "Good day, Miss Linwood. What brings you by so early on a Sabbath morn?"

"I came to say Bryony won't be working today. She's feeling poorly and needs to stay home."

"I'm so sorry. Is there anything—"

Michael appeared behind Jeremiah, cutting him off. "What's this about Bryony?"

Rose knew better than to let on she and Michael were acquainted. She removed her cap and curled her fingers around the brim. "She's not well, sir. Nothing serious, just working too hard, I reckon." She slanted him a meaningful glance. "Grandpa's run-in with those farmers over yonder in England kinda worried her, too."

"He was there?" Michael stepped past Jeremiah onto the porch, his gaze probing. "Anyone else with him?"

"He took a friend. They had a scare, but they came through all right." Rose was right proud of herself for managing this double-talk so well. "Least they took care of the business they went for." She winked. "Good news all around."

"I see." Michael exchanged glances with Jeremiah before turning his gaze back upon Rose. "And your sister? Does she need anything? Should she see a doctor?"

"Rest is what Bryony needs most of all." More rest than a single day could offer, if Rose were any judge. "Anyway, I just came to let y'all know. Best be on my way."

"Wait." Michael stayed her with his hand. "Jeremiah, have Odette pack up some food to send home with Miss Linwood. Something hearty and healthful."

The old servant nodded and bustled away.

Pulling the door partway closed, Michael peered into Rose's eyes. He kept his voice low as he asked, "Is she really all right?"

At the deep concern behind his question, Rose's assurance wavered. She pictured Bryony's tear-streaked face as she lay on the bed last night, exhaustion and hopelessness dimming her usually bright expression. To answer Michael, Rose could only shrug. "If you pray much, now would be a good time."

◈

"What's all the commotion about?" Michael's father caught him at the foot of the stairs.

"It was Rose Linwood, Bryony's sister. Bryony's ill and can't work today. I sent the girl home with a basket of food." Michael lifted his chin, daring his father to question his actions. "It seemed the least we could do."

"Another of your charitable gestures." His father nodded thoughtfully. "After your mother and I return from Mass, I'll have Odette put together baskets for the rest of our tenants. You and I will deliver them this afternoon."

Stunned into silence, Michael gave a shaky nod. Apparently, yesterday's incident in England had fully opened the man's eyes to the plight of Arkansas' tenant farmers and sharecroppers.

Michael's father strode across the foyer and peered into a gilt-framed mirror to adjust his tie. "Sure you won't come to church with us? Father Dempsey asks about you every week."

For the first time in a long time, Michael considered changing his mind. No doubt he'd benefit greatly from what counsel their perceptive family priest could offer, and perhaps one day soon he'd make a private appointment. But the idea of mingling with an entire congregation consisting of a few friends and many more who were strangers intimidated him far more than a trip into Eden or paying calls on tenant families. It had been strain enough attending the planters' meeting yesterday.

He spoke to his father's reflection in the mirror. "I can't, not yet. I don't expect you to understand what it's like for me, but I hope you can see I'm trying."

"I do, and I appreciate it." Dad checked his watch. The corner of his mouth twitched. "There's something else we must address, so don't leave on one of your solitary jaunts before I'm back from Mass."

Michael cringed inwardly at his father's tone. "That sounds ominous."

"We'll speak after church. Here comes your mother. Let's go in to breakfast."

Stepping regally down the stairs, Mother held to the rail with one hand, the other looped through Dancy's arm. Michael noticed his mother wore the garnet-studded bracelet Dad had given her for Christmas. In addition, she wore an aura of tranquility that Michael realized was typical of every Sunday morning, as if the anticipation of the worship service superseded her fretfulness and memory lapses.

An hour later, as Mother waited near the front door for Dad to bring the car around, she walked her fingers up the sleeve of Michael's sweater. Eyes clear and sparkling, she patted his shoulder. "I light a candle for you and your sister every Sunday. One Sunday soon you'll come with us." She whispered out a wistful sigh. "And someday Miranda will come home."

Dad pulled up outside, and Michael helped his mother into the LaSalle. Watching them drive away, he wondered again what his father had on his mind—and hoped it had nothing to do with his having learned where Miranda was staying.

He also hoped it had nothing to do with the odd look his father had given him moments before he followed Bryony downstairs yesterday after tea. Bryony was right—only a fragile wall separated the reality of his life and the dreams he refused to let go. If he didn't remain vigilant, he could lose everything.

At least while his parents were at Mass and half the servants had the day off, he could let down his guard briefly. At other times, even his own rooms weren't inviolate, for he could never be certain Dad wouldn't come barging upstairs and insist on discussing some facet of plantation business.

He'd like to drive over to the Rigby farm and check on Bryony. It was completely out of character for her to miss work on a whim, so Rose's report of her illness concerned him. Her tears yesterday, her look of utter hopelessness when she'd left the workroom, had worried him plenty, robbing him of sleep last night.

But something told him he should keep his distance for now, give her time to rest and perhaps to think more clearly than either of them had done these past weeks.

He needed to do the same. And he did his best thinking with pencil in hand.

Upstairs in his rooms, he latched the outer door, then took a key from his pocket and unlocked the bottom drawer inside his wardrobe. Since Christmas at Bryony's, he'd been stashing loose papers there, along with a few pencils—nothing so formal as a real sketchbook or quality drawing tools, but scraps and pencil nubs he'd confiscated from the office when Dad didn't notice. It seemed once Bryony's gift had reignited his passion for drawing, he couldn't snuff it out even when he returned home, and so sometimes late at night when everyone else was abed, he'd take out some paper and sketch whatever bloomed in his imagination.

This morning, he brought out the drawings he'd begun several nights ago after the last time he'd visited with Miranda and Callie together. Watching them, shades different in coloring yet as close and loving as a mother and daughter could ever be, Michael longed to capture the memory on paper. Until recently, he'd never attempted to draw a human likeness. Flowers, trees, and shrubs seemed far less threatening and judgmental than most people he'd known. He wasn't particularly good at human faces yet, either, but Miranda's and Callie's features grew more recognizable with each practice sketch he attempted. Someday, when he'd mastered his technique, he'd start fresh on good paper and then ask Jeremiah to have the portrait framed as a gift for his sister and niece.

With at least a couple of hours before his parents arrived home from church, Michael feasted on the chance to adjust and add to his latest attempt. As soon as he heard the LaSalle rumbling up the lane, he scooped up his papers and pencils and shut them away in the wardrobe. He reached the foyer a few moments before his parents entered through the front door.

Dad rang for Jeremiah to return the car to the garage, then escorted Michael's mother into the parlor and settled her into a comfortable chair. She looked tired but content. Dancy appeared from somewhere at the rear of the house, and while she attended to Michael's mother, his father motioned him down the hall to the office.

Whatever serenity Michael had garnered during his time alone instantly vanished. "Dad, it's Sunday. You aren't intending to talk business, are you?"

"Not the kind you're thinking of, at any rate." His father closed the door. "Sit down."

Michael wasn't sure he wanted to. "Odette will be calling us to dinner soon. Can't this wait?"

"No time like the present." A grim smile curved Dad's mouth as he drew up the chair on his side of the desk. "Hopefully this won't take long."

Michael swallowed and sat down. And waited.

Elbows on the chair arms, hands lying loosely in his lap, Dad inhaled long and slow, then blew out his breath between tight lips. "I'll be blunt. Are you having a fling with the hired help?"

"A *fling*?" Indignation propelled Michael to his feet. "How dare you—"

He snapped his mouth shut, all too aware of the dangers of saying the wrong thing.

With nothing more than a pointed look, his father instructed him to sit. "Let me rephrase my question. Michael, are you developing feelings for Bryony Linwood?"

There was no point in lying, because the truth was surely carved into every line of Michael's face. He curled his fingers around the arms of his chair. "Whatever you may suspect of me, be assured Bryony's virtue is unimpeachable. I beg you, Dad, don't take this out on her."

"I won't, unless you give me reason to. But you know what happened to your sister when she let herself be seduced by a workman." Michael's father sat forward, his gaze penetrating. "Don't repeat Miranda's mistakes."

⚜

Midweek brought a drop in temperature, so when Bryony finished work on Wednesday, she welcomed the sight of Grandpa's old pickup waiting for her at the end of the Heaths' drive. Her threadbare coat was usually plenty warm for Arkansas winters, but it didn't reach down to her toes, already going numb from the short walk down the lane.

Rose sat behind the wheel. "You're gonna love what Miranda's got in the oven tonight. Shepherd's pie—it'll warm you right up."

"Mmm, sounds wonderful." Bryony tucked her fingers deep into the opposite coat sleeves. "I hope she's teaching you all her recipes so you can make them after she leaves."

It was dark in the pickup, but Bryony could imagine her sister's eye roll. "She's trying," Rose said, "but I can guarantee you, if there's any way to mess 'em up, I'll find it."

Too tired to keep up conversation, Bryony replied with a weak chuckle. If not for the bumpy road, she might have dozed off. What she wouldn't give for a few more lazy days like she'd enjoyed last Sunday. Not that she'd intended to oversleep and miss work, but after learning Grandpa had sent Rose over to make excuses for her, she hadn't fussed for long. Especially when Miranda brought her breakfast on a tray and then let her drift back to sleep until nearly noon. She hadn't even heard Grandpa and Rose leave for church.

The respite had been good for her, in more ways than one. She hadn't realized how desperately she needed this time to herself to think and pray about what her future held . . . or didn't.

She roused as Rose drove up beside the barn and shut off the motor. Frowning toward the house, she murmured, "Is he here?"

Lips flattened, Rose shook her head. "Left about the time I came for you. He wanted to wait, but he'd already promised his mama he'd be home for supper."

Just as well. Easier on both of them the less they saw of each other.

Except she missed him something awful. It was pure torture going to work every day where only walls and doors separated them, where at any moment she might turn a corner and find him right in front of her and wearing a tender smile meant just for her. She cringed to think how often she'd wished exactly that, while praying for both their sakes that her wish didn't come true.

By the time Bryony and Rose hung up their coats, Miranda had supper on the table. The oniony aroma of shepherd's pie baked with a toasty topping of mashed potatoes made Bryony's stomach groan in anticipation.

"Hope it tastes as good with rabbit," Miranda said as she took her seat. "Beef's harder to come by these days, and your grandpa sure is handy with those traps."

Grandpa offered grace then dished up healthy servings onto each of their plates. "We got it mighty good compared to most folks. Best be grateful and enjoy the extra provisions while we got 'em."

"That reminds me." Rose chewed and swallowed. "I saw Caleb again when I picked up the mail. He said Mr. Heath and Michael came by on Sunday with a big basket of food."

Bryony's fork stopped midway to her mouth. "Both of them? Together?"

"Caleb and his mama could hardly believe how much there was." Rose scooped up another forkful. "And Caleb says he heard other tenants got food baskets, too."

A disbelieving laugh bubbled up from Miranda's chest. "Michael never said a word. He must have done some fancy talking to shake loose Daddy's tight fists."

Grandpa harrumphed. "More'n likely Sebastian saw the sense of staving off a food riot in Eden like they had over in England. The man may be stingy, but he ain't stupid."

Bryony wasn't so sure about the last part. What other word besides *stupid* so aptly described a man who'd cast aside one of his children and scorn the other's God-given talent?

On the other hand, no one could argue the fact of Michael's favorable influence on his father's business practices. Helping to manage the plantation might not be the life Michael would have chosen for himself, but he was definitely making a positive difference in the lives of the Brookbirch Plantation tenants.

After supper, Bryony helped with the dishes, then washed out her maid's dress and apron before crawling into bed. She dreamed Michael came to her door with a huge, gingham-covered basket. His warm smile promised abundance, but when he pulled the cloth aside to show her what he'd brought, a gaping black pit opened up, and she felt herself tumbling helplessly into the abyss.

She awoke in a cold sweat and gasping for air.

"It's just a dream, Bry." Rose loomed over her, stroking her hair off her face. "You're all right now. Let it go."

Bryony sat up and rubbed her eyes. If only it were so easy to scrub away the images from her dream. "Is it morning yet?"

"Barely. Your alarm would have gone off in another ten minutes." Rose shrugged into a tattered flannel robe that once belonged to their dad. She handed Bryony her own, then struck a match to light the kerosene lantern on the dresser. "What were you dreaming, anyway?"

"Just something crazy." She heard Grandpa rustling about in the kitchen and hurried in to help get breakfast started.

"Coffee's on—or what passes for coffee these days." Grandpa cast a wistful glance toward the canister where he'd stored the coffee beans Larkspur had given him for Christmas. He'd ground the last of them yesterday so was back to full-strength chicory.

Bryony helped herself to a cup, even knowing it wouldn't jolt her eyes open like real coffee would, and she could really use a good, strong kick this morning to banish the remnants of those unnerving dream images.

But the truth was, her life felt a whole lot like that deep, dark hole. A lot of nothing and falling fast.

Or was the dream trying to tell her something else, like maybe she was headed into an unknown future and only Michael could show her the way?

***

"Don't do this to me, Bryony." His face like flint, Michael blocked her exit from the servants' workroom.

She tried to laugh, but it sounded more like a whimper. "Do what? I'm just fetching my cleaning supplies."

"Don't keep pretending I don't exist." He set his right hand against the doorframe just above eye level.

Pretending is the only way I can survive working here, she wanted to say. She drew her glance away from the ink stains between his first and second fingers, evidence of the hours he spent keeping the Brookbirch ledgers up to date. She couldn't bring herself to look into his accusing expression, either, so she stared past his shoulder instead. "You shouldn't be here. Someone could see—"

He slapped his hand hard against the jamb, startling her into silence. Then his eyes fell shut, and he folded his fingers into a fist. His whole body trembled with a harsh exhalation. When he spoke again, his tone softened. "It's been nearly a week since you've so much as glanced my way. I see you coming down the hall, and you duck through an open door or turn in the opposite direction."

She found the courage to meet his gaze. "Tell me you haven't done the same thing."

His clenched jaw said he couldn't deny it. He stepped farther into the room, giving her no choice but to retreat. "Only to protect you, Bryony . . . and myself." He took the pail of cleaning supplies from her and set it on the table, then kicked the door shut with his heel.

"Michael—" She shouldn't be afraid, but she was. Not that Michael might try to take advantage, but of her own weak will. She *wanted* to be alone with him, wanted it desperately. She wanted his kisses, his whispered words of affection like gossamer against her ear. She wanted his arms around her, binding her to him so tightly that she could feel his heartbeat pulsing against her breastbone, her own thundering back in reply.

But he stayed near the door, hands at his sides. "Do you love me enough to trust me?"

She felt for the edge of the table, needing its support. With her throat clamped shut, she could only nod.

"Good. That's all I ask." Reaching behind, he found the knob and opened the door. His expression softening, he murmured, "I'll see you tonight."

Seconds later he was gone, leaving only the memory of his smile and a terrible, relentless yearning.

"I'll see you tonight."

The prospect of returning home at the end of the day to find him waiting brought more hope than she had any right to feel.

Michael had helped her make up her mind about one thing, though. Whatever the deep, dark, unknown future held, it didn't matter nearly as much as the decisions Bryony made right here in the present. She'd always been strong, determined, utterly unswerving in her commitment to protect and care for those she loved—a list that now included Michael. It wasn't enough merely that she'd encouraged him to draw again. Slipping away to Bryony's house for an hour or two at a time, only to leave his sketchbook and pencils behind at the end of his visit? The temporary escape might nourish his spirit, but it didn't change his circumstances. Anger bristled again over everything Sebastian Heath's cruelty had cost his son.

The familiar click of Miss Esther's heels sounded in the hallway. When the head housekeeper peered into the workroom and saw Bryony, her brows puckered in surprise. "Why aren't you upstairs yet? Alice has a good half-hour's head start on you."

Bryony snatched up the cleaning pail, then took one of the dust mops off the wall rack. "I was checking my supplies. I'm going up right now."

The steely-eyed woman didn't intimidate Bryony as she had at first, but Bryony still wasn't of a mind to get on her bad side. She ducked passed Miss Esther and scurried up the back stairs. At least Alice would be cleaning the bathrooms. Bryony's tasks for today included dusting, polishing furniture, and sweeping floors in the family's private rooms. Knowing Michael would be in the office with his father, she decided to clean his suite first and quickly. Her fragile emotions couldn't risk another encounter so soon.

As Bryony slipped inside Michael's sitting room, the comfortably masculine surroundings gave her pause. Morning sun angled a swath through the south-facing windows, and she could imagine Michael sitting at the table, his drawing supplies spread out before him. This was where he belonged—not in secrecy and self-imposed solitude, but with the freedom to pursue his true gifts.

With a quiet sigh, Bryony set to work. Once she'd made the rounds with her feather duster and polishing cloth, she gathered up the smaller rugs to take outside for a good shaking, then ran the dust mop across the bare wood floors. She'd come back later with the carpet sweeper for the big Persian rug in the sitting room.

When she swept beneath the wardrobe in Michael's bedroom, the dust mop brought out a wrinkled scrap of paper. Bryony bent to pick it up and recognized Odette's chicken-scratch printing: *salt, flour, lard, apples, rump roast* . . . Obviously a grocery list. Bryony was about to crumple the paper and stuff it in her pocket to discard later when she noticed something on the back.

"Oh . . . oh!" The mop handle clattered to the floor, and Bryony held her breath as she smoothed open the scrap for a better look. It was a crude sketch, but there was no mistaking the subjects—Miranda and Callie, side by side and looking so much like mother and daughter that no one could mistake them for anything else.

"Bryony, you in here?" Alice lumbered through the sitting room and dropped her cleaning supplies at the bedroom door. "There you are. Help me with the bathroom and I'll shake out those rugs for you. . . . Bryony?"

She realized her mouth hung open, the sketch pinched between the fingers of both hands. Still, she couldn't make herself move or speak.

"For Pete's sake, girl, you look like you've seen a ghost." Alice inched closer. "What is that you got there?"

With shaking hands, Bryony held the paper out for Alice to see.

Alice gasped, her stunned look fading into an admiring smile. "Ain't they the prettiest things ever! Mister Michael drew this? Why, he's—"

Men's voices sounded in the upstairs hallway, and both Alice and Bryony froze.

"Don't dally, Michael." Sebastian's tone grew louder with each step. "We can't be late for this appointment."

"Five minutes is all I need." Michael charged through the sitting room. At the bedroom door he stopped short, his gaze shifting from Alice to Bryony. His Adam's apple jerked. "Sorry, I'll just grab what I came for and get out of your way."

"Michael." The name tore from Bryony's throat on a raspy

whisper. She clutched the drawing against her abdomen and gave her head a rapid shake.

His glance slid to the paper, and she could tell the moment he guessed what she held. He started to back out of the room.

Before he could, his father came up behind him. "Get a move on, Michael. The banker won't wait all day." Then he glimpsed Bryony, and his impatient scowl deepened. He dismissed the women with a wave of his hand. "You can finish later. We're in a hurry."

Bryony would like nothing better than to escape Sebastian's scrutiny. If she tried to conceal the sketch now, though, she'd only draw Sebastian's attention, so she nonchalantly lowered the paper to her side. She nudged Alice, and they sidled toward the door.

Then Bryony stumbled over Alice's cleaning pail. When she tried to catch herself, the sketch fluttered to the floor.

And landed at Sebastian's feet.

$\maltese$ 2 0 $\maltese$

Michael's heart stopped. He lunged for the sketch.

But not quickly enough. His father snatched up the paper and held it out to Bryony. "You dropped a bit of trash."

Her face had turned a sickly pale. She darted a glance at Michael. "Yes. Thank you."

"Never mind, I'll dispose of it." Michael's father nodded toward the outer door. "Go along, now. We're in a hurry."

Bryony didn't move, her gaze riveted to the paper.

Striving for a casual air, Michael stepped between Bryony and his father and held out his hand. "I'll take it, Dad." He heard the tension in his own voice but hoped his father didn't. "Why don't you bring the car around? I'll meet you out front."

For the first time, Michael's father actually looked at the scrap he held. He glanced over the grocery list—the one Michael remembered all too well slipping into his pocket when he found it on the seat of the Chevrolet one afternoon—then flipped it over to see the other side. "What . . ."

"It's nothing." Michael tried again to take the paper. "Just rubbish. I'll toss it out."

Swiveling away, his father paced to the window. The grim set of his jaw hardened even more. His chest rose and fell in slow, deliberate breaths.

"Dad—"

A hand shot up, halting Michael mid-stride. "This is Miranda—that's obvious." His father glowered his disapproval, whether of the subject of the sketch or the fact that Michael had been drawing at all, Michael couldn't be certain.

Probably both.

"And the girl?"

Uncomfortably aware that both Bryony and Alice still watched from the doorway, Michael gathered what courage he had. It was long past time to confront his father with the truth. A touch of sarcasm lacing his tone, he said, "You don't recognize your own granddaughter?"

The glower deepened. Michael's father jabbed his finger at the drawing of Callie. "*This* is the half-breed child your sister gave birth to? You've seen her? Where?"

Michael took another step forward. His voice shook with indignation. "If you weren't so blind, so completely oblivious to everything beyond your own personal interests, you'd realize she's been living and working right here under your nose."

"Who? *Who?*" Michael's father whirled toward him, his face scarlet with rage.

Bryony's pleading voice sounded behind him. "Don't, Michael. Please!"

His father shot Bryony a disbelieving glare. "So now even the hired help knows more about my business than I do?" He looked again at the drawing, massaging his upper lip with the pads of two fingers. "Wait. I do know this face. She's the kitchen helper Esther hired awhile back—the girl who took over the laundry."

"Callie. Her name is Callie." Michael ignored Bryony's tug on his arm. He was sick to death of cowering before his father's supercilious tyranny. "When she was old enough, Miranda sent her here to work because she knew Esther and Odette would look after her."

Crushing the paper in his fist, Michael's father turned slowly to the window. Teeth clenched, he muttered, "I suppose you've known all along. Am I the only one besides your mother who's been kept in the dark?"

"I didn't know either, not until a few days after Miranda came back. Dad, please." Michael laid a hand upon his father's arm. "Do the right thing. Forgive Miranda and acknowledge Callie as—"

"I will *not*!" The thunderous retort shook the crystal globes of the dresser lamps. Michael's father flung the wad of paper across the floor and bolted from the room. Seconds later, the outer door slammed.

In the deafening silence, Michael could only stare at Bryony in shock and helplessness. Some distant part of his brain registered that Alice had left, most likely to inform Esther and Odette that the truth had finally come out.

"This is my fault," Bryony whimpered.

"No, no." Shaking off his stupor, Michael drew her into his arms. "We're all to blame, thinking we could keep him from discovering the truth." Waves of self-recrimination engulfed him. "Me most of all, for my stupid, stupid carelessness."

Bryony looked up at him, her tear-filled eyes dark with worry. "If he hurts Callie—"

"I'll make sure he doesn't, whatever it takes." Michael kissed her temple. "I'd better go after him. Will you be all right?"

She nodded, but as she eased from his embrace, she didn't look at all reassured. As he turned to go, her hand clamped down on his arm. "Promise me, Michael. Just like you asked your father to do the right thing, I'm asking you."

He cocked his head, not understanding.

"I know you, Michael. I know you're as determined as I am to protect the people you love." A tear slid down her cheek. "But sometimes . . . sometimes you have to protect yourself."

Her words cut to the marrow, releasing a different kind of anger to rise up in his chest. "All I've done—" He clenched his fists, his throat aching from the effort it took not to shout. "All I've done for years was protect myself. I didn't want to feel, didn't want to love, didn't want to *live.*

"But you, Bryony"—his tone mellowed, and a tremulous smile strained across his lips—"*you* are entirely to blame for waking me up, bringing me back to life. I'm still learning, still making mistakes, but I won't become that self-protective shell of a man again."

⚜

Michael left to find his father, and for long moments afterward, Bryony couldn't find the strength to do much more than stand in the bedroom doorway and pray. God surely wouldn't have allowed any of this to happen if he didn't have plans to bring something good out of it. *"I have purposed it, I will also do it,"* God spoke in Isaiah.

"Oh, Lord," she cried, her forehead pressed against her folded hands, "I beg you, bring peace to this family. Bring healing and love. Bring—"

The outer door burst open, and Alice careened into the room, breathless and red-faced. "Come downstairs, Bryony. Mr. Heath's calling all the house help together in the parlor."

Her stomach convulsed. She didn't dare move for fear she'd be sick all over the expensive Persian rug. "What's happening? Where's Michael?"

"Mr. Heath ordered him to keep the missus up here away from the commotion. Everybody else is lined up in the parlor like a firing squad." Alice signaled frantically for Bryony to hurry. "We gotta go *now.* He's not of a mind to wait."

As if appearances mattered, Bryony felt for loose pins in her bun and tucked straying strands behind her ears. When Alice huffed her impatience, Bryony coaxed her legs into motion. In the hallway, she paused only briefly to glance toward Mrs. Heath's closed door. Once again, Michael would be torn between standing up to his father and keeping his mother out of the fray.

When they reached the parlor, Alice slunk across the room to take her place in line next to Dancy. Jeremiah, grim-faced and arms tense at his sides, stood at the other end. Miss Esther and Odette shielded Callie between them, their eyes dark with defiance.

A few steps into the room, Bryony halted. She looked from the line of servants to Sebastian Heath, whose back was turned as he stared out the front windows. Fists propped low on his hips, he seemed intent on taking slow, deliberate breaths.

His head angled slightly in Bryony's direction, and his gaze hardened. "Do join us, Miss Linwood." He pivoted, glaring at her. "The day you showed up with your jar of pickles, I should have known trouble would follow. Not only have you turned my son's head and jeopardized his future, you've conspired with the rest of these miscreants to perpetuate a gross deception upon this family."

"Now, sir." Jeremiah stepped forward. "You can't be blamin' Bryony for what was done before she came here."

Sebastian whirled on him. "I'll be blaming the lot of you before this is over. Good-for-nothing lackeys—I should fire you all and be done with it!"

Tears poured down Callie's cheeks, and it tore at Bryony's heart to see how the girl cowered behind Odette's fleshy arm.

Sebastian Heath . . . a poor tenant farmer's son who'd never amount to anything.

Indignation rising, Bryony marched forward, though her knees trembled with every step. "Watch your words, Mr. Heath, or they might come back to bite you."

He stared at her in arrogant disbelief. "I should think you'd heed your own advice, Miss Linwood. One call to the sheriff is all it will take to get your family evicted—and good riddance."

She edged up beside him, praying for courage. Her tone dropped to a menacing whisper. "Unless you want everyone in this room to hear exactly how you came to be master of Brookbirch Plantation, you might want to dismiss the others to their duties so you and I can take this up in private."

"What are you—" Sebastian flicked a nervous glance her way.

At her arched-brow response, he firmed his jaw and spoke to the other servants. "It seems Miss Linwood and I have a few things to sort out. I suggest you return to your duties before you give me further reason to send you all packing."

One by one, the others filed from the room, each of them shooting Bryony a worried glance. She could offer only a shaky smile in return and hope they'd grown to respect her enough to trust her in this.

Jeremiah, the last to leave, looked back from the doorway, a curious gleam in his eye. His silent nod spoke his approval and gave Bryony much needed encouragement for what she was about to do.

❧

Michael hadn't felt so trapped and helpless since German gunners had his unit pinned down in a muddy foxhole—moments before the trench filled with the mustard gas that would soon have them all screaming in agony. The memory alone was enough to bring a burning ache to his chest. With one hand resting against his ribcage, he inhaled carefully and tried to look interested as his mother rambled on about the latest happenings in *Cimarron*.

"You should read the book when Bryony and I finish." She peeked through the curtains overlooking the north gardens. "I do hope she's coming over today. Certainly it's almost time for afternoon tea?"

"No, Mother, it isn't even noon yet." Michael thrust up from the chair. He'd gone after his father intending to have it out with him privately, knowing all too well what Sebastian Heath was capable of when angered.

But before Michael could stop him, Dad had ordered the entire household staff into the parlor, leaving Michael no choice but to see to his mother.

The distant rumble of his father's ranting had subsided, and

Michael couldn't restrain his curiosity a moment longer. He sidled to the door and eased it open.

Utter silence greeted him.

His stomach plummeted. There'd been the same deathly quiet in the seconds before the gas had seared his lungs. He edged farther into the hallway, listening. Holding his breath. Praying his father hadn't doomed seven loyal employees—one his niece, another the woman he loved—to starvation.

Plodding footsteps sounded on the staircase. Not his father's. Not Bryony's. When Dancy appeared on the landing, he whooshed out a relieved sigh.

The silver-haired maid came toward him, shaking her head. "Oh, Mister Michael, I'm sorry as I can be."

"Tell me what my father said." He kept his voice low. A quick glance through the sitting room door assured him his mother's attention was elsewhere.

"We was all near to bein' let go, till Bryony whispered something to your daddy. Couldn't make it out, but he sure didn't look happy about it. They's gone off to the office, and the door's shut tight."

Michael couldn't even guess what tactic Bryony might have used to divert his father's assault. With a firm but gentle grip on Dancy's elbow, he ushered her to the sitting room. "Stay with Mother. No matter what you hear, keep her here and keep her calm." At her wide-eyed look of panic, he slid his hand down to cradle hers. "It's going to be all right, Dancy. I don't know how yet, but I promise it will be."

Bryony was right—he was absolutely determined to protect the ones he loved, even at his own expense. *No one has greater love than this, to lay down one's life for one's friends*—it was the credo of every brother in arms Michael had served with during the war. And if he retained anything else from his years of memorizing Scripture in parochial school, it was the Lord's instruction to "love thy neighbor as thyself."

Then, as he made his way downstairs, two words echoed in his brain: *Love thyself.* He'd grown quite adept at self-protection, even self-sacrifice. But *loving* himself? Recognizing and addressing his own needs so that he could more fully meet the needs of others? When had he ceased believing himself worthy?

And how did a man of honor defend the people he loved while at the same time standing up for himself?

These plaguing thoughts slowed his steps as he neared his father's office. He pictured Bryony on the other side of the door. She'd be stiff-backed and steely-eyed, heedless of the wrath she was certain to pull down on herself by confronting Sebastian Heath in his own territory. Michael's veins throbbed with the overwhelming urge to charge into the room. *He* should be the one defending Miranda and Callie. He had to stop Bryony from putting her own family at risk.

Then he heard Bryony's voice, low but intense, and his breath stilled in his lungs.

⚜

"It's really too bad, Mr. Heath." Bryony kept her voice steady, though her insides quivered like a whole jarful of butterflies. "Seems your memory's even worse than your sweet wife's. She has trouble recalling what day it is sometimes, but she does really well at remembering the distant past."

On the opposite side of the desk, Sebastian propped his hips against a credenza in a poor attempt to appear unconcerned. His narrowed eyes and the subtle lift of his chin said otherwise. "Since you obviously think you have the upper hand here, suppose you tell me what it is you think you know?"

Bryony hesitated just long enough to feed his unease—and attempt to calm her own ratcheted nerves. "Unless you're going to call Mrs. Heath a liar, I understand you had much more humble beginnings than your wife's family. She told me her daddy once believed you'd never amount to anything."

Now he really began to squirm. He straightened, one hand stroking his jaw. "Fenella said this? When?"

"It was one week ago today." With a downward glance, Bryony let her fingertips drift across the polished wood of the partners desk. "The same day you had this fancy new piece of furniture delivered. Mrs. Heath was so proud that Michael would be working with you, learning everything he'd need to know someday about running the plantation."

Sebastian relaxed slightly, a smug smile edging out the worry. "Humble beginnings aren't a crime, Miss Linwood. They only tend to make a person work even harder to succeed."

"I reckon that's true. But how do you think Michael and Miranda will take the news that their father grew up poor, that your own daddy was a struggling tenant farmer just like my grandpa, and Nels Wieland—God rest his soul—and everybody else who's trying to scratch a living out of the dirt while their landlords live in big, fine houses and never have to—"

The door flung open with a bang. Michael stood there, lips parted and brow furrowed. His chest heaved with rapid breaths as he looked from Bryony to his father. "Is it true?" His voice scraped like sandpaper over rough wood.

"Michael—" His father extended one hand.

"I said, is it *true*?" The blaze of anger and disbelief in Michael's eyes made Bryony flinch.

"Son, you have to listen to me."

"No, Dad. This time, *you* have to listen to *me*." Michael marched around the desk and planted himself in front of Sebastian. "When I think of what you did to Miranda—" He paused, seething. "You threw her out because she fell in love with a hardworking man you were convinced—let me get this right—would *never amount to anything*."

Sebastian opened his mouth to speak, but no words formed. He had the look of a treed raccoon, dazed, scared, looking for a way to escape. Bryony felt a moment of pity for him, but even more, she felt sorry for Michael. He never should have been ambushed by the truth like this.

He turned away abruptly, whipped off his glasses, and drew a hand down his face. His shuddering sigh filled the room.

While Michael struggled to compose himself, Sebastian's gaze shifted to Bryony. "I hope you're happy now."

"No, sir, I am not." She thrust up her chin to hold back the tears she ached to cry for Michael's sake. For Miranda's and Callie's. "You have so much, and yet so little that really matters. At least when I go home tonight, it'll be to a family who loves and welcomes me. Too bad you can't say the same."

Sebastian looked away, defeat registering in his slumped shoulders. He sank heavily into his desk chair. "Get out, both of you, and leave me alone."

Planting her palms on the desktop, Bryony leaned toward him. "Not until I have your word that nobody gets fired. Including Callie—*if* she wants to keep working for her *grandfather*."

He cringed at the harshness of her tone. "Fine. Nobody gets fired." With a feral glance, he added, "Including *you*—although I wish it could be otherwise."

Bryony hadn't been sure she could count on that fact, but she gave an inward sigh of relief. It was time to let Sebastian Heath stew awhile over the mess he'd made of his life—and his family's. She circled the desk and tenderly slipped her arm through Michael's. "Let's go. I bet Odette's about worried enough to break some dishes."

Michael gave her a tentative smile, then looked briefly at his father. "I'll be along shortly. And don't say anything to anyone about what my mother told you. I want to be the one to tell my sister and Callie."

Bryony nodded. "Will you be okay?"

He laughed softly. "Eventually." Then he took her in his arms and held her as if he couldn't let go. His lips found her temple, his kiss fiercely passionate. "Thank you," he murmured against her hair. With a final squeeze, he released her and nudged her toward the door.

Before he closed it behind her, she caught a glimpse of Sebastian. He couldn't possibly have misread Michael's feelings for her in that moment, but his expression showed neither acceptance nor condemnation, only a sad, soundless emptiness.

⚜

Silence stretched between Michael and his father. Not a strained silence but an extended hush, not unlike the creeping, sweeping quiet on the battlefield when gunfire and cannon roar had ceased.

With an exhausted groan, Michael sank into the chair on his side of the partners desk. He folded his hands loosely in his lap. "We're alone now. Let's have the truth. All of it."

His father shot him a look of naked despair. "Why? So you can gloat about exposing your dear old man for a fraud?"

"No, Dad. So I can understand."

"What's to understand? I grew up on a tenant farm, just like the perceptive Miss Linwood said." Michael's father rubbed his palms back and forth over the chair arms. "And for the past forty years I've done everything in my power to wipe those memories from my mind."

Frustration clawed at Michael's nerves. "But clearly not from Mother's. She adores you, Dad. And you love her. But if you were so poor—"

"How did the two of us ever get together?" Glancing Michael's way, Dad coughed out a cynical laugh. "The easy answer? Pure luck. Or the Lord's providence, if you're so inclined to see things that way."

Michael had the feeling the truth ran much deeper. He locked his gaze on his father and waited for him to continue.

"All right, all right. If you want the unabridged version so badly, I'll give it to you." Rocking back in his chair, Dad heaved a long, noisy sigh. His eyes took on a faraway look, and he began his story.

It started on a tenant farm up toward Conway. Sebastian Heath had been the eldest of seven, a responsible kid who didn't balk at hard work. When he wasn't helping his family on the farm, he'd pick up odd jobs at their landlord's estate, including chauffeuring the landlord around when his regular driver wasn't available.

One of those trips was to Little Rock for a planters' association meeting, and it so happened a young lady named Fenella Gerhard had accompanied her father that day. For Sebastian it had been love at first glance, and though Fenella took a little more convincing, she didn't take exception to his efforts to get better acquainted. They'd meet up in Little Rock every time there was a planters' meeting, and soon were finding excuses even when there wasn't.

Sebastian quickly realized it wasn't only Fenella's affections he must win, but her father's approval as well. Though he couldn't afford college, he was an avid reader and studied up on all kinds of subjects, most especially agricultural management, that he thought would impress the iron-fisted Udell Gerhard.

"And it worked." Michael's father firmed his jaw. "When your grandfather realized I wasn't to be deterred, *and* that he could trust me to oversee this estate with a diligence to match his own, he freely gave his blessing for me to marry your mother."

Michael's maternal grandfather had died before he had a chance to know him, but he'd heard enough to know the man would never have turned over the plantation to someone he couldn't rely on to keep it prosperous. This land had been in the family for generations. "And yet you kept all this from your own children, as if, incomprehensibly, you're ashamed of the truth."

"Ashamed? Certainly not of what I've accomplished here." Dad shoved to his feet. Giving Michael his back, he ran his fingers along the spines of a dozen ledgers lining the shelf above the credenza. "But if you think it was hard gaining your grandfather's respect, imagine the struggle I'd have faced stepping into his shoes if our tenants had any clue their landlord had started out no better off than they are?"

"I don't know—maybe they'd respect you even more. I can say for a fact your children would." Michael stood, what patience he had wearing thinner by the minute. "Unfortunately, you didn't give us the chance."

$\clubsuit$ 2 I $\clubsuit$

Sebastian shifted in the chair, releasing a moan when his stiff back muscles screamed at him. It had been awhile since he'd spent a night at his desk. At least previous occasions involved productive work, usually necessitated by impending due dates for tax forms or agricultural reports.

Last night, however? Nothing but pondering the detritus of his crumbling life.

Sometime during the evening, Odette had ventured in with a supper tray. The bowl of soup remained untouched, a thin film congealed across the top. A cold, dry biscuit peeked out from its napkin wrapper. Sebastian nudged the tray to one side, then braced both elbows on the desk and scrubbed at his unshaven cheeks. His shirt reeked of his own nervous sweat, and he felt every bit the contemptible pig his children thought him to be.

The office door creaked open. He straightened, ready to order the intruder away. Then Fenella's radiant face appeared, her smile brighter than the morning sun slanting through the blinds.

"Darling, did you work all night again?" She wagged her finger at him, but there was no censure in her tone, only amused concern over her husband's reprehensible work habits. "Look at you— stubble on your chin, shadows beneath your eyes, your clothes a mass of wrinkles. You'll need a shower and shave before I'll allow you at the breakfast table."

He'd laugh if the whole situation weren't so atrociously sad. Rising, he took her hands and drew her over to the chair he'd just vacated. "Fenella, dearest, we need to talk."

"My, you look so serious." She settled in with a queenly air and smiled up at him. "If this is about plantation business, you know I don't have a head for such things. I trust you will handle any problems with your usual aplomb."

Aplomb? In this matter, he had none. Not for the first time since his wife's memory began to fail, he prayed for even a moment of clarity. He needed her wisdom, her strength, her assurance that the decisions he'd made over a lifetime hadn't been in vain.

He sank onto the edge of the desk and lowered his head. He twisted the gold band on his left ring finger, and the long, lonely night of introspection caught up with him—all the questions, all the doubts. "Why did you marry me, Fenella?"

Clucking her tongue, she took his hands and made him look at her. "After all these years, don't you know how completely I adore you?"

"But if your father hadn't approved, if he hadn't been convinced I could manage Brookbirch—"

"I'd have run away with you and married you anyway." His face must have registered his shock, because she peered up at him with a sad laugh. "You honestly didn't know? Darling, it wouldn't have mattered whether we were rich or poor, whether we lived in an elegant mansion or a ramshackle farmhouse. All I ever wanted was you."

Had he been too intent on proving himself, too caught up in the trappings of success to realize the wealth of blessings he had all along?

Fenella stood and patted his hand as if he were a naughty schoolboy. "Now do go upstairs and clean yourself up. After breakfast, you must drive into Little Rock and bring the children home for the weekend. I miss them so much when they're away at school."

Sebastian's heart sank, but he soldiered an obliging smile into place. "Of course, dear. Anything for you."

❦

Bryony stood before the kitchen window, her coat over her arm and an ache in her heart. It was already going on eight o'clock, nearly two hours later than she usually set out for the Heath mansion. But she'd slept horribly last night, too sick with worry over what might be happening between Michael and his father.

Grandpa came up beside her and jingled his pickup keys. "If you're bound and determined to go, least you can let me drive you. It's a right chilly morning for walking."

"Thanks, Grandpa." As if she hadn't walked to the Heaths' on much colder mornings than this. But when it came to his grand-daughters, Grandpa wasn't much good at hiding his worries. He knew the moment Bryony came home last night that something was amiss, and he hadn't let her rest until she confided every detail. Miranda had heard most of it, too, except for the part about Sebastian's humble roots. Honoring her promise to Michael, Bryony had kept that information between her and Grandpa.

Now, as incensed as he'd been over learning his uppity landlord was a lowly tenant farmer's son, Bryony feared he'd let something slip. She used their time alone on the ride over to remind him again about keeping the news to himself.

"Won't say a word," Grandpa said as he steered the pickup along the Heaths' main drive. "Leastwise, I'm going on into Brinkley from here to see about a part for the plow, and that could take the better part of the day." He slanted Bryony a troubled frown. "Why don't I swing by here on my way back, just in case—"

Bryony gave his arm a reassuring squeeze. "I'll be fine, Grandpa. Go on about your business and let me see to mine."

A growl sounded deep in Grandpa's throat, but he didn't argue.

He pulled into the paved area behind the Heath mansion and dropped her off, then drove away.

Michael was crossing the lawn as Bryony started toward the house. He quickened his pace and swept her into his arms. "I was afraid you weren't coming."

She didn't even care that anyone might see them. Sebastian may have had his suspicions before, but after yesterday he couldn't have doubted for a moment the depth of Michael's feelings—or hers. With a hand to his cheek, she searched his face. "Are you all right?"

A wry laugh rumbled through his chest. "We'll see after I talk to Miranda. I'm going there now."

"Will you tell Callie, too?"

"I'll let Miranda decide." Michael graced her lips with a brief but meaningful kiss. "Be careful of my father today. He's . . . unreadable. I've told Callie to steer clear of him, too."

The thought that Sebastian Heath paid his own granddaughter to do his washing, cooking, and cleaning made Bryony shudder with indignation. "How will we fix this, Michael? Things can't go back to the way they were. Not for your family. Not for the rest of us."

"And I don't want them to." Michael held her at arm's length. "I honestly don't know how all this will play out, but whatever happens, you and I *will* be together—that, I promise." After another quick kiss, he released her and continued to the garage.

Bryony watched from the veranda as he drove away in the green Chevrolet, then went inside.

Miss Esther met her in the back hallway. "Bryony, thank goodness. We're all in a state this morning." She cast an anxious glance over her shoulder. "It's Mrs. Heath. She raved on and on over breakfast about bringing 'the children' home from boarding school. You've always been so good with her. We're hoping you can talk her back to the present and calm her down."

Nerves prickling, Bryony slipped off her coat and draped it over a hook outside the workroom. "Where's Mr. Heath?"

"He drove off a little while ago, and nobody knows where to." Miss Esther wrung her hands. "The missus thinks he's gone to Little Rock for the children, and she's got Dancy taking all kinds of notes about menus and activities she's planning for the weekend."

Things had definitely gotten out of hand. Mrs. Heath must somehow have picked up on the tension in the house, and it had fed into her confused thoughts. And Sebastian's disappearance? Probably his way of avoiding a task that, sooner or later, he'd have to face—helping his wife understand the truth about her daughter and granddaughter.

Maybe Bryony could make it a little easier. Not for Sebastian's sake, but for everyone else involved. Instead of going straight upstairs, she detoured out to the kitchen in search of Callie. The girl paced between the stove and the table as Odette rolled out a pie crust.

"Ain't no good pining, child," Odette was saying. "Best you go on like things was and forget you even have a grandpappy. He ain't —" Seeing Bryony, she stopped.

"Sebastian Heath *is* Callie's grandfather," Bryony insisted, "and pretending won't change the fact." She motioned to Callie. "Come with me, honey. I think it's time you got better acquainted with your grandmother."

Callie balked at first, but Bryony took her firmly by the hand and marched her up the back stairs. She tapped on Mrs. Heath's outer door, then peeked inside. Dancy sat at the writing desk scribbling away on a thick pad of paper, while Mrs. Heath looked over her shoulder and rattled off recipe ingredients.

"Sorry to interrupt." Bryony stepped into the room and had to give Callie's arm a gentle tug to get her to follow. "I brought someone to see you, Mrs. Heath."

Dancy expelled a relieved breath. She shoved back her chair and gathered up several sheets of paper. "I'll just run these lists down to Miss Esther."

As Dancy scurried out, Mrs. Heath narrowed her gaze at Bryony. "Violet?"

"No, ma'am, it's Bryony. Bryony Linwood." She spoke slowly, deliberately. "Violet was my grandmother."

"Oh." The woman's expression dimmed. She put a hand to her forehead. "I get so confused lately."

"That's all right. Remember, I'm the one who's been reading to you in the afternoons." Bryony picked up the novel she'd left lying on a side table. "See? *Cimarron*." When Mrs. Heath showed signs of recognition, Bryony guided her to the chaise and helped make her comfortable. "I thought we'd read a bit this morning, if you'd like."

"Well, I was in the middle of making plans for . . . for . . ."

Bryony stilled her with gentle pats on her arm. "It's all being taken care of. In the meantime, I'm going to have Callie read to you." Ignoring the trepidation in the girl's eyes, Bryony nudged her into the chair beside the chaise and thrust the book into her hands. She bent near Callie's ear and whispered, "Share this time with your grandmother. Your voice will help her know you, even when she forgets."

Callie nodded uncertainly, then opened to the page Bryony had marked. She glanced at Mrs. Heath and managed a shaky laugh. "Looks like y'all were at chapter fifteen."

Bryony listened from across the room as Callie's confidence grew. The girl had a mellow tone, textured with Southern grit and refined by the schooling Miranda had provided. As the story captured Mrs. Heath's attention, the lines around the woman's eyes and mouth began to soften. With her gaze fixed on Callie, she rested her head against the cushions and smiled contentedly.

It was a start. Bryony could only pray that someday Mrs. Heath would come to love Callie as she loved her son and daughter.

As Michael expected, Miranda was outraged to learn their father had concealed his past. She pounded the table with a clenched fist. "And he had the nerve to look down his pompous, prideful nose at Daniel!"

While she rid herself of angry tears, Rose brought over three mugs and the steaming pot of chicory. "The man's a fool, is all I can say."

Miranda blotted her cheeks with a crumpled handkerchief. After a shaky sip of the hot drink, she seemed more in control. Then her gaze grew wistful. "Please, Michael, can I see the drawings?"

"I don't have them here. They're shut away in my wardrobe." He pursed his lips. "Where the smaller sketch *should* have been, if I hadn't been so careless."

"I'm not sorry." Miranda hiked her chin. "I'm glad he finally knows. Maybe now—"

An automobile roared up beside the house. Rose hurried to the window. "Um, y'all . . . we have company."

Michael joined her, then cast a worried glance at Miranda. "It's Dad."

She shot up from the chair. "Does he know I'm here?"

"No one told him, but I suppose he could have guessed." Taking his coat from the hook, Michael started for the door. "Stay here. I'll find out why he's come."

In the time it took Michael to don his coat and stride across the yard, Dad never moved from behind the steering wheel. When he turned his gaze toward Michael, pain and confusion marred his features.

Michael hesitated briefly before rounding the car and climbing into the passenger seat. "What are you doing here, Dad?"

He didn't answer right away. His knuckles whitened around the steering wheel. "Trying to figure things out. Trying to understand how I managed to turn both my children against me."

Another silent pause. "I suppose you know Miranda's inside?"

"I guessed as much. Your Miss Linwood's too much of a

bleeding heart." Dad released a harsh laugh. "Not to mention our grocery bill has nearly doubled over the past month."

Your Miss Linwood—the words lit a fire in Michael's chest. He had no idea how they'd ever sort through this awful mess, but he would forever bless the day Bryony walked into his life.

He looked over at his father, taking in the slumped shoulders, the shadowed eyes, defeat carved into every line of his face. Pity slowly edged out the resentment, and Michael stretched out his hand to touch his father's arm. "Come inside. Talk to Miranda."

"I—I don't know what I'd say to her."

"'I'm sorry' is never a bad way to begin."

Until his father actually stepped from the car and began his slow march to the house, Michael hadn't truly believed he'd make the attempt. Catching up, Michael showed his father into the Rigby kitchen.

One hand resting on the mound of her pregnancy, Miranda turned from where she'd been watching at the window. She heaved a tired sigh. "Hello, Daddy."

Rose slipped past. "I have some chores in the barn. Y'all make yourself at home."

Michael's father hadn't taken his eyes off Miranda. "That day you showed up at the house—I had no idea."

"That I was pregnant?" Miranda cocked her head. "Would it have made any difference?"

"I'm not completely devoid of feelings."

"Then you certainly had us all—"

Michael silenced his sister's cutting response with a pointed stare. "I think it's about time we all tried listening instead of attacking."

Both his father and his sister lowered their heads in acquiescence.

"Good." Moving purposefully to the table, Michael pulled out a chair, then waited for his father and Miranda to join him.

The conversation that ensued wasn't always civil, but Michael managed to deflect the worst of the verbal assaults. He insisted his father listen without comment as Miranda described her life since leaving home and marrying Daniel—the joys and the struggles. She painted a picture of a loving husband and devoted father, an intelligent, hardworking man bent on making the best life possible for his wife and daughter.

"I knew what I was getting into, Daddy, and there's not one thing I'd do differently, unless . . ." Miranda tentatively reached for her father's hand. "Unless I could have married Daniel with your blessing."

He gave his head a brusque shake. "This isn't what I wanted for you." His gaze shifted to Michael. "For either of you."

Clearly, he meant Bryony. Michael edged away from the table. "It isn't about what *you* want for us, Dad. It's about giving us the freedom to live our own lives."

His father harrumphed. "Your sister's choices brought her to the brink of starvation. Now I suppose you'll marry Bryony Linwood and end up living in a hovel while she cleans houses for rich folk and you draw your pretty pictures all day."

Michael's gut twisted, but he refused to be goaded by his father's distorted logic. Calmly, he stated, "No, Dad, *you* put Miranda's wellbeing at risk when you chose to disown her. You had the means to give her and Daniel a solid start in life, but you let your narrow-mindedness and pride get in the way." He gripped his father's arm. "You have a chance now to make things right—not just for Miranda but for your grandchildren."

"Callie." Eyes closed, Dad dropped his chin. "I can't believe I didn't know."

"She's a bright and beautiful girl," Miranda said. "If you'd only—"

Their father's chair scraped across the wood floor. He rose stiffly. "I've heard everything you said. Now, I need to think . . . and pray."

Michael followed his father to the door and watched him climb into the LaSalle and drive away. He turned to Miranda with a sad smile. "It's taken me entirely too long, I admit, but I've come to believe prayer is the only way we'll get through this mess."

"It's time I did more praying, too." Slanting her brow, Miranda studied him. "Have I told you lately how proud I am of you, little brother?"

"Don't go all soft on me now." Michael drew in a bolstering breath. "I should go home and see how Mother is doing."

Miranda stifled a sob. "I want to see her so badly."

"You will. Soon, I promise." With a warm hug and a kiss to the top of her head, Michael said goodbye.

At the mansion, he went directly upstairs, only to halt in surprise when he found Bryony sitting on the top step. She'd obviously been crying, and he sank down next to her and took her in his arms. "Tell me what's wrong."

"Nothing . . . and everything." She sniffled and dabbed her cheeks with the hem of her apron. With a quick nod toward his mother's suite, she cast Michael an ethereal mile. "Go look. It's wonderful!"

Now he was completely confused. And completely curious. He strode to the door, which stood slightly ajar, and quietly pushed it open. What he saw brought a catch to his throat—Callie and his mother, snuggled next to each other on the chaise, their heads touching as Callie read aloud from the book of Longfellow's poems Michael had given her for Christmas.

Bryony came up beside him and slipped her hand into his. "Isn't that the sweetest sight you've ever seen?"

Tearing his gaze away, Michael looked deep into Bryony's eyes. "Almost," he murmured. "Almost."

✣ 22 ✣

The weekend passed while Bryony watched and wondered. Out of both necessity and obligation, she and the rest of the staff carried out their usual household tasks, but it felt as if they all held their breaths, waiting to see what, if anything, would change.

One change quickly became obvious. Each day, Mrs. Heath specifically asked for Callie to spend the afternoon with her. Sometimes they read books together or simply sat and talked. On Sunday afternoon, they bundled up and went walking in the gardens. And though it meant Bryony had to take over many of Callie's chores, she didn't mind at all if it offered the girl this chance to get to know her grandmother. Mrs. Heath didn't yet comprehend who Callie was, but the two were already forming an unbreakable bond.

Clouds rolled in on Monday, and the temperature climbed into the fifties. As Bryony carried a load of wash out to the laundry room, she noticed the heaviness of moisture in the air. The promise of rain, no matter how little, made her heart swell. She dropped her wicker basket outside the door, lifted her face toward the sky, and inhaled the sweet, cool scent.

The next thing she knew, two solid arms encircled her from

behind, and Michael's throaty voice whispered in her ear. "You feel it, too. I'd be grateful for even a few sprinkles."

Bryony shouldn't be enjoying his nearness this much, especially when she ought to be working. But that was another change she didn't regret, Michael's freedom to be open about his feelings for her.

He turned her toward him but kept his arms around her. His long, thoughtful sigh blew warm across her cheek. "I spent the morning talking with Dad, and I've laid out some ideas for the future. I think he's agreeable."

A tremor started in her belly, curiosity mixed with concern. With a light laugh, she ducked from beneath his arms and gathered up the laundry basket. "Tell me all about it while I start the wash."

Michael followed her inside and helped her sort men's shirts from ladies' chemises as he spoke. "First of all, Dad's agreed that Miranda can come home. But we have to handle it just right for Mother's sake. She's liable to be very confused about what's happened in the intervening years."

"And Daniel—what about him?" Bryony inspected a stain on a shirt cuff.

"That's dicier. I doubt either Daniel or my father would ever be comfortable sharing the same living space." Michael voiced his thoughts about turning the loft over the garage into living quarters for Miranda, Daniel, Callie, and the new baby, at least until they could build a proper house close by.

"It sounds like a good plan." As the washer filled with water, Bryony chewed her lip. "I'm glad for them, but I can't help worrying about you."

Michael deposited the last of the shirts into the washer, then faced Bryony with a sad but knowing smile. "Trust me on this. As long as I continue working with Dad, I have a chance to make a difference in how things are run around here. My father's hardened heart won't fully heal in a day or a month or probably even a year, but for the first time since I went off to war, I see hope."

Hope was a good thing, but Bryony's chest ached at the

thought of Michael spending the rest of his days keeping books and overseeing tenant farms. It wasn't the life he was meant for, and she wouldn't rest until she made him see that for himself.

❧

Another month went by, and the household settled once again into a comfortable, if tentative, routine. Meals must still be prepared, clothes and linens washed and ironed, furniture dusted and floors swept.

The biggest difference was that Callie now held a privileged position as Mrs. Heath's almost constant companion. There were moments of clarity when the woman seemed to grasp that this was Miranda's daughter—her granddaughter—and the three of them spent many happy hours together.

By mid-February, the apartment over the garage had been made livable, and Miranda moved in with Callie. Daniel now had stable employment up north and didn't want to leave until he'd saved a little more for his family to live on. He'd written Miranda that the idea of taking charity from the man who'd formerly disowned his wife just didn't sit well with him.

But the odd thing was that Miranda showed an unexpected interest in plantation management. Growing up on the estate, plus all the years married to a sharecropper, had taught her much, and she'd inserted herself in the office right alongside Michael and their father. Bryony often heard her vehemently articulating her opinions about keeping the plantation solvent during the country's economic downturn while also accommodating the needs of their tenants.

One day, as Bryony ran the sweeper over the library carpet, she heard raised voices in the office. Moments later, Michael traipsed in and plopped into one of the library chairs. He looked up at Bryony with a wry grin. "I may soon be out of a job."

His remark pricked a nerve she hadn't realized was still so raw. She vigorously plied the carpet sweeper around Michael's feet.

"Isn't that dandy? Now you can return to your solitary life of drawing pictures nobody sees."

Michael's tone turned gruff. "And you can continue cleaning house for other people so your sisters can hope for a better life." He rose abruptly and moved the sweeper out of her reach. "Don't you think it's time we both stopped sacrificing our dreams for others and claimed some happiness for ourselves?"

"I don't have such luxury." She tried not to look at him, but he cornered her by the bookcase, leaving her no escape.

"Love isn't a luxury." He inched closer. When his warm fingers curled around her nape, her breath hitched. "Tell me, Bryony. What is it you want most in all the world? What would make you truly happy?"

How was she supposed to answer, much less think, when he looked at her that way? "I—I want to live in a lovely little house with gardens all around, and shade trees and a creaky old porch swing."

The corner of his mouth quirked. "Anything else?"

"A cat would be nice. A friendly one who'd sit on my lap and purr." She knew she sounded ridiculous, but he'd asked, and now all these nearly forgotten dreams sailed back in all their luminosity.

"I've never had a cat." Michael's lips hovered over hers. "But we could get one."

"We . . . ?"

"For our little house with the garden."

"Don't tease me, Michael." She really couldn't breathe now.

"I don't mean to, my darling." With a frustrated groan, Michael touched his forehead to hers, then guided her over to the sofa and pulled her down beside him. "I know how unsettling these past few weeks have been. Bringing Miranda home, trying to help Mother understand about Callie, working things out with my father—there's been so little time to make plans for *our* future. And I want a future with you, Bryony, more than anything."

The knot in her chest grew to the size of a melon. "What are you saying?"

He dipped his chin. When he looked up, yearning filled his gaze. "I'm asking you to marry me."

She gave a tiny cry and shook her head. "Oh, Michael—"

"Hush. Not another word"—he chuckled softly—"unless it's *yes*. Because I won't sit here and listen to all the reasons why you think it wouldn't work." Leaning against the sofa cushions, he drew Bryony next to him and cradled her head on his shoulder. "Your family will be all right, and so will mine. Making a home together doesn't mean we'll abandon them."

"But you're the heir to this huge estate, and I'm just a simple farm girl."

Michael tipped her head so that he could gaze into her eyes, and his own glistened with mirth. "Bryony Linwood, there is nothing simple about you."

When he lowered his mouth upon hers, she melted against him, her heart buoyant with happiness and hope.

A *tick-tick-tick* sounded outside the window. Bryony pulled away, gasping when she saw water droplets spattering the veranda. "Michael, it's raining!"

They hurried to the foyer and stood in the open front door, Michael's arms surrounding her. A chilly February wind swirled the mist around them, and Bryony opened her mouth to taste the clean, cold wetness. The rain didn't last long, barely dampening the parched ground, but it was a blessing nonetheless, and the sweetness of this moment would linger in her heart for the rest of her days.

EPILOGUE

"Hold still, will you?" Pencil poised over the sketchbook, Michael shot his new bride a mock scowl. "Honestly, it's so much easier drawing twigs, leaves, and berries."

"Yes, but twigs, leaves, and berries won't do this, will they?" Bryony popped off the porch swing and leaned down to tease Michael's lips with a kiss.

He gave an annoyed huff, not because he didn't relish her kisses but to show her she couldn't twist him around her little finger so easily. "You're impossible. Now sit down so I can finish."

"You're *supposed* to be finishing those illustrations for your editor, not wasting time and paper on silly sketches of your wife." Even so, Bryony flounced back to the swing, plopped down, and struck a pose.

Michael had to work hard to keep the amusement off his face. He'd already finished six of the ten botanical drawings he'd been commissioned to do for another university publication, with plenty of time to spare. Capturing his wife's pert smile was his reward.

Whenever he pondered all that had changed in his life over the past several months, it brought a clutch to his chest and a silent prayer of thanksgiving. Miranda's interest in the plantation had revealed a side of her Michael had never known, but her involvement had allowed him to significantly scale back his own while focusing on the one aspect that mattered most to him—seeing to the welfare of their tenants. With Bryony's encouragement, he'd contacted the university publishing house to ask for another chance, and the editor now kept him amply supplied with assignments.

Then, five weeks ago to the day, he'd made Bryony his wife. They'd moved into a charming little bungalow in Brinkley, with enough distance from both their families to allow them some breathing room but not so far that Bryony couldn't look in often on her grandfather and sisters. She'd always worry over her family like a mother hen, and that was one of the things Michael loved most about her.

Michael's mother remained a source of concern as well, but with both Miranda and Callie watching over her, and his father slowly coming to terms with the inevitable, Mother would be well cared for. And now, with a brand new baby grandson to cuddle and spoil, she seemed more content than ever.

As for Daniel Vargas, he was proving to be a blessing to both families. More and more, his hands-on farming experience and natural diplomacy had him serving as intermediary between Sebastian and the Brookbirch Plantation tenant farmers. At other times he lent his brawn to help out at the Rigby farm, a huge comfort to Bryony now that she and Larkspur had embarked on new lives and the bulk of the work fell to her grandfather and Rose.

So together, Michael and Bryony had found a path toward hope again, and Michael knew a depth of happiness he'd never expected could be his.

Bryony kicked the swing into motion. "I think you should draw a kitten on my lap."

"You're fidgeting again." Adjusting the sketchpad on his knee,

Michael narrowed his gaze. "And why, pray tell, should I add a nonexistent kitten?"

"Because in about a month I'm going next door to Mrs. Fritz's and choose one from the litter of five her cat Princess just gave birth to."

With a noncommittal "Mmm," Michael made a swift adjustment to the drawing. Satisfied, he laid his pencil on the side table and carried the sketchbook over to the swing. He sat down beside Bryony and laid the picture on her lap.

"Oh, it's perfect!" She folded her legs beneath her skirt and snuggled against Michael's chest.

Michael decided this moment was perfect, the two of them here together, their whole future before them like an unopened gift. There would be trials, yes—the drought lingered on, Arkansas farmers still struggled, and America's economy faced a long road to recovery—but right here, right now, life was good.

He pulled his pretty wife closer and kissed her temple. "What do you say, Mrs. Heath? Want to pay Mrs. Fritz and Princess a visit? I'd like to have a gander at those kittens."

Are you ready for the next book in the series?
Read Larkspur's love story in book 2,
Castles in the Clouds

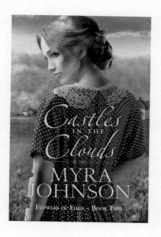

If you enjoyed *The Sweetest Rain*, please spread the word among your reader friends and wherever you share about books on Facebook, Goodreads, Instagram, or other social media.

Reviews are always deeply appreciated. A review doesn't have to be lengthy or eloquent, just a few brief words sharing your honest impressions. Reviews and personal recommendations are the best ways to help authors get discovered by new readers.

To receive regular updates about Myra Johnson's books and special events, subscribe to her newsletter (signup form on website, http://myrajohnson.com/newsletter-signup/).

Visit Myra online:
www.myrajohnson.com

ACKNOWLEDGMENTS

I'm forever thankful for my agent and cherished friend, Natasha Kern. Deepest gratitude for your continued confidence in my ability as a writer and for your tireless efforts to make sure my stories find the very best homes!

With gratitude to my editor, Ericka McIntyre, for your insights and gentle guidance. Working with you on each book of the Flowers of Eden series has been a joy.

I couldn't do what I do without my supportive and caring husband. Jack, you're becoming a better cook with every book I write! Thanks also to my dear daughters, Johanna and Julena, for your unfailing encouragement. Do you have any idea how proud I am of each of you?

The Lord has truly blessed me through family, friends, and vocation. To him be the glory!

AUTHOR'S NOTE

There is nothing quite so worrisome to a writer of historical fiction as the possibility of making a factual error that true historians will immediately recognize and call you out on. Digging into the research for a historical novel can be a daunting, but always quite enlightening, experience.

This has been no less true for *The Sweetest Rain*. When I set out to write about an Arkansas family at the onset of the Great Depression, I had little concept for the reality of life in the early 1930s except for one thing: it was *hard*. More than once during the writing and editing process, I told my husband the research was teaching me so much more than I ever remember learning in school about this grim era in American history.

A variety of reference books and websites helped provide the background for this novel, but none moved me as deeply as the memoirs collected in William D. Downs Jr.'s book *Stories of Survival: Arkansas Farmers during the Great Depression*. Those who made it through the worst hardships of the Great Depression and Dust Bowl years truly are survivors.

I chose Arkansas for the setting of *The Sweetest Rain* mainly because of my general familiarity with the state. My husband and I have vacationed in the Hot Springs area almost annually since the mid-1980s, and the city became the setting for my first historical series, Till We Meet Again (Abingdon Press). Also having driven I-40 between Memphis and Little Rock numerous times, I can readily envision the picturesque rolling farmlands of Central Arkansas.

The town of Eden as described in my story is entirely fictional. However, if you do an Internet search for "Eden, Arkansas," you will find a result calling Eden a "populated place" in Monroe County. On a map, it's pinpointed as a dot on country roads south of I-40 and about twenty-five miles southwest of Brinkley. When I settled on the early-1930s timeframe for my book and began reading about Arkansas' worst drought on record, the name Eden struck me for its symbolism. While everything green shrivels up and dies, my fictional farm family holds onto each other, their hope, and their faith in God's restorative promises.

The real-life farmers' struggles actually began in the years prior to the drought of 1930-31. Wild weather extremes brought killer tornadoes (the 1926 Thanksgiving Day tornado outbreak that ravaged central Arkansas is a historical fact), devastating floods (1927), and the stock market crash in 1929. According to the online Encyclopedia of Arkansas, the cotton yield in 1928 averaged six bales per twenty acres. In 1930 the number dropped to barely two bales per twenty acres, and the selling price per pound had fallen by almost half.

Today when natural disasters strike, we count on help from Red Cross, FEMA, and other relief agencies. In 1930, President Hoover was slow to respond. In Roger Lambert's article "Hoover and the Red Cross in the Arkansas Drought of 1930" (*Arkansas Historical Quarterly*, Volume 29, Spring 1970), Hoover is quoted as saying, "... the American people will proudly take care of the necessities of their countrymen in time of stress and difficulty." In other words, the starving tenant farmers and sharecroppers should depend upon the charity of neighbors who were better off than they. When the government finally did begin to act with legislation, initial relief focused on financial loans and *seed for planting* (note the irony during a time of drought!) rather than actually providing food for the many who were going hungry.

The England, Arkansas, food riot of January 3, 1931, is another historical fact. The Encyclopedia of Arkansas website states that a tenant farmer was visited by a neighbor who couldn't feed her children. The farmer and several other neighbors drove to England to demand food, but the Red Cross didn't have the necessary forms for people to apply for aid. Reports vary as to how many "rioters" were actually involved, but estimates run somewhere between the original group of around fifty farmers and some 300 to 500 desperate and angry people. Some eyewitness accounts deny that the scene became violent, stating that any actual rioting was averted when merchants generously provided food for those in need.

The tenant farming and sharecropping system developed as a result of the end of slavery after the Civil War, when plantation owners needed to find new ways of working the land. In Arkansas, common arrangements were for the tenant farmer to pay his landlord either in cash rent or twenty-five to fifty percent of the crop yield. Tenants supplied their own equipment and capital, and family members provided the labor. Sharecroppers were typically much poorer farmers and relied on the landowner for funding and equipment. The landowner also held title to a much larger share of the harvest. For a more complete description, see "Sharecropping and Tenant Farming" at the Encyclopedia of Arkansas website mentioned above.

At its core, *The Sweetest Rain* is a story about families—what holds them together, what drives them apart. The Heath family struggled with several issues, not the least of which was Michael's recovery from injuries both physical and emotional suffered while fighting in the Great War. Mustard gas caused severe blistering and excruciating pain, and since it could do as much damage externally as internally, gas masks offered limited protection. Even more unnerving, symptoms of mustard gas exposure might not appear for hours, and death could take days, usually from secondary respiratory infections. Length of recovery varied, depending upon the severity and type of exposure. If the lungs were damaged, as in Michael Heath's case, long-term effects might include shortness of breath, coughing, sensitivity to inhaled irritants, and increased susceptibility to respiratory tract infections. According to the American Journal of Public Health, an estimated thirty percent of all WWI casualties were the result of gas exposure. Another source reports total US casualties from gas at 72,807, with 1,462 deaths. The Medical Front WWI website offers an in-depth description of gas warfare and its consequences.

During the first World War, the psychological trauma of battle became known as "shell shock." Symptoms ran the gamut: physical pain, nightmares, psychologically induced blindness, insomnia, and unrelenting anxiety. Almost worse than the symptoms themselves was the stigma of being labeled weak or a coward, for there was little understanding or sympathy at the time for what we recognize today as post-traumatic stress disorder. Treatment took many forms, including hypnotism, electric shock therapy, and even shaming. Only as the condition was recognized as a psychological disorder did treatments become more humane.

A significant factor in 1930s Arkansas was the great racial divide. From the late 1800s through the 1960s, the discriminatory Jim Crow laws led to racial injustice and violence that became an ugly blemish on Arkansas history. The Latino population in Arkansas remained relatively small during the early twentieth-century, although the Mexican Revolution (1910-1919) drove many to migrate to the Southwestern U.S. to escape the war. Later, the first and second World Wars brought an influx of migrant workers from Mexico and Central America to fill labor shortages. These immigrant farm workers were low on the class scale, faring only slightly better than blacks.

Finally, a little about the history of Alzheimer's disease, which afflicted Fenella Heath, Michael's mother. The disease was first discovered in 1906 by Dr. Alois Alzheimer during the autopsy of a woman in her fifties who had suffered profound memory loss and psychological changes. Today, we know Alzheimer's to be a progressive brain disorder in which brain cells are destroyed and cognitive function slowly fails. Dr. Alzheimer's work has been called "groundbreaking" for the discoveries it led to about the plaque and nerve tangles that result in loss of mental function.

Even so, in the early twentieth century, dementia remained a puzzling ailment—was it simply age-related, due to arteriosclerosis, or was it this newly named Alzheimer's disease? Few options existed then, except to care for the patient at home or in a mental institution. Even today, though certain treatments have been found to slow the progression of Alzheimer's, the disease remains the sixth leading cause of death in the U.S. In 2015, an estimated 5.1 million Americans suffer from Alzheimer's, and almost two-thirds are women. For more information, visit the Alzheimer's Association website.

Thank you for coming along on this journey with Bryony, Michael, and their families. If you came across any historical discrepancies, I ask your indulgence and hope you will chalk them up to liberties taken for the sake of storytelling. I do love to hear from my readers, so feel free to contact me through my website, www.MyraJohnson.com, where you'll also find my social media links and information about my other books.

With blessings and gratitude,
Myra Johnson

ABOUT THE AUTHOR

Native Texan Myra Johnson is a three-time Maggie Awards finalist, two-time finalist for the prestigious ACFW Carol Awards, winner of Christian Retailing's Best for historical fiction, and winner in the Inspirational category of the National Excellence in Romance Fiction Awards. After a five-year sojourn in Oklahoma, then eight years in the beautiful Carolinas, Myra and her husband are thrilled to be home once again in the Lone Star State enjoying wildflowers, Tex-Mex, and real Texas barbecue!

Married since 1972, Myra and her husband have two beautiful daughters married to wonderful Christian men, plus seven amazing grandchildren and a delightful granddaughter-in-law. The Johnsons share their home with two pampered rescue dogs and a snobby but lovable cat they inherited from their younger daughter when the family moved overseas.

To receive regular updates about Myra's books and other news, be sure to subscribe to her newsletter (signup form on website).

Find Myra online:
www.myrajohnson.com

facebook.com/MyraJohnsonAuthor

x.com/MyraJohnson

instagram.com/mjwrites

bookbub.com/authors/myra-johnson

goodreads.com/MyraJohnsonAuthor

pinterest.com/mjwrites

MORE BOOKS BY MYRA JOHNSON

Find the complete list at Myra's website,

www.MyraJohnson.com

CONTEMPORARY INSPIRATIONAL ROMANCE

Autumn Rains

Romance by the Book

Where the Dogwoods Bloom

A Horseman's Heart

A Horseman's Gift

A Horseman's Hope

Rancher for the Holidays

Worth the Risk

Her Hill Country Cowboy

Hill Country Reunion

The Rancher's Redemption

Their Christmas Prayer

The Rancher's Family Secret

The Rebel's Return

The Rancher's Family Legacy

A Steadfast Companion

His Unexpected Grandchild

FLOWERS OF EDEN HISTORICAL SERIES

The Sweetest Rain

Castles in the Clouds

A Rose So Fair

TILL WE MEET AGAIN HISTORICAL SERIES

When the Clouds Roll By

Whisper Goodbye

Every Tear a Memory

CONTEMPORARY WOMEN'S FICTION

All She Sought[1]

One Imperfect Christmas

The Soft Whisper of Roses

NOVELLAS

The Oregon Trail Romance Collection: Settled Hearts

Designs on Love

Lifetime Investment

---

1. Previously published as *Pearl of Great Price*; see author website for details

Made in United States
North Haven, CT
10 February 2024